RANSOM

Also by Danielle Steel
available from Random House Large Print

Accident
Bittersweet
Safe Harbour
Johnny Angel
Dating Game
Answered Prayers
Sunset in St. Tropez
The Cottage
The House on Hope Street
Irresistible Forces
Journey
The Kiss
Leap of Faith
Lone Eagle
The Wedding

DANIELLE STEEL

RANSOM

RANDOM HOUSE
LARGE PRINT

This is a work of fiction. Names, characters, places, and incidents either are the product of the author's imagination or are used fictitiously. Any resemblance to actual persons, living or dead, events, or locales is entirely coincidental.

Copyright © 2004 by Danielle Steel

All rights reserved

Published in the United States of America by Random House Large Print in association with Delacorte Press, New York.
Distributed by Random House, Inc., New York

Library of Congress Cataloging-in-Publication Data
Steel, Danielle.
Ransom/Danielle Steel.
p. cm.
ISBN 0-375-72830-9

1. Police—California—San Francisco—Fiction. 2. San Francisco (Calif.)—Fiction. 3. Ex-convicts—Fiction. 4. Widows—Fiction. Large type books. I. Title.

PS3569.T33828R37 2004b
813'.54—dc22
2004042781

www.randomlargeprint.com

FIRST LARGE PRINT EDITION

10 9 8 7 6 5 4 3 2 1

This Large Print edition published in accord with the standards of the N.A.V.H.

To all of my wonderful children,
who are extraordinary people I admire, love,
and respect so much,
And especially to Sam, Victoria, Vanessa,
Maxx, and Zara for being brave, loving,
patient, and courageous.
And to the remarkable men and women
in state, local, and federal agencies,
often unknown and unseen,
who keep all of us safe.

with deepest thanks
and all my love,
d.s.

"Tenderness is more powerful than hardness.
Water is more powerful than the rock.
Love is more powerful than violence."

Hermann Hesse

RANSOM

Chapter 1

Peter Matthew Morgan stood at the counter, picking up his things. A wallet with four hundred dollars in it, from his cash account. The release papers he had to take with him, and give his parole agent. He was wearing clothes the state had given him. He was wearing jeans, a white T-shirt with a denim shirt over it, running shoes, and white socks. It was a far cry from what he had worn when he came in. He had been in Pelican Bay State Prison for four years and three months. He had served the minimum amount of time of his sentence, which was nonetheless a big hunk of time for a first offense. He had been caught with an extraordinary amount of cocaine, prosecuted by the state, convicted in a jury trial, and sentenced to state prison at Pelican Bay.

At first, he had only sold to friends. Eventually, it not only supported the habit he had developed inadvertently, it supported all his financial needs and at one time his family's as well. He had made nearly a million dollars in the six months before he'd been caught, but even that didn't fill the hole in the dam he'd created with the financial juggling he'd done. Drugs, bad investments, selling short, huge risks on commodities. He'd been a stockbroker for a while, and got in trouble with the SEC, not enough to be prosecuted, in which case he would have been arrested by the feds and not the state, but he never was. He had been living so far beyond his means, to such an insane degree, had so many potentially explosive balls in the air, and developed such a massive drug habit hanging out with the wrong people, that eventually the only way to negotiate his debt to his dealer had been to deal drugs for him. There had also been a small matter of bad checks and embezzlement, but he got lucky once again. His employer had decided not to press charges, once he got arrested for dealing cocaine. What was the point? He didn't have the money anyway, whatever he had taken, and it was in fact a relatively small amount in the scheme of things, and the money was long gone. There was no way he could recoup the funds. His employer at the time felt sorry for him. Peter had a way of charming people, and making them fond of him.

Peter Morgan was the epitome of a nice guy gone wrong. Somewhere along the way, he had opted for the low road too many times, and blown every golden opportunity he'd ever had. More than Peter, his friends and business associates felt sorry for his wife and kids, who became the victims of his crazy schemes and rotten judgment. But everyone who knew him would have said that at the core, Peter Morgan was a nice guy. It was hard to say what had gone wrong. In truth, a lot had, for a long time.

Peter's father died when he was three, and had been the scion of an illustrious family from the cream of social circles in New York. The family fortune had been dwindling for years, and his mother managed to squander whatever his father left, long before Peter grew up. Soon after his father died, she married another very social, aristocratic young man. He was the heir of an important banking family, who was devoted to Peter and his two siblings, educated and loved them, sent them to the best private schools, along with the two half-brothers who came into Peter's life during the course of their marriage. The family appeared wholesome, and moneyed certainly, although his mother's drinking increased steadily over time, and wound her up in an institution eventually, leaving Peter and his two full siblings technically orphaned. His stepfather had never legally adopted them, and remarried a year after Peter's mother died. His new wife saw no reason why her husband should be burdened, financially or otherwise, with three children who weren't his own. She was willing to take on the two children he had had by that marriage, although she wanted them sent away to boarding school. But she wanted nothing to do with the three children that had come into his previous marriage, with Peter's mother. All Peter's stepfather was willing to do after that was pay for boarding school, and then college, and an inadequate allowance, but he explained, somewhat sheepishly, that he could no longer offer them haven in his home, nor additional funds.

After that, Peter's vacations were spent at school, or at the homes of friends, whom he managed to charm into taking him home. And he was very charming. Once his mother died, Peter learned to live by his wits. It was all he had, and worked well for him. The only love and nurturing he got in those years were from friends' parents.

There were often little incidents, when he stayed with friends during school holidays. Money disappeared, tennis rackets vanished mysteriously, and seemed to be missing when he left. Clothes were borrowed and never returned. Once a gold watch seemed to evaporate into thin air, and a sobbing maid was fired as a result. As it so happened, it was later discovered, Peter had been sleeping with her. He was sixteen at the time, and the proceeds from the watch that he had talked her into pilfering for him had kept him going for six months. His life was a constant struggle to come up with enough money to cover his needs. And he did whatever he had to do to meet those needs. He was so kind, polite, and pleasant to have around, that he always appeared innocent when things went sour. It was impossible to believe that a boy like him could be guilty of any misdeed or crime.

At one point, a school psychologist suggested that Peter had sociopathic tendencies, which even the headmaster found hard to believe. The psychologist had wisely surmised that under the veneer, he appeared to have less of a conscience than he should. And the veneer was incredibly appealing. It was hard to know who Peter really was beneath the surface. Above all, he was a survivor. He was a

charming, bright, good-looking kid, who had
had a bunch of rotten breaks in his life. He had
no one to rely on but himself, and deep at his
core, he had been wounded. His parents'
deaths, his stepfather's distancing himself from
him, and giving him almost no money, the
two siblings he never saw once they were sent
to different boarding schools on the East
Coast, had all taken a toll on him. And later,
once in college, the news that his eighteen-
year-old sister had drowned was yet another
blow to a young soul already battered. He
rarely talked about the experiences he'd had,
or the sorrows that had resulted from them,
and on the whole, he appeared to be a level-
headed, optimistic, good-natured guy, who
could charm just about anyone, and often did.
But life had been far from easy for him, although to look at him, you'd never know it.
There was no visible evidence of the agonies
he'd been through. The scars were far deeper
and well hidden.

Women fell into his hands like fruit off trees,
and men found him good company. He drank
a lot in college, friends remembered later on,
but he never seemed out of control, and
wasn't. Not obviously at least. The wounds on
Peter's soul were deep, and hidden.

Peter Morgan was all about control. And he always had a plan. His stepfather lived up to his promise, and sent him to Duke, and from there he got a full scholarship to Harvard Business School, and graduated with an MBA. He had all the tools he needed, along with a fine mind, good looks, and some valuable connections he'd made in the elite schools he had attended. It seemed an absolute certainty that he was someone who would go far. There was no question in anyone's mind that Peter Morgan would succeed. He was a genius with money, or so it seemed, and he had a multitude of plans. He got a job on Wall Street when he graduated, in a brokerage firm, and it was two years after he graduated that things started to go wrong. He broke some rules, churned some accounts, "borrowed" a little money. Things got dicey for him for a while, and then, as usual, he landed on his feet. He went to work for an investment banking firm, and appeared to be the golden boy of Wall Street for a brief time. He had everything it took to make a success of his life, except a family and a conscience. Peter always had a scheme, and a plan to get to the finish line faster. He had learned one thing from his childhood, that life could fall apart in an instant, and he had to take care of himself. There were few, if any, lucky breaks in life. And whatever luck there was, you made yourself.

At twenty-nine, he married Janet, a dazzling debutante, who happened to be the daughter of the head of the firm where he worked, and within two years, they had two adorable little girls. It was the perfect life, he loved his wife and was crazy about his kids. It looked like a long stretch of smooth road ahead of him finally, when for no reason anyone could fathom, things started to go wrong again. All he talked about was making a lot of money, and seemed obsessed with that idea, whatever it took. Some thought he was having too much fun. It was all too easy for him. He had fallen into a golden life, played too hard, got greedy, and inch by inch, he let life get out of control. In the end, his shortcuts and old habit of taking what he wanted did him in. He started cutting corners and making shaky deals, nothing he could be fired for, but nothing his father-in-law wanted to tolerate either. Peter appeared to be on a fast track, heading for danger. Peter and his father-in-law had several serious talks, while walking the grounds of his parents-in-law's estate in Connecticut, and Janet's father thought he had made the point. To put it simply, he had tried to point out to Peter that there was no such thing as a free lunch or an express train to success. He warned him that the kind of deals he was making, and the sources he used, would come back to haunt him one day. Possibly even very soon. He lectured him about the importance of integrity, and felt sure that Peter would heed him. He liked him. In fact, all he succeeded in doing was make Peter feel anxious and pressured.

At thirty-one, first for the "fun of it," Peter started doing drugs. There was no real harm in it, he claimed, everyone was doing them, and it made everything more amusing and exciting. Janet was worried sick about it. By thirty-two, Peter Morgan was in big trouble, losing control over his drug habit, despite his protests to the contrary, and started running through his wife's money, until his father-in-law cut him off. A year later, he was asked to leave the firm, and his wife moved in with her parents, devastated and traumatized by the experiences she'd had at Peter's hands. He was never abusive to her, but he was constantly high on cocaine, and his life was completely out of control. It was then that her father discovered the debts he'd incurred, the money he'd "discreetly" embezzled from the firm, and given their relationship with him, and the potential embarrassment to them, and Janet, they covered his debts. He agreed to give Janet full custody of the girls, who were by then two and three. He lost his visiting rights subsequently, over an incident involving him, three women, and a large stash of cocaine on a yacht off East Hampton. His children had been visiting him at the time. The nanny had called Janet on her cell phone from the boat. And Janet had threatened to call the Coast Guard on him. He got the nanny and the girls off the boat, and Janet wouldn't let him see them again. But by then he had other problems. He had borrowed massive amounts of money to support his drug habit, and lost what money he had on high-risk investments in the commodities market. After that, no matter how good his credentials, or how smart he was, he couldn't get a job. And just as his mother had before she died, he spiraled down. He was not only short of money, but addicted to drugs.

Two years after Janet left him, he tried to get a job with a well-known venture capital firm in San Francisco, and couldn't. He was in San Francisco by then anyway, and settled into selling cocaine instead. He was thirty-five years old, and had half the world after him for bad debts, when he was arrested for possession of a massive amount of cocaine with intent to sell. He had been making a fortune at it, but owed five times as much when he was arrested, and had some frightening debts to some very dangerous people. As people who knew him said when they heard, he had had everything going for him, and managed to blow all of it to kingdom come. He was in debt for a fortune, in danger of being killed by the dealers who sold to him, and the people behind the scenes who financed them, when he was arrested. He had paid no one back. He didn't have the money to do it. Most of the time, in cases like that, when people went to prison, the debts were canceled, if not forgotten. In dire cases, people got killed in prison for them. Or if you were lucky, they let it go. Peter hoped that would be the case.

When Peter Morgan went to prison, he hadn't seen his children in two years, and wasn't likely to again. He sat stone-faced through his trial, and sounded intelligent and remorseful when he took the stand. His lawyer tried to get him probation, but the judge was smarter than that. He had seen people like Peter before, though not many, and certainly not one who'd had as many opportunities that he'd blown. He had read Peter well, and saw that there was something disturbing about him. His appearance and his actions didn't seem to fit. The judge didn't buy the pat phrases of remorse that Peter parroted. He seemed smooth, but not sincere. He was likable certainly, but the choices he'd made were appalling. And when the jury found him guilty, the judge sentenced him to seven years in prison, and sent him to Pelican Bay, in Crescent City, a maximum security prison, inhabited by 3,300 of the worst felons in the California prison system, three hundred and seventy miles north of San Francisco, eleven miles from the Oregon border. It seemed like an unduly harsh sentence for Peter and not where he belonged.

On the day Peter was released, he had been there for all the time he'd served, four years and three months. He had gotten free of drugs, minded his own business, worked in the warden's office, mostly with their computers, and hadn't had a single disciplinary incident or report in all four years. And the warden he worked for totally believed him to be sincerely remorseful. It was obvious to everyone who knew him that Peter had no intention of getting in trouble again. He had learned his lesson. He had also told the parole board that the one goal he had was to see his daughters again, and be the kind of father they could be proud of one day. Peter made it sound as if, and seemed to believe that, the last six or seven years of his life were an unfortunate blip on an otherwise clear screen, and he intended to keep it clear and trouble-free from now on. And everyone believed him.

He was released at the first legal opportunity. He had to stay in northern California for a year, and they had assigned him to a parole agent in San Francisco. He was planning to live in a halfway house until he found work, and he had told the parole board he wasn't proud. He was going to take whatever kind of work he could get, until he got on his feet, even manual labor if necessary, as long as it was honest. But no one had any serious worries that Peter Morgan wouldn't find a job. He had made some colossal mistakes, but even after four years in Pelican Bay, he still came across as an intelligent, nice guy, and was. With a little bit of luck, his well-wishers, which even included the warden, hoped that he would find the right niche for him, and build a good life. He had everything it took to do that. All he needed now was a chance. And they all hoped he'd get one when he got out. People always liked Peter and wished him well. The warden came out himself to say good-bye and shake his hand. Peter had worked for him exclusively for the entire four years.

"Stay in touch," the warden said, looking warmly at him. He had invited Peter to his own home for the past two years, to share Christmas with his wife and kids, and Peter had been terrific. Smart, warm, funny, and really kind to the warden's four teenage boys. He had a nice way with people, both young and old. And had even inspired one of them to apply for a scholarship to Harvard. The boy had just been accepted that spring. The warden felt as though he owed Peter something, and Peter genuinely liked him and his family, and was grateful for the kindness they'd shown him.

"I'll be in San Francisco for the next year," Peter said pleasantly. "I just hope they let me go back east for a visit soon, to see my girls." He hadn't even had a photograph of them for four years, and hadn't laid eyes on them in six. Isabelle and Heather were now respectively eight and nine, although in his mind's eye they were still considerably younger. Janet had long since forbidden him to have contact with them, and her parents endorsed her position. Peter's stepfather, who had paid for his education years before, had long since died. His brother had disappeared years before. Peter Morgan had no one, and nothing. He had four hundred dollars in his wallet, a parole agent in San Francisco, and a bed in a halfway house in the Mission District, which was predominantly Hispanic and a once-beautiful old neighborhood, some of which had gone downhill. The part Peter was living in had worn badly. The money he had wouldn't go far, he hadn't had a decent haircut in four years, and the only things he had left in the world were a handful of contacts in the high-tech and venture capital worlds in Silicon Valley, and the names of the drug dealers he had once done business with, and fully intended to steer clear of. He had virtually no prospects. He was going to call some people when he got to town, but he also knew there was a good chance he could be washing dishes or pumping gas, although he thought that unlikely. He was after all a Harvard MBA, and had gone to Duke before that. If nothing else, he could look up some old school friends, who might not have heard that he'd gone to prison. But he had no illusions that it was going to be easy. He was thirty-nine years old, and however he explained it, the last four years were going to be a blank on his résumé. He had a long uphill climb ahead of him. But he was healthy, strong, drug-free, intelligent, and still incredibly good-looking. Something good was going to happen to him eventually. Of that much, he was certain, and so was the warden.

"Call us," the warden said again. It was the first time he had gotten that attached to a convict who worked for him. But the men he dealt with at Pelican Bay were a far cry from Peter Morgan.

Pelican Bay had been built as a maximum security prison to house the worst criminal elements that had previously been sent to San Quentin. Most of the men were in solitary. The prison itself was highly mechanized and computerized, and state of the art, which allowed them to confine some of the most dangerous men in the country. And the warden had spotted instantly that Peter didn't belong there. Only the vast quantities of drugs he'd been dealing, and the money involved, had wound him up in a maximum security prison. Had the charges been less serious, he could just as easily have been incarcerated in a minimum security facility. He was no flight risk, had no history of violence, and had never been involved in a single incident during his time there. He was a quintessentially civilized person. The few men he chatted with over the years respected him, and he steered a wide berth of potential problems. His close relationship to the warden made him sacrosanct and gave him safe passage. He had no known associations with gangs, groups known for violence, or dissident elements. He minded his own business. And after more than four years, he seemed to be leaving Pelican Bay relatively unscathed. He had kept his head down, and done his time there. He had done a lot of legal and financial reading, spent a surprising amount of time in the library, and worked tirelessly for the warden.

The warden himself had written a glowing reference for him to the parole board. His was a case of a young man who had taken a wrong turn, and all he needed was a chance now to take the right one. And the warden was certain he would do that. He looked forward to hearing good things from and about Peter in future. At thirty-nine, Peter still had his whole life ahead of him, and a brilliant education behind him. And hopefully the mistakes he'd made would prove to be a valuable lesson of some kind. There was no question in anyone's mind that Peter would stick to the straight and narrow.

Peter and the warden were still shaking hands, as he was about to leave, when a re-

porter and photographer from the local newspaper got out of a van, and walked up to the
desk where Peter had just collected his wallet.
Another prisoner was just signing his release
papers, and he and Peter exchanged a look and
nodded. Peter knew who he was—everyone
did. They had met in the gym and in the halls
from time to time, and in the last two years,
he had frequently come to the warden's office.
He had spent years unsuccessfully seeking a
pardon, and was known to be an extremely
savvy unofficial jailhouse lawyer. His name
was Carlton Waters, he was forty-one years
old, and had served twenty-four years for
murder. In fact, he had grown up in prison.

Carlton Waters had been convicted of the
murder of a neighbor and his wife, and at-
tempting unsuccessfully to murder both their
children. He had been seventeen years old at
the time, and his partner in crime had been a
twenty-six-year-old ex-con who had be-
friended him. They had broken into their victims' home and stolen two hundred dollars.
Waters's partner had been put to death years
before, and Waters had always claimed that he
did none of the killing. He had just been there,
and he had never swerved once from his story.
He had always said he was innocent, and had
gone to the victims' home with no foreknowl-

edge of what his friend intended. It had happened quickly and badly, and the children had
been too young to corroborate his story. They
were young enough not to be a danger in
identifying them, so they had been badly
beaten but ultimately spared. Both men were
drunk, and Waters had claimed he blacked out
during the murders, and remembered nothing.

The jury hadn't bought his story, and he'd
been tried as an adult, despite his age, found
guilty, and lost a subsequent appeal. He had
spent the majority of his life in prison, first in
San Quentin, and then in Pelican Bay. He had
even managed to graduate from college while
there, and was halfway through law school.
He had written a number of articles, about the
correctional and legal systems, and had developed a relationship with the press over the
years. With his protestations of innocence
throughout his incarceration, Waters had become something of a celebrity prisoner. He
was editor of the prison newspaper, and knew
just about everyone in the prison. People
came to him for advice, and he was greatly respected within the prison population. He
didn't have Morgan's aristocratic good looks.
He was tough, strong, and burly. He was a
bodybuilder and looked it. Despite several incidents in his early days when he was still

young and hotheaded, in the past two decades he was a model prisoner. He was a powerful, fearsome-looking man, but his prison record was clean, and his reputation was bronze, if not golden. It was Waters who had notified the paper of his release and he was pleased that they were there.

Waters and Morgan had never been associates, but they had always been distantly respectful of each other, and had had a few minor conversations about legal issues while Waters waited to see the warden, and Peter chatted with him. Peter had read several of his articles in the prison newspaper, and the local newspaper, and it was hard not to be impressed by the man, whether innocent or guilty. He had a fine mind, and had worked hard to achieve something in spite of the challenge he had had growing up in prison.

As Peter walked through the gate, feeling almost breathless with relief, he looked back over his shoulder once, and saw Carl Waters shaking the warden's hand as the photographer from the local paper snapped his picture. Peter knew he was going to a halfway house in Modesto. His family still lived there.

"Thank you, God," Peter said as he stood still for a moment, closed his eyes, and then squinted up at the sun. This day felt like it had been a lifetime coming. He brushed a hand across his eyes so no one would see the tears springing from them, as he nodded at a guard, and set off on foot toward the bus stop. He knew where it was, and all he wanted now was to get there. It was a ten-minute walk, and as he hailed the bus and stepped aboard, Carlton Waters was posing for one last photograph in front of the prison. He told his interviewer again that he had been innocent. Whether or not he was, he made an interesting story, had become respected in prison over the past twenty-four years, and had milked his claims of innocence for all they were worth. He had been talking for years about his plans to write a book. The two people he had allegedly killed, and the children who had been orphaned as a result, twenty-four years before, were all but forgotten. They were obscured by his articles and artful words in the meantime. Waters was winding up the interview as Peter Morgan walked into the bus terminal and bought a ticket to San Francisco. He was free at last.

Chapter 2

Ted Lee liked working swing shift. He had done it for so long by now that it suited him. It was an old comfortable habit. He worked the four to midnight in General Works, Inspector Detective Lee in the San Francisco police force. He handled robberies and assaults, the usual smorgasbord of criminal activity. Rapes went to the Sex detail. Murders to Homicide. He had worked Homicide for a couple of years in the beginning and hated it. It was too grim for him, the men who made a career of it always seemed strange to him.

They sat around for hours looking at photographs of deceased victims. Their whole view of life got skewed by having to harden themselves to what they saw. What Ted did was more routine, but to him it seemed much more interesting. Every day was different. He liked the problem-solving aspect of matching criminals to victims. He had been in the police force for twenty-nine years, since he was eighteen. And a detective for nearly twenty, and he was good at what he did. He had worked Credit Card Fraud for a while too, but that seemed too boring. General Works was just his cup of tea, just as the swing shift was. He had been born and raised in San Francisco, right in the heart of Chinatown. His parents had come from Beijing before he was born, and both his grandmothers had come with them. His family was steeped in ancient traditions. His father had worked in a restaurant all his life, his mother was a seamstress. Both his brothers had joined the police force, just as he had, fresh from high school. One was a beat cop in the Tenderloin and didn't want to be more than that, the other was on horses. He outranked both, and they loved to tease him about it. Being a detective was a big deal to him.

Ted's wife was second-generation Chinese American. Her family was originally from Hong Kong, and owned the restaurant where his father had worked before he retired, which was how Ted had met her. They fell in love at fourteen, and he had never even dated another woman. He wasn't sure what that meant. He wasn't passionately in love with her, hadn't been in years, but he was comfortable with her. They were best friends now, more than lovers. And she was a good woman. Shirley Lee was a nurse in the intensive care unit at San Francisco General Hospital, and saw more victims of violent crimes than he did. They each saw more of their coworkers than they did of each other. They were used to it. He played golf on his day off, or took his mother to buy groceries, or whatever else she needed. Shirley liked to play cards or go shopping with her girlfriends, or get her hair done. They rarely had the same day off, and no longer worried about it. Now that the kids were grown, they had few obligations to each other. They hadn't planned it that way, but they had separate lives, and had been married since they were nineteen. Twenty-eight years.

Their oldest son had graduated from college the year before, and had moved to New York. The other two boys were still in college, in the University of California system, one in San Diego, and the other at UCLA. None of their three boys wanted to go into the police force, and Ted didn't blame them. It had been the right choice for him, but he wanted something more for them, although the department had been good to him. When he retired, he would have a full pension. He couldn't imagine retiring, although he would have thirty years in the coming year, and lots of his friends had retired long before that. He had no idea what he'd do when he retired. At forty-seven, he didn't want a second career. He still liked his first one. He loved what he did, and the people he did it with. Ted had seen men come and go over the years, some retire, some quit, some killed, some injured. He'd had the same partner for the last ten years, and before that for a few years, they had paired him off with a woman. She had lasted four years, and then moved to Chicago with her husband and joined the force there. He got Christmas cards from her every year, and in spite of his initial reservations, he had liked working with her.

The partner he'd had before that, Rick Holmquist, had left the force and joined the FBI. They still had lunch once a week, and Rick teased him about his cases. Rick always made it clear to Ted that what he did at the FBI was more important, or at least he thought so. Ted wasn't so sure. From what he could see, the SFPD solved more cases and put more criminals behind bars. A lot of what the FBI did was gathering information, and surveillance, and then other agencies stepped in and took it out of their hands. The Alcohol,

Tobacco, and Firearms guys interfered with Rick a lot of the time, the CIA, the Justice Department, the U.S. Attorney, and U.S. Marshals. Most of the time, no one interfered with Ted's cases at the SFPD, unless the suspect crossed state lines, or committed a federal offense, and then of course, the FBI stepped in.

Once in a while, he and Rick still got to work on a case together, and Ted always liked that. They had remained close friends in the fourteen years since Rick had left the SFPD, and they still had a lot of respect for each other. Rick Holmquist had gotten divorced five years before, but Ted's marriage to Shirley had never been in question. Whatever they had become, or their relationship had evolved into over the years, it worked for them. Rick was currently in love with a young FBI agent, and talking about getting remarried. Ted loved to tease him about it. Rick loved to pretend he was tough, but Ted knew what a sweet guy he was.

What Ted loved best about working swing shift, and always had, was the island of peace he found when he got home. The house was quiet, Shirley was asleep. She worked days, and left for work before he got up in the morning. In the old days, when the boys were young, it had worked for them. She dropped them off at school on her way to work, while Ted was still asleep. And he picked them up, and coached them in sports on his days off, whenever he could, or at least attended their games. When he was working, Shirley got home right after he left for work, so the boys were always covered. And when he got home everyone was asleep. It meant he didn't see a lot of the kids, or her, while they were growing up, but it brought in the bacon, and they had almost never needed to pay for a sitter, and never had to worry about day care. Between them, they had covered all their bases. It had taken a toll on them, in the time they hadn't spent together. There had been a time, ten and fifteen years before, when she had bitterly resented the fact that she never saw him. They had argued a lot about it, and eventually made their peace with his hours. They had both tried working days for a while, but they seemed to argue more, and he'd worked nights for a while, and then went back to swing shifts. It suited him.

When Ted came home that night, Shirley was sound asleep, and the house was quiet. The boys' rooms were empty now. He had bought a small house in the Sunset District years before, and on his days off, he loved to walk on the beach and watch the fog roll in. It always made him feel human again, and peaceful, after a tough case, or a bad week, or something that had upset him. There were a lot of politics in the department, which sometimes stressed him, but generally, he was an easygoing, good-natured person. Which was probably why he still got along with Shirley. She was the hothead in the family, the one who got angry and raged at him, the one who had thought their marriage and relationship should have been more than it turned out to be. Ted was strong, quiet, and steady, and somewhere along the way, she had decided that was enough, and stopped trying to get more out of him. But he also knew that when she stopped arguing with him, and complaining to him, some of the life had gone out of their marriage. They had given up something, passion for familiarity and acceptance. But as Ted knew, everything in life was a trade-off, and he had no complaints. She was a good woman, they had great kids, their house was comfortable, he loved his job, and the men he worked with were good people. You couldn't ask for more than that, or at least he didn't, which was what had always annoyed her. He was content to settle for what life offered him, without demanding more.

Shirley wanted a lot more than what Ted demanded of life. In fact, he demanded nothing. He was content with life as it was, and always had been. All his energies had gone into his work, and their boys. *Twenty-eight years.* It was a long time for passion to survive, and it hadn't for them. There was no question in his mind, he loved her. And he assumed Shirley loved him. She was not demonstrative, and rarely said so. But he accepted her the way she was, the way he accepted all things, the good with the bad, the disappointing with the comforting. He liked the security of coming home to her every night, even if she was sound asleep. They hadn't had a conversation in months, maybe even years, but he knew that if something bad happened, she'd be there for him, as he would be for her. That was good enough for him. The kind of fire and excitement Rick Holmquist was experiencing with his new girlfriend was not for him. Ted didn't need excitement in his life. He wanted just what he had. A job he loved, a woman he knew well, three kids he was crazy about, and peace.

He sat at the kitchen table, and had a cup of tea, enjoying the silence in the peaceful house. He read the paper, looked at his mail, watched a little TV. At two-thirty he slipped into bed next to her, and lay in the dark, thinking. She didn't stir, didn't know he was lying next to her. In fact, she rolled away from him and muttered something in her sleep, as he turned his back to her, and drifted off while thinking about his caseload. He had a suspect he was almost sure was bringing heroin in from Mexico, and he was going to call Rick Holmquist about it in the morning. As he reminded himself to call Rick when he woke up, he sighed softly, and fell asleep.

Chapter 3

Fernanda Barnes was staring at a stack of bills, as she sat at her kitchen table. She felt as though she had been looking at the same stack of bills for the four months since her husband died, two weeks after Christmas. But she knew only too well that even though the stack seemed the same, it grew bigger every day. Each time the mail came in, there were new additions. It had been a never-ending stream of bad news and frightening information since Allan's death. The latest being that the insurance company was refusing to pay on his life insurance policy. She and the attorney had been expecting that. He had died in questionable circumstances while on a fishing trip in Mexico. He had gone out on the boat late at night, while his traveling companions slept at the hotel. The crew members had been off the boat, at a local bar, when he took the boat out and had apparently fallen overboard. It had taken five days to recover his body. Given his financial circumstances at the time of his death, and a disastrous letter he'd left for her, filled with despair, the insurance company suspected it was a suicide. Fernanda suspected that as well. The letter had been given to the insurance company by the police.

Fernanda had never admitted it to anyone, except their attorney, Jack Waterman, but suicide had been the first thing she thought of when they called her. Before that, Allan had been in a state of shock and panic for six months, and kept telling her he was going to turn things around, but the letter made it clear that even he didn't believe that in the end. Allan Barnes had had one of those extraordinary lottery-ticket-type windfalls at the height of the dot-com era, and sold a fledgling company to a monolith for two hundred million dollars. She had liked their life fine before. It suited her perfectly. They had a small, comfortable house in a good neighborhood in Palo Alto, near the Stanford campus, where they had met in college. They had married in the Stanford chapel the day after graduation. Thirteen years later, he had hit the big time. It was more than she'd ever dreamed of, hoped for, needed, or wanted. She couldn't even understand it at first. Suddenly he was buying yachts and airplanes, a co-op in New York for when he had business meetings there, a house in London he claimed he had always wanted. A condo in Hawaii, and a house in the city so vast that she had cried when she first saw it. He had bought it without even asking her. She didn't want to move into a palace. She loved the house in Palo Alto that they had lived in since their son Will was born.

Despite Fernanda's protests, they had moved to the city four years before, when Will was twelve, Ashley was eight, and Sam was just barely two years old. Allan had insisted she hire a nanny so she could travel with him, which Fernanda hadn't wanted either. She loved taking care of her children. She had never had a career, and had been fortunate that Allan had always made enough to support them. It had been tight sometimes, but when it was, she tightened the belt at home, and they squeaked through it. She loved being home with their babies. Will had been born nine months to the day after their wedding, and she had worked part time in a bookstore while she was pregnant the first time and never since. She had majored in art history in college, a relatively useless subject, unless she wanted to get a master's, or even a doctorate, and teach, or work at a museum. Other than that, she had no marketable skills. All she knew how to be was a wife and mother, and she was a good one. Their kids were happy and wholesome and sensible. Even with Ashley at twelve and Will at sixteen, potentially challenging ages, she had never had a single problem with their children. They hadn't wanted to move into the city either. All their friends were in Palo Alto.

The house Allan had chosen for them was enormous. It had been built by a famous venture capitalist, who sold it when he retired and moved to Europe. But to Fernanda, it looked like a palace. She had grown up in a suburb of Chicago, her father had been a doctor and her mother a schoolteacher. They had always been comfortable, and unlike Allan, she had simple expectations. All she wanted was to be married to a man who loved her, and have wonderful children. She spent a lot of time reading up on experimental educational theories, she was fascinated by psychology in relation to childrearing, and she shared her passion for art with them. She encouraged them to be and become all that they dreamed of. And she had always done the same with Allan. She just hadn't expected him to make his dreams materialize to the extent he did.

When he told her he had sold his company for two hundred million dollars, she nearly fainted, and thought he was kidding. She laughed at him, and figured maybe with some extraordinary luck, he might have sold the company for one or two or five, or at a wild guess, ten, but never two hundred million. All she wanted was enough to get their kids through college, and live comfortably for the rest of their days. Maybe enough so Allan could retire at a decent age, so they could spend a year traveling in Europe, and she could drag him through museums. She would have loved to spend a month or two in Florence. But what his windfall represented to them was beyond dreaming. And Allan dove into it with a vengeance.

He not only bought houses and co-ops, a yacht and a plane, but he made some extraordinarily risky high-tech investments. And each time he did, he assured Fernanda that he knew what he was doing. He was riding the crest of the wave, and felt invincible. He was a thousand percent confident of his own judgment, more so than she was at the time. They started fighting over it. He laughed at her fears. He was plunging money into other companies that had yet to prove themselves, while the market was skyrocketing, and everything he touched turned to gold for nearly three years. It appeared that no matter what he did, or what he risked, he could not lose money, and didn't. On paper for the first year or two, their immense new fortune actually doubled. Notably, he invested in two companies that he had total faith in, and others warned him might plummet. But he didn't listen, not to her or the others. His confidence soared to dizzying heights, while she decorated the new house, and he chided her for being so pessimistic and so cautious. By then, even she was getting used to their new wealth, and starting to spend more money than she thought she should, but Allan kept telling her to enjoy it and not worry. She stunned herself by buying two important Impressionist paintings at a Christie's auction in New York, and literally shook as she hung them in their living room. It had never even dawned on her that one day she might own those paintings, or any like them. Allan congratulated her on her good decision. He was flying high and having fun, and wanted her to enjoy it too.

But even at the height of the market, Fernanda was never extravagant, nor did she forget her more modest beginnings. Allan's family was from southern California, and they had lived more lavishly than hers had. His father was a businessman, and his mother had been a housewife, and a model in her youth. They had had expensive cars, and a nice house, and belonged to a country club. Fernanda had been seriously impressed the first time she went there, although she thought them both somewhat superficial. His mother had been wearing a fur coat on a balmy night, as it dawned on her that even living in the frozen winters of the Midwest her mother had never owned one, and wouldn't want to. The show of wealth was far more important to Allan than it was to her, even more so once his overnight success broadsided them. His one regret was that his parents hadn't lived to see it. It would have meant the world to them. And in her own way, Fernanda was relieved that her parents were gone too, and couldn't see it. They had died in a car accident on an icy night ten years before. But something in her gut always told her that her parents would have been shocked at the way Allan was spending money, and it still made her nervous, even after she bought the two paintings. At least they were an investment, or at least she hoped so. And she truly loved them. But so

much of what Allan bought was about showing off. And as he kept reminding her, he
could afford it.

The wave continued to build for nearly
three years, as Allan continued to invest in
other ventures, and huge blocks of stock in
high-risk high-tech companies. He had enormous confidence in his own intuition, sometimes counter to all reason. His friends and
colleagues in the dot-com world called him
the Mad Cowboy, and teased him about it.
And more often than not, Fernanda felt guilty
about not being more supportive. He had
lacked confidence as a kid, and his father had
often put him down for not being more
brazen, and suddenly he was so confident she
felt that he was constantly dancing on a ledge
and totally fearless. But her love for him over-
came all her misgivings, and eventually all she
could do was cheer him on from the sidelines.
She didn't have anything to complain about
certainly. Within three years their net worth
had almost trebled, and he was worth half a
billion dollars. It was beyond thinking.

She and Allan had always been happy together, even before they had money. He was
an easygoing nice guy, who loved his wife and
kids. It had been a joy they shared each time
she gave birth, and he truly adored his chil-

dren, as she did. He was especially proud of Will, who was a natural athlete. And the first time he saw Ashley at her ballet recital, at five, tears had rolled down his cheeks. He was a wonderful husband and father, and his ability to turn a modest investment into a windfall was going to give their children opportunities that neither of them had ever dreamed of. He was talking about moving to London for a year at some point, so the kids could go to school in Europe. And the thought of spending days on end at the British Museum and the Tate was a major lure for Fernanda. As a result, she didn't even complain when he bought the house on Belgrave Square for twenty million dollars. It was the highest price that had been paid for a house there in recent history. But it was certainly splendid.

The children didn't even object, nor did she, when they went to spend a month there when school got out. They loved exploring London. They spent the rest of the summer on their yacht in the South of France, and invited some of their Silicon Valley friends to join them. Allan had become a legend by then, and there were others making nearly as much money as he had. But as with the gaming tables in Las Vegas, some took their winnings and disappeared, while others put them back on the table and continued to gamble. Allan was continually making deals, and huge investments. She no longer had any clear understanding of what he was doing. All she did was run their houses and take care of their kids, and she had almost stopped worrying about it. She wondered if this was what being rich felt like. It had taken her three years to actually believe it, and for the dream of his success to finally seem real.

The bubble burst finally, three years after his initial windfall. There was a scandal involving one of his companies, one he had heavily invested in as a silent partner. No one actually knew officially if, or to what extent, he had invested, but he lost over a hundred million dollars. Miraculously, at that point, it scarcely made a dent in his fortune. Fernanda read something about the company going under in the newspapers, remembered hearing him talk about it, and asked him. He told her not to worry. According to him, a hundred million dollars meant nothing to them. He was well on his way to being worth nearly a billion dollars. He didn't explain it to her, but he was borrowing against his ever-inflating stocks at that point, and when they started to collapse, he couldn't sell them fast enough to cover the debt. He leveraged his assets by borrowing to buy more assets.

The second big hit was harder than the first, and nearly twice the amount. And after the third hit, as the market plummeted, even Allan began to look worried. The assets he had borrowed against were worth nothing suddenly and all he had left was debt. What came after that was a swan dive so staggering that the entire dot-com world went with it. Within six months almost everything Allan had made had gone up in smoke, and stocks that had been worth two hundred dollars were worth pennies. The implication to the Barneses was disastrous, to say the least.

Complaining bitterly about it, he sold the yacht and the plane, while assuring Fernanda and himself that he would buy them back again, or better ones, within a year, when the market turned around again, but of course it didn't. It wasn't just that he was losing what they had, the investments he had made were literally imploding, creating colossal debt as all his high-risk investments fell like a house of cards. By year's end, he was staring at a debt almost as enormous as his sudden fortune. And just as she hadn't when he made the windfall on the first company, Fernanda didn't fully grasp the implications of what was happening, because he explained almost nothing to her. He was constantly stressed, always on the phone, traveling from one end of the world to another, and shouting at her when he got home. Overnight, he became a madman. He was absolutely, totally panicked, and with good reason.

All she knew before Christmas the year before was that he was several hundred million in debt, and most of his stock was worth nothing. She knew that much, but she had no idea what he was going to do to fix it, or how desperate their situation was becoming. And miraculously, he had made many investments in the name of anonymous partnerships and "letterbox" corporations, which were set up without his name being publicly disclosed. As a result, the world he did business in had not yet caught on to how disastrous his situation was, and he didn't want anyone to know. He concealed it as much out of pride as because he didn't want people to be nervous about doing business with him. He was beginning to feel as though he was surrounded by the stench of failure, just as he had once worn the perfume of victory. Fear was suddenly in the air all around him, as Fernanda silently panicked, wanting to support him emotionally, but desperately afraid of what was going to happen to them and their children. She was urging him to sell the house in London, the co-op in New York, and the condo in Hawaii, when he left for Mexico right after Christmas. He went there to make a deal with a group of men, and told her before he left that if it worked out, it would recoup nearly all their losses. Before he left, she suggested they sell the house in the city and move back to Palo Alto, and he told her she was being ridiculous. He assured her that everything was going to turn around again very quickly, and not to worry. But the deal in Mexico didn't happen.

He had been there for two days, when there was suddenly another catastrophe in his financial life. Three major companies fell like thatched huts within a week, and took two of Allan's largest investments with them. In a word, they were ruined. He sounded hoarse when he called her from his hotel room late one night. He had been negotiating for hours, but it was all bluff. He had nothing left to negotiate with, or trade. He started crying as she listened to him, and Fernanda assured him that it made no difference to her, she loved him anyway. That didn't console him. For Allan, it was about defeat and victory, climbing Everest and falling off again, and having to start at the

beginning. He had just turned forty weeks before, and the success that had meant everything to him for four years was suddenly over.
He was, in his own eyes at least, a total failure.
And nothing she said seemed to console him.
She told him she didn't care. That it didn't
matter to her. That she would be happy in a
grass hut with him, as long as they had each
other and their children. And he sat at the
other end and sobbed, telling her that life just
wasn't worth living. He said he'd be a laugh-
ingstock around the world, and the only real
money he had left was his life insurance. She
reminded him that they still had several houses
to sell, which all together were worth close to
a hundred million dollars.

"Do you have any idea what kind of debt
we're looking at?" he asked, his voice crack-
ing, and of course she didn't because he never
told her. "We're talking hundreds of millions.
We'd have to sell everything we own, and
we'd still be in debt for another twenty years.
I'm not even sure I could ever dig myself out
of this. We're in too deep, babe. It's over. It's
really, really over." She couldn't see the tears
rolling down his cheeks, but she could hear
them in his voice. Although she didn't fully
understand it, with his wild investment strate-
gies, leveraging their assets, and constantly

borrowing to buy more, he had lost it all. He had lost far more than that in fact. The debts he was facing were overwhelming.

"No, it's not over," she said firmly. "You can declare bankruptcy. I'll get a job. We'll sell everything. So what? I don't give a damn about all that. I don't care if we stand on a street corner selling pencils, as long as we're together." It was a sweet thought and the right attitude, but he was too distraught to even listen to her.

She called him again later that night; just to reassure him again, worried about him. She hadn't liked what he'd said about his life insurance, and she was more panicked about him than their financial situation. She knew that men did crazy things sometimes, over money lost or businesses that failed. His entire ego had been wrapped up in his fortune. And when she got him on the phone, she could hear that he'd been drinking. A lot presumably. He was slurring his words and kept telling her that his life was over. She was so upset that she was thinking of flying to Mexico the next day to be with him, while he continued his negotiations, but in the morning, before she could do anything about it, one of the men who was there with him called her. His voice was jagged and he sounded broken. All he knew was that Allan had gone out alone on the boat they'd chartered, after they all went to bed. The crew were off the boat, and he went late at night, handling the boat himself. All anyone knew was that he must have fallen overboard sometime before morning. The yacht was found by the local Coast Guard when the captain reported it missing, and Allan was nowhere to be found. An extensive search had turned up nothing.

Worse yet, when she got to Mexico herself later that day, the police handed her the letter he had left her. They had kept a copy for their records. It said how hopeless the situation was, that he could never climb back up, it was all over for him, and he'd rather be dead than face the horror and shame of the world finding out what a fool he'd been and what a mess he'd made of it. The letter was disastrous and convinced even her that he had committed suicide, or wanted to. Or maybe he was just drunk and had fallen overboard. There was no way to know for sure. But the greater likelihood was that he had killed himself.

The police turned the letter over to the insurance company, as they were obliged to. Based on his words, they had refused to pay the claim on his policy, and Fernanda's attorney said it was unlikely they ever would. The evidence was too damning.

When they recovered Allan's body finally, all they knew was that he had died by drowning. There was no evidence of foul play, he hadn't shot himself, he had either jumped or fallen in, but it seemed a reasonable belief that at that moment at least, he had wanted to die, given everything he had said to her right before that and what he'd written in the letter he had left behind.

Fernanda was in Mexico by the time they found his body, washed up on a beach nearby after a brief storm. It was a horrifying, heart-breaking experience, and she was grateful that the children weren't there to see it. Despite their protests, she had left them in California, and gone to Mexico on her own. A week later, after endless red tape, she returned, a widow, with Allan's remains in a casket in the cargo hold of the plane.

The funeral was a blur of agony, and the newspapers said that he had died in a boating accident in Mexico, which was what everyone had agreed to say. None of the people he had been doing business with had any idea how disastrous his situation was, and the police kept the contents of his letter confidential from the press. No one had any idea that he had hit rock bottom, and sunk even lower than that, in his own mind at least. Nor did anyone except she and his attorney have a clear picture of what the sum total of his financial disasters looked like.

He was worse than ruined, he was in debt to such a terrifying extent that it was going to take her years to clear up the mess he had made. And in the four months since he died, she had sold off all their property, except the city house, which was tied up in his estate. But as soon as they would let her, she had to sell it. Mercifully, he had put all their other properties in her name, as a gift to her, so she was able to sell them. She had death taxes hanging over her, which had to be paid soon, and the two Impressionists were going up for auction in New York in June. She was selling everything that wasn't nailed down, or planning to. Jack Waterman, their attorney, assured her that if she liquidated everything, including the house eventually, she might break even, without a penny to her name. The majority of Allan's debts were attached to corporate entities, and Jack was going to be declaring bankruptcy, but so far no one had any idea of the extent to which Allan's world had collapsed, and she was trying to keep it that way, out of respect for him. Even the children didn't know the full implications yet. And on a sunny May afternoon, she was still trying to absorb it herself four months after his death, as she sat in their kitchen, feeling numb and looking dazed.

She was going to pick Ashley and Sam up at school in twenty minutes, as she did like clockwork every day. Will drove himself home from high school normally, in the BMW his father had given him six months before, on his sixteenth birthday. The truth was that Fernanda barely had enough money left to feed them, and she couldn't wait to sell the house, to pay more of their debts, or even give them a slight cushion. She knew she would have to start looking for a job shortly, maybe at a museum. Their whole life had turned inside out and upside down, and she had no idea what to tell the children. They knew that the insurance was refusing to pay, and she claimed that their father's estate being in probate had made things tight for the moment. But none of the three children had any idea that before his death, their father had lost his entire fortune, nor that the reason the insurance wouldn't pay was because they thought he had killed himself. Everyone was told it was an accident. And unaware of the letter or his circumstances, the people who'd been with him weren't convinced it wasn't. Only she, her attorneys, and the authorities knew what had happened. For the moment.

She lay in bed every night, thinking of their last conversation and playing it in her head over and over and over again. It was all she could think of, and she knew she would forever reproach herself for not going to Mexico sooner. It was an endless litany of guilt and self-accusation with the added horror and constant terror of bills flooding in, endless debts he had incurred, and nothing with which to pay them. The last four months had been an indescribable horror for her.

Fernanda felt totally isolated by all that had happened to her, and the only person who knew what she was going through was their attorney, Jack Waterman. He had been sympathetic and supportive and wonderful, and they had just agreed that morning that she was going to put the house on the market by August. They had lived there for four and a half years, and the children loved it now, but there was nothing she could do about it. She was going to have to ask for financial aid to keep them in their respective schools, and she couldn't even do that yet. She was still trying to keep the extent of their financial disaster a secret. She was doing it as much for Allan's sake, as to avoid total panic. As long as the people they owed money to still thought they had funds, they would give her a little more time to pay them. She was blaming the delay on probate and taxes. She was stalling for time, and none of them knew it.

The papers had talked about the demise of some of the various companies he'd invested in. But miraculously, no one had strung the entire disastrous picture together, mostly because in many cases, the public had no idea that he was the principal investor. It was a tangle of horror and lies that haunted Fernanda day and night, while she wrestled with the grief of losing the only man she had ever loved, and trying to guide her children through the shoals and across the reefs of their own grief for their father. She was so stunned and terrified herself that most of the time it was hard to absorb what was happening to her.

She had been to see her doctor the week before, because she had barely slept in months, and he had offered to put her on medication, but she didn't want to. Fernanda wanted to see if she could tough it out without taking anything. But she felt utterly broken and in despair as she tried to put one foot in front of the other day after day, and keep going, if only for her children. She had to solve the mess, and eventually find a way to support them. But at times, especially at night, she was over-whelmed by waves of panic.

Fernanda glanced up at the clock in the enormous elegant white granite kitchen where she sat, and saw that she had five min-utes to get to the kids' school, and knew she'd have to hurry. She put a rubber band around the fresh stack of bills, and threw them into the box where she was keeping all the others. She remembered hearing somewhere that people got angry at those they loved who died, and she hadn't even gotten there yet. All she had done was cry, and wish he hadn't been foolish enough to go so wild with his success until it destroyed him, and their lives with him. But she was not angry, only sad, and to-tally panicked.

She was a small, lithe figure in jeans and a white T-shirt and sandals as she hurried out the door, holding her handbag and car keys. She had long straight blond hair she wore in a braid down her back that, at a rapid glance, made her look exactly like her daughter. Ashley was twelve, but maturing fast, and she was already the same height as her mother.

Will was coming up the front steps as she hurried out and slammed the door absentmindedly behind her. He was a tall dark-haired boy, who looked almost exactly like his father. He had big blue eyes, and an athletic build. He looked more like a man than a boy these days, and he was doing the best he could to be supportive of his mother. She was either crying or upset all the time, and he worried about her more than he let on. She stopped for a minute on the steps and stood on tiptoe to kiss him. He was sixteen, but looked more like eighteen or twenty.

"You okay, Mom?" It was a pointless question. She hadn't been okay in four months. She had a constant look of panic in her eyes, a look of shell-shocked distraction, and there was nothing he could do about it. She just looked at him and nodded.

"Yeah," she said, avoiding his eyes. "I'm going to pick up Ash and Sam. I'll make you a sandwich when I get home," she promised.

"I can do that myself." He smiled at her. "I have a game tonight." He played both lacrosse and baseball, and she loved going to his games, and practices, and always had. But lately she looked so distracted when she went, he wasn't even sure she saw them.

"Do you want me to pick them up?" he offered. He was the man of the house now. It had been a huge shock to him, as it was to all

of them, and he was doing his best to live up
to his new role. It was still hard to believe his
father was gone, and never coming back. It
had been an enormous adjustment for all of
them. It seemed like his mother was a different person these days, and he worried about
her driving sometimes. She was a menace on
the road.

"I'm fine," she reassured him, as she always
did, and convinced neither him, nor herself,
but kept moving toward her station wagon,
unlocked the door, waved, and got in. And a
moment later, she drove away, and he stood
watching her for a minute, as he saw her drive
right through the stop sign on the corner. And
then looking as though he had the weight of
the world on his shoulders, he unlocked the
front door with his key, walked into the silent
house, and closed the door behind him. With
one stupid fishing trip in Mexico, his father
had changed their lives forever. He had always
been going somewhere, doing something he
thought was important. In the last few years,
he had almost never been home, just out
somewhere, making money. He hadn't been
to one of Will's games in three years. And
even if Fernanda wasn't angry at him for what
he'd done to them when he died, there was no
question that Will was. Every time he looked

at his mother now, and saw the condition she was in, he hated his father for what he'd done to her, and all of them. He had abandoned them. Will hated him for it, and didn't even know the whole story.

Chapter 4

When Peter Morgan got off the bus in San Francisco, he stood looking around for a long moment. The bus deposited him south of Market, in an area he wasn't familiar with. All of his activities, when he lived there, had been in better neighborhoods. He had had a house in Pacific Heights, an apartment he used on Nob Hill to do drug deals, and he had had business dealings in Silicon Valley. He had never hung out in the low-rent neighborhoods, but in his state-issued prison hand-me-downs, he fit right in where he stood.

He walked along Market Street for a while, trying to get used to having people swirling around him again, and he felt vulnerable and jostled. He knew he would have to get over it soon. But after almost four and a half years in Pelican Bay, he felt like an egg without a shell on the streets. He stopped in a restaurant on Market, and paid for a hamburger and a cup of coffee, and as he savored it, and the freedom that went with it, it tasted like the best meal he'd ever had. Afterward, he stood outside, just watching people. There were women and children, and men looking as though they were going somewhere with a sense of purpose. There were homeless people lying in doorways, and drunks staggering around. The weather was balmy and beautiful, and he just walked along the street, with no particular goal in mind. He knew that once he got to the halfway house, he'd be dealing with rules again. He just wanted to taste his freedom first before he got there. Two hours later, he got on a bus, after asking someone for directions, and headed for the Mission District, where the halfway house was.

It was on Sixteenth Street. Once he got off the bus, he walked until he found it, and then stood outside, looking at his new home. It was a far cry from the places where he had lived before he went to prison. He couldn't help thinking of Janet, and their two little girls, wondering where they were now. He had missed his daughters terribly for all the years since he'd seen them. He had read somewhere that Janet had remarried. He had seen it in a magazine while he was in prison. His parental rights had been terminated years before. He imagined that the girls had probably been adopted by her new husband by now. The waters had closed over him long ago in her life, and his children's. He forced the memories from his mind, as he walked up the stairs of the dilapidated halfway house. It was open to recovering substance abusers and parolees.

The hallway smelled of cats and urine and burning food, and the paint was peeling off the walls. It was a hell of a place for a Harvard MBA to wind up, but so was Pelican Bay, and he had survived there for over four years. He knew he would survive here too. He was above all a survivor.

There was a tall thin black man with no teeth sitting at a desk, and Peter noticed that he had tracks on both his arms. He was wearing a short-sleeved shirt and didn't seem to care, and in spite of his dark skin, he had teardrops tattooed on his face, which was a sign that he had been in prison. He looked up at Peter and smiled. He looked welcoming and pleasant. He could see in Peter's eyes the shell-shocked dazed look of a new release.

"Can I help you, man?" He knew the look and the clothes and the haircut, and despite Peter's visibly aristocratic origins, he knew he had been in prison too. There was something about the way he walked, the caution with which he observed the man at the desk, that said it all. They instantly recognized each other as having a common bond. Peter had far more in common with the man at the desk now than he did with anyone from his own world. This had become his world.

Peter nodded and handed him his papers, saying that he was expected at the halfway house, and the man at the desk looked up at him, nodded, took a key out of the desk drawer, and stood up.

"I'll show you your room," he volunteered.

"Thanks," Peter said tersely. All his defenses were up again, as they had been for four years. He knew he was only slightly safer here than he had been at Pelican Bay. It was roughly the same crowd. And many of them would be going back. He didn't want to go back to prison, or have his parole violated, over a brawl, or having to defend himself in a fight.

They walked up two flights of stairs in the rancid-smelling halls. It was an old Victorian that had long since fallen into disrepair and had been taken over for this purpose. The house was inhabited only by men. Upstairs, the house smelled of cats, and seldom-changed litter boxes. The house monitor walked to the end of the hall, stopped at a door, and knocked. There was no answer. He opened it with the key and pushed open the door, as Peter walked past him into the room. It was barely bigger than a broom closet. There was badly stained old shag carpeting on the floor, a bunk bed, two chests, a battered desk, and a chair. The single window looked at the back of another house, badly in need of paint. It was beyond depressing. At least the cells in Pelican Bay had been modern, well lit, and clean. Or at least his was. This looked like a flophouse, as Peter nodded and looked at him.

"The bathroom's down the hall. There's another guy in this room, I think he's at work," the monitor explained.

"Thanks." Peter saw that there were no sheets on the top bunk, and realized he'd have to provide his own, or sleep on the mattress, as others did. Most of his roommate's belongings were spread all over the floor. The place was a mess, and he stood staring out the window for a long moment, feeling things he hadn't felt in years. Despair, sadness, fear. He had no idea where to go now. He had to get a job. He needed money. He had to stay clean. It was so easy to think of dealing drugs again to get himself out of this mess. The prospect of working at McDonald's or washing dishes

somewhere did not cheer him. He climbed
onto the upper bunk when the monitor left,
and lay there, staring at the ceiling. After a
while, trying not to think of all he had to do,
Peter fell asleep.

At almost the exact moment that Peter
Morgan walked into his room in the halfway
house in the Mission District in San Francisco,
Carlton Waters walked into his in the halfway
house in Modesto. The room he was assigned
to was shared with a man he had served a
dozen years with in San Quentin, Malcolm
Stark. The two were old friends, and Waters
smiled as soon as he saw him. He had given
Stark some excellent legal advice, which had
eventually gotten him released.

"What are you doing here?" Waters looked
pleased to see him, as Stark grinned. Waters
didn't let on, but after twenty-four years in
prison, he was in culture shock to be out. It
was a relief to see a friend.

"I just got out last month. I did another
nickel in Soledad, and got out last year. They
violated me six months ago, for possession of a
firearm. No big deal. I just got out again. This
place ain't bad. I think there are a couple of
guys here you know."

"What'd you do the nickel for?" Waters asked, eyeing him. Stark's hair was long, and he had a rugged, battered face. He'd been in a lot of fights as a kid.

"They busted me in San Diego. I got a job as a mule across the border." He had been in for dealing, when he and Waters first met. It was the only work Stark knew. He was forty-six years old, had been state raised, had been dealing drugs since he was fifteen, and using them since he was twelve. But the first time he'd gone to prison, there had been man-slaughter charges too. Someone had gotten killed when a drug deal went sour. "No one got hurt this time." Waters nodded. He actually liked the guy, although he thought he was a fool to have gotten caught again. And being a mule was as low as it got. It meant he had been hired to carry dope across the border, and obviously hadn't been smart about it, if he'd gotten arrested. But sooner or later, they all did. Or most of them anyway.

"So who else is here?" Waters inquired. For them, it was like a club or a fraternity of men who had been in prison.

"Jim Free, and some other guys you know." Jim Free, Carlton Waters remembered, had been in Pelican Bay for attempted murder and kidnap. Some guy had paid him to kill his wife, and he'd blown it. Both he and the husband had gotten a "dime." Ten years. A nickel was five. Pelican Bay, and San Quentin before it, were considered the graduate schools of crime. In some places equal to Peter Morgan's Harvard MBA. "So what are you going to do now, Carl?" Stark inquired, as though discussing summer vacations, or a business they were going to start. Two entrepreneurs discussing their future.

"I've got some ideas. I have to report in to my PA, and there are some people I've got to see about a job." Waters had family in the area, and he had been making plans for years.

"I'm working on a farm, boxing tomatoes," Stark volunteered. "It's shit work, but the pay is decent. I want to drive a truck. They said I had to box for three months, till they get to know me. I've got two months to go. They need guys if you want work," Stark suggested casually, trying to be helpful.

"I want to see if I can find a job in an office. I've gotten soft." Waters smiled. He looked anything but, he was in remarkable shape, but manual labor didn't appeal to him. He was going to see if he could talk his way into something better. And with luck, he might. The supply officer he'd worked for, for the last two years, had given him a glowing reference, and he had acquired decent computer skills in prison. And after the articles he'd written, he was a modestly skilled writer. He still wanted to write a book about his life in prison.

The two men sat around and talked for a while, and then went out to dinner. They had to sign in and out, and be back by nine o'clock. All Carlton Waters could think of as he walked to the restaurant with Malcolm was how strange it felt to be walking down a street again, and to be going out to dinner. He hadn't done that in twenty-four years, since he was seventeen. He had spent sixty percent of his life in prison, and he hadn't even pulled the trigger. At least that was what he had told the judge, and they had never been able to prove he had. It was over now. He had learned a lot in prison that he might never have learned otherwise. The question was what to do with it. For the moment, he had no idea.

Fernanda picked Ashley and Sam up at school, then dropped Ashley off at ballet, and went home with Sam. As usual, they found Will in the kitchen. He spent most of his time at home eating, although he didn't look it. He was an athlete, both lean and powerful, and just over six feet tall. Allan had been six two, and she assumed that Will would get there soon, at the rate he was growing.

"What time's your game?" Fernanda asked, as she poured Sam a glass of milk, added an apple to a plate of cookies, and set them down in front of him. Will was eating a sandwich that looked like it was about to explode with turkey, tomatoes, and cheese, and was dripping mustard and mayo. The boy could eat.

"It's not till seven," Will said between mouthfuls. "You coming?" He glanced at her, acting as though he didn't care, but she knew he did. She always went. Even now, with so much else on her mind. She loved being there for him, and besides, it was her job. Or had been till now. She would have to do something else soon. But for now, she was still a full-time mother and loved every minute of it. Being there with them was even more precious to her now that Allan had died.

"Would I miss it?" She smiled at him and looked tired, trying not to think of the fresh stack of bills she had put in the box before she left to pick up the kids at school. There seemed to be more every day, and they were growing exponentially. She had had no idea how much Allan spent. Nor how she would pay for it now. They had to sell the house soon, for as much as she could get for it. But she was trying not to think of it as she spoke to Will. "Who are you playing?"

"A team from Marin. They suck. We should win." He smiled at her, and she grinned, as Sam ate the cookies and ignored the apple.

"That's good. Eat your apple, Sam," she said, without even turning her head, and he groaned in answer.

"I don't like apples," he grumbled. He was an adorable six-year-old with bright red hair, freckles, and brown eyes.

"Then eat a peach. Eat some fruit, not just cookies." Even in the midst of disaster, life went on. Ballgames, ballet, after-school snacks. She was going through the motions of normalcy, mostly for them. But also for herself. Her children were the only thing getting her through it.

"Will's not eating fruit," Sam said, looking grumpy. She had one of every color, so to speak. Will had dark hair like his father, Ashley was blond like her, and Sam had bright red hair, although no one could figure out courtesy of whose genes. There were no redheads in the family, on either side, that they knew of. With his big brown eyes and multitude of freckles, he looked like a kid in an ad or a cartoon.

"Will is eating everything in the refrigerator,

from the look of it. He doesn't have room for fruit." She handed Sam a peach and a tangerine, and glanced at her watch. It was just after four, and if Will had a game at seven, she wanted to serve dinner at six. She had to pick Ashley up at ballet at five. Her life was broken into tiny pieces now, as it had always been, but more so than ever, and she no longer had anyone to help her. Shortly after Allan died, she had fired the housekeeper and the au pair who had helped take care of Sam previously. She had stripped away all of their expenses, and was doing everything including the housework herself. But the kids seemed to like it. They loved having her around all the time, although she knew they missed their father.

They sat at the kitchen table together, while Sam complained about a fourth grader who had bullied him at school that day. Will said he had a science project due that week, and asked her if she could get some copper wire for him. And then Will advised his brother what to do about bullies. He was in high school, and the other two went to grade school. Will was still holding his own scholastically since January, but Ashley's grades had plummeted, and Sam's first-grade teacher said he cried a lot. They were all still in shock. And so was Fernanda. She felt like crying all the time. The kids were almost used to it by now. Whenever Will or Ashley walked into her room, she seemed to be crying. She put up a better front for Sam, although he'd been sleeping in her bed for four months, and he heard her crying sometimes too. She even cried in her sleep. Ashley had complained to Will only days before that their mother never laughed anymore, she hardly even smiled. She looked like a zombie.

"She will," Will had said sensibly, "give her time." He was more adult than child these days, and was trying to step into his father's shoes.

They all needed time to recover, and he was trying to be the man in the family. More than Fernanda thought he should. Sometimes she felt like a burden to him now. He was going to lacrosse camp that summer, and she was glad for him. Ashley had made plans to go to Tahoe, to a friend's house, and Sam was going to day camp and staying in town with her. She was glad the kids would be busy. It would give her time to think, and do what she had to do with their attorney. She just hoped the house sold fast once they put it on the market. Although that would be a shock for the kids too. She had no idea where they were going to live once it sold. Someplace small, and cheap. She also knew that sooner or later it would come out that Allan had been totally broke and heavily in debt when he died. She had done what she could to protect him until now, but eventually the truth would come out. It wasn't the kind of secret you could keep forever, although she was almost certain that no one knew yet. His obituary had been wonderful and dignified and sung his praises. For whatever it was worth. She knew it was what Allan would have wanted.

When she left to pick up Ashley just before five, she asked Will to keep an eye on Sam. And then she drove to the San Francisco Ballet, where Ashley took classes three times a week. She wasn't going to be able to afford that anymore either. When all was said and done, all they were going to be able to do was go to school, keep a roof over their heads, and eat. The rest was going to be slim pickings, unless she got a great job, which was unlikely. It didn't matter anymore. Very little did. They were alive, and had each other. It was all she cared about now. She spent a lot of time asking herself why Allan hadn't understood that. Why he would rather have died than face his mistakes, or bad luck, or poor judgment, or all of the above? He had been in the grips of some kind of deal fever that had led him right up to the edge and past it, at everyone's expense. Fernanda and the children would much rather have had him than all that money. In the end, nothing good had come of it. Some good times, some fun toys, a lot of houses and condominiums and co-ops they didn't need. A boat and plane that had seemed pointless extravagances to her. They had lost their father, and she lost her husband. It was much too high a price to pay for four years of fabulous luxury. She wished he had never made the money in the first place, and they had never left Palo Alto. She was still thinking about it, as she often did now, when she stopped on Franklin Street outside the ballet. She got there just as Ashley walked out of the building in her leotard and sneakers, carrying her toe shoes.

Even at twelve, Ashley was spectacular looking with her long straight blond hair like Fernanda's. She had features like a cameo and was developing a lovely figure. She was slowly evolving from child to woman and often it seemed to Fernanda that it wasn't as slow as she would have liked. The serious look in her eyes made her look older than her years. They had all grown up in the past four months. Fernanda felt a hundred years older, not the forty she was turning that summer.

"How was class?" she asked Ashley, as she

slipped into the front seat, while cars backed up behind her on Franklin and started honking. As soon as Ashley was in and had her seatbelt on, her mother drove off toward home.

"It was okay." Although she was normally passionate about ballet, she looked tired and unenthusiastic. Everything was more effort now, for all of them. Fernanda felt as though she had been swimming upstream for months. And Ashley looked it too. She missed her father, as did the others, and her mother.

"Will has a game tonight. Do you want to come?" Fernanda asked as they drove north on Franklin in rush hour traffic.

Ashley shook her head. "I have homework." At least she was trying, although her grades didn't show it. But Fernanda wasn't giving her a hard time about it. She knew she couldn't have gotten decent grades either. She felt like she was flunking everything at the moment. Just making a couple of phone calls, dealing with their bills, keeping the house and kids in order, and facing reality on a daily basis was almost more than she could cope with.

"I need you to watch Sam tonight, while I'm out. Okay?" Ashley nodded. Fernanda had never left them alone before, but there was no one to leave them with now. Fernanda had no one to call to help her. Their instant success had isolated them from everyone. And their instant poverty more so. The friends she'd had for years had felt awkward with their sudden money. Their lives became too different, as their new lifestyle set them apart. And Allan's death and the worries he had left her with had isolated her further. She didn't want anyone to know how dire their situation was. She screened all her calls, and rarely returned them. There was no one she wanted to talk to. Except her kids. And the lawyer. She had all the classic signs of depression, but who wouldn't? She had been suddenly widowed at thirty-nine, and she was about to lose everything they had, even their house. All she had left were her children.

She cooked dinner for them when they got home, and put it on the table at six. She made hamburgers and salad, and put a bowl of potato chips out for them. It wasn't health food, but at least they ate it. She picked at hers, didn't even bother to put a hamburger on her plate, and pushed most of her salad into the garbage. She was seldom hungry, nor was Ashley. She had gotten taller and thinner in the past four months, which made her look suddenly older.

Ashley was upstairs doing her homework, and Sam was watching TV, when Fernanda

and Will left at a quarter to seven, and drove
to the Presidio. He was wearing cleats and his
baseball gear, and didn't say much to her. They
were both quiet and pensive, and once they
got there, she went to sit in the bleachers with
the other parents. No one spoke to her, and
she didn't try to engage them in conversation.
People didn't know what to say to her. Her
grief made everyone feel awkward. It was almost as though people were afraid the loss
would be contagious. Women with safe, comfortable, normal lives and husbands didn't
want to get near her. She was suddenly single
for the first time in seventeen years, and felt
like a pariah, as she sat watching the game in
silence.

Will scored two home runs. His team won
six to nothing, and he looked pleased when
they drove home. He loved winning, and
hated losing.

"Want to stop for a pizza?" she offered. He
hesitated and then nodded. He ran in with the
money she handed him, and got a large with
everything on it, and then he turned and
smiled at her when he got back in the car, and
sat in the front seat with the pizza box perched
on his lap.

"Thanks, Mom . . . thanks for coming . . ."
He wanted to say something more to her, but

didn't know how. He wanted to tell her that it meant a lot to him that she always came, and he wondered why his father hadn't. Not since he was a little kid. He had never even seen one of his lacrosse games. Allan had taken him to World Series games, and the Super Bowl, with some of his business associates. But that was different. He never went to Will's games. But she did, and as they drove home, she glanced over at him, and he smiled at her. It was one of those golden moments that happen once in a while between mothers and children, that you remember forever.

The sky was a gentle pink and mauve across the bay, as she pulled into their driveway, and she looked at it for a minute, as he got out of the car with his pizza. For the first time in months, she had a sense of competence and peace and well-being, as though she could handle what life had thrown at her, and they would all survive it. Maybe things were going to be okay after all, she told herself, as she locked her car, and followed Will up the steps to the house. She was smiling to herself, and he was already in the kitchen, as she closed the door gently behind her.

Chapter 5

Carlton Waters checked in with his parole agent on schedule, two days after he got out. As it turned out, he had the same parole agent as Malcolm Stark, and they went to report together. Waters was told to check in weekly, as Stark had been doing. Stark was determined not to go back this time. He had stayed clean since he'd been out, and was making enough at the tomato farm to stay afloat, to go out to eat at the local coffee shop, and be able to pay for a few beers. Waters had gone to apply for a job in the office of the farm where Stark worked. They said they'd let him know on Monday.

The two men had agreed to hang out together over the weekend, although Carl had said there were some family members he wanted to see on Sunday. They had been

warned to stay in the area, and needed permission to go out of the district, but Waters
told Stark his relatives were just a bus ride
away. He hadn't seen them since he was a kid.
They had dinner at a nearby diner on Saturday
night, and then went to hang out in a bar,
watching baseball on TV, and they were back
in the house by nine o'clock. Neither of them
wanted any problems. They had done their
time, now they wanted peace, freedom, and to
keep their noses clean. Waters said he hoped
he'd get the job he'd interviewed for the day
before, and if not, he'd have to start looking
for something else. But he wasn't worried
about it. The two men were asleep on their
bunks by ten o'clock, and when Stark got up
at seven o'clock the next day, Carl was gone,
and had left him a note. He said he'd gone to
see his relatives, and would see him that night.
Stark saw later that Carl had checked himself
out in the log at six-thirty that morning. He
spent the rest of the day hanging around the
house, watching the ballgame on TV, and talking to the others. He never gave any further
thought to where Carl had gone. He had said
he'd be with his relatives, and whenever anyone asked Stark where Carl was, he said so.

Malcolm Stark hung out with Jim Free from
about midday. They walked to the nearest Jack

in the Box and bought tacos for dinner. Free was the man who had been hired to kill a man's wife, had bungled the job, and wound them both up in prison instead. But they never spoke of their criminal life when they were together. None of them did. They did in prison occasionally, but out in the world, they were determined to put the past behind them. Free looked like he'd been in prison though. He had tattoos up and down his arms, and the familiar prison teardrops tattooed on his face. He seemed as though no one and nothing frightened him. He could take care of himself and looked it.

The two men sat talking about the ballgame that night, eating their tacos and talking about games they'd seen, players they admired, batting averages, and historical moments in baseball they'd wished they'd seen. It was the kind of conversation two men could have had anywhere, and Stark smiled when Free commented about the girl he'd just met. He met her at the gas station where he worked. There was a coffee shop next to it, and she worked there as a waitress. He said she was the prettiest thing he'd ever seen, and looked a lot like Madonna, which made Stark guffaw. He'd heard descriptions like that before, in the joint, and it always made him question the

guy's eyesight. The women never looked anything like the guy's descriptions when you saw
them. But if that was what Jim Free thought,
he wasn't going to argue with him. A man was
entitled to his dreams and illusions.

"She know you been in the joint?" Malcolm
Stark asked with interest.

"Yeah. I told her. Her brother did time for
grand theft auto as a kid. She didn't look too
worried." It was a whole world of people who
seemed to measure time by who went to
prison, for how long, and it didn't seem to faze
them. It was like a club, or a secret society.
They had a way of finding each other.

"You been out with her yet?" There was a
woman Stark had his eye on too, at the tomato
plant, but he hadn't dared approach her yet.
His dating skills were a little rusty.

"I thought I'd ask her about next weekend,"
Free said awkwardly. They all dreamed of romance and wild sexual exploits when they
were doing time. And once out, it was harder
to pursue than they'd expected. They were
neophytes in the real world, in a lot of ways.
And in some ways seeking out women was the
hardest. Most of the time, the men in the
halfway house just hung out together, except
for the ones who were married. But even they
took a while to get to know their wives again.

They were so used to a world of men, devoid of women, that in a lot of ways, it was easier staying in an all-male world, like priests, or men who had been too long in the military. Women were an uncomfortable addition to the equation. An all-male society was more familiar to them, and simpler.

Stark and Free were both sitting on the front steps, shooting the breeze when Carlton Waters walked in that evening. He looked relaxed and at ease, and as though he'd spent a pleasant day, as he smiled at the two men. He was wearing a blue cotton shirt open over a T-shirt, jeans, and cowboy boots, and his boots were dusty. He had just walked half a mile from the bus stop, on a dirt road, on a beautiful spring night. And he looked to be in good spirits. He was smiling and seemed relaxed.

"How were your relatives?" Stark asked politely. It was funny how out here manners mattered, and you were supposed to ask questions. In prison, it was always wisest to keep one's own counsel, and ask nothing. In places like Pelican Bay, people took offense at questions.

"Okay, I guess. Something must have happened. I took two buses all the way out to their farm, and damn if they hadn't gone somewhere. I told them I was coming, but I guess they forgot. I just hung around, and sat on their porch for a while, walked into town and had something to eat. And took the bus back." He didn't look bothered about it. It just felt good to be on a bus going anywhere, and walking in the sunshine. He hadn't had a chance to do anything like that since he was a kid. And he looked like one, as he sat down on the steps with them. He looked happier than he had the day before. Freedom agreed with him. He looked as though a weight had lifted off his shoulders, as he leaned back on the steps and Malcolm Stark grinned at him. When he did, you could see that Stark had almost no back teeth, just front ones.

"If I didn't know better, I'd say you were bullshitting me about your relatives, and you spent the day with a woman," Stark teased. Waters had the kind of sated, giddy look people had after great sex.

Carlton Waters laughed out loud at what Stark said, skipped a rock across the road, and offered no further comment. And at nine o'clock, they stood up, stretched, and went back inside. They knew their curfew. They signed the log, and went to their rooms. He and Stark talked for a while, sitting on their bunks, and Jim Free went to his room. They were used to the familiar peaceful routine of lockdown at night, and had no objection to the house rules or curfew.

Stark had to get up at six for work the next day, and by ten o'clock, both men were asleep, as was the whole house. Looking at them, sleeping peacefully, no one would have suspected how dangerous they were, or had been, or the damage they had done in the world, before they got there. But hopefully, for the most part, they had learned their lesson.

Chapter 6

As she always did, Fernanda spent the weekend with her children. Ashley had a rehearsal for a ballet recital she was preparing for in June, and afterward Fernanda dropped her off for a movie and dinner with friends. Fernanda chauffeured her to all of it, with Sam sitting in the front seat beside her. She had invited a friend in to play with him, on Saturday, and they went to one of Will's games while Ashley was at rehearsal. The children kept her busy, and she loved it. It was her salvation.

She had some paperwork she had to do on Sunday, while Ashley slept, Sam watched a video, and Will worked on his science project, with the Giants game droning in the background on the TV in his room. It was a boring game, and the Giants were losing, so he wasn't paying much attention. Fernanda was trying to concentrate unsuccessfully while she went over the tax papers the lawyer had given her to fill out. She would have liked to go for a walk on the beach with the kids. She suggested it at lunch, but none of them was in the mood. She just wanted to get away from her tax work. She had just taken a break, and walked into the kitchen for a cup of tea, when there was a sudden loud explosion that sounded very near them. It seemed as though it was right next to them, in fact, and afterward there was a long silence, as Sam ran into the room and stared at her. They both looked panicked.

"What was that?" he asked her, looking worried.

"I don't know. It sounded big though," Fernanda answered. They could already hear sirens in the distance.

"It sounded huge," Will corrected her, as he ran in, and Ashley came downstairs, looking confused a minute later, as they all stood in the kitchen, wondering what had happened. The sirens sounded as though they were on their street, and rapidly approaching. There were a lot of them, and three police cars sped past their windows, with lights flashing. "What do you think it is, Mom?" Sam asked again, looking excited. It sounded like a bomb had exploded at the home of one of their neighbors, although Fernanda knew that was unlikely.

"Maybe some kind of a gas explosion," she suggested, as they all looked out the window and saw more flashing lights speed by. They opened the front door and peeked out, and it looked like a dozen police cars had congregated down the street, as more arrived, and three fire trucks whizzed by. Fernanda and the children walked to the curb, and they could see a car in flames down the block, as firemen aimed hoses at it. People had come out of their houses, all up and down the street, and were chatting with each other. A few approached the burning car out of curiosity, but the police signaled them back, as a police captain's car arrived on the scene, but most of the excitement seemed to be over, as the flames on the car were extinguished.

"Looks like a car caught fire, and the gas tank must have exploded," Fernanda explained sensibly. The excitement was almost over. But there were police and firemen everywhere, as the captain got out of his car.

"Maybe it was a car bomb," Will said with interest as they stood outside, and eventually they went back into the house, while Sam complained. He wanted to see the fire trucks, but the police weren't letting anyone near the scene. There were a flock of cops down the block, circling the scene, and more still arriving. A car in flames didn't seem to warrant that much attention, but there was no denying the explosion had sounded impressive. She had jumped about a foot when it happened.

"I don't think it was a car bomb," Fernanda commented, once they were back in the house. "I think a gas tank exploding would make a pretty big bang. It was probably burning for a while, and no one noticed."

"Why would a car catch fire?" Ashley added, looking puzzled. It seemed dumb to her, but had sounded scary anyway.

"It happens. Maybe someone dropped a cigarette and didn't see it. Something like that. Maybe vandalism," although that seemed unlikely. Particularly in their neighborhood. Fernanda didn't know what else to suggest to explain it.

"I still think it was a car bomb," Will said, delighted to be distracted from his science project. He hated doing it, and any excuse to avoid it was valid, especially a car bomb.

"You play too much Nintendo," Ashley said to Will with a look of disgust. "No one blows up cars, except in movies or on TV."

They all went back to their respective activities then. Fernanda continued her tax work for her attorney, Jack Waterman. And as he left the room, Will said he couldn't finish his project without more copper wire, which they didn't have, and his mother promised to get him more on Monday. And Ashley sat with Sam, watching the end of the video with him. It was another two hours before the last of the police cars left, and the fire trucks left long before that. Everything was peaceful again, as Fernanda cooked dinner for them. She was just putting the dishes in the dishwasher when the doorbell rang. She hesitated at the front door, looked through the peephole, and saw two men standing outside, talking to each other. She'd never seen them before. She was wearing jeans and a T-shirt, and her hands were wet when she asked who it was through the door. They said they were police officers, but they didn't look like it to her. Neither was in uniform, and she was thinking about not opening the door, when one of them held his badge up to the peephole so she could see it. She opened cautiously and looked at them. They both looked respectable, and apologized for disturbing her, as she stood looking at them in confusion.

"Is something wrong?" It didn't occur to her at first that their visit had anything to do with the car they'd seen burning that afternoon, or the explosion they'd heard when the gas tank must have exploded. She couldn't imagine why they had come to see her. And for a moment it reminded her of the agonizing days after Allan's death, dealing with the authorities in Mexico.

"We were wondering if we could talk to you for a minute." They were two plain-clothes officers, one Asian, and the other Caucasian. They were both nicely dressed men somewhere in their forties, wearing sport coats, shirts, and ties. They said they were Detectives Lee and Stone, and handed her their cards, as they stood in the front hall, talking to her. There was nothing ominous about them, and the Asian man looked at her and smiled. "We didn't mean to frighten you, ma'am. There was an incident up the street from you this afternoon. If you were home, you probably heard it." He was pleasant and polite and put her instantly at ease.

"Yes, we did. It looked like a car caught fire, and I assumed the gas tank exploded."

"That's a reasonable assumption," Detective Lee volunteered. He was watching her, as though looking for something. There was something about her that seemed to intrigue him. The other detective said nothing. He let his partner take the lead.

"Do you want to come in?" Fernanda asked. It was obvious that they weren't ready to leave yet.

"Would you mind? We'll only take a minute." She walked them into the kitchen, and found her sandals under the kitchen table. They looked so respectable, she was embarrassed to stand there talking to them barefoot.

"Would you like to sit down?" She waved at the kitchen table, which was almost cleared. She used the sponge to get off the rest of the crumbs, tossed it into the sink, and then sat down with them. "What happened?"

"We're still working on it, we want to ask the neighbors some questions. Was anyone in the house with you when you heard the explosion?" She saw him glance around the room, taking in the elegant kitchen. It was a big handsome room, with white granite counters, state-of-the-art equipment, and a big white Venetian glass chandelier. It was in keeping with the grandeur of the rest of the house. It was an imposing, large, very formal house, in direct proportion to Allan's success at the time they acquired it. But she looked very normal and relaxed as Detective Lee took in the jeans, T-shirt, and hair loosely tied in an elastic. She looked like a kid, at first glance, and it was obvious that she had been cooking dinner, which seemed surprising to him. In a house like hers, he had expected to see a cook. Not a pretty woman in jeans and bare feet.

"My children were here with me," she said, as he nodded.

"Anyone else?" Along with a cook, he expected maids and a housekeeper too. It was the kind of house he presumed would be staffed. Maybe an au pair or two, or even a butler. It seemed odd to him that she was the only one there. Maybe they were off on Sunday, he assumed.

"No, just us. The kids and I," she said simply.

"Was your husband home?" he asked, and she hesitated, and then glanced away. She still hated to explain it. It was too new, and the word still hurt whenever she had to say it.

"No. I'm a widow." Her voice was soft and seemed to catch as she said it. She hated the word.

"I'm sorry. Did any of you go outside before you heard the explosion?" He sounded kind as he asked the questions, and she didn't know why, but she liked him. So far, Detective Lee was the only one doing the talking. The other inspector, Detective Stone, still said nothing. But she saw him glance around and notice the

kitchen. They seemed to be taking in everything, and studying her as well.

"No. We went outside afterward, but not
before. Why? Did something else happen? Did
someone set fire to the car?" Maybe it was
malicious mischief, and not an innocent fire
after all, she thought.

"We don't know yet." He smiled pleasantly.
"Did you look outside, or see anyone on
the street? Anything unusual, or anyone
suspicious?"

"No. I was doing some paperwork at my
desk, I think my daughter was asleep, one of
my sons was watching a video, and the other
one was doing a science project for school."

"Would you mind if we asked them?"

"No, that's fine. I'm sure the boys will think
it's exciting. I'll go get them." And then she
turned as an afterthought as she stood in the
doorway and Ted Lee watched her. "Would
you like something to drink?" She glanced at
both of them, and they shook their heads, but
both of them smiled at her and thanked her.
They seemed extremely polite to her. "I'll be
back in a minute," she said, and bounded up
the stairs to the children's rooms. She told
them that the police were downstairs and
wanted to ask them some questions. As she
had predicted, Ashley looked annoyed. She

was on the phone and didn't want to be interrupted. And Sam looked excited.

"Are they going to arrest us?" He looked both scared and hopeful. And Will tore himself away from a Nintendo game long enough to raise an eyebrow and look intrigued.

"Was I right? Was it a car bombing?" He looked hopeful.

"No, I don't think so. They said they don't know what it was, but they want to know if any of you saw someone or something suspicious. And no, Sam, they are not going to arrest us. They don't think you did it." Sam looked momentarily disappointed, and Will stood up and followed his mother to the stairs, while Ashley objected.

"Why do I have to come downstairs? I was asleep. Can't you tell them that? I'm talking to Marcy." They had serious matters to discuss. Like the eighth-grade boy in their school who had evidenced some recent interest in Ashley. As far as she was concerned, that was a lot more important, and more interesting than the police.

"Tell Marcy you'll call her back. And you can tell the detectives yourself that you were sleeping," Fernanda said, as she preceded them downstairs and they followed her to the kitchen. The children came into the room right behind her, as the two detectives stood up and smiled at them. They were a nice-looking bunch of kids, and she was a nice-looking woman. Ted Lee suddenly felt sorry for her, and from the look on her face when she'd answered him, he got the feeling her widowhood was recent. He had an instinctive sense of things, after almost thirty years of asking questions and watching people when they answered. She had looked wounded when she answered him, but she looked more comfortable now, surrounded by her children. He noticed that the little red-headed boy looked like an imp, and he was staring up at him with interest.

"My mom says you're not going to arrest us," Sam piped up, and everyone in the room laughed, as Ted smiled down at him.

"That's right, son. Maybe you'd like to help us with the investigation. How does that sound? We could deputize you, and when you grow up, you can be a detective."

"I'm only six," Sam said apologetically, as though he would have liked to help them out if he were older.

"That's all right. What's your name?" Detective Lee was good with kids, and instantly put Sam at ease.

"Sam."

"I'm Detective Lee, and this is my partner, Detective Stone."

"Was it a bomb?" Will interrupted, and Ashley rolled her eyes at her brother, convinced it was a dumb question. All she wanted was to go back upstairs and get back on the phone.

"Maybe," Ted Lee said honestly. "It might be. We're not sure yet. Forensics has to check it out. They're going to be going over the car pretty closely. You'd be surprised what they can find out." He didn't tell the kids, but they already knew it had been a bomb. There was no point frightening the neighbors by telling them yet. What they wanted to know now was who had done it. "Did any of you go outside, or look out your windows before you heard the explosion?"

"I did," Sam said quickly.

"You did?" His mother looked at him with amazement. "You went outside?" It seemed more than unlikely to her, and she looked at him skeptically, as did his brother and sister. Ashley thought he was lying to seem important to the police.

"I looked out the window. The movie got kind of boring."

"What did you see?" Ted asked with interest. The boy was cute as could be, and reminded him of one of his own sons, when he was little. He had had that same open, funny way of talking to strangers, and everyone he met loved him as a result. "What did you see, Sam?" Ted asked, sitting down on one of the kitchen chairs, so he didn't tower over him. He was a tall man, and once he sat down, Sam looked him right in the eye without hesitating.

"People were kissing," Sam said firmly with a look of disgust.

"Outside your window?"

"No. On the movie. That's why it was boring. Kissing is stupid."

Even Will smiled at that one, and Ashley giggled, while Fernanda watched him with a sad smile, wondering if he'd ever see kissing again in real life. Maybe not in her lifetime. Only in his. She forced the thought from her mind, as Ted asked him more questions. "What did you see outside?"

"Mrs. Farber walking her dog. He always tries to bite me."

"That's not very nice. Did you see anyone else?"

"Mr. Cooper with his golf bag. He plays

every Sunday. And there was a man walking down the street, but I didn't know him."

"What did he look like?" Ted asked almost casually.

Sam frowned as he thought about it. "I can't remember. I just know I saw him."

"Did he look weird or scary? Do you remember anything about him?" Sam shook his head.

"I just know I saw him, but I didn't pay any attention. I was looking at Mr. Cooper. He bumped into Mrs. Farber with his golf bag, and her dog started barking. I wanted to see if the dog would bite him."

"And did he?" Ted asked with interest.

"No. Mrs. Farber pulled on the leash, and yelled at him."

"She yelled at Mr. Cooper?" he asked, smiling, and Sam grinned. He liked him, and answering Ted's questions was fun.

"No," Sam explained patiently, "she yelled at the dog, so he wouldn't bite Mr. Cooper. And then I went back to the movie. And then after that, it sounded like something blew up."

"And that's all you saw?"

Sam concentrated again and then nodded. "Oh. And I think I saw a lady too. I didn't know her either. She was running."

"Which way was she running?"

Sam pointed away from the place where the car blew up.

"What did she look like?"

"Nothing special. She looked kind of like Ashley."

"Was she with the man you didn't know?"

"No, he was walking the other way, and she bumped into him. Mrs. Farber's dog barked at her too, but the lady just ran by them. And that's all I saw," Sam said conclusively, and then he glanced up at the others, looking embarrassed. He was afraid they would accuse him of showing off. Sometimes they did.

"That was very good, Sam," Ted complimented him, and then looked at his brother and sister.

"What about you guys? Did you see anything?"

"I was sleeping," Ashley said, but she was no longer hostile about it. She liked him. And the questions were interesting.

"I was doing my science project," Will added. "I didn't look up till I heard the explosion. I had the Giants game on, but the explosion was really loud."

"I'll bet it was," Ted said, nodding, and then stood up again. "If you think of anything else, any of you, give us a call. Your mom has our number." They all nodded, and as an after-thought, Fernanda asked him a question.

"Whose car was it? Any of our neighbors, or just a car parked on the street?" She hadn't been able to tell with the fire trucks all around it. The car had been unrecognizable by then, engulfed in flames.

"Judge McIntyre's, he's one of your neighbors. You probably know him. He's out of town, but Mrs. McIntyre was there. She was about to go out and drive somewhere, and it really scared her. Fortunately, she was still in the house when the incident occurred."

"It scared me too," Sam said honestly.

"It scared all of us," Fernanda admitted.

"It sounded like they blew up the whole block," Will added. "I bet it was a car bomb," he insisted.

"We'll let you know," Ted volunteered, but Fernanda suspected they wouldn't.

"Do you think it was meant for Judge McIntyre, if it was a bomb?" Fernanda asked with fresh interest.

"Probably not. It was probably just some random, crazy thing." But this time, she didn't believe him. There had been too many police cars on the scene, and the captain's car had arrived very quickly. She was beginning to think Will was right. They were obviously looking

for someone, and doing some careful checking. Too much so, she thought, for it to be just
a random fire.

Detective Lee thanked them, then he and his
partner said good night as they left, and
Fernanda closed the door behind them with a
thoughtful look.

"That was interesting," she said to Sam. He
was feeling very important after answering all
their questions. They talked about it all the
way up the stairs, and then went back to their
own rooms, and Fernanda went back to finish
cleaning up the kitchen.

"Cute kid," Ted Lee said to Jeff Stone as
they walked to the next house, where no one
had seen anything either. They checked all the
houses on the block, including the Farbers and
the Coopers Sam had mentioned. No one had
seen anything, or at least nothing they remembered. Ted was still thinking of the
adorable little red-headed kid three hours
later, when they went back to their office, and
he poured himself a cup of coffee. He was putting cream in it, when Jeff Stone made a random comment.

"We got a printout on Carlton Waters this
week. Remember him? The guy who killed a
couple of people when he was seventeen, was

tried as an adult, appealed about a million times, and tried to get a pardon. He never got it. He got out this week. Paroled to Modesto, I think. Wasn't McIntyre the sentencing judge on that case? I remember reading about it somewhere. He said he never doubted for a minute Waters was guilty. Waters claims his partner pulled the trigger and did the shooting, he was just standing there, innocent as a newborn babe. The other guy died by lethal injection at San Quentin a few years later. I think Waters was in Pelican Bay."

"So what are you telling me?" Ted asked as he took a sip of the steaming coffee. "That Waters did it? Not very smart of him, if he did. He tries to blow up the sentencing judge, twenty-four years later, a couple of days after he gets out of prison? He can't be that dumb. He's a smart guy. I read a couple of his articles. He's no fool. He knows he'd get a one-way ticket back to Pelican Bay on an express train on that one, and he'd be the first one they'd think of. It's got to be someone else, or just a random thing. Judge McIntyre must have pissed off a lot of folks before he retired. Waters isn't the only one he ever sent to prison."

"I was just thinking. It's an interesting coincidence. But probably only that. Might be worth a look though. Want to ride up to Modesto tomorrow?"

"Sure. Why not? If you think there's something to it. I don't. But I don't mind a ride in the country. We can go up there as soon as we come on, and be there by seven. Maybe something else will turn up between now and then." But no one had seen anything or anyone suspicious so far. They had come up dry at every house.

The only thing that did turn up was the confirmation from Forensics that it had in fact been a car bomb. A nice one. It would have done the judge and his wife some serious damage if they'd been in the car. As it turned out, it had gone off prematurely. The bomb had a timer, and the judge's wife had missed being blown to kingdom come, by at least five minutes. When they called the judge on the number his wife had given them, he said that he was convinced someone was trying to kill him. But like Ted, he thought Carlton Waters was too big a stretch. He had put too much effort into winning his freedom to take a risk like that after he'd only been out a few days.

"The guy's too smart for that," the judge commented on the phone. "I've read some of the articles he's written. He still claims he's innocent, but he's not dumb enough to try and blow me up the week he gets out." There were at least a dozen other possibilities, of people he suspected were furious at him, and who were out of prison. The judge had been retired for the last five years.

Ted and Jeff went to Modesto anyway, and arrived at the halfway house just as Malcolm Stark, Jim Free, and Carlton Waters were coming back from dinner. Jim Free had talked them into going to the coffee shop at the gas station, so he could see his girl.

"Good evening, gentlemen," Ted said pleasantly, as all three men looked instantly guarded and hostile. They could smell cops a mile away.

"What brings you here?" Waters asked, once he heard where they were from.

"A little incident in our neck of the woods just yesterday," Ted explained. "A car bombing of Judge McIntyre's vehicle. You may remember the name," he said, looking Waters in the eye.

"Yes, I do. Couldn't happen to a nicer guy," Waters said without hesitating. "Wish I'd had the balls to do it myself, but he's not worth going back to the joint for. Did they kill him?" he asked hopefully.

"Fortunately not. He was out of town. But

whoever did it nearly killed his wife. The bomb missed her by about five minutes."

"What a shame," Waters said, looking entirely undismayed. Lee was watching him, and it was easy to see how smart he was. He was as cool as a glacier in Antarctica, but Ted was inclined to agree with the judge. There was no way Waters was going to risk going back to the joint by doing something as dumb as blowing up the sentencing judge's car. Although there was always the possibility that he was in fact just that ballsy, and just that cool. He could have gotten there by bus certainly, planted the bomb, and gotten back to Modesto again, in time for curfew at the halfway house, with time to spare. But Ted's instincts told him that this wasn't their man. It was an unholy trio, though. He knew who the other two were, and how long they'd been out. Ted always read the printouts when they got them. And he remembered their names. They were a nasty piece of work. He had never bought Waters's claims of innocence either, and he didn't trust him now. All convicts claimed that they'd been framed, and set up either by their girlfriends, their running partners, or their attorneys. He'd heard it too many times. Waters was a tough customer, and smoother than Lee liked. He had all the earmarks of a sociopath, a man with little or no conscience, and he was definitely a smart guy.

"Where were you yesterday, by the way?" Ted Lee asked, as Waters stood watching him with an icy stare.

"Around here. I took a bus ride to see some relatives. They were out, so I hung out on their porch for a while, came back, and sat around with these guys." There was no one to corroborate the earlier part of his alibi, so Ted didn't bother to ask for names.

"How nice. Can anyone corroborate your whereabouts?" Ted asked, looking him right in the eye.

"A couple of bus drivers. I still have the ticket stubs, if you want."

"Let's see the stubs." Waters looked furious, but he went up to his room and brought them back. They showed a destination in the Modesto area, and had obviously been used. Only half the stubs were left. There was nothing to say he hadn't torn them himself, but Ted Lee didn't think he had. Waters looked totally unconcerned as Ted handed the tickets back. "Well, keep your noses clean, guys. We'll come back and see you sometime, if anything comes up." They knew he had the right to question them, or even search them, whenever he chose. All three were on parole.

"Yeah, and don't let the door hit you in the ass on the way out," Jim Free added under his breath as they left. Ted and Jeff heard what he said, but didn't react, got back in their car, and drove away, as Waters watched them with a look of hatred in his eyes.

"Pigs," Malcolm Stark commented, and Waters said nothing. He just turned on his heel and went back inside. He wondered if every time they had a wrinkle in their shorts in San Francisco, they were going to show up and question him. They could do anything they wanted with him, and he could do nothing about it, as long as he was on parole. The only thing he didn't want was to get sent back.

"So what do you think?" Ted asked his partner as they drove away. "Think he's clean?" Ted was of two minds, and thought anything was possible. His gut was still suspicious of him, but his head told him that the bomb had to have been put there by someone else. Waters couldn't have been dumb enough to do something like that. He was smart. But Ted had to admit, he looked like a bad guy. The bomb could have been set there as a warning of bigger things to come, since a timed bomb would only have killed the judge or his wife if they were in the car or standing near it when the bomb went off.

"Actually, no I don't think he's clean," Jeff Stone answered. "I think the guy's a nasty piece of work, and innocent on his first beef, my ass. I think he's ballsy enough to roll right into town, plant the bomb on McIntyre's vehicle, and come right back up here without missing lunch. I think he's capable of it. But I think he's too smart to do it. I don't think he did it this time. But I wouldn't trust the guy farther than I could throw him. I think he'll be back. We'll be hearing from him again." They had both seen men like him go back to the joint too many times.

Ted agreed. "Maybe we should run his mug shots, and show them up and down the street, just in case. Maybe the Barnes kid would remember him, if he saw a picture of him. You never know."

"It can't hurt," Jeff said, nodding, and thinking about the three men they had just seen. A kidnapper, a murderer, and a drug runner. They were an ugly group, and a bad lot. "I'll run the shots when we get back. We can take them around on Tuesday, and see if anyone remembers seeing him on the street."

"My guess is they won't," Ted said as they got back on the freeway again. It was hot in Modesto, and the trip hadn't produced anything for them, but he was glad they had gone anyway. He'd never seen Carlton Waters before, and there was something about seeing him in the flesh. The guy gave him the creeps, and Ted was absolutely dead certain they'd be seeing him again. He was that kind of guy. There was nothing rehabilitated about him. He had spent twenty-four years in prison, and Ted was certain that he was far more dangerous than he had been before he went in. He had been to gladiator school now for nearly two-thirds of his life. It was a depressing thought, and Ted just hoped he didn't kill someone again before he went back.

The two detectives drove in silence for a while, and then talked about the car bombing again. Jeff was going to run a list through the computer of all the people Judge McIntyre had sentenced in his last twenty years on the bench, and see who else was out. It was probably someone else who'd been out for a while, longer than Carl. The only thing they knew for sure was that it hadn't been a random act. It had been a gift meant exclusively for the judge, or failing him, his wife. It was not a reassuring thought, but Ted assumed they'd figure out who it was eventually. Carlton Waters wasn't entirely out of the running yet. He didn't have a corroborated alibi, but there was no evidence that pinned it to him either, and he and Jeff both suspected there wouldn't be. If Waters had done it, he was too smart for that. Even if he'd done it, they might never be able to pin it on him. But if nothing else, having seen him now, Ted was going to keep an eye out for him. And he figured that one of these days, Carlton Waters was going to drift across his screen again. It was almost inevitable. He was just that kind of guy.

Chapter 7

The doorbell rang at five o'clock on Tuesday, while Fernanda was in the kitchen, reading a letter from Jack Waterman, listing the things she had to sell and what she could expect to get for them. His estimate was conservative, but they were both hoping that if she sold everything, including the jewelry Allan had given her, and there was a lot of it, she might be able to start her new life at ground zero and not significantly below it, which was her worst fear. At best, she had to start from scratch, and she had no idea how she was going to support herself for the next several years, let alone get her kids through college when they got to that point. For the moment, all she could do was trust that she would come up with some idea. For now she would just get through each day, keep swimming, and do her best not to drown.

Will was upstairs doing homework, or pretending to. Sam was playing in his room, and Ashley was at rehearsal for her ballet recital, and due to finish at seven. Fernanda was going to make dinner late for all of them, which gave her more time to brood, as she sat in the kitchen, and gave a start when she heard the doorbell. She wasn't expecting anyone, and the car bombing of two days before was the last thing on her mind when she went to the door and saw Ted Lee through the peephole. He was alone, and he was wearing a white shirt, dark tie, and blazer. He had looked eminently respectable both times she'd seen him.

She opened the door with a look of surprise, and realized again how tall he was. He had a manila envelope in his hands, and seemed to hesitate, until she asked him to come in. He saw a look of strain in her eyes, her hair was loose, and she seemed weary. He wondered what was bothering her. She looked as though she had the weight of the world on her shoulders. But as he walked in, she smiled, and made an effort to be pleasant.

"Hello, Detective. How are you today?" she asked with a tired smile.

"I'm fine. I'm sorry to bother you. I wanted to stop by and show you a mug shot." He glanced around, as he had on Sunday. It was hard not to be impressed by the house, and the obviously priceless pieces in it. It looked almost like a museum. And in her jeans and T-shirt, as she had on Sunday, she looked somewhat out of place in her casual style. In the setting she lived in, she looked as though she should be sweeping down the stairs in an evening gown, trailing a fur coat behind her. But she didn't look like that kind of woman. Instinctively, Ted suspected he'd like her. She seemed like a normal person, and a gentle woman, although a sad one. Her grief was stamped all over her, and he sensed correctly that she was deeply attached to, and fiercely protective of, her children. Ted always had a good sense of people, and he trusted his own instincts about her.

"Did they find the person who blew up Judge McIntyre's car?" she asked as she led him into the living room, and gestured to him to sit on one of the velvet couches. They were soft and comfortable. The room was done in beige velvets and silks and brocades, and the curtains looked as if they'd been in a palace. He wasn't far wrong in thinking that. She and

Allan had bought them out of an ancient palazzo in Venice and brought them home.

"Not yet. But we're checking out some leads. I wanted to show you a photograph, and see if you recognize someone, and if Sam's around, I'd like him to take a look too." He was still bothered by the unidentified man Sam said he had seen, but couldn't remember in detail. It would have been too easy, if Sam ID'd the mug shot of Carlton Waters. Stranger things had happened, although Ted didn't expect it. His luck wasn't usually that good. Finding suspects generally took longer, but once in a while the good guys got lucky. He hoped this would be one of the times.

Ted pulled a large blow-up out of the envelope and handed it to her. She stared at the face, as though mesmerized by it, and then shook her head and handed it back to him. "I don't think I've ever seen him," she said softly.

"But you might have?" Ted pressed, watching her every move and expression. There was something both strong and fragile about her. It was odd to see her so sad in these splendid surroundings, but then again she had just lost her husband only four months before.

"I don't think so," she said honestly. "There's something familiar about his face, maybe he just has one of those faces. Could I have seen him somewhere?" She was frowning, as though dredging her memory and trying to remember.

"You might have seen him in the newspapers. He just got out of prison. It's a famous case. He was sent to prison for murder at seventeen, with a friend of his. He's been claiming for twenty-four years that he was innocent, and the other guy pulled the trigger."

"How awful. Whoever pulled the trigger. Do you think he was innocent?" He looked capable of murder to her.

"No, I don't," Ted said honestly. "He's a smart guy. And who knows, maybe by now he believes his own story. I've heard it all before. The prisons are full of guys who say they're innocent, and wound up there because of bad judges or crooked lawyers. There aren't a lot of men, or women for that matter, who tell you they did it."

"Who did he kill?" Fernanda almost shuddered. It was an awful thought.

"Some neighbors, a couple. They almost killed their two kids too, but they were hardly more than babies and didn't bother. They were too young to identify them. They killed their parents for two hundred dollars, and whatever else they found in their wallets. We see it all the time. Random violence. Human life discarded for a few dollars, some dope, or a handgun. That's why I don't work in Homicide anymore. It's too depressing. You start to ask yourself questions about the human race that you don't want the answers to. The people who commit these crimes are a special breed. It's hard for the rest of us to understand them." She nodded, thinking that what he did instead wasn't much better. Car bombings were not particularly pleasant either, and they could easily have killed the judge or his wife. But it was certainly less brutal than the crime that he had just attributed to Carlton Waters. Even the photograph of him made her blood run cold. There was something icy and terrifying about him, which came across even in a photograph. If she had seen him, she would have known it. She had never seen Carlton Waters before.

"Do you think you'll find the person who blew up the car?" she asked with interest. She wondered what percentage of crimes they solved, and how much energy they put into it. He seemed very earnest about it. He had a nice face, and gentle eyes, and an intelligent, kind demeanor. He wasn't what she would have expected a police detective to be like. She somehow expected him to be harder. Ted

Lee seemed so civilized somehow, and so normal.

"We might find the bomber," Ted said honestly. "We'll try to certainly. If it really was a random act, that makes it that much harder, because there's no rhyme or reason to it, and it could be almost anyone. But it's amazing the things that come out, when you dig below the surface. And given the fact that it's a judge, my guess is that there was a motive. Revenge, someone he sent to prison who thinks he didn't deserve the sentence he got, and wants to get even. If it's someone like that, we're more likely to find them. That's why I thought of Waters, or actually my partner did. Waters just got out last week. Judge McIntyre was the judge at the trial, and sentenced him.

"Twenty-four years is a long time to hold a grudge, and it wouldn't be smart to bomb the judge's car the week he gets out. Waters is smarter than that, but maybe he's more comfortable in prison. If it's someone like that, it'll surface eventually. Whoever did it will talk, and we'll get a phone call from an informant. Most of the leads we get are either anonymous tips, or paid informants." It was a whole subculture Fernanda knew nothing about, and didn't want to. And although it was frightening, it was also fascinating to hear him talk about it. "A lot of these people connect and are linked to each other in some way. And they're not great at keeping secrets. They're almost compelled to talk about it, which is lucky for us. In the meantime, we have to check out every lead we've got, and all our hunches. Waters was nothing more than a hunch, and it's probably too obvious, but it's worth checking out anyway. Do you mind if I show Sam the mug shot?"

"Not at all." She was curious herself now if Sam would recognize him, although she didn't want him put at risk by identifying a criminal who might try to hurt him and get revenge for it later. She turned to Ted then with a question. "What if he does recognize him? Will Sam's identity be kept secret?"

"Of course. We're not going to put a six-year-old child at risk," he said gently. "Or even an adult for that matter. We do everything we can to protect our sources." She nodded, relieved, and he followed her up the sweeping staircase to Sam's bedroom. There was an immense chandelier overhead that dazzled him when he looked at it. Fernanda had bought it in Vienna, from yet another crumbling palace, and had it shipped, in tiny individual crystal pieces, to San Francisco.

She knocked on the door of Sam's room,

and opened it with Ted standing right behind her. Sam was playing with his toys on the floor.

"Hi." Sam grinned up at him. "Are you going to arrest me now?" It was obvious that he wasn't the least concerned about Ted's visit, and even seemed pleased to see him. He had felt very important on Sunday, when Ted asked him what he'd seen and let him go into detail. And even though Sam had only seen him once before, he sensed that Ted was sympathetic and friendly, and liked children. Sam could tell.

"Nope. I'm not going to arrest you. But I brought you something," Ted said, reaching into his coat pocket. He hadn't told Fernanda he was going to give the boy a gift. While he was talking to her, he'd forgotten about it. He handed something to Sam then, who reached out and took it and gave a gasp when he saw it. It was a shiny brass star, much like the silver one that Ted carried in his wallet. "You're a deputy police inspector now, Sam. It means you always have to tell the truth, and if you see any bad guys hanging around, or suspicious people, you have to call us." It had a number one on it, under the initials of the SFPD, and was a gift they gave to friends of the department. Sam looked as though his new friend had just handed him a diamond. Fernanda smiled at the look on his face, and then at Ted, to thank him. It was a nice thing to do. And Sam was thrilled.

"That's pretty impressive. *Very* impressive." She smiled at her son, and walked into the room with Ted behind her. As everything else was in the house, the room was beautifully decorated. It was done in dark blue with accents of red and yellow, and there was everything in it a boy could want, including a large TV to watch videos on, a stereo, and a bookshelf with games and toys and books on it. And in the middle of the room were a pile of Legos and a remote-controlled car he'd been playing with when they walked in. There was a window seat too, which was where Ted suspected Sam had been when he'd been watching the street on Sunday, and saw the adult male he didn't remember in detail. Ted handed him the mug shot of Carlton Waters then, and asked Sam if he'd ever seen him.

Sam stood and stared at it for a long time, as his mother had. There was something about Waters's eyes that hooked you into them in an eerie way, even on paper. And Ted knew after his visit to him in Modesto the day before that Waters's eyes were even colder in person. Ted said nothing to distract the boy, he just stood quietly and waited, while both adults watched him with interest. Sam was clearly thinking and combing his memory for some sign of recognition, and finally he handed the photograph back and shook his head, but he still seemed to be thinking. Ted noticed that too.

"He looks scary," Sam commented, as he gave Ted back the mug shot.

"Too scary to say you've seen him?" Ted asked him carefully, watching his eyes. "Remember, you're a deputy now. You have to tell us what you remember. He's never going to know you told us, if you did see him, Sam." As he had Fernanda, Ted wanted to reassure him, but Sam shook his head again.

"I think the man had blond hair like him, but he didn't look like him."

"What makes you say that? Do you remember more about what the man on the street looked like?" Sometimes things came back later. It was a phenomenon that happened to adults too.

"No," Sam said honestly. "But when I look at the picture, I know I don't remember seeing him. Is he a bad guy?" Sam asked with interest, and he didn't look frightened. He was safe at home with his new police detective friend, and his mother, and he knew that nothing could harm him. Bad things had never happened to him, except for losing his dad, but it never even occurred to him that someone would want to hurt him.

"A very bad guy," Ted responded to his question.

"Did he kill someone?" Sam found it extremely interesting. To him it was just an exciting story, there was no reality to it. And as a result, no sense of danger.

"He killed two people, with a friend." Fernanda looked instantly worried by what Ted told him. She didn't want Ted to tell Sam about the two children they had harmed as well. She didn't want Sam to have nightmares, as he had frequently since his father died. He was afraid she would die too, or even that he would. It was age appropriate for him, but also normal after what had just happened to his father. Ted instinctively knew that. He had children of his own, and was not going to frighten Sam unduly. "They put him in prison for a long time for it." Ted knew it was important to tell him that he had been punished for it. He wasn't just a random killer roaming the streets, without consequences for his behavior.

"But he's out now?" Sam asked with interest. He had to be, if Ted thought he had been walking down their street on Sunday and wanted to know if Sam had seen him.

"He got out last week, but he was in prison for twenty-four years. I think he learned his lesson," he continued to reassure him. It was a fine line to walk with a child his age, but Ted was doing his best. He had always been good with children, and loved them. Fernanda could see that, and guessed that he must have kids of his own. He wore a wedding band on his left hand, so she knew he was married.

"Then why did you think he blew up the car?" Sam asked sensibly, which was another good question. Sam was a bright boy, and had a strong sense of logic.

"You never know when someone will turn up where you don't expect them to. Now that you're a deputy, you'll have to learn that, Sam. You have to check out every lead, no matter how unlikely it seems. Sometimes you get a big surprise, and find your man that way."

"Do you think he did it? The car, I mean?" Sam was fascinated by the process.

"No, I don't. But it was worth coming over here to check it out. What if this photograph was the man you'd seen and I hadn't bothered to show it to you? He might have gotten away with it, and we don't want that to happen, do we?" Sam shook his head, as the two adults smiled at each other and Ted put the mug shot back in the manila envelope. He hadn't thought Waters was dumb enough to do something as obvious as that, but you never knew. And now he had an additional piece of information from Sam at least. He knew the suspect was blond. A small piece of the car bombing puzzle had fallen into place. It didn't hurt. "I like your room, by the way," he said congenially to the boy. "You've got a lot of great stuff."

"Do you have kids?" Sam asked, looking up at him. He was still holding his star, as though it was now the most precious thing he owned, and to him, it was. It had been a thoughtful gift from Ted, and Fernanda was touched.

"Yes, I do." Ted smiled at him and ruffled his hair in a fatherly way. "They're all big guys now. Two of them are in college, and one works in New York."

"Is he a cop?"

"No, he's a stockbroker. None of my boys want to be cops," he said. He'd been disappointed at first, but now he'd decided it was just as well. It was tiresome, often tedious, dangerous work. Ted had always loved what he did, and was glad he had. But Shirley had always stressed academics and education to them. One of his boys in college wanted to go to law school after he graduated, and the other was in pre-med. He was proud of them.

"What do you want to be when you grow up?" Ted asked with interest, although Sam was way too young to know. But he suspected the boy missed having his father around, and it was nice for him to have a few minutes to chat with a man. He didn't know Fernanda's circumstances since her husband's death, but on the two occasions he'd come to the house, he didn't have the feeling there was a man around, other than her oldest son. And she had the stressed, nervous, vulnerable look of a woman who was coping with a lot on her own.

"I want to be a baseball player," Sam announced, "or maybe a cop," he said, glancing down lovingly at the brass star in his hands, and the two adults smiled again. Fernanda stood there thinking what a good boy he was, just as Will walked in. He had heard adult voices in the room next to his and wondered who it was. He smiled when he saw Ted, and Sam instantly told him he was a deputy now.

"That's cool." Will grinned, and then looked at Ted. "It was a bomb, right?"

Ted nodded slowly. "Yes, it was." He was a good-looking, bright kid, much like his brother. Fernanda had three nice kids.

"Do you know who did it?" Will inquired,

and Ted pulled out the mug shot again and handed it to him.

"Have you ever seen this man around here?" Ted asked quietly.

"He did it?" Will looked intrigued and stared at it for a long time. Carlton Waters's eyes had the same mesmerizing effect on him, and then he handed it back to Ted and shook his head. None of them had ever seen Carlton Waters, which was something. It didn't totally confirm Waters's innocence, but it made his guilt a lot more unlikely.

"We're just checking out possibilities. There's nothing to link him to it for now. Have you ever seen him, Will?"

"No, I haven't." The boy shook his head. "Anyone else?" Will enjoyed talking to him, and thought he was a good man. He conveyed decency and integrity, and he had an easy way with kids.

"Not yet. We'll let you know." Ted looked at his watch then, and said he had to go. Fernanda walked him back downstairs and he stood in the doorway for a minute and looked at her. It was a strange thing to feel about a woman who lived this well, but he felt sorry for her. "You have a beautiful house," he commented, "and lovely things. I'm sorry about your husband," he said sympathetically. He knew the value of companionship after twenty-eight years with his wife. Even if they were no longer close, they meant a lot to each other. And he could sense Fernanda's loneliness and solitude like a pall that hung over her.

"Me too," she said sadly in response to Ted's sympathy.

"Was it an accident?"

Fernanda hesitated and looked at him, and the pain he saw in her eyes took his breath away. It was naked and raw. "Probably . . . we don't know." She hesitated for a moment, and felt surprisingly comfortable with him, more than she had reason to, and for no reason she could explain, even to herself, she trusted him. "It could have been a suicide. He fell off a boat in Mexico, at night. He was alone on the boat."

"I'm so sorry," he said again, and then opened the door and turned back to look at her again. "If there's anything we can ever do for you, let us know." Meeting her and her children was part of what he liked about his job, and always had. It was the people he met who made it worthwhile for him. And this family had touched his heart. No matter how much money they had, and they appeared to have a lot of it, they had their sorrows too.

Sometimes it didn't matter if you were rich or poor, the same things happened to people in all walks of life, at all economic levels, and the rich ones hurt just as much as the poor ones. No matter how big her house was, or how fancy her chandelier, that didn't keep her warm at night, and she was still alone, with three kids to raise on her own. It was no different than if something had happened to him, and Shirley had wound up alone with his boys. He was still thinking about her when he went back to his car, and drove away, and she quietly closed the door.

She went back to her desk after that, and read Jack Waterman's letter again. She called to make an appointment with him, and his secretary said he would call her back the next day. He had left for the day. And at a quarter to seven, she got in her car, and drove to pick Ashley up at ballet. She was in good spirits when she got in the car, and they drove home chatting about the recital, school, and Ashley's many friends. She was still on the cusp of puberty, and liked her mother more than Fernanda knew she would in another year or two. But for now at least, they were still close, and Fernanda was grateful for that.

As they got to the house, Ashley was talking excitedly about her plans to go to Lake Tahoe in July. She could hardly wait for school to be over in June. They were all looking forward to it, although Fernanda knew she would be even lonelier over the summer while Ashley and Will were away. But at least she would have Sam with her. She was glad that he was still so young, and not nearly as independent yet. He liked sticking close to her, even more so now without his dad around, although Allan hadn't paid much attention to him in recent years. He was always too busy. He would have been better off, Fernanda thought to herself as she walked up the front steps, spending more time with his kids than creating the financial disaster he had, that had destroyed their life, and his own, in the end.

She cooked dinner for the kids that night. Everyone was tired, but in better spirits than they'd been in for a while. Sam wore his new star, and they talked about the car bombing up the street again. Fernanda felt slightly better knowing that more than likely it was specifically directed at the judge by someone he had sentenced harshly over the years, than if it had been just a random act of violence directed at anyone. But even at that, it was an unpleasant feeling knowing that there were people out there willing to hurt others and destroy property. She and her children could easily have been injured in the blast if they'd been walking by, and it was just blind luck that no one was, that Mrs. McIntyre was in her house, and the judge was out of town. All three of the Barnes children were fascinated by it. The idea of something so extraordinary happening right on their block, to someone they knew, seemed incredible to them, and to her. But incredible or not, it had happened, and could again. The vulnerability it left Fernanda still feeling when she went to bed that night made her miss Allan more than ever.

Chapter 8

Peter Morgan called every contact he'd ever had in San Francisco before he left, hoping to find a job, or at least line up some interviews. He had just over three hundred dollars in his wallet, and he had to show his parole agent that he was doing his best. And he was. But within his first week back in the city, nothing had panned out. People had moved, faces had changed, people who remembered him either wouldn't take his calls, or did and fobbed him off, sounding stunned to hear from him at all. Four years in a normal life was a long time. And almost everyone who'd ever known him knew he had gone to prison. No one was anxious to see him again. And by the end of the first week, Peter realized he was going to have to lower his sights dramatically, if he wanted to find a job. No matter how useful he had been to the warden while he was in prison, no one in Silicon Valley, or the financial field, wanted anything to do with him. His history was too checkered, and they could only imagine he'd have learned worse tricks than the ones he knew previously, after four years in prison. Not to mention his predilection for addiction, which had ultimately brought him down.

He inquired at restaurants, then small businesses, a record store, and finally a trucking firm. No one had work for him, they thought he was overqualified, overeducated, one man openly called him a smart-ass and a snob. But worse than that, he was an ex-con. He literally could not find work. And at the end of the second week, he had forty dollars in his wallet, and not a single prospect. A tortilla shop near the halfway house offered him half of minimum wage, in cash, to wash dishes, but he couldn't live on it, and they didn't need to pay him more. They had unlimited numbers of illegal aliens at their disposal, who were willing to work for pennies. And Peter needed more than that to survive. He was feeling desperate as he flipped through his old address book again, and when he started at the beginning for the tenth time, he stopped at the same place he always did. Phillip Addison. Until that moment, he had been determined not to

call him. He was bad news, and always had
been, in every way, and had caused trouble for
Peter before. Peter had never been absolutely
sure in fact that he hadn't been responsible for
the drug bust that had sent him to prison.
Peter had owed him a fortune, and was using
so much cocaine himself that he had no way
to repay him, and still didn't. For whatever
reason, Addison had chosen to ignore the debt
for the past four years. He knew there had
been no way to collect while Peter was in
prison. But with good reason, Peter was still
leery of him and worried about reminding
Addison of the outstanding debt. There was
no way he could repay him or ever would,
and Addison knew that.

Phillip Addison owned an enormous company openly, it was a high-tech stock listed
publicly, and he had half a dozen other, less legitimate, companies he kept concealed, and
extensive connections in the underworld. But
someone like Addison could always find a
place for Peter in one of his shadier companies, and if nothing else, it was work, and decent money. But Peter hated to call him. He
had been sucked in by him before, and once
he had you, for whatever reason, he owned
you. But there was no one else to call at this

point. Even gas stations wouldn't hire him. Their clients pumped their own gas, and they didn't want a guy fresh out of prison handling their money. His Harvard MBA degree was virtually useless to him. And most of them laughed at the warden's reference. Peter was truly desperate. He had no friends, no family, no one to call, no one to help him. And his parole agent told him he'd better find work soon. The longer he was out of work, the closer they would watch him. They knew the kind of pressure it put on parolees not to have money, and the kind of activities they resorted to in desperation. Peter was getting panicked. He was nearly out of money, and he had to eat and pay rent, at least.

Two weeks after he'd stepped through the gates of Pelican Bay, Peter sat staring at Phillip Addison's number for nearly half an hour, and then picked up the phone and called him. A secretary told him Mr. Addison was out of the country, and offered to take a message. Peter left his name and number. And two hours later, Phillip called him. Peter was in his room looking grim, when someone shouted up the stairs that there was a call for him from some guy called Addison. Peter ran to the phone, with a sick feeling in the pit of his stomach. It could be the beginning of disaster for him. Or salvation. With Phillip Addison, it could be either.

"Well, this is a surprise," Addison said in an unpleasant tone. He always sounded like he was sneering. But at least he had called him. And quickly. "When did you wash up on the beach? How long have you been out of prison?"

"About two weeks," Peter said quietly, wishing he hadn't called him. But he needed the money. He was down to fifteen dollars, and his parole agent was keeping the heat on him. He had even thought of going on welfare. But by the time he got it, if he did, he'd be starving, or homeless. He realized now that that was how those things happened. Desperation. No options. And there was no question in his mind that it could happen. Phillip Addison was his only option at the moment. Peter told himself that as soon as he got something better, he could always dump him. What he was worried about and trying not to focus on were the shackles Addison put on those he helped, and the unscrupulous methods he used to keep people beholden to him. But Peter had no choice. There was no one else to call. He couldn't even get a job washing dishes for a decent wage.

"What else did you try before you called me?" Addison laughed at him. He knew the drill. He had other ex-cons working for him. They were needy, desperate, and loyal, just like Peter Morgan. Addison liked that. "There's not much work out there for guys like you," he said honestly. He didn't pull any punches. "Except washing cars or shining shoes. Somehow, I can't see you doing that. What can I do for you?" he said, almost politely.

"I need a job," Peter said bluntly. There was no point playing games with him. He was careful to say he needed work, not money.

"You must be down to your last buck if you called me. How hungry are you?"

"Hungry. Not hungry enough to do anything ridiculous. I'm not going back to prison, for you or anyone. I got the point. Four years is a long time. I need a job. If you have something legitimate for me to do, I'd really appreciate it." Peter had never felt so humble, and Phillip knew it. He loved it. Peter didn't mention his debt to him, but they were both aware of it and of the risk Peter had taken when he called him. He was that desperate for work.

"I only have legitimate businesses," Addison said, sounding huffy, as he ruffled his feathers. You never knew if a line was wired, although as far as he knew, he was on a safe line. He was on an untraceable cell phone. "You still owe me money, by the way. A lot of it. You took down a lot of people when you went down. I ended up having to pay them all off. If I hadn't, they'd have come after you and killed you in prison." Peter knew it was possibly an exaggeration, but there was some truth to it. He had borrowed money from Addison for his last buy, and never paid it back when he got arrested, and they confiscated the bulk of the shipment before he sold it. In real terms, he knew he probably owed Addison a couple of hundred thousand dollars, and he didn't deny it. For whatever reason, Addison hadn't collected. But they both knew Peter owed him.

"You can take it out of my paycheck, if you want. If I don't have a job, I can't pay you back at all." It was a sensible way to look at it, and Addison knew it was true too, although he no longer expected to recoup the money. It was one of those losses that happened in that kind of business. What he liked about it was that Peter had an obligation to him.

"Why don't you come in and talk to me," he said, sounding pensive.

"When?" Peter hoped it would be soon, but didn't want to push. And the secretary had said he was out of the country, which was probably a smokescreen.

"Five o'clock today," Addison said, without asking if it was convenient for him. He didn't care if it was or not. If Peter wanted to work for him, he had to learn to jump when Addison told him to. Addison had fronted money for him before, but he had never actually employed him. This was different.

"Where do I go?" Peter asked in a dead voice. He could still say no if whatever Addison offered him was too outrageous, or too insulting. But Peter was fully prepared to be insulted, and used, and even mistreated. As long as it was legal.

Addison gave him the address, told him to be on time, and hung up on him. The address he gave Peter was in San Mateo. He knew it was where he held his legitimate business. He had a high-tech company that had been a mammoth success at first, and had trouble after that. It had gone up and down over the years, and had been booming at the height of the dot-com craze. The stock prices had fallen drastically after that, just as everything else had. They made high-tech surgical equipment, and Peter knew he had also made some big investments in genetic engineering. Addison himself was both an engineer and had a medical background. And for a while, at least, he had been thought to be a genius with money. But eventually, he had proven that like everyone else, he had clay feet, and he had overextended himself pretty badly. He had shored up his own finances by running drugs out of Mexico, and the bulk of his net worth now was in crystal meth labs in Mexico, and a land office business he did selling heroin in the Mission. And some of his best clients were yuppies. They didn't know they were buying it from him, of course, no one did. Even his own family thought he ran a respectable business. He had a house in Ross, children in private schools, he served on all the respectable charity boards, and belonged to the best clubs in San Francisco. He was thought to be a pillar of the community. Peter knew better. They had met when Peter was in trouble before, and Phillip Addison had quietly offered to help him. He had even supplied the drugs at discount rates at first, and told Peter how to sell them. If his own use hadn't gotten out of hand, and his judgment with it, Peter would probably never have gone to prison.

Addison was smarter than that. He never touched the drugs he sold. He was clever, and ingenious about how he ran his underground empire. Most of the time, he was a good judge of horseflesh. He had made a mistake in Peter, he had thought he was more ambitious than he was, and more devious. In the end, Peter was just another nice guy gone wrong, who had no idea what he was doing. A guy like him was a real risk to Phillip Addison, because he had all the wrong instincts. Peter had been a petty criminal, forced into it by circumstance and poor judgment, and eventually his own addiction. Addison was a major criminal. For him, it was a lifetime commitment. And for Peter, only a pastime. But in spite of that, Addison thought he could use him. He was smart, well educated, and had grown up with the right people in the right places. He had gone to good schools, was good-looking and presentable, had married well, even if he had screwed it up. And a Harvard MBA degree was nothing to sneeze at. When Peter and Phillip Addison had met, Peter even had the right connections. Now he had blown them, but if he could get on his feet again, with Phillip's help, Addison thought he could be useful. And with what he'd learned in prison in the last four years, perhaps even more so. He had been an amateur conman before, an innocent gone wrong. But if he'd turned pro, Addison wanted him, no question. What he needed to assess now was what Peter had learned, what he was willing to do, and how desperate he was at the moment. His minor claims of only wanting to work legally were of no interest to Phillip. He didn't care what Peter said. The question was what would he do, and the debt he still owed was only a plus in their dealings, from Phillip's viewpoint. It gave him a hold over Peter that appealed to Phillip immensely, and a lot less to Peter. It also hadn't gone unnoticed by Addison that Peter had never divulged his name or exposed him once he was arrested, which showed that he could be trusted. Addison liked that about Peter. He hadn't taken anyone down with him when he went down. It was the main reason why Addison hadn't had him killed. Peter was, in some ways at least, a man of honor. Even if it was honor among thieves.

Peter rode the bus to San Mateo wearing the only clothes he now owned. He looked neat and clean, and had gotten himself a decent haircut. But all he had to wear were the jeans and denim shirt and running shoes they'd given him in prison. He didn't even own a jacket, and he couldn't afford to buy a suit for the interview. As he reached the address on foot, he felt overwhelmed with trepidation.

And in his office, Phillip Addison was sitting at his desk, reading through a thick file. It had been in a locked drawer in his desk for over a year, and was a life's dream for him. He had been thinking about it for nearly three years now. It was the only project he wanted Peter's help with. And whether or not he was willing to do it was of no interest to Phillip. Whether he was capable of pulling it off was the only question. This was the one thing he was not willing to risk, or do badly. It had to be done with the precision of the Bolshoi Ballet, or the surgical instruments he made, with the infinite pinpoint perfection of a laser. There was no room here for slippage. Peter was perfect for it, he thought. It was why Addison had called him back. He had thought of it the moment he got the message. And when his secretary told him Peter was there, he put the file back in the locked drawer, and stood up to greet Peter.

What Peter saw when he entered the room was a tall, impeccably groomed man in his late fifties. He was wearing a custom-made English suit, a handsome tie, and a shirt that had been made for him in Paris. Even his shoes were shined to perfection when he came around the desk to shake Peter's hand, seeming not to notice the garb Peter wore, which he wouldn't have deigned to wash his car with, and Peter knew it. Phillip Addison was so smooth, he was like a greased marble egg sliding across the floor. You could never get a grip on him, or get the goods on him. No one ever had. He was above suspicion. And it made Peter feel uneasy to find him so friendly. His mild threats about the money Peter owed when he called seemed to have been forgotten.

They chatted inanely for a while, and Phillip indulged him by asking what he had in mind. Peter told him the areas that were of interest. Marketing, finance, new investments, new divisions, new business, anything entrepreneurial that Addison thought would be suited to him. And then he sighed and looked at Phillip. It was time to be honest.

"Look, I need the work. If I don't get a job, I'm going to be out on the street with a shopping cart and a tin cup, and maybe only the tin cup and no cart. I'll do whatever you need me to, within reason. I don't want to go back to prison. Short of that, I'd like to work for you. In your legitimate business obviously. The other stuff is just too risky for me. I can't do it. And I don't want to."

"You've gotten very noble in the last four years. You didn't have quite as many compunctions five years ago, when I met you."

"I was stupid and a lot younger, and pretty crazy. Fifty-one months in Pelican Bay gets your feet on the floor, and your head out of your ass. It was a good wake-up call, if you can

call it that. I'm not going back there. Next
time, they'll have to kill me." He meant it.

"You were lucky they didn't kill you last
time," Addison said openly. "You pissed off a
lot of people when you left. What about your
debt to me?" Addison asked, not so much because he wanted it, but he wanted to remind
Peter that he owed him. It was a fortuitous beginning. For Addison, if not for Peter.

"I told you, I'd be happy to work for it, and
have you take it out of my paycheck over
time. It's the best I can do for now. I have
nothing else to give you." Addison knew it
was the truth. They both did, and Peter was
being honest with him. As honest as you could
be with a man like Addison. Honesty wasn't
something he valued. For him, choirboys were
useless. But even Phillip knew you couldn't
get blood from a stone. Peter had no money to
give him. All he had were brains and motiva-
tion, and for now that was enough.

"I could still have you killed, you know,"
Addison said quietly. "Some of our mutual
friends in Mexico would be happy to do it.
More particularly there's one in Colombia
who wanted to have you taken out in prison.
I asked him not to. I always liked you,
Morgan," Addison said as though discussing
his golf game with him. He played golf regu-

larly with heads of industries and heads of state alike. He had important political connections. He was a fraud of such a lofty degree that Peter knew he would be helpless to go after him, if anything ever went wrong. He was a powerful man, an evil force, with absolutely no integrity or morals. None whatsoever. And Peter knew it. He was outclassed in every possible way. If Peter went to work for him, he would be a pawn in one of Addison's chess games. But if he didn't, sooner or later, out of sheer desperation, he could wind up back in Pelican Bay, working for the warden.

"If that's true, about the guy from Colombia, then thank you," Peter said politely. He didn't want to lie to him, and in response to Addison saying he had always liked him, Peter didn't respond. He never had liked Addison. He knew too much to like him. Addison looked good, but was rotten. He had a very social wife, and four very lovely children. To the few who knew him well, and knew the many masks he wore, they compared Phillip Addison to Satan. To the rest of the world, he seemed successful and respectable. Peter knew better.

"I figured you'd be more useful to me alive one day," Addison said thoughtfully, as though he had something in mind for him, which he did. "And that time may have come. It seemed like a waste having you die in prison. I have an idea for you. I was thinking about it after we talked today. It's sort of a precision issue of sorts. A highly technical, carefully organized, synchronized combined effort between experts." He made it sound like open heart surgery, and Peter couldn't figure out what kind of project it was, from what he was saying.

"In what field?" Peter asked, relieved to be talking about work finally, and not threats to have him killed, or the money he owed him. They were getting down to business.

"I'm not prepared to explain it to you yet. I will. But I want to do some more research. Actually, you're going to do the research. I want to think about the execution of the project. That's my job. But first, I want to know that you're in. I want to hire you as the project coordinator. I don't think you have the technical knowledge to do the job. Neither do I. But I want you to line up the experts who will do it for us. And together, we'll share in the profits. I want to cut you in on this deal, not just hire you as an employee. If you do this right, you'll have earned it." Peter was intrigued as he listened. It sounded interesting and challenging, and profitable. It was just what he needed to get on his feet and make a few investments of his own again, maybe start his own company. He had a keen sense for investments, and had learned a lot before he got off on the wrong track. This was the chance he needed to start over. It was too good to hope for. Maybe his luck was turning. Addison was finally doing something decent for him, and Peter was grateful.

"Is it a long-term research project, to be developed over several years?" There was job security in that, although it might tie him to Addison for longer than he wanted. But it would also give him plenty of time to get on his feet, which was something. He might even get visitation rights with his girls again, which Peter still dreamed of, when he allowed himself to. He hadn't seen his daughters in five years, and his heart ached when he thought of it. He had screwed everything up so badly in the past, even his relationship with his children, while they were still babies. He hoped one day to get to know them. And with financial stability again, he could approach Janet more reasonably, even if she had remarried.

"Actually," Addison went on to explain the project he had in mind for him, "it's relatively short term. I think we can accomplish it in months, or even weeks. There will be some research and set-up time, of course, the project itself, which might take a month or even two to handle, and the clean-up afterward. I don't think we're talking long term here. And the profit sharing could be extraordinary." It was hard to guess what it was. Maybe some new high-tech invention he was planning to release on the market, and he wanted Peter to organize the launch, in terms of marketing and PR. He couldn't think what else it was. Or some start-up venture he wanted Peter to handle while it was being shot out of the cannon into the public at first, to be handed over to other people once it was. Addison was being mysterious about it, as Peter listened and tried to guess what it was.

"Are you talking about product introduction or development, or market testing of some kind?" Peter was groping to understand it.

"In a way." Addison nodded and then paused. He had to say something to him, even before he took him into his confidence entirely. "I've been considering this project for a long time, and I think the time is right for it. I think your call to me this morning was strangely providential," he said with an evil smile. Peter had never seen eyes as cold or terrifying as his.

"When would you want me to start?" He

was thinking of the fifteen dollars he had in his wallet, which weren't going to get him past dinner that night and breakfast in the morning, provided he ate at McDonald's. If not, it would be gone by that night. And after that, he'd be begging on the street, and could be violated for that, if he got caught.

Addison looked him dead in the eye. "Today, if you like. I think we're ready to start. We need to handle this project in stages. Over the next four weeks, I would want you to take on research and development. In fact, I want you to do the hiring." Peter's heart gave a hopeful leap. This was better than he'd hoped for, and the answer to his prayers.

"What kind of people are we talking about hiring here?" He still didn't understand the scope, or even the focus, of the project. But obviously, it was something top secret and high tech.

"Who you hire is up to you. I want to be consulted of course but I think your connections in this area are better than mine," Addison said generously. And with that, he unlocked the drawer he had locked as Peter walked in, and took out the heavy file he had been compiling for years, and handed it to him. In it were clippings and reports on virtually every project Allan Barnes had under-

taken for the past four years. Peter took the
file from him and opened it, and then looked
up at Phillip. He was impressed. He knew
who Allan was. There was no one in the financial or high-tech world who didn't. He
was a dot-com genius, the biggest of them all.
There were even several photographs of him
with his family in the file. It was extraordinarily complete.

"Are you thinking of a joint venture with
him?"

"I was. Not anymore. You've been a little
out of the loop apparently. He died in January,
leaving a widow and three children."

"That's too bad," Peter said sympathetically,
wondering how he had missed it, although
there had been times in Pelican Bay when he
didn't read the papers. The real world had
seemed too remote.

"The project would actually have been
more interesting while he was still alive. I
think we would have gotten better response
from him, but in this case, I'm actually willing
to work with his widow," Phillip said magnan-
imously.

"On what?" Peter looked blank. "Is she running his empire now?" He really was out of
the loop. He hadn't read anything about it.

"I assume he left her his entire fortune, or

most of it, whatever he didn't leave to his kids," Phillip explained. "I understand from a friend that she was his sole beneficiary. And I know for a fact that he made half a billion dollars before he died. He died on a fishing trip in Mexico. He fell overboard and was lost at sea. They're being close-mouthed about their plans for his companies, but I assume she is going to be making most of those decisions, or some of them."

"Have you approached her directly about a joint investment of some kind?" Peter had never had the impression that Allan Barnes's interests lay in the same fields as Addison's, but it was an interesting concept, and whatever money problems Addison still had were going to be solved by an alliance with an empire as solvent as the one Allan had left, or so Peter thought. It hadn't occurred to either of them that the empire had crashed and burned before he died, let alone that that was why he had. Barnes had done such a masterful job of hiding companies behind other companies, and concealing the insane gambles he had taken, that, for the moment at least, even a man with Addison's connections had no idea of the depth of the rubble Allan Barnes had left in his wake. Fernanda, the attorneys, and the heads of Allan's defunct companies had done a brilliant job keeping it quiet, although they couldn't do it forever. But for the four months since he died, they had managed, and the legend of Allan Barnes had not been tarnished yet. Fernanda wanted it that way for as long as possible, to honor her husband's memory and for her children's sake. The benefit to Addison of an alliance with Barnes, from what Peter could see, was that the world Barnes had created around him was so respectable, it would gild his ventures with the same golden brush. In fact, any kind of joint project between them was a stroke of genius, and Peter approved. Allan Barnes's name and reputation were respectable and admired in the extreme. And certainly a project involving both groups of companies was exactly what Peter needed to put him back on the map. For good. It was a dream come true, and he sat smiling at Phillip Addison with new respect, as he held the thick file that Phillip had handed to him.

"I haven't approached Mrs. Barnes directly myself," Addison went on to explain. "We're not ready to do that yet. You have to do the hiring first."

"I guess I'd better read the file, in order to fully understand the nature of the project."

"I don't think so," Phillip said, reaching across the desk, and taking it back from him.

"All that is, is a history and chronology of his accomplishments. It's relevant, of course, but you probably know most of it anyway," he said vaguely, as Peter looked confused again. The entire project seemed to be shrouded in mystery, so much so that he was being asked to hire people for a nameless project, in a field that hadn't been explained to him, to do a job that Addison had yet to outline. It was more than a little confusing, which was precisely what Addison had intended. He smiled across the desk at Peter again, as he locked the file back in the drawer.

"Who am I supposed to hire, if I don't have a clear idea of what we're doing?" Peter sounded puzzled.

"I think you have a clear idea, Peter. Don't you? Do I have to spell it out for you? I want you to hire some of your friends from the last four years."

"What friends?" Peter looked even more confused.

"I'm sure you've met some very interesting people, some entrepreneurial sorts who would like to make a very large amount of money, and then quietly disappear. I want you to do some serious thinking, and we'll handpick them to do a very special job for us. I don't expect you to do the manual labor here, but

I do expect you to oversee it, and run the project."

"And the project is what?" Peter was frowning, he suddenly didn't like what he was hearing. From a business standpoint, the last four years of his life had been a blank. All he had met were criminals and rapists, murderers and thieves. And suddenly, as he looked at Addison, his blood ran cold. "Where does Allan Barnes's wife fit in?"

"It's very simple. After we put together the project, or you do more precisely, we make our proposal to her. We provide a little incentive for her to accept our offer. She pays us handsomely. In fact, I am prepared to be reasonable with her, given the size of her fortune, and the estate taxes she is probably required to pay. Assuming he was worth half a billion dollars when he died, the government will want just over fifty percent of that. Conservatively, I'd say she'll be worth two hundred million dollars when all is said and done. And we're only asking her for half of that. At least that's what I have in mind."

"And what is she going to be investing in?" Peter asked in a chilled voice, but he had already guessed.

"The lives and safe return of any and all of her children, which would be cheap at twice the price. Essentially, we are asking her to split her net worth with us, which I think sounds very fair, and I'm sure she'll be happy to pay it. Don't you?" Addison was smiling evilly, as Peter Morgan stood up.

"You're telling me that you want me to kidnap her children for a ransom of a hundred million dollars?" Peter looked like he'd been shot out of a cannon, as he stared at the man across the desk from him. Phillip Addison was insane.

"Absolutely not." Phillip shook his head calmly and leaned back in his chair. "I'm asking you to locate and handpick people who will. We want professionals doing this, not amateurs like you and me. You were only a petty criminal when you went in, and a very sloppy drug dealer. You're no kidnapper. And neither am I. I wouldn't even call this a kidnapping. It's a business deal. Allan Barnes came up with a winning lottery ticket. That's all it ever was. A very lucky one, I'll admit. There is no reason why his widow should hang on to all of it. You or I could just as easily have won the same lottery he did, and there's no reason for him not to share that with us now posthumously. We're not going to hurt the children. We're just going to hang on to them for a short time, and return them to her safe and sound, in exchange for a slice of the pie Allan left her with. There's no reason not to share that pie. He didn't even earn it, for God's sake. He just got lucky. Now, so will we." Phillip's eyes glinted evilly as he smiled.

"Are you nuts?" Peter was standing and staring at him. "Do you know anything about the sentences for kidnapping? We could be put to death if they catch us, whether we harm them or not. In fact, just committing conspiracy to commit kidnap could get us the death penalty. And you expect me to organize this? I won't do it. Find yourself another guy," Peter said, and started to walk away. Addison looked unmoved.

"I wouldn't do that, if I were you, Morgan. You have a stake in this too." Peter turned to look at him blankly. He didn't give a damn what he owed Addison. He would prefer to let him kill him first than to risk the death penalty for him. Besides, it was a heinous idea, preying on other people's misfortune and grief, and the survival of their kids. The thought of it made him sick.

"No, I don't," Peter answered him. "What stake could I possibly have in your kidnapping someone's kids?" He spat the words at Phillip. Addison disgusted him. He was even worse than Peter had feared. Much, much worse. He was inhuman, and so greedy as to be insane. But what Peter didn't know was that Addison's empire was in trouble, and without a major shot in the arm of this magnitude, his own house of cards was about to fall. He had been laundering money for his Colombian associates for quite some time, and investing it in high-risk dot-com deals, which promised a tremendous return. The results had been extraordinary for a while, until the tides had begun to turn. They had not only turned finally, but damn near drowned him when they did. And he knew the Colombians would be lethal once they discovered the money he had lost for them. He had to do something about it soon. Peter's call had been a godsend for him.

The answer to Peter's question to Addison was simple. "The stake you have in this," Phillip Addison said with an evil smile at Peter, "is saving your own children."

"What do you mean, 'saving my own children'?" Peter looked suddenly nervous.

"I believe you have two little girls, whom you haven't seen in a number of years. I used to know your ex-father-in-law in my youth. Nice man. And I'm sure they're lovely kids." Phillip Addison's eyes never left his, as something icy cold and terrifying ran down Peter's spine.

"What does that have to do with anything?" Peter said, as he felt something turn over in his stomach. The beast he felt churning within him now was terror. Not for himself this time, but for his kids. Without even meaning to, he had put them at risk by talking to Addison. The thought of it made him sick.

"It wouldn't be very difficult to locate them. I'm sure you could too, if you were interested. If you stand in the way, or expose us somehow, we'll settle for your two daughters. And there won't be any ransom involved. They will just quietly disappear, never to be seen again." Peter's face went pale.

"Are you telling me that if I don't kidnap the Barnes children for you, or orchestrate it, you're going to kill my children?" Peter's voice cracked and shook as he asked. But he already knew the answer.

"That's precisely what I'm telling you. You have no choice here, as I see it. But I have every intention of making it worth your while. There are three Barnes children, and I'll settle for any one of them. If you can get all of them, fine. If not, any one will do. I want you to hire three good men to do the job. Professionals, not amateurs like you. I want the real thing, so nothing gets bungled. You find them and hire them. I will pay each of them five million dollars, paid into either a Swiss or South American account. I'll pay them a hundred thousand dollars up front, and the rest when the ransom is delivered into our hands. I will pay you ten million dollars to run the show. Two hundred thousand up front, and the balance into a Swiss account. I'll even cancel your debt to me, as of now. The rest is mine." Peter did a rapid calculation and realized that out of the hundred-million-dollar ransom he was talking about, Addison was keeping seventy-five. He and the three men he hired were supposed to divide up the rest, like so much pie. But Addison had made very clear to him what the ground rules were. If he didn't agree to do it for him, his own two children would be killed. This was beyond playing hardball. This was nuclear warfare. Whatever way Peter turned, he was screwed. He wondered if he could warn Janet of the danger to the girls, before Addison got to them, but he didn't want to rely on that. Addison was capable of anything, he knew now. And Peter wanted none of these children hurt, neither his, nor the Barneses. Suddenly there were five lives at stake, as well as his own.

"You're a maniac," Peter said, and sat down

again. He couldn't see a way out of this, and was afraid there was none.

"But a clever one, you'll have to admit," Addison said with a smile. "I think the plan is sound. Now you have to find the men. Offer them one hundred thousand each up front. I'll pay you the two hundred thousand up front. That ought to buy you some decent clothes and get a place to stay until you get things up and running. You have to find a location to take them, of course, while we wait for the ransom to be paid. Having just lost her husband, I don't think Mrs. Barnes will take a long time to pay for her children's return. She's not going to want to lose them too." He correctly assumed that this was a vulnerable time for her, and he wanted to strike while the iron was hot. It was sheer providence that Peter had called. This was the omen he had been waiting for, and the man he needed to run the project. He was sure Peter would know the right men after his years in Pelican Bay. He did, of course, but this was not the job Peter had wanted from him. In fact, he was thinking of just walking out. But then what would happen to his girls? Addison had him by the balls. There was no other way to see it. And if his own children's lives were in fact at stake, then he had no choice. How could he possibly take the risk? He didn't think Janet would even talk to him, and by the time he found her to tell her of the danger their children were in, his own daughters might be dead. There was no way he was going to take that risk, with a man as dangerous as this. Addison would have had them killed without a second glance.

"And if things go sour with the Barnes children, and something goes wrong? What if one of them is killed?"

"It's your job to see that doesn't happen. Parents aren't generally as enthusiastic about paying ransom for dead kids. And it upsets the cops."

"Never mind the cops. We're going to have the FBI on our asses the minute those kids disappear."

"Yes, we will. Or you will. Or someone will," Addison said pleasantly. "Actually, I'm going to Europe this summer. We're going to the South of France, so I'm going to be leaving this matter in your very capable hands." And avoiding any possible implications that he was involved in it, of course. "By the way, if one of your men gets caught in the process of this, I am prepared to pay them half the promised amount. That should cover their attorney fees, and even a fairly reliable escape." He had thought of everything. "And you, my friend, can either brazen it out here afterward, or disappear very comfortably to South America, where ten million dollars will buy you a very agreeable life, whichever you think best. We might even do some business together after that. You never know." And Addison would be blackmailing him forever, of course, threatening to expose him to the FBI, unless he did whatever Phillip wanted. But no matter how he looked at this, what clinched it for Peter was his own children's lives on the line. Even if he hadn't seen them since they were toddlers, he still loved them, and he would die before he'd put them at risk. Or risk prison, or even the death penalty to protect them. All he could think now was that it was his responsibility to see to it that the Barnes children weren't killed in the course of the kidnap. It was the only thing he wanted, even more than the ten million dollars.

"How do I know you'll pay?" When Peter asked the question, Phillip knew he was in. It was done.

"You get two hundred thousand in cash up front. The rest paid into a Swiss account when the job is over. That ought to give you enough play money for now. The rest will come when we get paid. Not a bad petty cash account for an ex-con without a pot to piss in. Wouldn't you say?" And he had already said that Peter's previous debt to him was canceled. Peter didn't answer, he just stared at him, shaken by all he'd heard. In the last two hours, his entire life had gone down the drain again. There was no way he would ever be able to explain the money, and he would be on the run for the rest of his life. But Addison had thought of that too. "I'm prepared to say that I fronted you the money for a business deal with me, and the investment paid off brilliantly. No one will ever know." But Addison would. And no matter how he cooked his books, there was always the risk that someone would talk. The prisons were full of guys who thought their asses were covered, until someone sold them out. And Addison would own his ass for the rest of his life. But he already did. The moment he explained the plan to him, it was all over for Peter. Or his kids. And the Barnes children for sure.

"What if she doesn't have the money? If he lost some of it?" Peter asked sensibly. Stranger things had happened, particularly in the current economic climate. Fortunes had come and gone in the last few years, leaving in their wake a veritable Everest of debt. Addison only laughed at the idea.

"Don't be ridiculous. A year ago the man was worth half a billion dollars. You can't lose that much money if you try." But others had. Addison just refused to believe it about Barnes. He had been too smart to lose it all, or even most of his fortune, or so Addison thought. "The man was pure gold. Trust me. It's all there. And she'll pay. Who wouldn't? All she has now are her kids, and his money. And all we want is half of it. That leaves her plenty to play with, and her family intact." As long as they stayed that way. That was going to depend now on the men Peter chose. It was all resting on him. His life had turned into a nightmare in the past two hours. Worse than ever before, and beyond anything he could imagine. He was risking the death penalty, or life in prison at the very least.

Addison opened a drawer in his desk and pulled out an envelope of money. He had prepared it before Peter arrived. And he threw it across the desk.

"There's a hundred thousand dollars in there, to give you a start. The other hundred thousand will be delivered to you next week, in cash, for whatever your petty cash needs are.

It's against the ten million you'll get in the end. You walked in here a bum and an ex-con two hours ago, and you're walking out of here a rich man. Keep that in mind. And if you ever implicate me in any way in this, or even so much as breathe my name, you'll be dead within a day. Is that clear? And if you get cold feet, and try to back out, just think of your girls." He had Peter by the ass, the balls, and the throat. And he knew it. There was nowhere for Peter to turn. "Start looking for your men now. Pick the right ones. I want to start watching her by next week. And when you pick your men, make clear to them that if they run with their hundred thousand, and skip out on us, they'll be dead within two days. I can guarantee that." His eyes said he meant it, and Peter believed him, and knew it applied to him too.

"When do you want to do this?" Peter asked, slipping the envelope into his pocket, and feeling numb. "What's your target date?"

"If you hire all three men within the next week or two, I think if we watch them for the next four to six weeks, we'll know all we need to know about them. You should be able to make your move at the beginning of July." He was leaving for Cannes on the first of July. He wanted to be out of the country before they did it. Peter could guess that much.

Peter nodded and looked at him. His entire life had changed in the last two hours. He had an envelope full of money in his pocket with a hundred thousand dollars in it. And by the following week, he would have another hundred thousand dollars, and it meant nothing to him. All he had accomplished in the single afternoon he had spent with Phillip Addison was selling his soul in exchange for his daughters' lives. And with any luck at all, he would keep the Barnes kids alive too. The rest meant nothing to him. The ten million dollars was blood money. He had sold his soul to Phillip Addison. He might as well have been dead, as far as he was concerned. In fact, he was. He turned to walk out of the room, without saying another word to Addison, who watched him go, and just as Peter reached the doorway, Addison spoke up.

"Good luck. Stay in touch." Peter nodded and walked out of the office, and took the elevator downstairs. It was seven-thirty when he stepped outside. Everyone had left hours before. There was no one else around as Peter leaned over the garbage can on the corner and threw up. He stood there retching for what seemed like a long time.

Chapter 9

As Peter lay in bed in the halfway house that night, he thought about contacting his ex-wife. He wanted to warn her to be especially careful with the girls. But he knew she'd think he was insane. He didn't want Addison pulling a stunt on him, and holding them hostage until he accomplished the task he'd been assigned. But Addison was smarter than that. He knew that if he put Peter's kids at risk or worse, Peter would have nothing left to lose, and would expose him. So as long as Peter did what he had been hired to do, the girls were safe. It was the only thing he had done for his daughters in the last six years, or maybe their entire lives. He had bought their safety at the expense of his own. He was still having trouble believing they would be able to pull it off. But if he picked the right people, maybe he could. It was all about who he hired now. If he picked a bunch of sloppy, careless criminals, they might panic and kill the kids. What he had to find now was the real thing. The smoothest, toughest, coldest, most competent men in the business, if there was such a thing. The men he knew from prison had already proven their ineptitude by being caught, or maybe their plans had been flawed. Peter had to admit that Addison's strategy was very smooth. As long as Allan Barnes's widow had the money he wanted at her disposal. It was unlikely she kept a hundred million dollars in cash at home, in a cookie jar.

He was thinking about all of it, as he lay on his bunk, and his roommate walked in. He was going to look for a room in a decent hotel the next day, nothing too showy or expensive. He didn't want to make a sudden show of wealth he couldn't explain, although Phillip Addison had told him he was going to put him on the books of one of his minor subsidiary companies as a consultant. It was allegedly a market research firm, and was in fact a front for one of his drug rings. But it had been operating for years without a problem, and could be traced nowhere to him.

"How'd it go today?" the roommate asked. He had spent a killing day working at Burger

King, and reeked of burgers and french fries. It was only a modest improvement over the way he'd smelled the week before, when he'd worked in a place that served fish and chips. The whole room had smelled of fish. The burger smell was only slightly better.

"It went okay. I got a job. I'm going to move out tomorrow," Peter said in a dead voice. The roommate was sorry to see him go. Peter was quiet and didn't bother him, and minded his own business.

"What kind of job?" He could see Peter was a classy guy, he just had that look about him, even in jeans and T-shirts, and he knew he was educated. But even with an education, he was in the same boat as everyone else when he got out of prison.

"Doing market research. It's no big deal, but it'll pay rent and food." Peter looked unenthused. He was still feeling sick about it. He felt like his life was over. He almost wished he was back in prison. At least there, life was simple and he still had hope of a decent life one day. Now he no longer did. It was over for him. He had sold his soul to Satan.

"That's nice, man. I'm glad for you. Want to go out and eat something to celebrate?" He was a decent guy, who'd done time in the county jail for dealing marijuana, and Peter liked him, although he was a slob to live with.

"No, that's okay. I have a headache. And I have to go to work in the morning." In fact, he was going to start thinking, and already was, about the men he was going to hire for Addison's project. It was going to be excruciatingly delicate to find people who wouldn't expose him if they turned him down or he decided to reject them, if he thought they were too risky. He wasn't going to share the plan with them until he met them, trusted them, and had checked their credentials. But it was still going to be a delicate matter hiring them. He had a pain in the pit of his stomach just thinking about it. So far, he had only one man in mind. He hadn't been convicted of kidnapping, but Peter suspected he was the right kind of person for the job. He knew who he was, and roughly where he had gone when he left prison. All Peter had to do now was locate him. He was going to start in the morning, after he moved to a hotel. Just thinking about it, he tossed and turned all night.

He went to look for a hotel the next morning when he got up. He took a bus downtown, and found a place on the fringes of the Tenderloin, at the southern base of Nob Hill.

It was small and impersonal, and just busy enough so no one would pay attention to him. He paid a month's rent in advance, in cash, and then went back to the Mission, to the halfway house, to pack his things. He signed out at the desk, left a note for his roommate, wishing him luck, and then took a bus downtown again. He went to Macy's and bought some clothes. It was nice being able to do that again. He bought some slacks and shirts, a couple of ties, a sport coat, a leather baseball jacket, and some sweaters. He bought new underwear, and a few pairs of decent shoes. And then he went back to the hotel where he had taken the room. He felt like a human being again when he cleaned up, and walked down the street, looking for someplace to eat. There were hookers wandering by, and drunks in doorways. There was a drug deal going down in a car parked outside, and other than that, there were businesspeople and tourists. It was the kind of neighborhood where no one paid much attention to you, and you could get lost easily, which was exactly what he wanted.

He had no desire to draw attention to himself.

After dinner, he spent half an hour on the phone. He knew who he was looking for, and he was surprised how easy it was to find him. He decided to take a bus to Modesto in the morning. And before he did, he bought a cell phone. One of the conditions of his parole was not having a cell phone. It was a standard condition for parolees who had gone to prison for dealing drugs. Addison had told him to buy one. And now, without question, Addison was the boss. Peter knew there was no way his parole agent would know he'd bought the phone. He had notified him of his job and change of address that morning and his P.A. sounded pleased.

Peter called Addison in the office, and left him the cell phone number on his voice mail, and also the phone number at his hotel.

Fernanda was cooking dinner for the children that night. They were getting more and more excited about getting out of school for the summer. Will was particularly excited about playing lacrosse at camp for three weeks. And the others were excited about their plans too. And when they left for school the next day, she drove downtown, to meet with Jack Waterman. They had a lot to talk about. They always did. She liked him, she always had, although these days he was the voice of doom. He was the attorney who was handling Allan's estate, and before that they had been friends for years. He had been stunned by the mess Allan's affairs were in, the catastrophic decisions he had made, and how they impacted Fernanda and the kids.

His secretary poured her a cup of coffee when she walked in, and Jack sat across the desk from her with a grim expression. He hated Allan for what he'd done sometimes. She was such a nice woman, she didn't deserve this. No one did.

"Have you told the kids yet?" he asked, as she set the coffee down and shook her head.

"About the house? No, I haven't. They don't need to know yet. We're not putting it on the market till August. It'll be soon enough then. They don't need to worry about it for three months. Besides, it may take a while to sell."

It was a huge house, and an expensive one to keep up. And the real estate market hadn't been doing well. Jack had already told her that she absolutely had to sell it and have the money in her hands by the end of the year. He had also told her to strip the place and sell as much as she could separately. The furniture certainly. They had spent nearly five million dollars furnishing the house, some of which couldn't be recouped, like the marble they'd put in all the bathrooms, and the state-of-the-art kitchen. But the Viennese chandelier they had paid four hundred thousand dollars for could be sold at auction in New York, and might even bring a profit. And there were other things she could remove and sell throughout the house. She also knew that once they started stripping the place, it would be upsetting for the children, and she was dreading it. She tried not to think of it as she smiled at him, and he smiled back. She had been a hell of a good sport for the past four months, and he admired her for it. Fernanda said she wondered if Allan had ever considered what this would do to her. Knowing him, Jack suspected it had been the farthest thing from his mind. All he thought about was business, and money. There were times when Allan only thought of himself, both during his meteoric rise to dot-com celebrity, and as he plummeted at record speed on his way down. He was a handsome, charming, brilliant guy, but there had also been something very narcissistic about him. Even his suicide had been all about his own despair, without even thinking about her, or the kids. Jack wished he could do more for her, but for the moment he was doing all he could.

"Are you going anywhere this summer?" he asked, as he leaned back in his chair. He was a nice-looking man. He'd gone to business school with Allan, and then law school after that. The three of them had known each other for a long time. He had had his own griefs over the years. He had been married to an attorney, and she died of a brain tumor at thirty-five. He had never married again, and they hadn't had time to have kids. His own loss made him sympathetic to Fernanda's grief, and he envied her the kids. He was particularly worried about what she was going to live on after they paid Allan's debts. He knew she was thinking about getting a job in a museum, or teaching school. She had figured out that if she taught at Ashley and Sam's school, or even Will's, they might give her a break on their tuitions. But they needed a lot more than that to live on. They had gone from rags to riches to rags again. A lot of people had, in the wake of the dot-com blaze, but their story was more extreme than most, thanks to Allan.

"Will is going to camp, and Ash is going to Tahoe," she explained. "Sam and I are staying here. We can always go to the beach."

Listening to her made him feel guilty that he was going to Italy in August, and he almost wanted to invite her and the kids to join him, but he was traveling with friends. There was no current woman in his life, and he had had a soft spot for Fernanda over the years, but he also knew from his own experience that it was far too soon to approach anything of the kind with her. Allan had been gone for four months. And when his own wife died, he hadn't dated anyone for a year. But the thought of it had crossed his mind several times in the past few months. She needed someone to take care of her, and so did her children, and he was very fond of all of them. Fernanda knew nothing of his feelings for them.

"Maybe we can go to Napa for the day or something when the kids get out of school," he suggested cautiously, and she smiled at him. They had known each other for so long that she thought of him as a brother. It never even occurred to her that he wanted to ask her out and was biding his time. She had been off the dating market for seventeen years, and hadn't even thought of reentering it. She had more important things to think of first. Like their survival, and how she was going to feed her kids.

"They'd like that," Fernanda said in answer to his invitation to Napa.

"I have a friend who has a boat too. It's a beautiful sailboat." He was trying to think of ways to cheer her up, and entertain her children, without being pushy or offensive. And she looked at him sheepishly as she finished her coffee.

"The kids would love it. Allan took them out on boats a number of times. I get seasick." She had hated Allan's yacht, although he loved it. She got sick just standing on the dock. And now the mere mention of boats reminded her of how Allan had died. She never wanted to see a boat again.

"We'll think of something else," he said kindly. They spent the next two hours going over business matters, and finished the last of their paperwork shortly before noon. She had a good understanding of all of it, and she was being responsible about the decisions she made. There was nothing frivolous about her. He just wished that there was more he could do.

He invited her out to lunch, but she said she had some errands to do, and a dentist appointment that afternoon. In truth, the time she spent with him was so stressful, talking about how dire her situation was, that after seeing him, she felt as though she needed a breather and some time to herself. Inevitably, if they went to lunch, they would talk about her problems and Allan's debts. She knew Jack felt sorry for her, which was kind of him. But it made her feel waiflike and pathetic. She was relieved when she said good-bye to him, and drove back to Pacific Heights on her own. She heaved an enormous sigh, and tried to get rid of the sensation of panic in her stomach. She had a knot in it the size of a fist whenever she left his office, which was why she had declined his invitation to lunch. Instead, he had volunteered to come to dinner the following week, and promised to call her. At least seeing him with the children would buffer the horror of facing the grim realities with him. He was a very pragmatic person, and he spelled things out much too clearly. She would have been shocked to realize he had romantic intentions toward her. It had never even occurred to her in the course of their many meetings. She had always thought Jack was wonderful, and as solid as a rock, and she had been sorry for him that he had never remarried. He always claimed to her and Allan that he hadn't met the right person. She knew how much he had loved his wife, and Allan had warned her several times not to bug him about fixing him up with friends, so she hadn't. It never even dawned on her that she might wind up with him one day. She had been deeply in love with Allan, and still was. And for all his failings, and the mess he'd made of things in the end, she thought he was a great husband. She had no desire to replace him, in fact the reverse. She could imagine herself feeling married to him for the rest of her life, and never dating anyone else. And she had said as much to her children, which in some ways comforted them, particularly Sam, but it also made them sad for her.

Ashley had talked to Will about it several times when they were alone, if her mother was out with Sam, or busy doing something else.

"I don't want her to be alone forever," Ashley had said to her older brother, who was always startled when she brought it up. He tried not to think of his mother involved with someone other than his dad. Ashley was a born matchmaker, like her mother, and far more romantic.

"Dad just died," Will always said, looking upset when she talked about it. "Give her time. Did Mom say something?" Will had asked, looking worried.

"Yeah, she says she doesn't want to go out with anyone. She wants to be married to him forever. That's so sad." She still wore her wedding band. And she never went out at night anymore, except with them, for a movie or a pizza. And a couple of times they had gone to Mel's Diner after Will's ballgames. "I hope she meets someone and falls in love one day," Ashley concluded as Will rolled his eyes.

"It's none of our business," Will said sternly.

"Yes, it is. What about Jack Waterman?" Ashley had suggested, being far more perceptive than her mother. "I think he likes her."

"Don't be stupid, Ash. They're just friends."

"Well, you never know. His wife died too. And he never remarried." And then she suddenly looked worried. "Do you think he's gay?"

"Of course not. He's had a bunch of girlfriends. And you're disgusting," Will said, and stormed out of the room, as he always did when she brought up the subject of their mother's nonexistent love life. He didn't like thinking of his mother in that context. She was his mother, and he didn't see anything wrong with her staying alone, if she was happy that way, and she said she was. That was good enough for him. His sister was far more astute, even at her tender age.

They spent the weekend engaged in their usual pursuits, and while Fernanda sat in the bleachers, watching Will play lacrosse in Marin on Saturday, Peter Morgan was on his way to Modesto on a bus. He was wearing some of the new clothes he'd bought with the money Addison had given him. And he looked respectable and discreet. The person who had answered the phone at the halfway house told him Carlton Waters was registered there. It was the second one he had called. He had no idea what he was going to say when he got there. He needed to feel Waters out and see how things were going for him. And even if Waters didn't want to do the job himself, after twenty-four years in prison, with a conviction for murder, he would certainly know who would. How Peter was going to get the information from him was another story, particularly if he didn't want to do the job himself, or took umbrage at being asked. The "research," as Addison had referred to it, wasn't as easy as it looked. Peter was thinking about how to approach it, as he rode to Modesto on the bus.

As it turned out, the halfway house was only a few blocks from the bus station, and he walked there in the late spring heat. Peter took his leather baseball jacket off, and rolled up the sleeves of his shirt. And by the time he got to the address they'd given him on the phone, his new shoes were covered with dust. But he still looked like a businessman when he walked up the front steps and inside to the desk.

When he asked for Waters, he was told he had gone out, and Peter went back outside to wait. They had no idea where he'd gone or when he was due back. The man at the desk said he had family in the area and might have gone there, or he might have gone almost anywhere with friends. All he would confirm was that curfew was at nine o'clock, and he'd be back by then.

Peter sat on the porch waiting for a long time, and at five o'clock, he was thinking about getting something to eat, when he saw a familiar figure sauntering slowly down the street, with two other men. Waters was an imposing figure. He looked like a basketball player, or a linebacker. He was powerfully built, both tall and broad, and he had spent years in prison bodybuilding with impressive results. In the wrong place, at the wrong time, Peter knew he would be a frightening man, although he also knew that in twenty-four years, he had had no history of violence in prison. He found that information only slightly reassuring. There was a good chance that the offer Peter wanted to make to him would infuriate him, and he might beat the hell out of Peter for even asking. Peter wasn't looking forward to broaching it with him.

Waters was looking straight at Peter as he walked slowly across the street. They recognized each other instantly, although they had never been friends. He was exactly who and what Addison wanted him to find, a pro as opposed to an amateur criminal like Peter Morgan. Although now, thanks to Addison, he was in the big leagues too, and Peter was anything but proud of it. In fact, he hated what he was doing, but had no choice.

The two men nodded at each other, as Peter stood watching him from the porch, and Waters looked him in the eye with a hostile expression as he came up the steps. Peter wasn't reassured.

"You looking for someone?" Waters asked him, and Peter nodded, but didn't volunteer who it was.

"How've you been?" They were circling each other like pit bulls, and Peter was afraid that Waters would attack. The other two men, Malcolm Stark and Jim Free, hung slightly back, watching to see what would happen.

"I've been fine. You?" Peter nodded in answer, and their eyes never left each other, like magnets that were glued to metal, and could not release. Peter wasn't sure what to say to him, but he had the feeling Waters knew he had come to talk to him, and without saying anything to Peter, he turned to Malcolm Stark and Jim Free. "I'll be inside in a minute." They looked at Peter as they walked by, and let the screen door slam, as Waters looked back at Peter again, with a question in his eyes this time. "You want to talk to me?" Peter nodded again, and sighed. This was harder than he thought, and a lot scarier. But there was also a lot of money on the table. It was hard to predict how Waters would react, or what he'd say. And this wasn't the place to talk about it. Waters sensed easily that it was important. It had to be. The two men hadn't exchanged ten words in prison in the four years they'd both been there at the same time, and now he had ridden all the way from San Francisco to talk to him. Waters was curious to hear what it was about, to bring Peter up three hours on a bus from the city, and have him wait all day. Peter looked like a man with something important on his mind.

"Can we talk somewhere?" he said simply, and Waters nodded.

"There's a park down the street." He sensed correctly that Peter didn't want to go to a bar or a restaurant, or the living room in the halfway house, where they might be overheard.

"That'll do," Peter said tersely, and followed him down the steps off the porch.

He was hungry and nervous, and he had a rock in his stomach as they walked down the street without saying a word to each other. It was a full ten minutes before they reached the park, and Peter sat down on a bench, as Waters hesitated for a long moment and then lowered himself onto the bench next to him. He sat there, and took some chewing tobacco out of his pocket. It was a habit he had acquired in prison, and he didn't offer any to Peter. He just sat there, and finally looked at him, half annoyed and half curious.

Peter was exactly the kind of convict he had no respect for. He was some fool with money who had gotten himself busted out of sheer stupidity, and then kissed the warden's ass to get a job in the office. Waters had done hard time, and spent a lot of time in solitary. He hung around with murderers and rapists and kidnappers, and guys who had done a lot of time. Peter's little four-year stint meant nothing to him compared to his twenty-four. And Waters had claimed he was innocent to the end, and still did. Whatever his history, his innocence or guilt, he had spent most of his life in prison, and he had no interest in Peter Morgan. But if the man had come all the way from San Francisco to see him, he was going to listen to him, but that was all he was going to do. It was written all over him as he spat a wad of tobacco several feet and turned to look

at Peter. Waters's eyes nearly made Peter
shiver, as they had when he saw him in the
warden's office. He was waiting, and there was
no avoiding it. Peter knew he had to talk, he
just didn't know what to say, as Waters spat
again.

"What's on your mind?" Waters asked him,
looking him right in the eye. The force of his
stare took Peter's breath away. He was in
it now.

"Someone offered me a business deal," Peter
started as Waters watched him. Waters could
see that his hands were shaking, and he had
noticed the new clothes. The jacket looked
expensive, and so did the shoes. He was obviously doing okay. Waters was loading boxes at
the tomato farm, for minimum wage. He
wanted a job in the office, but they had told
him it was too soon. "I don't know if you'd be
interested, but I wanted to talk to you. I need
your advice." As soon as he said that, Waters
knew he was up to no good. He leaned back
against the bench and frowned.

"What makes you think I'd be interested, or
want to help you?" he said cautiously.

"I don't. I have no idea." He decided to be
honest with him, it was the only way to go
with someone as dangerous as he was. He figured it was the only shot he had. "I've got my

ass on the line. I owed someone money when I went to prison, a couple of hundred thousand dollars, and I walked right into his arms. He says he can have me killed anytime he wants, which is probably about right, although he hasn't till now. He offered me a deal. I have no choice. If I don't do this for him now, he says he'll kill my kids, and I think he would."

"Nice people you're hanging out with," Waters commented, stretched out his legs, and looked at his dusty cowboy boots. "Has he got the guts to do it?" Waters was curious, and felt sorry for him.

"Yeah. I think he would. So I'm in this up to my ass. He wants me to do a job for him."

"What kind of job?" His voice was noncommittal, as he continued to observe his boots.

"A big job. A very big job. There's a lot of money on the table. Five million bucks to you, if you're in. A hundred thousand in cash up front, the rest on the back end." Peter decided as he said it to him that maybe it wasn't as insulting as he had at first feared. Even if Waters didn't want it, it was a hell of an offer. For either of them. Waters nodded, he had figured that out too, but he didn't look impressed. He was very cool.

"How much to you?"

Honesty again. It was the only way to go here. Honor among thieves. "Ten on completion. Two hundred thousand cash up front. He wants me to put it together and hire the guys for him."

"How many?"

"Three, including you. If you do it."

"Drugs?" He couldn't even imagine how much heroin that represented, or cocaine. He couldn't think of anything else that would generate that much income. But that was high even for a drug deal, unless it was incredibly high risk, which it had to be, if anyone was offering to pay that much. But as Waters looked at him, Peter shook his head.

"Worse. Or better. Depending on how you look at it. In theory, it's pretty clean. They want us to kidnap someone, sit on them for a couple of weeks, collect the ransom, send them home, and split. With luck, no one gets hurt."

"Who the fuck is it?" Waters bellowed at him. "The president?"

Peter almost smiled but didn't. This was serious business, for both of them. "Three kids. Or as many as we can get. One'll do."

"Is he crazy? He's paying us twenty-five million bucks between the four of us to nab three kids, and send them home. What's in it for him? How much is the ransom?"

Peter was nervous giving him all the details, but he had to tell him enough to rope him in. "A hundred million. He keeps seventy-five. It's his idea." Waters whistled and stared at Peter for a long moment, and then with no warning, he reached across the bench and grabbed Peter so hard by the throat with one hand, he nearly choked the life out of him. Peter could feel his veins and arteries exploding in his viselike grip as Waters moved his face to within an inch of Peter's.

"If you're fucking with me, I'll kill you, you know that, don't you?" With his free hand, he ripped Peter's shirt open and tore all the buttons off to see if he'd been wired by the cops, but he hadn't been.

"This is for real," Peter managed to choke out with the last of his breath. Waters held him there until Peter saw stars and nearly lost consciousness, and then let go, and lay back against the bench again, looking unconcerned.

"Who's the guy?"

"I can't tell you," Peter said, rubbing his neck. He could still feel Waters's hand on his throat. "That's part of the deal." Waters nodded. It sounded right to him.

"Who're the kids?"

"I can't tell you that either, until I know you're in. But you'll know soon, if you are. He wants us watching them for a month or six weeks, so we know what we're doing, their routine, and when to grab them. And I have to set up a place for us to go."

"I can't do surveillance. I've got a job," Carl Waters said practically, as though he were organizing a work schedule or a car pool. "I can do it on weekends. Where is it, Frisco?" Peter nodded.

"I could do it during the week. It's probably less noticeable if we mix it up a little." That made sense to both of them.

"They've really got that kind of money? Or is this guy dreaming?"

"They had half a billion dollars a year ago. It's hard to spend that kind of money in a year. The guy died. We're hitting his wife up for the ransom. She'll pay to keep her kids." Waters nodded. That made sense to him too.

"You realize we could get the death penalty if they catch us," Waters said matter-of-factly. "Who's to say this guy won't sell our asses out if we do it. I don't trust people I don't know." He didn't say it, but he trusted Peter, although he also thought he was naïve. He'd always heard he was okay in prison. He was no hardass, but he had done his time and stayed clean. That meant a lot to him.

"I think we'd all need to figure out where to go afterward. I guess we do it, and we're on our own. If anyone talks, we're all screwed," Peter said quietly.

"Yeah, and so is he, if you do. He must trust you."

"Maybe. Greedy fucker. I had no choice. I can't risk my kids." Waters nodded again, that much he understood, although he had none of his own.

"Who else have you talked to?"

"No one. I started with you. I figured if you didn't want to do it, you'd give me some ideas. Unless you beat the shit out of me and told me to get fucked." They exchanged a smile on that one, and Waters laughed.

"You've got a lot of balls asking me something like this. I could have beaten the crap out of you."

"Or choked me," Peter teased, and Waters laughed again. It was a deep rumble that went with his looks. "What do you think?"

"I think this guy's a lunatic, or he has some mighty rich friends. You know the hit?"

"I know who they are."

"And they're for real?"

"Very much so," Peter reassured him, and

Waters looked impressed. He'd never heard of that kind of money except on drug deals, and Peter was right, this sounded clean. "I still have to find a place for us to go, with the kids."

"That's not hard. All you need is a mountain cabin, or an RV parked in the desert somewhere. Hell, how complicated is it to baby-sit three kids? How old are they?"

"Six, twelve, and sixteen."

"Shit, what a pain in the ass. But I guess for five million bucks I could baby-sit Dracula and his kids."

"But the deal is we don't hurt them. They go back untouched. That's the deal," Peter reminded him.

"I get it," Waters said, looking irritated. "No one's going to pay a hundred million bucks for three dead kids. Or even one." He got the point.

"Presumably, she'll pay the ransom quickly. She lost her husband, she won't want to lose her kids. It may take her a week or two to free up the money, but it shouldn't take too long. Not for her kids."

"I like the fact that it's a woman," Waters commented, thinking about it. "She's not going to make us sweat it for six months. She'll want those kids." Waters stood up then, and

looked down at Peter, still sitting on the
bench. He'd heard enough, and he wanted to
get back to the house. He had enough to think
about for now. "I'll think about it, and let you
know. How do I find you?" Peter handed him
a slip of paper with his cell phone on it. He'd
written it down while he was waiting on the
porch.

"If you do it, can you find the other guys?"
Peter asked, as he stood up.

"Yeah. It's gotta be guys I can trust. Anyone
can nab someone, but can they keep their
mouth shut afterward? Our asses are going to
be on the line after that. I want to make sure
mine won't rot in prison." He had a point, and
Peter agreed with him.

"He wants us to make a move in July. He'll
be out of the country then, and he wants it
over by the time he comes back." They had
just over a month to set it up, find the men,
and watch her. And take the kids.

"That shouldn't be a problem," Waters said,
and after that they walked along in silence,
while Peter wondered what he was thinking
and when he'd hear from him. Waters didn't
even look at him when they reached the
halfway house. He just started up the steps and
then turned around to look at him. And in
a voice no one could hear but Peter, he

mouthed the words "I'm in." And with that, he walked onto the porch and into the house. Peter stood staring after him, and the screen door slammed. Twenty minutes later, Peter was back on the bus and heading home.

Chapter 10

Peter heard from Carlton Waters on his cell phone later that week. He had the two other guys they needed. Malcolm Stark and Jim Free. He said he was sure they could do the job, and keep their mouths shut. The three of them had decided they would go to South America via Canada or Mexico after they did it. They wanted their five million dollars each in accounts in South America, where they could access it. Between themselves, they had talked about getting into the drug business, but they didn't have to figure that out yet. Waters knew people who could get them passports, and run them into Mexico. And from there, they could go anywhere. All they wanted was to do the job, get their money, and get the hell out. None of them had serious attachments, or were married. The girl in the coffee shop hadn't panned out for Jim Free. It turned out she had a boyfriend, and wasn't interested in Jim after all. She was just flirting with him.

There was a whole new life waiting for them in South America. All they needed now was a place to stay while they waited for the ransom, once they'd kidnapped the Barnes children. Peter said he'd take care of it. And Waters agreed to start watching them that weekend. Next, they had to get a car. Peter said he'd buy one for him and Waters to use for surveillance, something ordinary and innocuous that wouldn't attract attention. And they needed a van to do the job. Waters agreed to meet Peter at his hotel on Saturday. Carl could cover it from nine A.M. till six o'clock on weekends. Peter would follow them during the week, and on weekend nights. They were covered. Peter had a feeling she didn't go out much anyway, if she was alone with three kids. And it was only for a month. For ten million bucks, he could sit in a car all day, and cover nights. He reported in to Addison and told him they had the guys. Addison sounded pleased and said he was willing to pay for both the van and the car. They could dump both a month later, after the job was done.

Peter bought a Ford station wagon that afternoon. It was five years old and had a lot of mileage on it, and conveniently, it was black. He bought an old van at a different lot the next day and rented a space for it in a public garage. At six o'clock that night, he was parked outside Fernanda's house. He recognized her and the children from the photograph in Phillip's file, and remembered their names. They were emblazoned on his mind.

He saw Fernanda come in with Ashley, and then go out again, and he followed her. She drove erratically, and ran through two red lights. He wondered if she drank. He parked within three cars of her near the playing field in the Presidio and watched her get out. She sat in the bleachers watching Will play lacrosse, and as he walked back to the car with her afterward, Peter saw them hug before they got back in the car. Something about the way they did it made his heart ache, and he wasn't sure why. She was beautiful and blond and very small, and when they got to the house again, the boy was laughing when he got out of the car. He was in good spirits. They had won. Peter watched them walk up the steps to the house arm in arm. Seeing them made him want to be next to them, and he felt left out in an odd way when they went inside and shut the door. And as she went in, he watched her through the window to see if she was setting the alarm, which was important information for him. She didn't. She walked straight into the kitchen.

Peter saw the lights go on in the kitchen, and he imagined her cooking dinner for them. He had seen both Ashley and Will by then, but hadn't seen Sam yet. He remembered him from the photograph as being a smiling, red-headed little boy. Late that night, he saw her standing by the window in her bedroom. He watched her with binoculars, and saw that she was crying. She just stood there with tears rolling down her cheeks in her nightgown, and then she turned and walked away. It was a strange feeling, watching her like that. He kept getting glimpses into their life. The girl in the ballet leotard, the boy she hugged after he won his lacrosse game, and the tears running down her cheeks as she stood in her bedroom window, crying for her husband probably. It was two in the morning when Peter drove away. The house was dark, and had been for three hours. He realized now he didn't need to stay that late, but these were all things he needed to learn about them.

He was back the next morning at seven o'clock. Nothing happened until nearly eight. He couldn't see any activity in the kitchen, be-cause he couldn't tell if she'd turned the lights on. That side of the house was lit by morning sun, and at ten to eight she came flying out. She turned to talk to someone in the hallway behind her, and the ballerina came out dragging a heavy bag. The lacrosse player helped her with it, and then walked to the garage for his own car. The door to the house was still standing open, and Fernanda was looking impatiently toward it, and finally the youngest one came out. And as Peter sat watching him, he couldn't suppress a smile. Sam was wearing a bright red T-shirt with a fire engine on his back, with navy corduroy pants and red high-top sneakers, and he was singing at the top of his lungs, while his mother laughed and waved him to the car. He got into the back seat, because his sister was in the front seat, with the bag on her lap. And when they got to school, with Peter in the traffic behind them, Fernanda helped her out. He couldn't imagine what was in the bag as she dragged it up the steps. Sam bounced into school behind her like a puppy, and turned with a grin to wave at his mom, as she stood there for a minute, blew him a kiss, waved, and got back in the car. She waited until he'd gone inside before she drove away.

She drove to Laurel Village to the grocery store then, and pushed a cart around for a while, reading labels, and checking produce before she put it in the cart. She bought a lot of kid food, cereals and cookies and snacks, half a dozen steaks, and at the counter where they sold flowers, she stopped and looked at them, as though tempted to buy them, and then rolled past, looking sad. Peter could have stayed in the car, but he had decided to follow her, to get a better sense of who she was. And as he watched her, he found himself fascinated by her. She was the epitome of the perfect mom, in his eyes. All she did and all she thought about and all she bought seemed to be about and for her kids. He stood behind her in the check-out line as she picked up a magazine, glanced at it, and put it back. He was impressed by how simply dressed she was. No one would have thought for a minute that her husband had left her half a billion dollars. She was wearing a pink T-shirt, jeans, and clogs, and she looked like a kid herself. She turned to look at him, as they both waited, and unexpectedly she smiled at him. He looked immaculate in a new blue button-down shirt, loafers, and khaki pants. He looked like all the men she'd grown up with, or friends of Allan's. He was tall and good-looking and blond, and he knew from things he'd read about her now that he was only six months younger than she. They were virtually the same age. They had both gone to good colleges. She had gone to Stanford, and he had gone to Duke. He had gone to graduate school, while she married and had babies. And their kids were almost the same age. Sam was six, and Isabelle and Heather were eight and nine. She looked a little like Janet, but prettier, and more than he realized, he looked like Allan with blond hair. She had noticed it when she put back the magazine, and then stared at him. And when she dropped a roll of paper towels, while putting them on the check-out stand, he picked them up and handed them to her.

"Thanks," she said pleasantly, and he noticed her wedding band. She was still wearing it, and he found it a loving gesture. He liked everything about her, and listened to her chatting with the man adding up her groceries, who seemed to know her well. She said the kids were doing okay, and Will was going to camp to play lacrosse. Peter had to remind himself of what his mission was, and wondered when the boy was going to camp. It might mean, if it was in July, that Waters and his buddies would only be able to get two of the kids. And as he thought of it, he felt sick. This woman was so obviously decent, so loyal to her husband, and so devoted to her kids, that what they were about to do to her seemed more than ever like a heinous thing to him. They were going to make her pay a hundred million dollars just to keep all that she had and cherished now.

The thought of it weighed on him, as he watched her go through two more red lights and a stop sign on California Street on the way home. Her driving stank. He wondered what she was thinking about when she cruised through the red lights. And he was puzzled by what he saw when he got back to the house. He expected a housekeeper, or even a fleet of them to come out and unload the car. Instead she opened the front door, left it standing open, and carried the groceries in herself, bag by bag. He wondered if it was the maid's day off. After that, he didn't see her again till noon. She came back out for something she had forgotten in the car, and dropped the roll of paper towels again, but this time he didn't pick them up as he had in the store. He didn't move. He couldn't let her see him. He just watched.

She looked slightly disheveled when she came out in a rush at three o'clock. She jumped in her station wagon and drove off toward school, driving too fast, and nearly hit a bus. Just watching her for a day, he already knew that the woman was a menace on the road. She drove too fast, she went through lights, she changed lanes without signaling, and nearly hit pedestrians in crosswalks twice. She was obviously distracted, and she came to a rapid stop outside the two younger kids' school. Ashley was on the street waiting for her, talking to friends and laughing, and Sam bounced out carrying an enormous papier-mâché airplane five minutes later with a huge grin and a hug for his mom. Just watching them made Peter want to cry. Not for what he and Waters were going to do to them, but for all that he himself had missed as a child. Suddenly, he realized what life could have been like, if he hadn't screwed up, and were still with Janet and their kids. They'd be hugging him. And he'd have a loving wife like this pretty blond. It made him feel lonely thinking of all he didn't have, and never had.

They stopped at the hardware store on the way home, where she bought lightbulbs and a new broom, and a lunch pail for Sam to use at day camp. She dropped him off at the house, said something to Will when he came to the door for his brother, and then drove Ashley to ballet. And that afternoon, after she picked Ashley up, she went to another one of Will's games. Her entire life seemed to revolve around them. By the end of the week, Peter had seen her do nothing except drive them to and from school, take Ashley to ballet, and go to Will's games. She did nothing else. And when he checked in with Addison, he mentioned that they had no domestic staff, which seemed odd to him for someone with their means.

"What difference does it make?" Addison said, sounding annoyed. "Maybe she's cheap."

"Maybe she's broke," Peter said, ever more curious about her. She looked like a serious person, and when she was alone, she looked sad. But when she was with the kids, she smiled and laughed and hugged them a lot. And he saw her crying in her bedroom window every night. It made him want to hold her in his arms, the way she did her kids. She needed that, and had no one to do it for her.

"No one can spend half a billion dollars in a year," Phillip answered, sounding unconcerned.

"No, but you can sure as hell blow that and more on bad investments, especially with the bottom falling out of the market the way it has." Phillip knew that only too well. But what he had lost, he assumed would have been a drop in the bucket to Allan Barnes.

"I haven't read anywhere about any of Barnes's deals going sour. Believe me, Morgan, they've got it. Or he did and she does now. She probably just doesn't like to spend it. Are you keeping track of her?" Addison asked, pleased with the way things were going. Peter had put the team in place quickly, and he said he was going to Tahoe over the weekend to find a house. He wanted to find a cabin somewhere in an isolated area where they could keep the kids for as long as it took for her to come up with the ransom. As far as Addison was concerned, this was just business. For him, there was nothing personal or sentimental about it. Peter was feeling more intense, after watching her drop off, pick up, and constantly hug and kiss her children. Not to mention the nightly tears in her bedroom window.

"Yes, I'm keeping track of her," Peter said tersely. "She doesn't do anything except drive her kids around and go through red lights."

"Great. Let's hope she doesn't kill them before we get them. Does she drink?"

"I don't know. She doesn't look it. I think she's distracted or upset." The day before, he had watched her nearly hit a woman in yet another crosswalk. Everyone had honked at her, and she had jumped out of the car and apologized profusely, and when she did, he saw that she was crying. Fernanda was driving him crazy. She was all he could think of now, not only because of what they had in store for her, but because of what he wished he could say to her, and the time he wished he could spend with her, if things were different. In other circumstances, he would have liked to get to know her. In his mind, she had become the perfect woman. Seeing her with her children, he had come to admire her so much. He loved watching her, and wondered what she'd been like when Barnes married her. Thinking of her as a young girl nearly drove him insane.

Why hadn't he met her then? Why was life so cruel? While he had been busy screwing up his life, and his ex-wife's, Fernanda had been married to a lucky guy, and building a family. She was spectacularly beautiful. And Sam had won his heart the first day he saw him. Ashley was a beauty. Will looked like the kind of son every man wanted. Whatever else Allan Barnes had done, and the name he had made for himself in the business world, it was obvious to Peter Morgan that he had left the perfect family behind. Peter felt like a Peeping Tom watching her, and when he went back to his hotel to sleep at night, invariably he found himself dreaming of her, and couldn't wait to go back in the morning to see her again. She had begun to haunt him like an old friend, or a lost love. In fact, for him, she was like a reminder of a lost world. A world he had always wanted to be part of, and had been for a time, but seeing her reminded him of the life and opportunities he had blown. She was everything he had always wanted and would never have again.

He hated to turn her over to Carlton Waters on Saturday, when he gave him the car, and used the van to go to Tahoe. He had a listing of houses to rent he'd gotten on the Internet. He didn't want to work with a realtor. But as long as no one saw Carl and his boys, there was no problem. If anything happened, Peter could always say that the men had broken in and used the house while he was in San Francisco. They were all making painstaking efforts to keep all of the various elements separate, and so far, there had been no problems. No one in Modesto, other than Stark and Free, knew that Carl was in the city. He was going to be back by curfew.

No one was going to follow Fernanda after six o'clock that night, until Peter got back from Tahoe sometime around ten. And if she followed her usual pattern, she'd be home with her children long before that. The only time she went out at night was to drop off Will or Ashley at friends' houses, or pick them up after a party. She didn't like Will driving at night, although as he told her frequently, and Peter could have verified, her driving was far worse than his was. From everything Peter had seen, she was a total menace.

"What's she liable to do today?" Carl asked Peter when he picked up the car keys. He was wearing a baseball cap that shielded his face, and changed his looks, and dark glasses. When Peter followed her, he looked as he always did, and if there were too many people on the street, he drove around the block a few times, and came back again. But so far he didn't have the feeling anyone had spotted him, least of all Fernanda.

"She'll probably take the older boy to a game, maybe in Marin. Or the girl to ballet. She usually has the little one with her on Saturdays. They don't seem to do much, probably even on weekends." The weather had been great, but she didn't seem to go out much. In fact, almost never. "You'll get a good look at the kids. She's with them pretty much all the time, and the little guy never leaves her." Peter had a sense of betraying them, and Waters nodded. Carl wasn't interested in making friends with them. This was a reconnaissance mission for him, and nothing more than that. To him, this was business. To Peter, it was becoming an obsession. But Carlton Waters didn't know that. He took the keys, got in the car, and drove to the address Morgan had given him. It was ten o'clock on a brilliantly sunny Saturday in May as Peter left for Tahoe.

He thought about her all the way, wondering what would happen if he backed out now. It was simple, Addison would have his daughters killed, and Peter himself shortly thereafter. And if he confessed to the police and did time for it, or was violated, Addison would have him killed in prison. It was all so simple. There was no turning back. They were on a roll now. And as he reached Truckee finally, Waters was following her to Marin, to one of Will's lacrosse games. He had seen all three kids by then, and she looked about the way he had expected her to. To him, she looked like a suburban housewife, which was of no interest to him. To him, she was a victim, and a lucrative one, and nothing more. To Peter, she looked like an angel. But in some ways, Waters didn't know what he was seeing. The kind of women that appealed to him were a lot jazzier-looking than Fernanda. He thought she looked pretty but plain, and noticed that she didn't wear makeup. At least not when she

went out with her children. In fact, she hadn't
worn any since Allan died. It no longer mattered to her. Nor did fancy clothes, high heels,
or any of the jewelry he'd given her. She had
already sold most of it, and the rest had been
in the safe since January. She didn't need jewelry or fancy clothes for what she was doing,
or what her life was now.

Peter drove to the first address on his list,
and saw that it was bordered on three sides,
and within two feet in each case, by other
houses, which made it impossible for their
purpose. He had the same problem with the
next four. The sixth one was insanely expensive. The next four were equally unsuitable.
And much to his relief, the last one was the
right one. It was perfect. It had a long winding driveway that was full of potholes and
weeds, the house itself looked ramshackle, and
was so overgrown, you couldn't even see in
the windows, which were shuttered, which
was yet another bonus. The house had four
bedrooms, a kitchen that had seen better days
but was functional, and a large living room
with a fireplace Peter could have stood up in.
And behind it, there was a cliff of sheer rock
face. The man who owned it showed it to
him, and said he no longer used it. It had been
used by his sons, and they had moved away

years before, but he kept it as an investment. He was renting it since his daughter didn't want it either. Both his sons lived in Arizona, and he was spending the summer in Colorado with his daughter. Peter took it as a six-month rental, and asked the man if he minded if he cleaned it up a bit, and weeded the yard, since he was going to be using it to entertain clients, and the owner looked delighted. He couldn't believe his good fortune to have Peter as a tenant. Peter hadn't even quibbled about the price. He signed the lease, paid three months' rent and a security deposit in cash, and by four o'clock he was back on the road when he got a call on his cell phone from Carlton Waters.

"Something wrong?" Peter sounded worried and wondered if something had happened, or if Waters had been spotted. Or even scared her, or one of the children.

"No, she's fine. They're at the kid's ballgame. She doesn't do much, does she? And she's always got one of the kids with her." It was going to complicate things for them eventually, not that it really mattered. She was too small to give them any trouble. "I just thought of something. Who's getting the weapons?"

Peter looked blank for a moment as he thought about it. "I guess you are. I can ask, but he probably doesn't want to supply us anything that can be traced back to him. Can you handle it?" Peter knew Addison had the connections to supply them. But he also knew Addison wanted no link whatsoever to this project.

"Maybe I can. I want automatic weapons." Waters was clear about it.

"You mean like machine guns?" Peter sounded startled. "Why?" The kids weren't going to be armed. Nor was she. But the cops would be if there was ever a showdown. To Peter, machine guns sounded excessive.

"That keeps things nice and simple," Waters said bluntly, and Peter nodded. These were the professionals Addison had wanted.

"You take care of it," Peter said, sounding worried. He told him about the house then, and Waters agreed with him. It sounded perfect. They were all set now. All they needed to do was pick a date in July. And go for it. It all seemed so simple, but as soon as Peter hung up, he had the now familiar pain in his stomach. He was beginning to think it was his conscience. Following her around from ballet to baseball games was one thing. Taking her children away from her, using machine guns, and demanding a hundred million dollars ransom for them was another. And Peter knew the difference.

Chapter 11

In the first week of June, on the last day of school, Fernanda had her hands full. Ashley and Sam both had performances at school. She had to help them get all their art projects and books home afterward. Will had a playoff game for his baseball team, and later that night he had a lacrosse game, which she had to miss, in order to attend Ashley's ballet recital. She felt like a rat in a laboratory, running all day, to get from one child to the other. And as usual, there was no one to help her. Not that Allan would have, if he were still alive. But until January, she had had a nanny to help her cover the bases. Now there was no one. She had no family, had lost touch with even her closest friends for a variety of reasons, and realized now how totally dependent she had been on Allan. With him gone, all she had left now were her children. And their circumstances were too awkward for her to want to contact their old friends again. She might as well have been living on a desert island with her children. She felt completely isolated.

Peter had spoken to her twice by then, once in the supermarket on the first day, and another time in a bookshop, when she glanced up at him and smiled, and thought he looked vaguely familiar. She had dropped some of the books she was carrying, and with an easy smile, he handed them to her. After that, he had stood watching her from the distance. He sat in the bleachers at one of Will's games in the Presidio once, but he was behind her, and she never saw him. He never took his eyes off her.

He noticed that she had stopped crying at the bedroom window. He saw her standing there sometimes, looking out at the street vacantly, as though she were waiting for someone. It was like looking straight into her soul, when he saw her there at night. It was almost as though he knew what she was thinking. She was almost certainly dreaming of Allan. Peter thought he'd been a lucky guy to have a wife like her, and wondered if he knew it. Sometimes people didn't. But Peter appreciated every gesture she made, every time she picked up her kids, and every time she hugged them. She was exactly the kind of mother he would have wanted, instead of the one he'd had, who had been an alcoholic nightmare, and had eventually left him unloved, unwanted, and abandoned. Even the stepfather she'd left him with had ultimately left him stranded. But there was nothing abandoned or unloved about Fernanda's children.

Peter was almost jealous of them. And all he could think of when he saw her at night was how much he would have loved to put his arms around her, and console her, and he knew he could never do it. He was confined to watching her, and condemned to cause her more grief and pain, by a man who had threatened to kill Peter's children. The irony of it was exquisite. In order to save his own children, he had to risk hers, and torture a woman he had come to admire, and who aroused a flood of powerful emotions in him, some of which confused him, and all of which were bittersweet. He had a sense of longing every time he saw her.

He followed her to Ashley's recital that night, and stopped behind her at the florist where she had ordered a bouquet of long-stemmed pink roses. She had bought one for the ballet teacher as well, and emerged carrying both of them.

Ashley was already at the ballet school. And Sam was at Will's game, with the mother of one of Will's friends, who also had a son Sam's age and had volunteered to take him. He had announced that afternoon that ballet was for sissies. And Peter realized, as he watched them leave, that if Waters and the others had been planning to hit that night, they could have gotten both boys, if not Ashley.

By then, Waters had bought the machine guns, through a friend of Jim Free's. The man they bought them from had shipped them from L.A. by Greyhound, in golf bags. They arrived undisturbed, and it was obvious that no one had checked them. Peter had been shaking from head to foot when he went to get them. And after he picked the guns up, he left them in the trunk of his car. He didn't want to risk keeping them in his hotel room. Technically, he was obliged to submit to a search of his premises, without warrant or notice, if his parole agent ever decided to show up, which so far he hadn't. He wasn't worried about Peter, especially now that he was employed. But there was no point taking chances. Up till then, everything had gone smoothly.

Peter waited for Fernanda and Ashley outside the ballet school that night, and saw Ashley come out beaming, carrying the bou-

quet of pink roses. Fernanda looked incredibly
proud of her, and after the performance, they
met up with Will and Sam for a celebratory
meal at Mel's Diner on Lombard. And once
they were sitting down, Peter slipped quietly
into a corner booth, and ordered a cup of coffee. He was so close, he could almost touch
them. And when she walked by him, he could
smell Fernanda's perfume. She had worn a
khaki skirt that night, a white cashmere
V-neck sweater, and high heels for the first
time since he'd seen her. Her hair was down,
she had lipstick on, and she looked happy and
pretty. Ashley had makeup on, and was still
wearing her leotard from the performance.
And Will was in his lacrosse uniform, while
Sam told them all about the game. Will's team
had won, and earlier that day, his baseball team
had won the playoff. They had multiple victories to celebrate that night, and Peter felt sad
and lonely as he watched them. He knew
what was coming. And his heart ached for
Fernanda. He felt almost like a ghost watching
them. One who knew the future, and the
heartbreaks that would come, and could do
nothing to stop them. In order to save his own
children, his voice and his conscience had
been silenced.

They hung out at the house for the rest of

June. Friends came and went. Fernanda did
errands with Sam, and went shopping with
Ashley for a few things for Tahoe. She even
went shopping herself one day, just for the fun
of it, but all she came home with was a single
pair of sandals. She had promised Jack Waterman in January that she would buy nothing,
or close to it. He had invited her and the children to spend a day in Napa with him on the
Memorial Day weekend, but they couldn't go,
since Will had a lacrosse game, and his mother
wanted to drive him. She didn't like him driving to Marin on holiday weekends. Jack had
given them a rain check for the Fourth of July
weekend, when Will would be away at camp,
and Ashley would be in Tahoe. Fernanda had
promised that she and Sam would come, and
Jack was taking them to a friend's Fourth of
July picnic. She and Sam were looking forward to it. As Jack was, more than she imagined. Their friendship always seemed innocent
to her, and always had been. But things were
different now, in his mind, if not hers. As far
as Jack was concerned, she was single. Ashley
had teased her about it when her mother told
her about the picnic. She said Jack had a crush
on Fernanda.

"Don't be silly, Ash. He's an old friend.
You're disgusting." Ashley had said in no un-

certain terms that Jack Waterman had the hots for her.

"Does he, Mom?" Sam had looked up from a stack of pancakes with interest.

"No, he doesn't. He was a friend of Daddy's." As though that made all the difference. But Daddy was gone now.

"So? What difference does that make?" Ashley commented, as she took a bite of Sam's pancakes, and he swatted her with his napkin.

"Are you going to marry him, Mom?" Sam looked at her sadly. He liked having her to himself. He was still sleeping in her bed most of the time. He missed his dad, but he had grown even closer to his mother, and he wasn't anxious to share her.

"Of course not," Fernanda said, looking flustered. "I'm not going to marry anyone. I still love Daddy."

"Good," Sam said, looking satisfied, as he stuffed a forkful of pancakes into his mouth, and dripped syrup down his T-shirt.

On the last week in June Fernanda hardly left the house. She was too busy packing. She had Will's lacrosse gear to organize and pack, and everything Ashley was taking to Tahoe. It was endless. It seemed like every time she packed something, one of them took it out of the bag again, and wore it. By the end of the week, everything was dirty, and she had to start over. Ashley had tried on everything she owned, and borrowed half of her mother's clothes. And Sam suddenly announced that he didn't want to go to day camp.

"Come on, Sam, you'll love it," she encouraged him as she did a load of laundry, just as Ashley breezed through the laundry room wearing her mother's high heels, and one of her sweaters.

"Take those off," she scolded her, as Sam wandered off, and Will walked in, to ask her if she'd packed his cleats, because he needed them for practice.

"If either of you touch the bags I've packed again, I'm warning you both, I'm going to kill you." Ashley looked at her as though she was weird, and Will rushed back upstairs to find his own shoes.

Their mother had been testy all morning. In fact, she was sad to see them both going. She counted on them now, more than she ever had, for company and distraction, and it was going to be lonely with only Sam home. She suspected that he was feeling it too, which was why he had balked at camp. She reminded him then of the Fourth of July picnic they were going to in Napa. She thought it would be fun for him, and he even looked unenthusiastic about that. He was going to miss his sister and brother. Will was leaving for three weeks, and Ashley for two. It seemed like an eternity to both Sam and Fernanda.

"They'll be back before you know it," Fernanda reassured him. But she said it as much to comfort herself, as him. And outside, Peter was doing some mourning of his own. In six days they were going to make their move, and his part in her life would be over. Maybe they would meet somewhere one day, and with luck, she would never know the part he had played in the horror that was about to strike her. He had fantasies about running into her, or following her again, just so he could see her. He had been following her for over a month now. And she had never for a single second sensed it. Nor had the children. He had been careful and wise, as had Carl Waters on the weekends. Waters was far less en-chanted with her than he was. He thought her life incredibly mundane and boring, and won-dered how she stood it. She hardly went any-where, and wherever she did go, she took her children. It was precisely that that Peter loved about her.

"She ought to thank us for taking those kids off her hands for a week or two," Waters had commented to Peter one Saturday. "Christ, the woman never goes anywhere without them."

"You have to admire her for that," Peter said quietly. He did certainly, but Carl Waters didn't.

"No wonder her husband died. The poor bastard must have died of boredom," Carl muttered. He thought tailing her had been the dullest part of the assignment, unlike Peter, who loved it.

"Maybe she went out more before she was widowed," Peter commented, and Waters shrugged, as he turned the car over to Peter, and headed for the bus station to go back to Modesto. He was glad the surveillance was almost over and they could get on with it. He was anxious to get his hands on the money. Addison had proved to be true to his word. He, Stark, and Free had each received their one hundred thousand dollars. It was locked in suitcases, in lockers at the bus terminal in Modesto, where they'd put it for safekeeping. They were going to take it with them when they left for Tahoe. Everything was ready. And the clock was ticking.

All had gone on schedule so far, and Peter had assured Addison it would continue to do so. He anticipated no glitches, on their end at least. The first problem they encountered unexpectedly emanated not from them, but from Addison. He was sitting at his desk, dictating to his secretary, when two men walked in, holding their badges up to him, and informed him that he was under arrest. The secretary ran out of the room, crying, and no one stopped her, as Phillip looked at them and didn't so much as blink.

"That's the most ridiculous thing I've ever heard," he said calmly, with a wry look on his face. He thought the visit had something to do with his crystal meth laboratories; if so, it was the first time his underworld life had crossed over into his serious business. The men still holding out their badges were wearing plaid shirts and blue jeans. One was Hispanic, and the other was African American, and he had no idea what they wanted. As far as he knew, his drug business was running smoothly. Nothing was traceable to him, and the people running it were totally efficient.

"You're under arrest, Addison," the Hispanic man repeated, and Phillip Addison started laughing.

"You must be joking. What in God's name for?" He looked anything but worried.

"Apparently, there's been a little funny business with transfers of monies. You've been running cash across state lines in large amounts.

It looks like you've been laundering money," the agent explained, feeling slightly ridiculous himself. The two agents had been doing some undercover work on another case that morning, and hadn't had time to change before they were sent to Addison's office. Given his casual reception of them, they felt a little foolish, and as though they should have looked more official, in order to intimidate him, or at least impress him. Addison just sat there and smiled at them, as though they were badly behaved children.

"I'm sure my attorneys can handle this, without your having to arrest me. Would either of you like some coffee?"

"No, thank you," the black agent said politely. They were both young agents. And the special agent in charge of the investigation had told them not to underestimate Addison. There was more to him than met the eye, which both of the younger agents had assumed meant he might be armed and dangerous, which obviously he wasn't.

The young Hispanic agent read him his rights, as Phillip realized they weren't cops, they were FBI, which he found slightly more disturbing, although he didn't show it. In fact, the arrest was a stretch, but their superiors were hoping more would come out in the investigation. They'd been keeping an eye on him for a long time. They knew something was wrong, but they weren't entirely sure what, and they were using what they had.

"I'm sure there must be some mistake here, Officer . . . er . . . I mean, Special Agent." Even the title sounded foolish to him, and very cops-and-robbers.

"Maybe there is, but we still have to take you to the office. You're under arrest, Mr. Addison. Shall we cuff you, or will you come with us under your own steam?" Phillip had no intention of being dragged out of his office in handcuffs, and he stood up, looking angry, and no longer amused. However youthful they looked, the two agents apparently meant business.

"Do you have any idea what you're doing? Do you realize the lawsuit I could slap you with, for false arrest and defamation of character?" Phillip was suddenly in a white fury. As far as he knew, they had absolutely no reason to arrest him. Or surely none that they knew of.

"We're just doing our job, sir," the black agent, Special Agent Price, said politely. "Will you come with us now, sir?"

"As soon as I call my attorney." He dialed his lawyer's phone number, while the two agents stood on the other side of his desk and waited. Phillip told him what had happened. He promised to meet Phillip in the FBI office in half an hour, and advised him to go with the two agents. It was going to take Phillip at least a half hour to get from San Mateo to the city. The warrant for Phillip's arrest had been filed by the U.S. Attorney, and there was mention of tax evasion in the complaint, for some ridiculous amount. This was the last thing Phillip wanted. "I'm leaving for Europe in three days," he said, looking outraged as they escorted him out of his office. His secretary had vanished, but he could tell from the looks on people's faces as they watched him leave that she had told everyone what had happened. He was livid.

When he got to the FBI office and was greeted by Special Agent Rick Holmquist, the agent in charge, he was more so. He was under investigation for tax evasion, tax fraud, and transporting funds illegally across state lines. This was no small matter, nor were they prepared to make light of it. And when his attorney arrived, he advised Phillip to cooperate fully. He was being formally charged by the U.S. Attorney, and the FBI had been assigned to handle the investigation. He was asked to step into a locked room with his attorney and

Special Agent Holmquist, who did not look in the least amused, nor cowed by Phillip's grandeur. And his claims of innocence and outrage didn't impress him either. In fact, there was absolutely nothing about Phillip Addison that Special Agent Holmquist liked, not the least of which was the condescending way he had treated his agents.

Special Agent Holmquist allowed attorney and client to confer, and after that he spent three hours interrogating Phillip, and wasn't satisfied by any means with Phillip's answers. Holmquist had signed an order for the search of his offices, which was already under way while they were speaking. A federal judge had signed the search warrant requested by the U.S. Attorney. They had some serious questions in their minds about the legitimacy of Addison's business, and suspected that he might be laundering money, maybe even by the millions. As usual, a paid informant had tipped them off, but this one at an interestingly high level. And Phillip nearly burst an artery when he heard that at that exact moment, half a dozen FBI agents were searching his office.

"Can't you do something about this? This is an outrage!" he shouted at his lawyer, who shook his head, and explained to him that if the search warrant was in order, which it was apparently, there was absolutely nothing he could do to stop it.

"I'm leaving for Europe on Friday," he told them, as though he expected them to put their investigation on hold while he left on vacation.

"That remains to be seen, Mr. Addison," Holmquist said politely. He had dealt with men like him before, and always thought them extremely unpleasant. In fact, he enjoyed playing with them whenever possible. And he had every intention of tormenting Phillip, after they booked him of course. He knew that whatever bail they set for him, given the size of his net worth, he would be out in minutes. But until bail was set, he had all the opportunity he wanted to question Phillip.

Holmquist spent the rest of the afternoon interrogating him. After which, he was formally booked, and informed that it was too late in the day for a federal judge to set bail. He would have to cool his heels in jail for the night, and could only be released after a hearing to set bail at nine o'clock the next morning. Phillip Addison was beyond outraged, and there was nothing his lawyer could do to help him. Addison was still unclear about what had set the investigation off in the first place. It appeared to be a matter of irregular debits and deposits and money disappearing over state lines, notably to a bank where he had an account under another name in Nevada, and the government wanted to know why, what he was doing with it, and where the money came from. He knew by now it had nothing to do with his crystal meth labs. All the money he used to run those came from an account he kept in Mexico City under another name, and the proceeds went into several numbered Swiss accounts. This current situation truly appeared to be a matter of tax evasion. Agent Holmquist said that over eleven million dollars had come in and out of the Nevada account in the past several months, and mostly out, and from what they'd been told, he had never paid taxes on any of it, nor on the interest. Phillip continued to look unconcerned as they took him away to a cell for the night, although he gave a look of fury to both Holmquist and his attorney.

Holmquist met with the agents who had searched his offices after that, and nothing much had turned up. They had gone through computers and files, which would be used as evidence against him. They had brought boxloads of them back to the office. They had also unlocked his desk, and found a loaded handgun in it, a number of personal files, and four hundred thousand dollars in cash, which Holmquist found interesting. That was a lot of cash for the average businessman to keep in his desk drawer, and they said he had no permit for the gun. They had two boxes with everything they'd found in Phillip's desk, and one of the agents handed them to Holmquist.

"What do you want me to do with this?" Rick looked at them, and the agent who had handed it to him said he thought he'd want to go through it. Rick was going to tell them to put the boxes with the rest of the evidence, and at the last minute thought better of it, and carried them into his office.

The gun had been put in a plastic evidence bag, and there were several plastic envelopes with small scraps of paper in them, and for no reason in particular, he started to read through them. There were notes with names and phone numbers on them, and he noticed that two of them had the name Peter Morgan on them, but the phone numbers were different. He was halfway through the second box when he found the file on Allan Barnes, which spanned three years of his career, and was as thick as the San Francisco phone book. It seemed like an odd file for him to keep, Holmquist thought to himself, and set it aside.

He wanted to ask Addison about it. There were several photographs of Barnes from old magazine and newspaper articles, and there was even one of Barnes with his wife and children. It was almost as though Addison were obsessed with him, or even jealous. The rest of what Rick found in the boxes was meaningless to him. But might mean something to the U.S. Attorney's office. They had used master keys to open all his desk drawers, and the special agents who'd gone through them assured Rick that when they left Addison's office, his desk was empty. They had brought everything back with them, and seized it all as evidence, even his cell phone, which he had forgotten to take with him.

"If he has a phone book in it, remember to mark those numbers down too."

"We already did." One of the agents smiled at him.

"Anything interesting?"

"It's all the same stuff that was in his desk. Some guy called Morgan called while we were working on it, and when I said I was FBI, he hung up." The agent laughed, and so did Holmquist.

"I'll bet he did." But the name struck him again. His name and number were on the two pieces of paper from Phillip's desk, and he was obviously someone he spoke to regularly, if he had called looking for Phillip. It was probably nothing, but it was one of those odd instincts he had sometimes, like a tic, that gnawed at him and clicked later. He had a sixth sense about the name. It stuck in his mind, and for some reason he couldn't forget it.

It was after seven when Rick Holmquist left his office that night. Phillip Addison was in custody for the night. His lawyer had stopped harassing them to make an exception and let him out, and he had finally gone home. Most of the agents were gone by that hour. Rick's girlfriend was out of town, and on his way home, Rick decided to call Ted Lee. They had been best friends since they had gone through the police academy together, and been partners for fifteen years. Rick had always wanted to join the FBI, and the cut-off was thirty-five. He had just made it by joining at thirty-three. And he had been a special agent now for fourteen years. He had another six to go before he retired at fifty-three, after twenty years with the FBI at that point. Ted liked reminding him that he only had a year before he could retire with thirty, but neither of them intended to retire anytime soon. They both still loved what they did, Ted even more than Rick. A lot of what Rick did for the FBI was tedious, the paperwork nearly killed him sometimes. And there were times, like tonight, when he wished he was still working with Ted at SFPD. He hated people like Addison. They wasted his time, their lies were less convincing than they thought, and their attitudes disgusting.

Ted answered his cell phone on the first ring, and smiled as soon as he heard Rick. They had dinner or lunch religiously once a week, and had for the last fourteen years. It was the best way for them to stay in touch.

"What are you? Bored?" Holmquist teased. "You sure picked up quick. It must be a dead night downtown."

"It's quiet tonight," Ted admitted. Sometimes it was nice that way. And Jeff Stone, his partner, was out sick. "What about you?" Ted had his feet on his desk. He was doing paperwork on a robbery that had happened the day before. But other than that, Rick was right. He was bored.

"I had one of those days that make me wonder why I left the force. I'm just leaving the office. I handled more paper today than a printing press. We busted a real sonofabitch for tax evasion and laundering money. He was one incredible pompous prick."

"Anyone I know? We get a few of those too."

"Not like this. Give me an assault and robbery or a shooter any day. You've probably heard of him. Phillip Addison, he's head of a bunch of corporations, and he's a big-deal socialite. He has about two hundred businesses, that are probably all fronts for the taxes he doesn't pay."

"He is a big fish," Ted commented. It always struck him as odd when people like that got arrested, but they did sometimes. It happened to them too. "What did you do with him? Let him out on bail, I assume," Ted teased Rick. Suspects like that usually had a battalion of lawyers or one very good one. Very few of the people Rick arrested were flight risks, except for the guys carrying weapons or drugs over state lines. But the paper pushers and the tax evaders always bailed.

"He's cooling his heels in jail tonight. By the time he stopped talking, none of the judges were around to set bail." Rick Holmquist laughed, and Ted grinned. The irony of a man like Addison spending a night in jail amused them both.

"Peg's in New York with her sister. You want to grab something to eat? I'm too tired to cook," Rick suggested as Ted glanced at his watch. It was still early, and other than his robbery reports, he had nothing else to do. He had his beeper, his radio, and his cell phone on. If they needed him, they could find him, and he'd come in. There was no reason why he shouldn't have dinner with Rick.

"I'll meet you at Harry's in ten minutes." Ted suggested a familiar haunt. It was a hamburger joint they had gone to for years. They would give them a quiet table in the back, as they always did, so they could talk quietly. There would be only a few stragglers left at that hour. Most of the business they did at night was at the bar.

Rick was already there when Ted arrived, and he was relaxing at the bar with a beer. He was going off duty so he could drink. Ted never did. He needed his wits about him when he was working.

"You look like shit," Ted said with a grin, when he saw his friend. Actually he looked fine, just tired. It had been a long day for him, and Ted's was just beginning.

"Thanks, you too," Rick returned the compliment, and they settled down at a corner table and ordered two steaks. It was nearly eight o'clock by then. Ted was on duty until midnight. They ate their steaks and talked about work until nine-thirty. And then Rick remembered something.

"Listen, do me a favor. It's probably nothing.

I had one of those weird hunches I get sometimes. They're usually bullshit, but once in a while they pay off. There were a couple of pieces of paper in this guy's desk today, with a name on it. I don't know why, but it grabbed me, like I was meant to see that or something." The fact that the name appeared twice told Rick it might be something.

"Don't go *Twilight Zone* on me," Ted said, and rolled his eyes. Rick had a profound respect for his own intuition, and sometimes he was right. But not often enough for Ted to trust it completely. But he had nothing else to do. "So what's the name? I'll run it for you when I go back. You can come with me, if you want." They could see if the person in question had a rap sheet of arrests, or a prison record with the state.

"Yeah, maybe I will hang around while you check. I hate going home when Peg's away. This is bad, Ted. I think I've gotten used to her." As he said it, he looked worried. He'd managed to stay single in the years since his divorce, and liked it that way. But as he'd said to Ted a lot recently, this girl was different. They had even vaguely discussed marriage.

"I told you you're going to wind up marrying her. You might as well. She's a good woman. You could do a lot worse." And had frequently. He had a weakness for loose women, but this one wasn't.

"That's what she says." He grinned. Rick paid the check since it was his turn, and the two men walked back to Ted's office. Rick had jotted down the name with both phone numbers and handed it to Ted. He had checked for federal charges on him, but there were none. But sometimes what the feds didn't have, the state did.

When they got back to his office, Ted fed the name into the computer, and poured them each a cup of coffee while they waited, and Rick talked about Peg in glowing terms. He was obviously crazy about her. Ted was pleased to hear how serious Rick was about her these days. As long as he was married, he thought everyone else should be. And Rick had been avoiding that for ages.

They were still drinking coffee when the computer spat the answer out at them. Ted glanced at it, and raised an eyebrow as he handed it to Rick.

"Your tax evasion guy has some interesting friends. Morgan got out of Pelican Bay six weeks ago. He's on parole in San Francisco."

"What did he do time for?" Rick took the printout from him and read it carefully. All of Peter Morgan's charges were there, along with the name of his parole agent, and the address of a halfway house in the Mission. "What do you suppose Mr.-Fancy-Pants-Social-Leader-of-the-Community is doing with a guy like this?" Rick said aloud, as much to himself as to Ted. It was a new piece of the puzzle.

"Hard to say. You never know why people hook up. Maybe he knew him before he went to prison, and the guy called him when he got out. Maybe they're friends," Ted said, as he poured them both another round of coffee.

"Maybe so." There were bells going off in Rick's head, and he had no idea why, as he looked at Ted. "He had a lot of strange stuff in his desk. A loaded gun notably, four hundred thousand bucks in cash, for pocket money apparently. And a file on a guy called Allan Barnes that was about three inches thick. He even had a picture of Barnes's wife and kids." This time Ted looked at him strangely. The name had struck a chord with him.

"That's weird. I met them about a month ago. Cute kids."

"Don't give me that. I saw the photograph. She looks pretty cute too. What got you to her?" Rick was well aware of who they were. Allan Barnes had made the front page often enough for his deals and meteoric success. He wasn't like Addison, flaunting himself in the social columns for going to the opening of the symphony. Allan Barnes was an entirely different breed, and there had never been any rumors of monkey business around him. He had appeared to be a straight shooter till the end. Rick had never read otherwise, nor had Ted. There had never been any question of tax evasion, and he was surprised to hear Ted had met his widow. That was a pretty fancy group of people for Ted to meet in the line of duty.

"There was a car bombing up the street," Ted explained.

"Where do they live? Hunter's Point?" Rick teased.

"Don't be such a smart-ass. They live in Pacific Heights. Someone hit Judge McIntyre's car, about four days after Carlton Waters got out of prison." And then Ted looked at Rick strangely. Something had just clicked for him too. "Let me see that printout again." Rick handed it back to him, and Ted reread it. Peter Morgan had been in Pelican Bay too, and had gotten out at the same time as Carlton Waters. "You're making me feel *Twilight Zone* too. Waters was in Pelican Bay. I wonder if these two guys know each other. Was there anything in your guy's desk with Waters's name on it?" That would have been too much to ask, and Rick shook his head.

Ted noticed the date of Peter Morgan's release then, and fed something else into the computer. When he got it, he looked at his friend. "Waters and Morgan got out on the same day." It probably didn't mean anything, but it was an interesting coincidence certainly. Although Ted knew it probably meant nothing.

"I hate to say it, but it probably doesn't mean shit," Rick said sensibly. And Ted knew that more than likely, he was right. As a cop, you couldn't get carried away by coincidences. Once in a while, they panned out, but the rest of the time they went nowhere. "So what happened with the car bombing?"

"Nothing. We don't have anything on it yet. I went up to see Waters in Modesto, just for the hell of it, and to let him know we were paying attention. I don't think he had anything to do with it. He's not that stupid."

"You never know. Stranger things have happened. Did you run it all through the computer to see if any of the judge's other fans had just gotten out?" But knowing Ted, Rick was sure he had. He had never worked with anyone as thorough and persistent as Ted Lee. He often wished he had been able to convince him to come to the FBI with him. Some of the people Rick worked with there drove him nuts. And he still missed working with Ted.

They traded a lot of information, and talked about their cases with each other frequently. More than once, in fact many times, they had cracked a case together, just by talking it out. Even now they used each other as sounding boards, as they had tonight, and it always helped them. "You still didn't tell me what the Barnes woman had to do with the car bombing. I assume she wasn't a suspect." Rick smiled at him, and Ted shook his head, amused. They loved teasing each other.

"She lives down the block from Judge McIntyre. One of her kids was looking out the window, and I showed him Waters's mug shot the next day. Nothing. He didn't recognize him. We came up cold. So far, no leads."

"I gather she wasn't a lead," Rick teased again, with a meaningful look. He loved doing that to him. And Ted always gave it right back. Particularly about Peg. She was the first serious romance Rick had had in years. Maybe ever. Ted knew nothing about that kind of thing. He had been faithful to Shirley since they were kids, which Rick always told him was sick. But he admired him for it, although he had known for years from things Ted said, and didn't, that their marriage wasn't all that it used to be. At least they were still together, and they loved each other in their own way. You could hardly expect it to be exciting after twenty-eight years, and it wasn't.

"I didn't say anything about her," Ted pointed out to him. "I said the kids were cute."

"So no car bombing suspect, I gather," Rick commented, and Ted shook his head.

"Not a one. It was interesting to see Waters though. He's a tough customer. He seems to be keeping his nose clean, for now at least. He wasn't too happy with my visit."

"Tough shit," Rick said bluntly. He had no use for convicts like Carlton Waters. He knew who he was and didn't like anything he'd read about him.

"Those were pretty much my sentiments on the subject." And as Ted said it, Rick looked at him again. There was something rolling around in his head. He couldn't figure out the connection between Peter Morgan and Phillip Addison, and it was bothering him. And the fact that Carlton Waters had gotten out on the same day as Morgan probably meant nothing. But it had just occurred to him that it might not hurt to have a look. And as a parolee, Peter Morgan was in Ted's jurisdiction.

"Will you do me a favor? I can't justify sending one of my boys over. Can you send someone out to Morgan's halfway house tomorrow?

He's on parole, you don't need a search warrant to go through his stuff. You don't even need to clear it with his parole agent. You can go anytime you want. I just want to know if there's something there that ties him to Addison, or anyone else of interest. I don't know why, but I'm drawn to this guy, like a bee to honey."

"Oh Christ, don't tell me the FBI has turned you gay." Ted laughed at him, but he agreed to go. He had a certain amount of respect for Rick's instincts. They had panned out for both of them before, and it couldn't hurt this time. "I'll go tomorrow, when I get up. I'll call you if anything turns up." He had nothing else to do in the morning, and with luck, Morgan would be out, which would make it easier to search. He'd have a look around his room, and see what he found there.

"Thanks a lot," Rick said comfortably, picked up Morgan's printout, folded it, and put it in his pocket. It might come in handy at some point, particularly if Ted found something at the halfway house the next day.

But all Ted found when he got there was his forwarding address. The man at the desk told him that Morgan had moved out. Peter's parole agent had obviously not gotten around to updating the address in the computer, which was sloppy, but they were busy. Ted glanced at it and saw that it was a hotel in the Tenderloin, and determined to do what he'd promised Rick he would the night before, he went there. The clerk at the desk said Morgan was out. Ted showed him his star and asked for the key. The desk clerk wanted to know if he was in trouble, and Ted said it was a standard check of a parolee, which didn't seem to bother him. There had been others who had stayed there before. The desk clerk shrugged and handed Ted the key, and he walked upstairs.

The room he walked into was spare and neat. The clothes in the closet looked new. The papers on the desk were neatly stacked. There was nothing exceptional about the room. Morgan had no drugs, no weapons, no contraband. He didn't even smoke. And he had a fat address book sitting on the desk, held together by a rubber band. Ted flipped through it and found Addison's name and number under the A's. And when he rifled through the desk, two pieces of paper caught Ted's eye, and stopped him dead in his tracks. One had Carlton Waters's number in Modesto on it, and the other piece of paper made his blood run cold. On it was written Fernanda's address. There was no telephone number and no name. Only the address, but he recognized it immediately, even without a name. He closed the book and put the rubber band on it, closed the desk drawer, and after a last look around, he walked out of the room. And as soon as he got back to his car, he called Rick.

"Something smells. And I'm not sure what. In fact, I'm beginning to think it stinks." Ted was worried, and he looked it. Why did a guy like Morgan have Fernanda's address? What was his connection to Waters, or had they just met in prison? But if so, why did he have his number in Modesto? And what was Addison doing with Morgan's telephone number? Why did Morgan have his? Why did Addison have a file three inches thick on Allan Barnes, and a photograph of Fernanda and the kids? Suddenly there were too many questions, and not enough answers. And two convicts, one of them convicted of murder, who had gotten out of prison on the same day. There were too many coincidences floating in the air. Rick could hear something in his voice that he hadn't heard in years. Ted was panicked, and he wasn't sure why.

"I just left Morgan's room," he explained. "He's not living at the halfway house anymore. He's living in a hotel in the Tenderloin, and he's got a closet full of new clothes. I'm going to call his parole agent and find out if he got a job."

"How do you suppose he knows Addison?" Rick asked with interest. He had just come from the hearing to set bail. Addison had gotten off nearly scot free, as far as bail went anyway. He had been asked to put up a two-hundred-and-fifty-thousand-dollar bond, which was peanuts to him. And the judge was letting him leave for Europe with his family in two days. The federal investigation was still on, but his attorney said it could continue during his absence, it was the FBI's problem, not his, and the judge agreed. They had no doubt that Addison would return to San Francisco in four weeks. He had an empire to run. Rick had watched Addison drive off with his attorney, and he was intrigued by what Ted had found in Morgan's room.

"Maybe they're old friends. The ink on the entry with Addison's name and phone number looks old," Ted explained. But why Carl Waters's phone number in Modesto? And Fernanda Barnes's address on a piece of paper? No phone number or name. Just the address.

"Why?" Rick echoed the single word in Ted's head.

"That's my point. I don't like this, and I'm not even sure why. Something's coming down, I can smell it, but I'm not even sure what it is." And then he had a thought. "Can I come look at the file Addison has on Barnes?" Maybe something would turn up there. "And do me another favor," Ted said, as he turned the key in the ignition. He was going straight to Rick's office to see the file, and whatever else Rick had. He was interested in it now. He had no idea what Fernanda had to do with this, but something told him that she was at the hub of the wheel. She was an obvious target for a lot of reasons. But Ted had no idea for what, or who was involved, let alone why. Maybe the answer was in that file.

"What's the favor?" Rick reminded him. Ted sounded distracted, and he was. He was trying to figure it out, and so far nothing had clicked. There were a lot of pieces flying around in midair. Morgan. Waters. Addison. Fernanda. The car bombing. And there were no obvious connections between any of them. Not yet.

"Check into Addison's finances for me. Go as deep as you can, and see what comes up," Ted asked as he started the car. He knew Rick would be doing it anyway, but now Ted wanted it fast or as much as he could get in a short trip.

"We already did check, superficially anyway.

That's why we arrested him yesterday. There's some smoky business in Nevada, some taxes he hasn't paid. A lot of money going back and forth across state lines." There was no state tax in Nevada, so it was a haven for guys like Addison, with illegal money on his hands. "It's a lot of nickel-and-dime stuff right now. The worst he'll probably get is a stiff fine. I don't think he'll do time for this. He's got good lawyers," Rick said, sounding disappointed. "We're still checking." But they both knew it took time.

"I mean really look into it. Pull up the rug. Take the floor out of the car."

"Literally?" Rick was stunned. He couldn't imagine what Ted was looking for. And neither could Ted at this point. But he had a powerful sixth sense something was there.

"No, not literally. I mean check him out thoroughly. I want to know what kind of money this guy has, and if he's in trouble anywhere. Shine a bright light on him. Not over the next two months. Find out everything you can now. I want whatever you can get, as fast as you can get it." He knew how long their investigations could take, especially if they were about money, and lives weren't at stake. But maybe they were in this case. Maybe something else was going on. "Pull out all the stops.

I'll be there in ten minutes," Ted said as he sped downtown.

"It'll take me longer than that," Rick said apologetically.

"How long?" Ted sounded anxious, and he himself didn't know why.

"Couple of hours. A day or two. I'll try to get you everything I can today." He was going to have his agents contact the computer analysis and response team in Washington, D.C., and their informants in the underground financial network. But it all took time.

"Christ, you guys are slow. Do whatever you can. I'm halfway there. I'll be there in five."

"Let me get started. You can read the file he has on Allan Barnes while we dig up whatever else we can. See you in a minute," he said, and hung up.

By the time Ted walked into his office, Rick had the Barnes file on his desk, and he had three agents working full time on the computers and calling other agencies and a few select informants, to see what they could find out. It was what they had been planning to do on Addison anyway. He had just speeded it up. By a lot. And three hours later, as Ted and Rick sat talking over sandwiches, it paid off. All three agents walked into his office together and handed him a stack of papers.

"What's the bottom line?" Rick asked, looking at them. Ted had finished the Barnes file by then. There was nothing in it but articles and clippings about Allan Barnes's victories and accomplishments, and the single photograph of Fernanda and the kids.

"Addison is thirty million in debt. The *Titanic* is going down," one of the agents said. One of their best informants had turned out to be a gold mine.

"Shit," Rick said, and looked at Ted. "That's quite a debt."

"His holding company is in trouble," one of the agents explained, "and he's managed to keep it quiet till now. But it won't stay quiet for long. He's got a juggling act going worthy of Ringling Brothers Circus. We think he's been investing funds for some South American connections. And his investments went bad. He's been borrowing from other companies he's got to cover them, he's got a shitload of bad debts. I think there's probably some credit card fraud at the shallow end. At the deep end, he's in so much trouble, my informant says he'll never bail out. He needs a huge influx of money to clean it up, and no one will give him any. My other informant says he's been laundering money for years. That's what the setup in Nevada is all about, and we have no idea why. But if you wanted to know if he's in trouble, he is. A lot of it. Deep, deep shit. If you want to know why and how, and who he's been investing for, it'll take time. And a lot of guys. This is the rough and dirty. We've still got a lot of checking to do. But it looks pretty bad."

"I think that'll do it for now," Rick said quietly, and thanked all three of them for the fast work, particularly with their informants. As soon as they left, he turned to Ted. "So what do you think?" He could see Ted's mind racing at full speed.

"I think we have a guy whom we know is at least thirty million dollars in debt, maybe more. A woman whose husband left her roughly half a billion dollars, according to the press anyway, if you can believe what you read, and I don't. But even if she's worth half of that, she's a sitting duck, with three kids. You have two convicted felons who got out of the slammer six weeks ago, and seem to be floating around loose. They're both tied to Addison in some way and each other. And you have a car bombing down the street from our sitting duck. She's a victim waiting to be born, if you ask me, and so are those kids. You know what I think? I think Addison is after her, I think that's what that file is about. You could never pin it on him in court and make it stick, but something's happening, and if I really let my imagination run wild, I think Addison used Morgan as a conduit to Waters. Maybe now they're in it together, maybe not. I think Waters was watching her when he set the bomb on Judge McIntyre, if he did. And now I think he did. It's too big a coincidence that they just happen to live on the same street. He was probably there anyway, and figured he'd get a twofer for his time. Why not? It's shit luck the Barnes boy didn't recognize him, but you can't have everything all at once. I think what we're looking at here is a conspiracy against Fernanda Barnes. I know I sound like a lunatic, and I can't substantiate any of it, but that's what I think, and my gut says I'm right."

Over the years, they had both learned to trust their guts, and they were seldom wrong. More than that, they had learned to trust each other's, and Rick did now. Everything Ted had just said made sense to him. In the criminal world, it was how people thought, and how things worked. But between knowing it and proving it there was often a dizzying leap over the abyss, and a lot of time. And sometimes the time it took to prove a theory could cost lives. If Ted was right, this one could. They had nothing to go on but instinct at this point, and there was nothing they could do for her, until someone made a move on her or her kids. It was all theory and intuition right now.

"What kind of a conspiracy?" Rick asked him seriously. He believed everything Ted had just said. They had been cops for too long to be entirely wrong. "To extort money from her?"

Ted shook his head. "Not with a guy like Waters hanging around. We're not talking white-collar crime. I think she's a kidnapping victim waiting to happen, and so are her kids. Addison needs thirty million dollars, and he needs it fast. She's worth five hundred million, or thereabouts. I don't like the way those two facts match up. Or Waters hanging around, if he is. And even if he isn't, that doesn't change the fact that Addison has a file on her the size of the Manhattan phone book. And a picture of her and the kids."

Rick didn't like it either, but he just remembered something else. "He's leaving for Europe in two days. What the hell is he doing that for, if he's broke?"

"His wife probably doesn't know. And his leaving the country doesn't change anything.

He's not going to do this himself. In my opinion, someone else is. And if he's out of the country when it happens, he has an airtight alibi. At least that's what he thinks, I'll bet. The question is who is doing this, and when, if I'm right." And they didn't even know for sure what "this" was yet. But whatever it was, they both agreed, it was nothing good.

"Are you going to haul Morgan's ass in and talk to him?" Rick asked with interest. "Or Waters?" Ted shook his head.

"I don't want to tip them off. I want to wait and see what they do. But I want to warn her. I owe her that."

"Do you think they'll let you put guys on her?"

"They might. I want to see the captain tonight. But I want to talk to her first. Maybe she's seen something, or knows something we don't, something she doesn't even know she knows." They had both seen that before. You turned the dial just a little bit, and the whole picture came clear. Although Ted suspected the captain would think he was nuts. He'd been a good sport about going with Ted's hunches before, and they had paid off often enough. It was like money in the bank, and Ted was going to use it now. He was absolutely sure he was right. And so was Rick.

He would have offered his FBI agents to help him out, but there wasn't enough to justify it for him. This was SFPD's baby for now. Although Addison had the file. Rick didn't think the U.S. Attorney would authorize him to assign agents to protect the Barnes family, but he was going to call him anyway, to keep him informed. There wasn't enough evidence against Addison to warrant a conspiracy-to-commit-kidnap charge against him. Yet. But Rick thought they were heading that way, and Ted looked scared as he stood up. He hated cases like this. Someone was going to get hurt. Unless they could do something about it, but he was not yet sure what. He wanted to discuss that with the captain, after he talked to her. He looked at Rick as he got ready to leave.

"Do you want to come with me, just for the hell of it? See what you think after we talk to her. I could use your head on this." Rick nodded and followed him out. It had been a crazy two days in his office, and it had all started with Addison, a piece of paper in his desk with a name on it, and a file on Allan Barnes that made no sense. None of it did. But it was starting to. Rick and Ted had been at it for a long time. Together and apart. They knew the criminal mind. It was all about thinking the way they did, and being nearly as sick as they were. It was about being one step ahead of them all the time. Ted just hoped they were.

Ted called Fernanda from his cell phone, after he and Rick got in the car. Rick told his office he'd be gone for a couple of hours, which seemed reasonable. He really missed working with Ted. This was almost fun. But he didn't dare say that to Ted. Ted was too worried to be amused at the moment. Fernanda was home, and sounded breathless when she answered. She said she'd been packing for her son, who was leaving for camp.

"Is it about the car bombing again?" she asked, sounding distracted. He could hear loud music in the background, so he knew some of the kids were home. Ted hoped all of them were. He didn't want to frighten them, but she had to know. He wanted to tell her what he thought. Even if it scared her, she needed to be warned.

"It's not directly about the car bombing," Ted said evasively. "It's indirectly related, but it's actually something else." She said she'd be home when he arrived, and then they hung up.

Ted parked in her driveway, and glanced around as he walked up to the front door, wondering if they were watching her, if

Waters or Morgan was somewhere in the street outside her house. In spite of that possibility, he had made a conscious decision to enter the house through the front visibly. There was no reason for Peter Morgan to recognize him, and even if he or Waters did, Ted had always preferred the theory of a visible police presence in circumstances like that as a deterrent. The FBI often preferred keeping out of sight, which Ted had always personally felt put victims in the position of being used as live bait.

Peter Morgan saw them go in. For a minute, he thought they looked like cops, and then decided he was crazy. There was no reason for cops to show up at her house. He was getting paranoid, because he knew the day was coming close. He also knew Addison had been arrested the day before, on Mickey Mouse charges connected to his taxes. Addison said he wasn't worried. He was still leaving for Europe on schedule, and their plans hadn't changed. Everything was in order, and whoever the guys were who had gone into her house, she seemed to know them. She smiled broadly at the Asian man who had rung the doorbell. Peter wondered if they were stockbrokers or attorneys, or people who managed her money. Sometimes money men looked like cops too. He didn't even bother to call Addison and tell him. There was no reason to, and he had told Peter not to call for a while, unless he had a problem, even though he said his cell phone couldn't be traced. But Peter's could. He hadn't had time to buy one of the ones Phillip had recommended, although he was planning to in the next week. And as Peter sat outside the house, thinking about it, Ted was sitting down with her in the living room. She had no idea why he had come to see her. And even less idea that in the next five minutes, what Ted Lee was going to say to her would change her life forever.

Chapter 12

When Fernanda opened the door to Ted and Rick, she smiled up at them for a moment and then stood aside to let them in. She noticed that Ted's partner was different this time, and there was an unmistakable ease and warmth between the two men, which seemed to extend itself to her. And she saw immediately that Ted looked concerned.

"Are the kids home?" Ted asked as she walked them into the living room, and she laughed. The music was blaring so loud from upstairs that it nearly shook the chandelier.

"I don't usually listen to that stuff myself." She smiled and offered them something to drink, which they declined.

She noticed that there was an air of authority about the second man, and wondered if he was Ted's superior, or just someone to replace the partner he had brought with him before. Ted saw her looking at Rick, and explained that he was a special agent with the FBI and an old friend. She couldn't imagine what had brought the FBI into it, and was momentarily intrigued as Ted asked again if all the kids were at home, and she nodded.

"Will's leaving for camp tomorrow, if I can ever get him organized, and keep all his stuff in his bag long enough to get him out of here." It was like packing an Olympic team, she'd never seen so much lacrosse equipment for one kid. "Ashley's leaving for Tahoe the day after tomorrow. Sam and I are going to hang out together for a couple of weeks." And before they even left, she already missed Ashley and Will. It was going to be the first time that any of them had been apart since Allan's death, and being separated from them now was harder for her than it had ever been. She sat looking at the two men expectantly, wondering why they had come to see her. She had no clue.

"Mrs. Barnes, I'm here on a hunch," Ted started cautiously. "That's all it is. An old cop's intuition. I think it's important. That's why we came. I could be wrong, but I don't think I am."

"This sounds serious," she said, frowning

slowly, looking from one to the other. She couldn't imagine what it was. And until two hours ago, neither could they.

"I think it is. Police work is like putting a puzzle together, one of those ones with a thousand pieces, where about eight hundred of them are sky, and the rest are water. It all looks like nothing for a long time, and then little by little, you get a chunk of sky put together, or a little bit of ocean, and pretty soon enough starts to fit together, and you figure out what you're seeing. Right now, all we have is a piece of sky, a very small piece of it, but I don't like what I'm seeing." For a crazy minute, she wondered what he was saying, and if she or the kids had done something wrong, although she knew they hadn't. But there was a vague, uneasy feeling in the pit of her stomach as she looked at him. He seemed so earnest, and so concerned, and sincere. And she could see that Rick was watching her.

"Did we do something?" she asked openly, her eyes searching Ted's, and he shook his head.

"No. But I'm afraid someone might do something to you, that's why we're here. I have a feeling, that's all I have, but I'm sufficiently worried to come to you. This could be nothing, or it could be serious." He took a breath, as she listened carefully, suddenly her whole being was on red alert, and he wanted it to be.

"Why would anyone want to do something to us?" She looked puzzled, as Ted realized how naïve she was. She had lived in a protective bubble all her life, particularly in recent years. In her world, people didn't do bad things, not the kind of things Ted and Rick knew about. She didn't know those kinds of people, and never had. But they knew her.

"Your husband was a very successful man. There are dangerous people out there. People with no scruples or morals, who prey on people like you. They're more dangerous than you can imagine, or want to believe. I think some of them may be watching you, or thinking about you. They may be doing more than thinking. I don't know anything for sure, but the pieces started falling into place for me a few hours ago. And I want to talk to you about it. I'll tell you what I know, and what I think, and we'll take it from there." Rick was watching his old partner at work, as he listened to Ted talk to her, and as he always had, he admired his gentleness and style. He was forthright without being unduly frightening. He also knew Ted was going to tell her the truth, as he saw it. He always did. He believed in informing victims, and then giving his all to protect them. And Rick loved him for it. Ted was a man of dedication, integrity, and honor.

"You're scaring me," Fernanda said softly, searching Ted's eyes to see how bad it was, and she didn't like what she saw.

"I know I am, and I'm sorry," he said gently. He wanted to reach out and touch her to re-assure her, but he didn't.

"Special Agent Holmquist arrested a man yesterday." He glanced at Rick as he said it, and Rick nodded as Ted went on. "He runs a mammoth business. He is apparently success-ful, he's done some fancy footwork with his taxes, and he's probably been laundering money, which got him into trouble. I don't think anyone really knows the whole story on him yet. He's very social, he seems respectable. He has a wife and kids, and to the world at large, he appears to be a huge success." She nodded, listening carefully, taking it all in. "We did some checking this morning, and things aren't always what they appear. He's thirty million dollars in debt. Possibly thirty million dollars of other people's money, and more than likely the people he's investing for are not honest, law-abiding people. They don't like losing money and will go after him.

Things are closing in on him. According to our sources, he's desperate."

"Is he in jail?" She recalled the beginning of the story, when Ted said he'd been arrested the day before.

"He's out on bail. It'll probably take a long time to get him to court. He has good lawyers, powerful connections, he's good at what he does. But underneath the surface, there's a giant mess. Probably worse than we think. He needs money to stay afloat, maybe even to stay alive, and fast. That kind of desperation makes people do crazy things."

"What does he have to do with me?" It made no sense to her.

"I don't know yet. His name is Phillip Addison. Does that name mean anything to you?" He searched her face, but there was no sign of recognition as she shook her head.

"I think I've seen his name in the papers. But I've never met him. Maybe Allan knew him, or who he was. He knew a lot of people. But I've never met this man. I don't know him."

Ted nodded thoughtfully, and went on. "He had a file in his desk. A big file, very big, about three or four inches thick, full of clippings about your husband. From the look of it, he was obsessed with him, and his success. Maybe he admired him, or thought he was a hero. But I suspect he followed everything your husband did."

"I think a lot of people did," Fernanda said with a sad smile. "He was every man's dream. Most people thought he just got lucky. He did. But it was some luck and a lot of skill. Most people don't realize that. He had a sixth sense for business, and high-risk deals. He took a lot of chances," she said sadly, "but all most people see are the successes." She didn't want to betray him by exposing his failures, which had been equally huge, in fact greater in the end. But to the naked eye, and those who read about him, Allan Barnes had been the personification of the American dream.

"I'm not sure why Barnes kept that file on him. It goes back a lot of years. It may be innocent, but it may not be. It's very thorough. Maybe too thorough. He even has magazine and newspaper pictures of your husband, and one of you and the kids."

"Is that why you're worried?"

"Partly. It's a little piece of that puzzle right now, a piece of sky. Maybe two pieces. We found a name in his desk. Special Agent Holmquist did. And old cops have good instincts, sometimes they don't even know why.

They're used to seeing something that looks like nothing, and bells go off. Bells went off for him. We checked the guy out, the name on the piece of paper is Peter Morgan. He's an ex-con. He got out of prison a few weeks ago. He's a small-time operator, but kind of an interesting guy. He graduated from Duke, got an MBA from Harvard, went to the right prep schools before that. His mother married money, or something like that." He had read Peter's probation report, and all of that was in it, which was how Ted knew of it. He had read everything before he came to her. "He got himself in some trouble working in a brokerage house when he got out of Harvard, switched to investment banking, and married well. He married the daughter of the head of the firm, had a couple of kids, and started getting in trouble again. He got into drugs, started dealing, or using heavily, which probably led him into dealing. He embezzled some money, did a lot of stupid stuff, his wife left him, he lost custody and visitation of his kids, and came out here. And made a bigger mess. Eventually, he got arrested for dealing drugs. He was a small-time operator fronting for bigger fish, and he took the fall for them. But he deserved it. He sounds like a bright guy gone wrong. It happens. Sometimes people with the best opportunities do everything in their power to screw them up. He did. He spent just over four years in prison. He had a job working for the warden, who seems to think he's a great guy. I have no idea what his connection is to Addison, but he had Morgan's name written down twice. I don't know why. And Addison's name is in Morgan's address book. It looks like an old entry, not a new one.

"A few weeks ago Morgan was living in a halfway house, without a penny to his name. Now he's living in a second-rate hotel in the Tenderloin, with new clothes in his closet. I wouldn't call it a windfall, but he seems to be doing okay. We checked, he has a car, he's paying his rent, he hasn't gotten into trouble since he got out, and he has a job. We don't know about his connection with Addison. They may have known each other before he went to prison, or Morgan may have met him more recently. But something about that connection doesn't feel right to me, and it didn't to Special Agent Holmquist either.

"The other thing I don't like is that Morgan got out of prison on the same day as a man named Carlton Waters. I don't know if that rings any bells for you. He's been in prison for murder since he was seventeen years old. He's written a number of articles about his innocence, he tried to get a pardon a few years ago, and didn't. He lost on appeal several times. He finally got out after serving twenty-four years. He and Morgan were both in Pelican Bay prison, at the same time, and got out on the same day. We haven't connected Addison to Waters, but Morgan had Waters's number in his room. There's a link between these people, maybe a very thin link, but it's there. We can't ignore it."

"Isn't that the man you showed us the mug shot of, after the car bombing?" The name sounded familiar to her, and Ted nodded.

"That's the one. I went to see him in Modesto, where he's living in a halfway house. And it may not mean anything, but I don't like the fact that you're living on the same street where I think he put a bomb under Judge McIntyre's car. I have absolutely no evidence, but I have my gut. My gut tells me he did it. Why was he here? For the judge, or for you? Maybe he decided to kill two birds with one stone. Have you noticed anyone watching you, or following you, a face that has turned up more than once? A strange coincidence of someone you keep running into?" She shook her head, and he made a mental note to himself to show her Morgan's mug shots. "I'm not certain, but my instincts tell me you're part of this somehow. Morgan had your address on a scrap of paper in his hotel room. Addison was fascinated by your husband, and maybe with you. I'm worried about that file. Addison is linked to Morgan. And Morgan is linked to Waters. And Morgan had your address. These are bad people. Waters is as bad as it gets. He and his buddy killed two people, no matter what he says, for two hundred dollars and some small change. He's dangerous, Addison is desperate for money, and Morgan is a small-time crook, and possibly the link between the other two. We have a car bombing, no suspect we can nail it on, and I think Waters did it, although I can't prove it." Listening to himself, his suspicions sounded far-fetched, even to him, and he was afraid he probably appeared totally insane to her. But he knew with his entire being that something was wrong, very wrong, and something bad was about to happen, and he wanted to convey the seriousness of that to her. "I think what clinches it for me here is that Addison needs money. A lot of it. Thirty million dollars in a very short time before his ship goes down. And I'm worried about what he and the others may do to get that money for him. I don't like the file on your husband, or the photograph of you and your children."

"Why would he go after me, because he needs money?" she asked with a look of innocence that made Rick Holmquist smile. She was a pretty woman and he liked her, she seemed like a genuine and kind person, and she obviously felt comfortable with Ted, but she had been so protected all her life that she had no idea what kind of danger she could be in. It was impossible for her to imagine. She had never in her life been exposed to people like Waters, Addison, and Morgan.

"You're sitting here like a prize," Ted explained. "For people as unscrupulous as this, you're a gold mine. Your husband left you a lot of money, you have no one to protect you. All they see you as, I think, is a cash box they can run off with to solve their problems. If they can get their hands on you, or your kids, they may figure that to you, thirty million dollars, or even fifty, would mean nothing. People like this get delusional, they believe their own fantasies and stories. They talk to each other in prison, they dream of things they think they can pull off. Who knows what Addison told them, or what they told each other? We can only imagine it. They may figure it's no big deal to you, or there's nothing wrong with it. All they know is violence, and if that's what they have to use to get what they want, they figure it's worth it. They don't think like you and me. Maybe Addison doesn't even know what they have in mind. Sometimes people like him get a ball rolling that gets out of control, and the next thing you know, people are hurt, or worse. I can't show you anything concrete to prove what I think, but I can tell you that something is wrong with this picture. Suddenly there is a lot of sky on the table, and I think there's a storm coming, maybe even a very bad one. I don't like what I'm seeing." Even more than that, he didn't like what he was feeling.

"You're telling me that you think the children and I are in danger?" She wanted to get this straight and hear it clearly from him. It was so inconceivable to her that she needed a minute to absorb it, and sat there looking pensive as the two men watched her.

"Yes, I am," Ted said simply. "I think one or all of these guys, and maybe even others, are after you. They may be watching you, and I think something ugly could happen. There's a lot of money at stake here, and they probably don't see why you should have all that, and they'd be more than happy to take it from you." She had understood him.

She looked straight into Ted's eyes then, and spoke clearly. "There is none."

"None what? No danger?" His heart sank as he realized that she didn't believe him. She obviously thought he was crazy.

"No money," she said simply.

"I don't understand. What do you mean, no money?" She clearly had a lot of it. The others didn't. They all understood that much.

"I have no money. None. Zero. We've managed to keep everything out of the press, for my husband's sake, but we can't cover for him forever. He had lost everything he'd ever made, in fact, he was hundreds of millions of dollars in debt. He committed suicide, or let something happen to him in Mexico, we'll never know, because he couldn't face it. His whole world was about to implode, and it has. There's nothing left. I've been selling everything since he died, the plane, the boat, houses, co-ops, my jewelry, art. And I'm putting this house on the market in August. We have nothing. I don't even have enough in the bank to live on till the end of the year. I may have to take the kids out of their schools." She looked at Ted dispassionately as she said it. She had lived with the shock of it all for so long, that after five months of constant panic over it, she was numb. This was just where her life was now. She was adjusting to it. It was the situation Allan had left her with, whether she liked it or not. And she would still rather have had him than all the money he had lost. She didn't care about the money, what she missed most was him. But in addition, he had certainly left her in dire circumstances, and Ted looked stunned.

"Are you telling me that there is no money? No investments, no nest egg somewhere, a few million in a Swiss bank account?" It seemed as impossible to him as it once had to her.

"I'm telling you we can't buy shoes. I'm telling you I won't have money for groceries by November. After I settle this mess, I have to get a job. Right now, just orchestrating what we sell and how we do it, and how we juggle the debts and the taxes and the rest of it, is full-time work. What I'm telling you, Detective Lee, is that we have nothing. All we have left is this house, and if we're lucky, whatever we sell it for may cover the last of my husband's personal debts, if I'm fortunate enough to get a big price for it and whatever is in it. His attorneys are going to declare bankruptcy on the corporate side, which will get us off the hook. But even at that, it may take me years, and a lot of clever attorneys I can no longer afford, to dig us out. If Mr. Addison thinks he's going to get thirty million dollars out of me, or even thirty thousand, he's going to be very disappointed. Maybe someone should tell him," she said, looking small and dignified as she sat on the couch.

There was nothing pathetic, or even embarrassed about her. She was very real. And Rick Holmquist was impressed, as was Ted. Talk about a rags-to-riches story, and riches-to-rags just as quickly. She was a hell of a good sport about it, as far as they were concerned. Her husband had left her holding one hell of a bag, with nothing in it. And she didn't even say anything critical of him. As far as Ted was concerned, she was a saint. Particularly if what she was saying was true, and she hardly had enough to feed her kids. He and Shirley were in much better shape than she was, and they both had jobs and each other. But what upset him about what she had just told him was that her situation was even more dangerous than he had thought. The world perceived her as having hundreds of millions of dollars, which made her an automatic target, like a bull's-eye painted on a barn, when in fact she had nothing, which was going to make someone crazed and even more violent, if she got grabbed, or the kids did.

"If someone kidnaps me or the children, they're not going to get ten cents," she said simply. "There's nothing to pay. And no one who would. Allan and I had no family to speak of, except each other, and there's just no money anywhere. Believe me, I've looked. They could have my house, but that's about it. No cash." She had no pretensions about it, and made no apology for it. And what Ted found himself loving about her as he listened to her, as much as her dignity, was her quiet grace. "I guess we haven't done ourselves a favor by keeping it out of the press. But I thought I owed Allan that, for as long as I could. The letter he left was so distraught and full of shame. I wanted to preserve the legend for him as long as I could. But eventually, it'll get out. Very soon, I think. There's just no way to keep it quiet. He lost everything. He risked it all on bad deals, made some terrible assumptions and calculations. I don't know what happened. Maybe he lost his mind, or his insight, or it all went to his head, or he thought he was invincible. But he wasn't. No one is. He made some terrible mistakes." It was a polite understatement, considering the fact that he had left his wife and children penniless, and hundreds of millions in debt. He'd had quite a fall. And she and the kids were the ones paying for it. It took a few minutes for Ted to absorb it, and the implications for her, particularly now.

"What about the children?" Ted asked, trying not to look as panicked as he felt. "Is there some kind of kidnap insurance policy on them, or you?" He knew they existed, and assumed they came out of Lloyd's of London. But he knew that people like Allan had them, in case they or some family member got kidnapped. There were even policies for extortion.

"There's nothing. All our policies have lapsed. We don't even have health insurance right now, although my lawyer is trying to get some for us. And our insurance company told us that they're not going to pay up on Allan's life insurance. The letter he left is too damning, and makes it look like a suicide, which we assume it was. The police found the letter. And I don't think we ever had kidnapping insurance. I don't think my husband thought we were at risk." God knows he should have, Ted thought, and Rick silently echoed his thoughts. With the kind of money he had made, and so publicly, they were at risk for everything. Even Fernanda and the kids. Maybe especially them. His family was his Achilles' heel, as they were for anyone in his position. Apparently, he didn't notice, which made Ted feel suddenly angry, although he didn't show it. But he didn't like any of what he'd been hearing, for a number of reasons, and neither did Rick Holmquist.

"Mrs. Barnes," Ted said quietly, "I think this puts you at even greater risk. As far as these men or anyone else knows, you look like you have a lot of money. Anyone would assume that. And in fact, you don't. I think the faster we can get that word out there, the better off you'll be. Although people may not believe it. Most people won't, I think. But right now, you've got the worst of all possible worlds. You look like a major target, and you've got nothing to back it up. And I think the danger here is very real. These men are up to something. I don't know what. I don't even know how many of them might be in it, but I think they're cooking up something. These are three very bad guys, and who knows who else they've been talking to. I don't want to panic you, but I think you and your children are in grave danger." Fernanda sat very quietly for a long moment, looking at him, and trying to be brave, and for the first time, her facade of calm strength began to crack, and her eyes filled with tears.

"What am I going to do?" she whispered, as the music continued to blare from upstairs, and both men looked at her uncomfortably, not sure what to do for her. She was in a major mess. Thanks to her husband. "What can I do to protect my kids?"

Ted took a long breath. He knew he was speaking out of turn, he hadn't talked to his captain yet, but he felt desperately sorry for her, and he trusted his instincts. "That's our job. I haven't talked to my captain yet. Rick and I came straight here from the FBI office. But I'd like to put a couple of my men here for a week or two, till we check this out further, and see what they do. Maybe this is all fantasy on my part. But I think it's worth keeping an eye on you. I'll see how the captain feels about it, but I think we can commit a couple of men to this detail. I have a feeling someone may be watching you." Rick nodded. He agreed. "What about you?" Ted turned to him, and Rick looked uncomfortable. "Addison is your guy." The FBI was investigating him, which gave Rick the authority he needed, and he and Ted both knew that. "Can you give us an agent for a week or two, to watch the house and the kids?" Rick hesitated and then nodded. In his case, the decision was his. He could spare one man. Maybe two.

"I can't justify it for more than a week or two. Let's see what happens." She was a major entity after all. And her husband had been an important man. More important, Addison was

a big fish for them, if they could catch him up
to no good, and tie him to some kind of conspiracy. Stranger things had happened in both
their lives as detectives. And Ted was convinced he was right. So was Rick.

"I want to make sure no one is following
you or the kids." She nodded. Suddenly her
life was turning into a worse nightmare than
the one she'd been living since Allan's death.
Allan was gone. Terrible people were after
her. The children were in danger of being kidnapped. She had never felt so totally lost and
vulnerable in her life, even when Allan died.
She had a sense of impending doom suddenly,
as though there was nothing she could hu-
manly do to protect her family, and she was
terrified that one or all of her children would
get hurt, or worse. She tried valiantly to control herself, but in spite of her best efforts,
tears rolled down her cheeks, and Ted looked
sympathetic.

"What about Will going to camp?" she asked
through her tears. "Is that all right?"

"Does anyone know where he's going?" Ted
asked quietly.

"Just his friends, and one of his teachers."

"Has there been anything about it in the papers?" She shook her head. There was no reason to write about them anymore. She had

hardly left her house in five months. And Allan's fascinating career was over. They weren't even old news now, they were no news, and she was relieved. She had never enjoyed that, and would have even less now. Jack Waterman had already warned her that there would be a lot of bad press, and curiosity about them, when the news of Allan's financial disaster finally came out, and she was bracing herself for it. He thought it would hit them in the fall. And now this. "I think he can go," Ted said in answer to her question about Will going to camp. "You'll have to warn him and the camp to be careful. If anyone asks for him, or strangers show up, people claiming to be relatives or friends, they have to say he's not there, and call us right away. You need to talk to Will before he leaves." She nodded, pulled a tissue out of her pocket, and blew her nose. She always had tissues on her now, because she was always finding something in a drawer or a cupboard that reminded her of Allan. Like his golf shoes. Or a notebook. Or a hat. Or a letter he had written years before. The house seemed to be full of reasons to cry. "What about your daughter going to Tahoe? Who's she going with?"

"A friend from school and her family. I know the parents. They're nice people."

"Good. Then let her go. We'll have local

law enforcement in the area assign surveillance to them. They can keep it to one man in a car outside their house. It's probably better to get her out of here. It gives us one less victim to worry about." She literally flinched when he said the word, and Ted looked apologetic. In his mind, this was a case now, or a potential one, not just a family or a person. And Rick was thinking along the same lines. For him, it was an opportunity to put Phillip Addison away and cement his case. To Fernanda, it was only about her children. She wasn't even thinking about herself. And she was scared, more than she ever had been in her entire life. Looking at her, Ted knew it. "When are they leaving?" Ted inquired, his mind was already racing. He wanted two men to check the street as soon as he could get them out there. He wanted to know if there were men sitting in parked cars, and if so, who.

"What about you and Sam? Are you going anywhere? Any plans?"

"Just day camp for him." She couldn't afford to do much else. Camp for Will had been a stretch, but she didn't want to deny him that. None of the children knew the full extent of their financial ruin yet, although they were aware that things were less lavish than they had been. She still had to explain the full implications of it to them, but she was waiting to do that when she put the house on the market. After that, she knew the ceiling would fall in. In fact, it already had. The kids just didn't know it.

"I'm not crazy about that idea," Ted said carefully. "Let's see how it goes. When do the others leave?"

"Will leaves tomorrow. Ashley the day after."

"Good," Ted said bluntly. He was anxious for them to leave, and reduce the number of targets. Half of them were going. He looked at Rick then. "I'm putting plainclothes boys on this, or should we use guys in uniform?" He knew as soon as he said it that he was asking the wrong man. They constantly disagreed about the concept of protecting potential victims. The police force preferred to make the protection visible, in order to scare perpetrators off, while the FBI liked luring them in to entrap them. But in this case, he wanted to see what, if anything, their suspects would do, and he was inclined to agree with Rick's theories on the subject, to a point. He had already been considering it when they walked into the house.

"Does it matter?" Fernanda asked, confused by all that was happening. Her head was spinning.

"Yes, it does," Ted said quietly. "It can make a big difference. We may see some action faster if we use plainclothesmen." She got the point.

"So no one knows they're cops?" He nodded. It all sounded terrifying to her.

"I don't want any of you going anywhere till I get a couple of men assigned to this. Probably later tonight. Did you have plans to go out?"

"I was just going to take the kids out for pizza. We can stay home."

"That's where I want you," Ted said firmly. "I'll call you as soon as I talk to the captain. With luck, I can have two men here by midnight." He was suddenly all business.

"Are they going to sleep here?" She looked startled. She hadn't thought of that, as Ted laughed and Rick smiled.

"Hopefully not. We need them to stay awake and be aware of what's happening. We don't want anyone climbing in your windows, while everyone's asleep. Do you have an alarm?" he asked, but it was obvious that they would, and she nodded. "Use it till they get here." And then he turned to Rick. "What about you?"

"I'll send two agents over in the morning." She wouldn't need them before that if she had

Ted's guys. And he had to pull two men off other details, and replace them, which took a little time. He turned to Fernanda then, and his eyes were sympathetic. She seemed like a nice woman, and he felt sorry for her, as did Ted. He knew how tough situations like this were. He'd seen a lot of them, both in police work and with the FBI. Potential victims. And witness protection. It could get ugly, and often did. He hoped it wouldn't for her. But there was always that risk. "That means you'll have four men with you, two SFPD and two FBI agents. That should keep you safe. And I think Detective Lee is right about the other two children. It's a good idea to get them out of here."

She nodded and asked the question that had been tormenting her for the last half hour. "What happens if they try to kidnap us? How would they do it?"

Ted sighed. He hated to answer her question. One thing was for sure. If they wanted money from her, they were not going to kill her, so she could pay the ransom. "They'd probably try to take you by force, ambush you while you're driving, and take a child if you had one with you. Or get in the house. It's not likely to happen if we have four men with you all the time." And if it did, he knew from experience that someone would get killed, either cops or kidnappers, or both. Hopefully, not her or a child. The men assigned to the detail would be fully cognizant of the risk they were taking. That was part of the job for them, and what they did for a living.

Rick looked at Ted then. "We need fingerprints and hair from the kids before they leave." He said it as gently as he could, but there was nothing gentle about what he'd just said, and Fernanda looked panicked.

"Why?" But she knew. It was obvious even to her.

"We need it to identify the kids if they get snatched. And we should get prints and hair on you too," he said apologetically, and Ted intervened.

"I'll send someone over later today," he said quietly, as Fernanda's mind raced. This was actually happening to her, and her children. It was beyond belief, and she hadn't fully understood it yet, and wondered if she ever would. Maybe they were just imagining it. Maybe they were both crazy and had been doing this for too long. Or worst of all, maybe it was really happening and they were right. There was no way to know. "I'm going to get someone out on the street right away and check plates," he said more to Rick than to her. "I want to know who's out there." Rick nodded. And Fernanda wondered if there were really people watching her, or the house. She had had no sense of it whatsoever.

Shortly after that, both men stood up. Ted looked down at her and could see easily how stressed she was. She looked like she was in shock. "I'll call you in a little while, and let you know what's happening and who to expect. In the meantime, lock the doors, turn on the alarm, and don't let the kids go out. For any reason." As he said it, he handed her his card. He'd given it to her before, but knew she might have lost it, which she had. It was in a drawer somewhere, and she couldn't have found it. She didn't think she'd need it. "If anything unusual happens, call me immediately. My cell phone's on there. And my pager. I'll be in touch in a few hours." She nodded, unable to answer him, and walked them to the front door. Both men shook hands with her, and as he walked out, Ted turned to look at her with a reassuring expression. He didn't have the heart to leave without saying something to her. "It'll be all right," he said softly, and then followed Rick down the stairs, as she closed the door behind them and set the alarm.

As they walked out, Peter Morgan saw them

leave, and didn't think much of it. This was his first experience with surveillance, which was fortunate for them. Waters would have smelled them five seconds after spotting them. Peter didn't.

Rick got in Ted's car again and looked at his old partner with a dazed expression. "Christ, can you believe anyone could lose that kind of money? The papers said he was worth half a billion dollars, and it can't be that long ago, a year or two maybe. The guy must have been crazy."

"Yeah," Ted said, looking unhappy. "Or an irresponsible sonofabitch. If she's telling the truth"—and he had no reason to think she would lie to him, she didn't seem like that kind of person—"she's in a hell of a situation. Particularly with Addison and his boys after her, if they are. They're not going to believe she's out of money."

"And then what?" Rick said pensively.

"It gets ugly." Then, they both knew, it was all about SWAT teams, and hostage negotiations, and commando tactics. He just hoped they never got there. If there really was something coming down, Ted Lee was going to do everything in his power to stop it. "My captain's going to think we've been smoking crack," he said with a grin at Holmquist. "Seems like every time we get together, we get into something."

"I sure miss that," Rick said, smiling, and then Ted thanked him for giving him two agents for the detail. He knew he couldn't commit them for long, if nothing happened. Ted didn't know, but he had a feeling something would happen soon. Maybe Addison's arrest the day before would make them anxious, or even panic. He also had a feeling that Addison's leaving the country had something to do with it. If that was the case, something was going to happen in two days, or anytime thereafter. Maybe soon.

Ted drove Rick back to his office, and half an hour later, he walked into his.

"Is the captain in?" he asked the senior officer's secretary, a pretty girl in a blue uniform, and she nodded.

"He's in a rotten mood," she whispered.

"Good. Me too," Ted said to her with a grin, and strode into his office.

Will bounded down the stairs from his room, and reached for the front door. Fernanda was at her desk, and instantly stopped him.

"Stop! The alarm is on," she shouted at him, louder than she needed to, and he stopped in his tracks and looked startled.

"That's weird. I'm just going out for a minute. I need to get my shin guards out of the car." She had left the station wagon in the driveway when she came in, and knew she couldn't go out to it until the police arrived sometime that night.

"You can't," she said sternly, and Will looked at her strangely.

"Is something wrong, Mom?" He could see that it was, as she nodded and tears filled her eyes.

"Yeah . . . no . . . actually there is. I have to talk to you, Ash, and Sam."

She had been sitting at her desk trying to figure out what to say to them, and when. She was still trying to absorb what had happened, or might, and all she'd heard from Ted and Rick. It was a lot to swallow, and would be even more so for her kids. They didn't need this any more than she did. They'd been through enough in the past six months, and so had she. But now all she could do was look at Will. There was no point putting it off. She had to tell them. And it looked like now was the time, since Will had just discovered that something was up. "Will you go upstairs and get them, sweetheart? We need to have a family meeting," she said somberly, and almost choked on the words. The last family meeting they'd had was when their father died and she had told them the news. And the full impact of what she had just said hadn't been lost on Will. He looked at her, with terror in his eyes, and without another word, turned and ran up the stairs to find the others, as Fernanda sat shaking where she sat. All she cared about now was keeping them safe. And she just prayed that the police and the FBI would be able to do that.

Chapter 13

Fernanda's meeting with her children went as well as it could have gone, under the circumstances. They came down the stairs to the living room five minutes after she had sent Will up for them, after conferring briefly in Sam's bedroom about what might be wrong. Finally, Will told them to just get downstairs, and they did, trailing down the stairs, by order of age, with Will first. All three of them looked worried, as did their mother, as she waited.

She waited until Ash and Sam had settled on the couch, and Will sprawled out in the chair that had been his father's favorite. Instinctively, he had taken it over as soon as Allan disappeared. He was the man of the family now, and did his best whenever possible to fill his father's shoes.

"What's wrong, Mom?" Will asked quietly,

as Fernanda looked at them, not sure where to start. There was so much to say, and none of it good.

"We're not sure," she said honestly. She wanted to tell them as much of the truth as she could. They needed to know, or at least Ted said they did. And she suspected he was right. If she didn't warn them of the potential danger, they might take risks they wouldn't otherwise. "It may be nothing," she tried to reassure them, and as she said the words, Ashley suddenly panicked, fearing her mother might be sick. She was all they had now. But as their mother went on, they knew it wasn't that. Fernanda thought it was worse. "Maybe nothing will ever come of this," she started again, as the moments ticked by agonizingly for all of them, "but the police were just here. Apparently they arrested someone yesterday whom they think is a bad man, and something of a crook. He had a big file on your dad with pictures of all of us in it. And apparently he was very interested in your father's success"— she hesitated—"and our money." She didn't want to tell them yet that they no longer had any. They had enough other problems apparently at the moment, and there was still time for that. "They also found in his desk the name and phone number of a man who recently got out of prison. Neither your father nor I know any of these people," she reassured them, and even to her, this sounded crazy as she told it. The children were staring at her in fascination, without comment or expression. The story was too foreign to them, and too unfamiliar, to even fathom the implications. "They went to search the hotel room of the man who came out of prison, and found the name and number of another man, who is thought to be extremely dangerous, and also just got out of prison. They don't know what the connection is between these three men. But apparently the man the FBI arrested yesterday is in a lot of trouble, and needs a lot of money. And they found our address in the hotel room of one of the men. What the police are afraid of"—she swallowed hard, trying to keep her voice steady with considerable effort—"what they're afraid of is that the man who was arrested might try to kidnap one of us to get the money he needs." That was it, in a nutshell. The children stared at her for an interminable moment.

"Is that why the alarm is on?" Will looked at her strangely. The whole saga sounded incredible when you heard it, or tried to tell it.

"Yes. The police are going to send two policemen to protect us, and so is the FBI, just for a few weeks, until they see if anything happens. Maybe their theory is all wrong, and maybe no one wants to hurt us. But just in case, they want us to be careful, and they're going to be with us for a while."

"In the house?" Ashley looked horrified, as her mother nodded. "Can I still go to Tahoe?" Fernanda smiled at the question. At least no one was crying. She suspected correctly that they hadn't fully understood it. Even to her, it sounded like a bad movie, as she nodded at Ashley.

"Yes, you can. The police think it's a good idea for you to get out of town, in fact. You just have to be careful, and keep an eye out for strangers." But she knew the family Ashley was going with was extremely cautious and attentive, which was why she had agreed to let her go. And she was going to call them and warn them of what was happening before Ashley left.

"I'm not going to camp," Will suddenly said sternly, with an anguished look at his mother. He got it. More than the others. But he was older. And he was playing the role of protector now, in his father's absence. Fernanda didn't want him to have that burden. At sixteen, he still needed to enjoy the last of his boyhood and childhood.

"Yes, you are," she said firmly. "I think you should. If anything happens, or it gets worse here, I'll call you. You're safer there, and you'd go crazy stuck in the house with me and Sam. I don't think we're going to be doing much for the next few weeks till this gets sorted out, or they figure out what's really happening. You're much better off in camp, playing lacrosse." Will didn't answer as he sat in the chair, mulling it over. And Sam was watching her reactions.

"Are you scared, Mom?" he asked openly, and she nodded.

"Yes, I am. A little," which was an understatement. "It sounds scary. But the police will protect us, Sam. They'll protect all of us. Nothing is going to happen." She wasn't as certain as she sounded, but she wanted to reassure them.

"Will the policemen wear guns when they're here?" he asked with interest.

"I think so." She didn't explain the theory about the risks of being protected by cops in uniform or plainclothesmen, and their being used as live bait to catch the criminals quicker. "They'll be here by midnight. Until then, we can't go out, at all. And the alarm is on. We have to be careful."

"Do I have to go to day camp?" Sam asked,

hoping he wouldn't, since he'd had cold feet about it anyway, and had changed his mind about it. He liked the idea of men wearing guns around the house. That part sounded like fun to him.

"I don't think you have to go to camp, Sam. You and I will find lots of things to do here." They could go to museums and the zoo, and do art projects, or go to the Exploratorium at the Museum of Fine Arts, but she wanted him with her. He looked pleased.

"Yayy!!!" he said, dancing around the room, as Will glared at him and told him to sit down.

"Don't you realize what this means? All you're worried about is Tahoe and day camp. Someone wants to kidnap us, or Mom. Don't you get how scary that is?" Will was seriously upset, and after the others went back upstairs, slightly mollified after his outburst, he argued with his mother again. "I'm not going to camp, Mom. I'm not going to leave you here, just so I can play lacrosse for three weeks." He was old enough, at sixteen, nearly seventeen now, for her to be honest with him.

"You're safer there, Will," she said, with tears in her eyes. "They want you there. And Ash in Tahoe. Sam and I will be fine with four men to protect us. I'd rather you go away so I don't have to worry about you too." It was as honest as she could be with him and it was true. He could get lost in the anonymous shuffle of other boys at camp, and be safe there. And Ashley would be protected in Tahoe. Now all she'd have to worry about was Sam. One child instead of three.

"What about you?" He looked genuinely worried about her, and put an arm around her shoulders, which brought tears to her eyes again, as they walked back up the stairs to his room.

"I'll be fine. No one is going to do anything to me." She sounded so certain of it that he looked surprised.

"Why not?"

"They'd want me to pay the ransom, and if they take me, no one could." It was a horrifying thought, but they both knew it was true.

"Will Sam be okay?"

"With four policemen to protect him, I can't imagine he wouldn't be." She tried to smile bravely, for Will's sake.

"How did this happen, Mom?"

"I don't know. Bad luck, I guess. Your dad's success. It gives some people a lot of crazy ideas."

"That's so sick." He still looked horrified, and she hated to expose any of them to so much risk and fear, but as long as it was happening to them, or could be, they had to know. She had had no choice but to tell them. And she was proud of the way they took it. Especially Will.

"Yes, it is sick," she agreed. "There are a lot of crazy people in the world, I guess. And bad ones. I just hope these people lose interest in us quickly, or figure we're not worth the trouble. Maybe the police are wrong. They're not entirely sure about any of it. Right now, it's all theories and suspicions, but we have to pay attention to that too. You haven't seen anyone watching us, have you, Will?" she said more out of form than any real belief that he had, and was shocked to see him pause for a minute, and nod his head.

"I think I have . . . I'm not sure . . . I saw a guy in a car across the street a couple of times. He didn't look weird or anything. Actually, he looked nice. He just seemed normal. He smiled at me. The reason I think I noticed him"—Will looked embarrassed at what he said next—"I think I noticed him because he looked kind of like Dad." What he said rang some kind of bell for her too, but she couldn't figure out what it was.

"Do you remember what he looked like?" Fernanda asked, looking worried. Maybe the police were right, and there were men watching them. She kept hoping that they were wrong.

"Sort of," Will said. "He looked kind of like Dad, but with light hair, and he dressed like Dad too. He was wearing a blue button-down shirt one time, and a blazer another time. I just thought he was waiting for someone. He seemed okay." Fernanda wondered if he had dressed that way intentionally so he would fit into the neighborhood. They talked about it for a few minutes and then Will went to his room to call his friends to say good-bye before he left for camp. She had already warned him not to tell anyone about a possible kidnapping threat. Ted had told her that it was important that they kept it quiet, or if word got out, it might hit the press, and they'd have copycats all over the place. Will and the others had promised. The only people she was going to tell were the family in Tahoe who would be taking care of Ash.

Fernanda called Ted as soon as possible. She wanted to report to him about what Will had said. The secretary told her that he was in a meeting with the captain, and would call her back. She stood, looking out the window then, thinking about all of it, and wondering if there were people out there, watching her, whom she couldn't see. And as she did, Ted

and the captain were shouting at each other.
He said it was an FBI problem, not theirs. The
primary suspect had been arrested by the FBI,
mostly on financial issues, this had nothing to
do with the SFPD, and he wasn't going to tie
up his men baby-sitting some Pacific Heights
housewife with three kids.

"Give me a break, for chrissake," Ted
shouted back at him. They knew each other
well and were old friends. The captain had
been two years ahead of him in the Academy,
and they had worked on countless cases together. He had profound respect for Ted's
work, but this time he thought he was nuts.
"What if one of them gets kidnapped? Whose
problem is that going to be?" They both knew
it was going to be everyone's problem then.
The FBI and the SFPD. "I'm onto something
here. I know it. Trust me. Just give me a few
days, a week, maybe two, let me see what I
come up with. If I come up dry, I'll shine your
shoes for a year."

"I don't want my shoes shined, nor the tax-
payers' money thrown out the window for
baby-sitting service. What in hell makes you
think Carl Waters is involved in this? There's
no evidence to prove that, and you know it."

Ted looked him right in the eye fearlessly.
"All the evidence I need is here." He pointed

at his gut. He had already sent an undercover policewoman out, dressed as a meter maid, to check the cars lining Fernanda's street. There were no meters, but cars had to have permit stickers in order to park for longer than two hours, so the meter maid's presence would seem entirely reasonable to anyone who saw her. Ted was anxious to know what she'd come up with, who was sitting in parked cars, what they looked like, and he had told her to run a check on every license plate on the block. She called while Ted and the captain were still going at it, when Ted's bureau secretary came in to tell him that Detective Jamison had something for him, and said it was urgent. The captain looked annoyed when Ted took the call, and Ted stood there for a long moment, holding the phone and listening. He made a few unintelligible comments and thanked her, and then looking at the captain, he hung up.

"Now, I suppose you're going to tell me that Carlton Waters and the guy the FBI busted are standing on her doorstep with shotguns." He rolled his eyes, he'd heard it all before. But Ted looked serious as he looked him in the eye.

"No. I'm going to tell you that Peter Morgan, the parolee who had Waters's number in his hotel room, is sitting in a parked car across the street from the Barnes house. Or it sounds like him. The car is registered to him. And one of the neighbors said he's been sitting there, or up the block, for weeks. They said he looked like a nice man and they never thought anything of it. They didn't seem worried."

"Shit." The captain ran a hand through his hair and looked at Ted. "This is all I need. If they kidnap that woman, it will be all over the papers that we didn't do a damn thing about it. All right, all right. Who've you got on it?"

"No one yet." Ted smiled at him. He didn't want to be right about this, but he knew he was. And it had been a lucky break that Jamison had found Morgan sitting there. He was going to instruct his men not to touch him. He didn't want to scare him off. What Ted wanted was to catch all of them, whoever they were, and however many, whether Carlton Waters was involved or not. Whatever this conspiracy was against her, all Ted wanted was to blow it sky high, arrest the men involved, and keep her and her kids safe. It would be no small feat.

"How many of them are there, the Barnes woman and her kids, I mean?" the captain asked, sounding surly, but Ted knew him better than that.

"She's got three kids. One leaves for camp tomorrow. Another one leaves for Tahoe the day after, and we can cover that through the sheriff at Lake Tahoe. After that, it will just be her and a six-year-old kid."

The captain nodded in answer. "Give her two guys around the clock. That ought to do it. Is your buddy Holmquist giving us anyone?"

"I think so," Ted said cautiously. It was a little awkward that he had told Rick about it, before he'd gone to the captain, but it happened that way sometimes. When they traded information, cases got solved more quickly.

"Tell him what you just found out about Morgan, and tell him to kick in two guys for sure, or I'll kick his ass the next time I see him."

"Thank you, Captain." Ted smiled at him and left his office. He had some phone calls to make to set up the protection for Fernanda and Sam. He called Rick and told him about Morgan. And he had a junior officer print out a mug shot of Morgan so he could show it to Fernanda and the kids. And then he took a folder out of his desk, and wrote a case number on it, to make it official. *Conspiracy to commit kidnap,* he wrote in bold letters. He wrote in Fernanda's name, and those of her children. And where it said to list suspects, he wrote Morgan's name. For the moment, the others were too remote, although he jotted down Phillip Addison's name, and wrote a brief description of the file he had on Allan Barnes. This was just the beginning. Ted knew the rest would come. The little pieces of sky were falling into place. It had just gotten a little bigger. All he had in that piece of sky now was Peter Morgan. But he felt in his gut that the others would be in the puzzle with him before too long.

Ted drove back to Fernanda's house at six o'clock that evening. And as he had earlier, he made a decision to enter the house visibly, like a guest, and look casual about it. He had taken off his tie, and was wearing a baseball jacket. The policeman he had brought with him was wearing a baseball cap, sweatshirt, and jeans. He could have been one of Will's friends, and Ted his father. She and the children were eating pizza in the kitchen when they walked in. They had let Ted in as soon as they saw him through the peephole. And the young man he had brought with him had brought some things with him in an athletic bag slung over his shoulder, which coordinated well with his youthful, athletic demeanor. Ted quietly asked him to set up in the kitchen, and then after asking Fernanda's permission, he sat down at the kitchen table with her and the kids. He had brought an envelope with him.

"Did you bring us more pictures?" Sam asked with interest, as Ted smiled at him.

"Yes, I did."

"Who is it this time?" Sam was acting like the official deputy Ted had made him the last time. He tried to sound blasé about it, as his mother smiled. There wasn't much to smile at right now. Ted had called and told her about Morgan. Apparently, he'd been outside for weeks, and she'd never seen him once. It didn't say much for her powers of observation, and she was worried. Ted had told her that there would be four men at her house shortly after midnight. Two SFPD and two FBI. Sam was very excited about it, and wanted to know from Ted if they'd be wearing guns. Sam had asked his mother earlier, but wanted confirmation from him.

"Yes, they will," Ted responded, as he took the mug shot out of the manila envelope he had brought with him, and handed it to Will. "Is this the man you saw in the car across the street?"

Will looked at it for less than a minute, nodded, and handed it back to Ted. "Yes, it is." He looked slightly sheepish. It had never occurred to him to tell his mother that he had seen a man in a car who had smiled at him. He just thought it was a random coincidence that he had seen him twice. He looked like a nice guy. And something like his dad.

Ted circulated the mug shot around the table. Neither Ashley nor Sam recognized him, but when the photograph reached Fernanda, she sat and stared at it for a long time. She knew she had seen him somewhere, but couldn't remember where. And then suddenly, she remembered him. It had either been at the supermarket, or the bookshop. She remembered dropping something and his picking it up, and just as Will had said, it had struck her at the time that he looked like Allan. She explained the circumstances to Ted.

"Do you remember when that was?" he asked calmly, and she said that it had been sometime in the past few weeks, but she wasn't sure when, which confirmed that he had been watching them for a while. "He's out there now," he explained quietly to the kids, and Ashley gasped. "And we're not going to do anything about it. We want to see who comes to talk to him, if anyone, who spells him off, and what they're up to. When you go outside, I don't want you to look for him, or notice him, or acknowledge him. We don't want to scare him off. Just act like you don't know anything about it," Ted said calmly.

"Was he out there just now?" Ashley asked, and Ted nodded. He knew the car now, from Detective Jamison's description, and where it was. But he hadn't even appeared to notice it. Ted was driving his own car, and chatted and smiled with the young cop he'd brought with him, trying to propagate the myth that he was a friend bringing his son over to visit. They actually looked convincing. The young policeman looked the same age as her older children and in fact, wasn't too much older.

"Do you think he knows you're a cop?" Will asked him.

"I hope not. But you never know. He might. I'm hoping he just thinks I'm a friend of your mom's for now." But there was no question, when they put four men on the detail, it was going to attract attention and would inevitably warn Morgan and his cohorts of something. It would be a double-edged sword once that happened. The police lost the advantage of anonymity, but it also warned the kidnappers to proceed with caution, or it could scare them off completely, although Ted considered that unlikely. They had no other choice. Fernanda and her family needed protection. And if it scared the man off for good, that was all right too. But above all, she needed a police presence there to protect her and her children. Some of the cops on the detail were probably going to be women, which might create a distraction at first, and make it less obvious that cops were on the scene. But sooner or later, four adults arriving twice a day, going everywhere with Fernanda and the children, and staying there twenty-four hours a day was going to attract considerable attention, and more than likely alarm them. Ted knew there was nothing else they could do for the moment. The captain had also discussed putting what he called a 10B out front, which was an unmarked police car with a plainclothes policeman in it. But Ted didn't think they needed one, and having Peter Morgan and a cop staring at each other in parked cars seemed foolish, even to him. The local station was going to be making passing calls to keep an eye on them, and that would be helpful too, and enough for the moment.

By the time they finished talking about it, the young officer Ted had brought with him was ready. He had put paper towels down, and set up his kits on them. His briefcase lay open, and two full fingerprinting kits were lying next to the sink. One had black ink, and the other red. Ted asked them all to step up to the sink. He asked Will to go first.

"Why do you have to fingerprint us?" Sam asked with interest. He was just tall enough to see what Will and the detective were doing. It was a fine art, as he rolled Will's fingers expertly side to side across the pad, and then rolled them again on a chart, which showed each finger of his hands. He rolled them to make sure they were clear, and Will was surprised to discover that the ink didn't leave his fingers dirty. They did red ones first, and then black. Will understood why they were being fingerprinted, as did Ashley and Fernanda, but no one wanted to explain it to Sam. It was in case one of them got kidnapped, or killed, with the fingerprints, their bodies could be identified. It was not a cheering prospect.

"The police just want to know who you are, Sam," Ted said simply. "There are a lot of ways to do that. But this one works. Your fingerprints will stay the same for the rest of your life." It was a piece of information he didn't need, but it helped. Ashley went next. Then her mother, and finally Sam was last. His fingerprints looked tiny on the cards.

"Why are we doing red and black?" Sam inquired as the detective took his prints for a second time.

"The black ones are for SFPD," Ted explained, "the red ones are for the FBI. They like to be fancier than we are." He smiled at him, as the others stood by and watched. They were huddled together as though they took strength in standing close to one another, and Fernanda was hovering over them like a mother hen.

"Why does the FBI like red?" Fernanda asked.

"Just to be different, I guess," the detective doing them said. Other than that, there was no real reason. But fingerprints done in red always belonged to the FBI.

As soon as he finished doing the fingerprints, he took out a small pair of scissors, and he turned to Sam with a cautious smile. "Can I snip a little piece of your hair, son?" he asked politely, as Sam looked at him wide-eyed.

"Why?"

"We can tell a lot of things from people's hair. It's called a DNA match." This was a lesson none of them needed, but like the rest of it, they had no choice.

"You mean like if I get kidnapped?" Sam looked frightened, and the man hesitated, as Fernanda stepped in.

"They just want us to do it, Sam. I'm going to do it too." She took the scissors from the man, snipped a tiny wisp of Sam's hair, then her own, and then her other children's. She made as little fuss about it as she could, and thought it seemed less ominous if she did it for them, rather than a stranger. Shortly after that, talking quietly amongst themselves, the children went upstairs. Sam wanted to stay with her, but Will took him by the hand and said he wanted to talk to him. He thought his mother wanted to talk to Ted about what was happening, and he assumed correctly that Sam would get scared. There was a lot happening to them. A lot had already occurred in a very short time. And Fernanda knew that after midnight, with four armed policemen in the house night and day, their lives would dramatically change.

"We're going to need photographs of them," Ted said quietly to Fernanda, after the others left the room. "And descriptions. Height, weight, distinguishing marks, everything you can give us. But the hair and fingerprints will help."

"Will all this really make a difference if they get kidnapped?" She hated even asking him that, but she needed to know. All she could think of now was what it would be like if they took one of her children. It was so frightening, she couldn't even hold the thought in her mind for long.

"It could make a big difference, especially with someone as young as Sam." He didn't want to tell her that sometimes children that age got snatched, and only turned up ten years later, living other lives with other people, having been kept prisoner in another country or state, and fingerprints and hair would help the authorities identify him, whether dead or alive. In the case of Will or Ashley, the circumstances that would lead them to need hair or fingerprints would be far more dire. And in this case, with a ransom involved, these kids weren't going to disappear into other lives. They were going to be taken, held, and hopefully returned when the ransom was paid. All Ted could hope, if it happened, was that no one would get harmed, and the kidnappers would keep the kids alive. He was going to do everything he could to see that it didn't happen. But they had to be prepared for all contingencies, and the hair and fingerprints they'd taken were important for them to have. He told Fernanda to get him the rest of the information as soon as possible. And a little while later, they left.

She sat alone in the kitchen with the empty

pizza box after that, staring into space, wondering how all this had happened, and how soon it would be over. All she could hope now was that the men plotting against her, if they really were, would be caught. She still clung to her doubts, hoping that it was all someone's imagination, and not something that would really happen. The prospect of that was so terrifying that if she had let herself think about it, she would have gotten hysterical, and never let her children out of the house. She was doing everything she could to stay calm, and not frighten them excessively, given the circumstances. And she thought she was doing a good job of staying calm, until she put the empty pizza box in the fridge, poured orange juice in a cup of tea, and put the clean towels in the garbage.

"Okay, calm down," she said to herself out loud, "everything's going to be fine." But as she put the towels away in the right place, she saw that her hands were shaking. It was all too terrifying to imagine, and she couldn't help but think of Allan and wish he were there. She wondered what he would have done about it all. She had the feeling that he would have handled it far more competently and coolly than she had.

"You okay, Mom?" Will asked as he walked

into the kitchen for some ice cream, just as she was leaving to come upstairs.

"I guess," she said honestly, looking tired. The day had left her feeling exhausted. "I don't love this." She sat down in a chair at the table next to him, while he ate his ice cream.

"You still want me to go to camp?" he asked, looking worried, and she nodded.

"Yes, I do, sweetheart." She wished Sam were going with him. She didn't want any of them to be waiting in the house with her, for bad things to happen. But Sam was too young, and she was going to keep him close to her. Ted had suggested that they go out as little as possible. He wasn't crazy about her being in a car, waiting to be ambushed. They had already discussed whether the officers would ride with her, or follow her. Ted preferred them in the car. Rick and the captain wanted her followed. It was the issue of being live bait again. And as a result, Ted suggested that if at all possible, she go nowhere.

Fernanda called the family hosting Ashley at Tahoe that night, and explained the situation to them, in strictest confidence. They told her how sorry they were, and assured her that they'd keep a close eye on Ashley, and she thanked them. They said they understood about the rotation of sheriff's deputies that would be watching, and felt more comfortable knowing someone would be there to protect Ashley. Neither Ted nor Rick felt she would be pursued in Tahoe, but they both felt it was a good idea to be cautious. And Fernanda was relieved to know that she'd be safe there.

Fernanda was lying on her bed that night, when the doorbell rang, and all four officers arrived together. Peter Morgan had gone home by then, and never saw them. He knew from her normal routines that she was in for the night by then. He usually left at nine-thirty or ten, and rarely later, except when she and the kids went to the movies. But that night, he had gone home early. She'd been at home all night, as had the kids, and he'd gone back to his hotel. He was almost sorry it was almost over. He liked knowing he was close to her and the children, and loved imagining what they were doing, as he glimpsed them from time to time at the windows.

Fernanda thought of calling Jack Waterman that night, to tell him what was happening, but she was too tired, and it sounded too crazy. What was she going to tell him? That a bunch of bad guys had a file about them, and one of them had been sitting in a parked car for weeks, watching them? And then what? There was still no concrete evidence that anyone wanted to kidnap them, just endless suspicions. It all sounded insane, even to her. And there was nothing he could do anyway. She thought she should wait a few days to see what happened, before she called him. He had been through enough drama with her about the money. And she and Sam were seeing him that weekend anyway. He was taking them to Napa the day after Ashley left for Tahoe. There was plenty of time to tell Jack then, so she never called him.

The officers who arrived at midnight were extremely polite, and after looking around the house, they decided to base themselves in the kitchen. There was coffee and food. She offered to make sandwiches for them, and they told her it wasn't necessary, but they thanked her for her kindness, and settled in.

There were four men, two from the San Francisco Police Department, two from the FBI, as Ted told her there would be, and they sat down and engaged in friendly banter, as she made coffee for them. They knew the alarm was on, and she showed them how to work it. Two of them took their jackets off, and she saw their guns hanging in their shoulder holsters, and another on their belt. She suddenly felt as though she were involved in some sort of resistance movement, or underground, surrounded by guerrillas. Seeing their artillery made her feel at the same time vulnerable and protected. No matter how friendly they were, their very presence in the house seemed ominous. And just as she was about to go upstairs, the doorbell rang. Two of the police officers came out of the kitchen rapidly, and went to answer it. She was surprised to see Ted a moment later in the hallway.

"Is something wrong?" she asked him, as she felt her heart beat faster in panic. Or maybe for once, it would be good news. She realized instantly that if it had been good news, he probably would have called her.

"No, everything's fine. I just thought I'd stop by on the way home and see how things were going." The men had gone back to the kitchen by then. She knew they were planning to be there till noon. The next shift after that would be there from noon to midnight. Which meant that the next day, her children would be having breakfast with men in holsters at their kitchen table. It reminded her of *The Godfather,* when they went to the mattresses. The only problem was that this was her life, and not a movie. And if it was a movie, it was a very bad one. "Are the boys behaving?" Ted asked as he looked at her. She looked so tired that just as a friendly gesture, he wished he could put his arms around her, but he didn't.

"They've been very nice to me," she said in a small voice, and he wondered if she'd been crying. She looked so tired and so frightened, although he had been impressed earlier by how calm she was in front of the children.

"They're supposed to be nice to you." He smiled at her. "I don't want to intrude. You must be exhausted. I just thought I'd check on them, and show the flag. It never hurts. If you have any problems with them, call me." He spoke of them like his children, and they were in some ways. A lot of the men and women who worked for him were young, and seemed like kids to him. He had also asked that they assign some women to the detail. He thought it might be easier and less frightening for Fernanda and the children. But the first shift was all male, and they were talking quietly in the kitchen, while Ted and Fernanda chatted in the hallway. "Are you holding up all right?"

"More or less." It was an incredible amount of pressure, waiting for something to happen.

"Hopefully, it'll be over soon. We'll catch these guys doing something stupid. They always do. Like hold up a liquor store right before they were supposed to pull off something much more important. You've got to remember, all these guys were in prison, which tells you that they weren't a great success at whatever they did before this. We're counting on that factor to help us. Some of them even want to get caught. It's a lot of work being outside, and having to make an honest living. They'd rather go back to prison and have three free meals a day, and a roof over their heads courtesy of your taxes. We're not going to let anything happen to you or the kids, Fernanda." It was the first time he had called her by her first name, and she smiled at him. Just listening to him, she felt a little better. He was quiet and reassuring.

"It's just so scary. It's horrible to think of people like that who want to hurt us. Thank you for everything you're doing," she said sincerely.

"It is horrible. And scary. And you don't have to thank me. What I'm doing is what I get paid for." She could tell that he was good at what he did, and she had been impressed by Rick Holmquist too, the man who had done the fingerprints so carefully, and even the four armed men in her kitchen. There was an air of calm competence about all of them.

"It looks like a movie," she said with a rueful smile, as she sat down on the stairs under the Viennese chandelier, and he sat down next to her. They sat whispering like two kids in the darkness. "I'm glad Will is leaving tomorrow. I wish I could get them all out of here, not just Will and Ash. This is scary for Sam." It was for her too, and Ted knew that.

"I was thinking about something tonight. What about a safe house? Is there anywhere you and Sam could go to get away for a few days? We don't need to do that now. We're comfortable with the plan we have in place to protect you. But for instance, if an informant tells us they've added more men, or we get information that things could get out of hand. It would have to be somewhere where no one would think to look for you, where we could spirit you away and hide you." In some ways, it would be a lot easier than protecting her in the city, although one of the big advantages of keeping her in the city was that it would only take them minutes to get back-up assistance and manpower in an attack or hostage situation. However many men ambushed her, if they did, the police and FBI could have reinforcements there in minutes from all the surrounding police stations. That was an important factor, but Ted always liked to have a backup plan. Fernanda shook her head in answer to his question.

"I sold all our other houses." It reminded him again of the incredible story she had told them that afternoon, of Allan losing all their money. It was still hard for him to believe that anyone could be so foolish and so foolhardy as to lose half a billion dollars. But apparently Allan Barnes had done it. And left his wife and kids with literally no money.

"Any friends or family you could stay with?" She shook her head again. She could think of no one. She couldn't think of a single friend she was still close enough to, to impose on in that way. And she had no other family at all.

"I'd hate to put anyone else at risk," she said pensively, but there was no one she could think of anyway, and certainly no one she wanted to admit her circumstances to, neither about their financial situation, nor the potential kidnap. Allan had somehow managed to alienate all their close friends from them, with his vast success and huge show of wealth that in the end had finally made even good friends feel awkward and avoid them. And on the way down from his lofty pinnacle, he didn't want anyone to know it. All that was left now, after his death, were acquaintances she didn't want to confide in. And Jack Waterman, their old friend and attorney. She was planning to tell him what was happening on the weekend, but he had no safe house either. All he did was stay at a hotel in Napa occasionally on random weekends, and he had a tiny apartment in town.

"It would do you good to get out of here," Ted said thoughtfully.

"Sam and I were supposed to go to Napa for the day this weekend. But it's beginning to seem like it would be pretty complicated to orchestrate, unless the police go with us." And that wouldn't be much fun for her or Jack or Sam, squashed in a car with them.

"Let's see what happens before that," Ted said, and she nodded.

He went in the kitchen to check on his men then, bantered with them for a few minutes, and left at one. And Fernanda walked slowly up to her bedroom. It had been an endless day for her. She took a long hot bath, and was just climbing into her bed, next to Sam, when she saw a man walk past her room and jumped a foot, as she stood shaking next to her bed, in her nightgown, and the man appeared in the doorway. It was one of the policemen, and he stood there with his guns on, as she stood staring at him in her nightgown.

"Just doing the rounds," he said comfortably. "You're okay?"

"I'm fine. Thank you," she said politely. He

nodded and went back downstairs, and she got into bed, still trembling. It was going to be very strange having them there. And as she fell asleep finally, she clung to Sam, and dreamed of men running around her house with guns drawn. She was in a movie. It was *The Godfather.* Marlon Brando was there. And Al Pacino. And Ted. And all her children. And as she drifted deeper into sleep, she saw Allan coming toward her. It was one of the few times she had ever dreamed of him since he died, and she remembered it vividly in the morning.

Chapter 14

When Will and Sam came down to breakfast the next day, Fernanda was making bacon and eggs for the two agents and two policemen sitting at her kitchen table. She set their plates in front of them, and Will and Sam took their places between them. She saw Sam staring at their guns with interest.

"Are there bullets in them?" he asked one of the men, and the police officer smiled at him and nodded, while Fernanda cooked her children's breakfast. It was more than a little surreal watching four heavily armed men eat breakfast with her children. She felt like a gun moll.

Sam wanted pancakes, and Will wanted eggs and bacon like the men, so she cooked both. Ashley hadn't woken up yet and was upstairs sleeping. It was still early. Will had to catch the

bus at ten o'clock, and she had already discussed with two of the officers whether or not
she should go with him to see him off. They
thought it was a bad idea and would draw too
much attention to the fact that he was leaving.
If someone was following her, it was better for
her to remain home with the other children.
One of the officers was going to take Will to
the bus. He had suggested that Will get in the
car in the garage, and lie on the back seat, so
no one would see that he was leaving. It was a
little far-fetched, but she could see that it made
sense. So at nine-thirty, she kissed Will good-
bye in the garage, he lay down on the back
seat, and a few moments later the officer drove
out of the garage, and appeared to be driving
alone. He had Will wait a few blocks before he
sat up, and once he did, they chatted on the
way to the bus. He put Will on the bus, with
his bag and his lacrosse stick, waited until the
bus took off, and waved as though it were his
own son. He was back at the house an hour
later.

Peter was in place down the street by then,
and saw a man driving Fernanda's car back
into the garage. He had seen him leave earlier
that morning, and had never seen him come
in the night before, as the night shift had all arrived after he left. And this was the only one

he'd seen so far. Peter was a little shocked to see a man there so early, which was something he had never seen before. It didn't even occur to him that the man who had driven into the garage was a policeman. Nothing seemed chaotic or out of place. And Peter himself was a little surprised to realize that he was annoyed at her for having a man there with the kids. It seemed irrational even to him, but he hoped he was just a friend, who had arrived early to help her and nothing more. The man left the house at noon, looking unconcerned, and Sam waved to him as he left, as though he were a friend.

When the new shift arrived that afternoon, there were two male FBI agents, and both police officers were women, so it looked like two couples coming to visit. Peter never saw the other three men go out the back of the house, and cross the neighbor's property, so no one would see them leaving.

He left that evening before her guests went home. They seemed to stay forever, and Peter saw no reason to stay. He already knew everything he needed to know about her. He also was almost certain that she never put the alarm on. And if she did, Waters was going to cut the wires before they went in. At this point, his surveillance was more out of habit of the past weeks than because he needed to learn anything new about her routine. He knew everywhere she went, what she did, who she went with, and how long it took her. If anything, his watching her now was for his own pleasure and because he had told Addison he would. It was no hardship to do so. He loved being near her, and watching her with her children. It seemed pointless to sit there now while she entertained two couples all day. The two couples had looked benign and friendly when they arrived in one car, talking and laughing. Ted had handpicked them and told them what to wear so they looked like friends. And although Peter had never seen her entertain, she seemed so happy when she greeted them, that it never occurred to Peter for an instant that they were FBI and SFPD. There was nothing to suggest to him that the atmosphere had changed. In fact, he felt sufficiently relaxed that he left early that night before the couples did. He was tired, and there was nothing to see. Other than greeting her guests, neither Fernanda nor the kids had moved all day. He had seen Sam playing in the window of his room, and Fernanda in the kitchen, cooking for her friends.

The next day was his last day of surveillance. Carlton Waters, Malcolm Stark, and Jim Free were going to stay with him that night. He still had a few things to get for them in the morning, which got him to Fernanda's late. Ashley had already left for Tahoe with her friends, and the shift had changed. By sheer luck, he never saw the cops of the previous shift leave at noon, nor the new ones come in, all through the back door again. And when he left for the last time that night, regretfully, at ten o'clock, he had no idea that there was anyone in the house with her. He wasn't there to see them leave at midnight, and others arrive. In fact, he didn't see Fernanda at all that day, nor her children. He wondered if she was tired from entertaining the day before, or just busy. And as the kids were out of school for the summer, they didn't have to go anywhere, and he suspected they were enjoying their vacation and being lazy. He saw her at the windows in the day, and he had noticed that she had drawn her shades at night. He always felt lonely when he couldn't see her, and as he drove away for the last time, he knew just how much he was going to miss her. He already did. He hoped he'd see her again one day. He couldn't imagine what his life would be like now without her. It saddened him, almost as much as what they were about to do to her. He still felt sick at the thought of it. And worrying about it distracted him from any sense that she and the children were being protected. He didn't repeat it to Addison because he was completely unaware of it. Surveillance was unfamiliar to him.

Caring about her as he did, he finally forced himself to stop thinking about what it was going to do to her when his associates kidnapped one or all of her children. He couldn't allow himself to continue thinking of it, and forced his mind toward more agreeable subjects, as he drove away that night, and went back to the hotel, thinking of her. When he got there, Stark, Waters, and Free were already waiting for him and wanted to know where he'd been. They were hungry and wanted to go to dinner. He didn't want to admit to them how hard it had been for him to leave her, even if leaving her meant only driving away from a parking space on the street where she lived. He had never admitted to any of them how much he had come to respect and like her, nor how fond he had become of the children.

As soon as Peter got to the hotel, the four of them went out to dinner. They went to a taco place Peter knew and liked in the Mission. All four of them had been to their parole agents the day before, and as they were on two-week check-in status now, no one would realize they were gone until they were out of the country. Just as Addison had assured him, Peter in turn had assured them that Fernanda would pay the ransom quickly for her children. Presumably within a few days. The three men who would be executing the plan had no reason to disbelieve him. All they wanted out of this was their money. They didn't care about her or her kids, one way or the other. It made no difference to them who they took, or why, as long as they got the money. They had already been paid a hundred thousand each in cash. The balance was to be paid to all four of them out of the ransom. Peter had detailed instructions from Addison as to where she was to transfer the money. It was to be wired into five accounts that could not be traced, in the Cayman Islands, and from those accounts into two in Switzerland for Addison and Peter and three in Costa Rica for the others. The children were to be held until the money was wired and Waters was to warn her at the outset that if she called the police, they'd kill the children, although Peter did not intend to let that happen. Waters was to make the ransom demand, according to the instructions Peter had already given him.

There was no need for an honor system among the men. The three others still did not know Phillip Addison's identity, and if any of them squealed on the others, they would not only lose their share but be killed, and each of them knew it. The plan appeared to be failsafe. Peter was to leave his hotel the next morning, while the others took whatever kids they got to the house they had rented in Tahoe. He had already booked a motel room on Lombard under another name. The only contact between Peter and the other three men was to be when they had dinner the night before the kidnap, and slept in his hotel room. They had brought sleeping bags and put them on the floor, and Peter got up, dressed, and left when they did, separately, early the next morning. The van was gassed up and ready for them. They picked it up at the garage. They were not yet sure at exactly what time they would make their move. They were going to watch for a short while, and pick their moment while things were still quiet in the house. There was no set time schedule, and no hurry. Peter arrived at his motel on Lombard by the time they got to the garage to pick up the van. He still kept his other room so as not to arouse suspicion. Everything was set up. They had moved the golf bags with the machine guns out of the car into the van. There was rope and plenty of duct tape, and a startling amount of ammo. They shopped for groceries on the way to the garage, and had enough to keep them going for several days. They didn't expect it to last long. They weren't worried about feeding the children. Hopefully, from their point of view, they wouldn't have them long enough to worry much about it. They had bought peanut butter, jelly, and bread for the kids, and some milk. The rest of what they bought was for themselves, which included rum, tequila, a lot of beer, and canned and frozen food, since none of them liked to cook. They had never had to cook for themselves in prison.

It was the third day of cops and FBI agents in the house, when Fernanda called Jack Waterman early that morning and said that she and Sam had the flu and couldn't go to Napa for the day. She still wanted to talk to him about what was happening, but things were too crazy, and it still seemed too unreal. How could she explain the men camping out in her living room, sitting around the table with holsters in her kitchen? It almost made her feel foolish. Particularly if it turned out to be unnecessary. She was hoping that she'd never have to tell him about it. Jack said he was sorry they both had the flu, and offered to come by on his way to Napa, but she said they still felt too lousy, and she didn't want him to catch it.

After that, she tucked Sam into bed with her, and put on a movie. She had fed the four men breakfast by then, and she and Sam were cuddling, with his head on her shoulder, when she heard an unfamiliar sound downstairs. The alarm wasn't on, and didn't need to be with two policemen and two FBI agents protecting her. With all that trained protection and armed firepower at hand, the alarm seemed redundant, so she hadn't put it on the night before, or in fact since they'd been there. Ted had told her they could set it off accidentally with the movements of the men going in and out of the back door from time to time to check on things. It sounded as though something had fallen in the kitchen, a chair or something comparable. She didn't worry about it with four men downstairs, and lay there with Sam dozing on her shoulder. Neither of them was sleeping well at night, and sometimes it was easier dozing in the daytime, as Sam did now, in his mother's arms.

She heard muffled voices then, and footsteps on the stairs. She was just beginning to wonder what was going on and assumed they were coming upstairs to check on them, but didn't want to get up and disturb Sam, when three

men in ski masks exploded through her bedroom door and stood at the foot of her bed,
pointing M16 machine guns with silencers at
them. As Sam saw them, his eyes flew open
wide, and he stiffened in his mother's arms, as
one of the men came toward them. Sam's eyes
were huge with terror, as were Fernanda's,
who was praying the men wouldn't shoot
them. Even to her untrained eye, she knew
they were carrying machine guns.

"It's okay, Sam . . . it's okay . . ." she said
softly in a shaking voice, not even knowing
what she'd said. She had no idea where the
men protecting her were, but there was no evidence of them, and no sound from downstairs. She clutched Sam to her and backed up
in the bed, as though it would save her and
Sam from the men, as one of them wrenched
Sam out of her hands without a sound, and she
screamed as he took him from her. "Don't
take him," she pleaded pitifully. The moment
they had feared had come, and all she could do
was beg him. She was sobbing uncontrollably,
as one man held a machine gun on her, and
another tied Sam's hands with rope, and put a
piece of tape over his mouth, as her son
looked wild-eyed at her in helpless terror.
"Oh my God!" she screamed as two of them
forced Sam into a canvas bag, with hands and

feet tied, like so much laundry. There were terrified grunts from Sam, and screams from her, as the man closest to her yanked her hair back so hard with one hand, it felt like he had torn it from her scalp.

"If you make another sound, we'll kill him, and you don't want that, do you?" She could tell that he was powerfully built, in a rough jacket and jeans and workmen's boots. There was a wisp of blond hair peeking from the ski mask. One of the other men was stockier, but powerful as he slung the canvas bag over his shoulder. Fernanda didn't dare move for fear that they would kill Sam.

"Take me with him," she said in a shaking voice, and the two men said nothing. They were following orders and had been told clearly not to. She had to stay back to pay the ransom. There was no one else who could do it. "Please . . . please . . . don't hurt him," she begged them, falling to her knees, as all three ran out of the room and down the stairs carrying him, and then she got up and ran down the stairs after them, and on the stairs she suddenly saw footprints in blood everywhere.

"If you tell the cops or anyone about this, we'll kill him." She nodded her understanding to the man who had spoken in a voice muffled by the mask.

"Where's the door to the garage?" one of the men asked her, and she saw blood splashed on his pants leg and his hands. She hadn't heard a single shot ring out. All she could think about was Sam, as she pointed to the door to the garage. One of the men was pointing his machine gun at her, and another tossed Sam to the third one. He slung the bag with Sam in it over his shoulder, and there was no sound and no movement, but she knew that nothing they had done to him so far could have killed him. The heavy-set man spoke to her again then. They had been in Will's and Ashley's bedrooms before they got to her, and hadn't found them.

"Where are the others?"

"Away," she said, and they nodded and ran down the back stairs, while she wondered where the cops were.

The kidnappers had backed up their van to the garage, and no one had seen them do it. They had looked innocuous when they arrived, looking like workmen, went around to the back, broke a window using a towel, unlocked it, and climbed in. They had disabled the alarm and cut the wires before they broke the window pane. It was a skill they had developed over the years and knew well. No one had seen anything. And no one did now, as they opened the garage door to access their van, and she watched them open the back door to throw Sam in. If she had had a gun, she would have shot them, but as things were, there was nothing she could do to stop them, and she knew it. She was afraid to even scream for her protectors, for fear that the kidnappers would kill Sam.

The man carrying the bag with Sam in it climbed in and dragged him in, bumping Sam across the back bumper. The others threw their weapons in, ran around to the front, as the back door slammed. And seconds later they drove away, as Fernanda stood sobbing on the sidewalk. And much to her horror, no one heard or saw her. The windows of the van had been heavily tinted, and by the time the men took their ski masks off, they had turned the corner, and she saw nothing. She hadn't even seen their license plate and only thought of it afterward. All she could do was watch them drive her son away and pray that they wouldn't kill him.

She ran back inside, still sobbing then, flew up the back stairs and into the kitchen, across the bloodstained hall carpet, to find the policemen. And what she found there was a scene of total carnage. One with his head bashed in, another with the back of his head blown off by an M16. His brains were splattered all over her kitchen wall. She had never seen anything so horrible, and was too terrified to even cry. They could have done this to her or Sam, and still could. The two FBI agents had been shot in the chest and heart, one of them was sprawled across the table with a hole in his back the size of a dinner plate, the other was lying on his back on the kitchen floor. The two FBI men were holding their Sig Sauer .40 calibers, and the two policemen held semiautomatic .40-caliber Glocks, but none of them had had time to fire off a round before the kidnappers shot them. They had been distracted for just a moment, talking and drinking coffee, and had been taken completely unaware. All of them were dead. And she ran out of the room to use the phone and call someone. She found the card with Ted's phone number, and dialed his cell phone. She was so panicked she didn't think to call 911, and she remembered the kidnappers' warning "not to tell anyone." That seemed impossible now with four officers dead at their hands.

Ted answered on the first ring, and was at home, doing some paperwork and cleaning his .40-caliber Glock, which he'd been meaning to do all week. All he heard were strange gutteral moaning sounds, like some wild wounded beast. She could not find the words to tell him, and sobbed pathetically into the phone.

"Who is this?" he said sharply. But he was afraid to know. Something deep in his soul told him instantly it was Fernanda. "Speak to me," he said, sounding powerful, as she clamped her teeth shut and fought for air, sucking the air through them. "Talk to me. Where are you?"

"They . . . toooookkkkk . . . himmmm . . ." she finally managed to say, shaking violently from head to foot, barely able to breathe or speak.

"Fernanda . . ." He knew it. Even in extremis, he knew her voice. "Where are the others?" She knew he meant his men, and couldn't tell him.

She sobbed uncontrollably again then. All she wanted now was her son back. And this was only the beginning. "Dead . . . all dead," she managed to say. He didn't dare ask her if Sam was too, but he couldn't be. It would do them no good if they had killed him in front of his mother. "They said they'd kill him if I told . . ." Ted and she both believed them. "I'll be right there." He cut her off without asking more questions, called central dispatch, and gave them her address and a warning to keep it off the radio to keep the press out of it.

They did the dispatch in code. His next call was to Rick, and he told him rapidly to get their media rep to Fernanda's house. They had to control what was said, if anything, so as not to risk Sam. Rick sounded as upset as Ted was, and was running out the door with his cell phone as they talked, and both hung up within seconds.

Ted ran out his front door, having just re-assembled his gun, and shoved it in the holster. He didn't even bother to turn his lights off. He put a red light on top of his car, turned it on, and drove as fast as he could to where she was. But long before he got there, her street was filled with police cars, flashing lights, and sirens. They had sent three ambulances. And there were nine police cars up and down her street, and another blocking the entrance to her block when he got there, only minutes af-ter they did. Two more ambulances arrived as he got out, and Rick was just behind him.

"What the hell happened?" Rick ran along-side him as they reached the front steps. There were police already in the house, and Ted could see no sign of Fernanda, the agents, or policemen who had been protecting her and Sam.

"I don't know yet . . . they have Sam . . . that's all I know . . . she said 'all dead,' and then

I cut her off, called dispatch, and you." As they rushed into the house, Ted saw the blood on the steps and the hall carpet, and as though drawn to it, they walked into the kitchen, and saw all that Fernanda had. And as much horror as they had both seen in their careers, what they saw there hit them hard.

"Oh my God," Rick said in a whisper, as Ted stared in silence. All four of their men were dead, and their deaths had been brutal and ugly. Animals had done it. That was what these men were. Ted felt rage overcome him as he turned to look for her, and ran back into the hallway. There were twenty policemen in the house by then, all shouting and running, and checking for suspects. Ted had to fight his way past them as the FBI media rep was giving orders to keep the press out. Ted was about to run up the stairs, when he saw Fernanda on her knees in the living room, just lying there and sobbing, with her head on the carpet. She was hysterical when he knelt beside her and took her in his arms, stroked her hair, and knelt there with her and held her. Ted just held her and rocked her and said nothing. Her eyes were wild and terrified as she looked at him and then leaned against him.

"They took my baby . . . oh my God . . . they took my baby . . ." She had never fully believed they would do it. Nor had he. It was too bold and too outrageous and too crazy. But now they'd done it. And killed four men when they took him.

"We'll get him back. I promise." He had no idea if he could live up to it, but he would have told her anything to calm her. Two paramedics walked in then, and looked at him. He didn't think she was injured but she was in bad shape, and one of them knelt beside her and talked to her. She was suffering from extreme trauma.

Ted helped them lay her down on the couch, and took off her shoes before he did it. There was blood on them, and she had tracked it all over the room. There was no point getting it on the couch too. There were police photographers everywhere by then, taking photographs and videos of the crime scene. It was beyond gruesome. Policemen were crowding in everywhere, some were crying, all were talking, as FBI agents began to arrive by the carful. Within half an hour, there were forensic experts everywhere, collecting fibers, glass, fabrics, fingerprints, and DNA evidence for FBI and SFPD crime labs. And there were already two kidnap negotiators standing by the phones, waiting for a call. The general mood was one of outrage.

It was late afternoon before they left, and
Fernanda was in her room by then. They had
put yellow caution tape on the kitchen doorway, indicating that it was a crime scene and
had to be left intact, or "sterile" as they called
it. Most of the police cars had left. There were
four more men assigned to her. The captain
had come to survey the damage, and left again
looking shaken and grim. They had explained
nothing to the neighbors. And barred all access to the press. The official statement was
that an accident had happened. And they took
the bodies out the back door, after the press
left. The police knew without question that
there could be no public statement until they
had the boy back. Anything said publicly
would jeopardize him further. Nothing more
could be said.

"For a while there," the captain said to Ted
before he left, "I thought you were crazy. It
turns out they are." He hadn't seen anything as
grisly in years, and he had asked Ted immediately if Fernanda had heard or seen anything
that could help them, like the license plate, or
their destination. But she hadn't. They had all
been wearing ski masks, and said little or nothing. She had been too frantic to even notice details about the van. All they knew was what
they'd known before it happened. Who it

might be, and who might be behind it. There was nothing new, except that two policemen and two FBI agents had died, and a six-year-old boy had been kidnapped. Detectives had gone to Peter's Tenderloin hotel within minutes of Fernanda's call to Ted, but the desk clerk said he'd gone out that morning and not come back. Peter's guests of the night before had gone out a service entrance and never been seen or linked to him. The police were staking out his room, but there was no sign of him, and Ted knew there wouldn't be. He was gone for good, although what seemed like all his belongings were still in the room. And there were coded all points bulletins out for Peter and Carlton Waters, and Peter's car. Everyone knew they had to act with extreme caution so as not to alert the kidnappers or jeopardize the boy.

Carlton Waters and his two friends had called Peter as soon as they crossed the Bay Bridge and were driving through Berkeley. They used the new number he'd given them, on his brand-new nontraceable cell phone.

"We had a little problem," Waters said to him. He sounded calm but angry.

"What little problem?" For a terrifying moment, Peter was afraid that they'd killed her, or Sam.

"You forgot to mention she had four cops

with her, sitting in her kitchen." Waters sounded livid. They hadn't expected to have to kill four cops to get to the kid. That was not part of the deal. And Peter hadn't warned them.

"She what? That's ridiculous. I never saw them go in. She had a few friends in the other day, but that was it. There was no one with her." He sounded certain. But he had also left before ten o'clock the night before, maybe they had gone in after he left. He wondered if that was why he hadn't seen much of her for the past few days. But there was no one to tip her off to what was happening. No way for her to know. Nothing had happened, except Addison getting himself arrested for tax problems. But nothing about that could have warned the police or the FBI, unless he had said something inadvertently. Peter knew he was too smart for that. He couldn't figure out what had happened, or what had gone wrong.

"Well, whoever wasn't with her is no longer a problem. If you get my drift," Waters said, spitting a wad of chewing tobacco out the van window. Stark was driving. And Free was in the back seat. The boy was in the bag they'd put him in, in the back of the van, with their weapons and the groceries. Free had an M16 at his feet, and an arsenal of handguns, mostly

.45-caliber Rugers and Berettas, both were semiautomatic weapons. Carl had brought his favorite, an Uzi MAC-10, a small fully automatic machine gun he'd grown fond of and learned to use before he went to prison.

"You killed them?" Peter asked, sounding stunned. That was going to complicate everything, and he knew Addison wasn't going to like it. Nothing like that was supposed to happen. He'd been watching her for over a month. How the hell did four cops get into the picture? And who had they been watching? Suddenly, Peter felt a chill run down his spine. As Addison had said, there was no such thing as a free lunch. All of a sudden, Peter knew he was about to earn his ten million.

Carlton Waters did not comment on Peter's question. "You'd better warn the cops not to say how those guys died. If they put any of this in the newspapers, we'll kill the kid. I told her that, but maybe you'd better remind them too. We want everything nice and quiet, till we get the money. If they put it on TV, every asshole in the state will be looking for us. We don't need that too."

"Then you shouldn't have killed four cops. Christ, what am I supposed to do here? You can't expect me to keep them quiet."

"You better do something fast. We left there

half an hour ago. If the cops talk, it's going to be all over the news in the next five minutes."

Peter knew his phone was untraceable, but he hated testing the limits. He had no choice though. Waters was right. If the kidnapping hit the press along with the murder of four cops, there would be a statewide search on every freeway, on every road, in every corner of the state, and on every border, even more so than just for Sam, which would be bad enough. But killing four cops added a whole new dimension. Sam was still alive, and the police would know he would be. But four men had died now. That was a very different story. It was against his better judgment, but Peter called a central police number, and asked to speak to a sergeant. He knew it didn't matter where he called, whoever he gave the message to would get it into the right hands within seconds. So he passed on what Carl had told him.

"If anything about the dead cops or the kidnapping hits the press, the boy is dead," he said, and hung up. Ted and his captain got the message in less than two minutes. It presented a problem for them because two officers and two FBI agents had died, but a child's life was hanging in the balance.

The captain called the chief of police, and what they came to was that a statement would be made to the press that four men had been killed in the line of duty. They were going to say that an accident had occurred involving a high-speed chase. Details would be released at the appropriate moment, to give the families time to notify their loved ones. It was all they could do, and the simplest and cleanest explanation for the deaths of four law enforcement officers, from two agencies, both city and federal. It was going to be tough to cover. But they all knew they had to, until the kidnappers were found, or the boy reclaimed. After that, all hell could break loose and the boy's life would no longer be at stake. The captain wrote the press release himself with the FBI media rep, and Carl Waters heard it on the radio two hours later, while they were still on the road to Tahoe. He called Peter and said he had done a good job. But by then, Peter was facing a serious dilemma, as he sat in his motel room on Lombard. Things had not gone entirely according to plan, and he felt he owed it to Addison to tell him. He didn't tell Carl he was thinking of doing that, although he expected Peter to contact his superiors after what had happened. Waters was still angry at

Morgan for his sloppy surveillance, which had led to the problem. The murder of four cops was definitely a problem.

Peter had Addison's phone number in the South of France, and called him from his cell phone, while Phillip was sitting in his hotel room. There had never been any plan for Peter to join the others in Tahoe. In fact, he was to stay as far away from them as possible, so there would be no link to him, or Addison. He was going to say that his rented house had been broken into, long after they claimed the ransom.

Addison had arrived in Cannes the day before, and had just begun enjoying his vacation. He knew what was happening, and the schedule they were on. What he wanted to hear about was good results, not problems. He had told them to wait a couple of days before making their ransom request. He wanted to give Fernanda time to panic about it. He knew if they did, she'd pay faster. He assumed she would pay quickly.

"What are you telling me?" he said as Peter beat around the bush for a minute. Peter hated telling him that Waters and the others had killed four cops. It was also going to be difficult to explain why he hadn't known they were in there in the first place. Peter began by telling him they only got Sam, the others were away.

"I'm telling you there was a problem," Peter said, holding his breath for a minute.

"Did they hurt the boy or his mother?" Addison's voice was icy. If they killed the boy, there would be no ransom. Only headaches. Big ones.

"No," Peter said, pretending to be calm, "they didn't. Apparently, four cops got into the house last night after I left. There haven't been any till now, I'd swear to it. There's been no one in the house except her and the kids. There isn't even a maid. I don't know how the cops got into it. But Waters said they were there when he and the others got there."

"And then what happened?" Addison said slowly.

"Apparently, they killed them."

"Oh, for chrissake . . . my God . . . is it all over the news yet?"

"No. Waters called me from the road. I called the police and left a message. I said that if anything about the dead cops or the kidnapping hit the press, we'd kill the boy. They just issued a press release on the radio that four officers were killed in a high-speed chase. There

were no other details. And there's no mention
of the kidnap. Our guys warned her they'd kill
the boy if she or the cops talk."

"Thank God you did that. They'll be looking for the boy everywhere anyway, but if they
warn the public, it'll be that much worse.
There would be random 'sightings' of the kidnappers from here to New Jersey. All we need
are cops combing the state, looking for cop
killers. They care a lot more about that than a
kidnap. They know you'll keep the boy alive
to get the ransom money. But four dead cops
are another story." He was anything but
pleased. They both knew that for Sam's safety,
the police would keep their mouths shut, so as
not to put Sam in even greater jeopardy.

"It sounds like you handled it, but how stupid of the others. I suppose they had no
choice. They couldn't take four cops with
them."

Addison sat on the balcony of his suite at the
Carlton in Cannes for a long moment, watching the sunset, thinking about what to do.
"You'd better go up there." It was a change of
plan, but might make an important difference.

"To Tahoe? That's insanity. The last thing I
need is to be identified with them." Or worse,
caught with them, if they did something
equally stupid, like rob a 7-Eleven for a sand-

wich, Peter thought, but didn't mention it to his boss. Addison was upset enough about the four dead cops, and Peter was too.

"The last thing any of us needs is to lose a hundred million dollars. Consider it protecting our investment. I'd say it's worth it."

"Why in hell do you want me to go up there?" Peter sounded panicked.

"The more I think about it, I don't trust them with the boy. If they hurt him, or kill him accidentally, we're screwed. I'm not sure their baby-sitting skills are quite what they should be. I'm relying on you to protect our principal asset." They were turning out to be more violent than he thought they would be. All they needed was for one of them to get out of control. It wouldn't take much to kill the boy, and they might be dumb enough to do something like that. And with only one child to bargain with, Addison didn't want to take any chances. "I want you to go up there," he said firmly.

It was the last thing Peter wanted to do, but he could see Addison's point. And he knew that if he was there, he could keep an eye on Sam. "When?"

"No later than tonight. In fact, why don't you go now? You can keep an eye on them. And the boy. When are you going to make the call to his mother?" He was just checking. They had worked out all the details before he left. Although he certainly didn't expect them to kill four cops. That was not part of the plan.

"In a day or two," Peter said. It was what they had planned and agreed on.

"Call me from there. Good luck," he said, and hung up, as Peter sat in his hotel room staring at the wall. Things were not going according to plan. He hadn't wanted to go anywhere near Tahoe while they were there. All he wanted was his ten million dollars and to get out. He wasn't even sure he wanted that. The only reason he was doing this was to save his daughters. And going to Tahoe to be with Waters and the others put him at much greater risk for being caught. But he knew, as he had from the beginning of this mess, there was no way out. He tried not to think of Fernanda and what she must be going through, as he picked up his bag of toiletries and shaving gear, the two clean shirts and underwear he'd brought in a paper bag, and walked out of the motel ten minutes later. But whatever she was feeling now, or how terrified she was, one thing he was sure of, with a hundred million dollars at stake, they'd be sending back her son. So no matter how sick she was over it, it was going to turn out all right in the end. Peter re-

assured himself with that thought, as he left
the motel and hailed a cab. He had it drop him
off at Fisherman's Wharf, where he took another cab to a used car lot in Oakland. He had
left the car he'd been using for the past month
in a back alley in the Marina. He had removed
the license plates and dropped them in a
dumpster before walking half a dozen blocks
to the motel, where he had paid cash for the
room.

In Oakland he bought an old Honda, paid
cash for it, and an hour after his call to Phillip
Addison, he was on the road to Tahoe. It
seemed a lot safer to use a different car than
he'd been using while following her for the
past month, in case someone in the neighborhood had seen him. Now that Waters and the
others had murdered four cops, the risk was
greater for all of them, and for Peter, going to
Tahoe increased the risks further. But he knew
he had no choice in the matter. Addison was
right. Peter didn't trust them with Sam, and he
didn't want anything worse to happen than already had.

Long before he reached Vallejo, photographs
of Peter and Carlton Waters had been circulated all over the state on police computers.
Peter's now-abandoned license plates and the
description of his previous car were circulated

with them, along with extreme confidential warnings not to publish any information, as there was a kidnap in progress. Peter didn't stop along the way, and drove within the speed limit, to avoid incident. And by then, Addison was already under surveillance by the FBI in France. And all Fernanda needed now was a phone call from the kidnappers, so the police and FBI could find Sam.

Chapter 15

All the police photographs they needed had been taken by that night. The men's families had been notified, the bodies were at funeral parlors, what was left of them. The wives and families had been told the circumstances, that a child's life was hanging in the balance, and no one could talk, or tell the truth until the boy had been released by his captors. They understood, and all had agreed. They were good people, and as cops' and agents' wives, they knew the difficulties of the situation. They were dealing with their own and their families' grief, with the help of trained psychologists in both departments.

By then profiling experts were at work on Peter Morgan and Carl Waters. Their respective rooms had been searched extensively, friends interviewed, and the manager of the

Modesto halfway house had supplied the information that Malcolm Stark and Jim Free, both parolees, had left with Waters, which spawned fresh investigations, and the dispersal of more mug shots, profiles, and APBs over the Internet to law enforcement agencies around the state. The FBI profilers in Quantico were adding their expertise to that of the SFPD. They had spoken to Waters's, Stark's, and Free's parole agents and employers, Peter's parole agent, who said he scarcely knew him, and a man who claimed to be Peter's employer but appeared not to know him at all. Three hours later, the FBI profilers had ferreted out the fact that the company that alleged to employ Peter was actually an indirect subsidiary of a company Phillip Addison owned. Rick Holmquist correctly suspected that Peter's job was a front, which made sense to Ted as well.

Ted had also called the industrial cleaning service they used at homicide scenes, or the one they recommended. They were tearing Fernanda's kitchen apart that night. They even had to pull out the granite and strip the room, thanks to the weapons that had been used and the devastating physical damage they had caused. Ted knew that by morning, the place would be stripped and no longer elegant, but it would be clean, and there would be no visible evidence, in terms of bloodstains at least, of the grim carnage that had taken place there when the officers were killed and the kidnappers got Sam.

Four more officers had been assigned to her, all cops this time. Fernanda was upstairs lying on her bed. Ted had been there all day and evening. He never left. He made whatever calls he had to make from his cell phone, while camping out in her living room. And there was a trained negotiator standing by, waiting for the kidnappers' call. There was no question in anyone's mind that it would come. The only question was when.

It was nearly nine o'clock at night when she came downstairs, looking gray. She hadn't eaten or had anything to drink all day. Ted had asked her a few times, and then finally he had left her alone. She needed some time to herself. He was there for her, if she wanted him. He didn't want to intrude on her. He had called Shirley a few minutes before, and told her what had happened, and that he was going to spend the night with his men. He wanted to keep an eye on things. She said she understood. In the old days, when he was on a stakeout, or working undercover in his youth, sometimes he'd been gone for weeks. She was used to it. Their crazy lives and schedules had essentially kept them apart for years, and it showed. Sometimes she felt she hadn't been married to him in years, not since the kids were small, or even before that. She did what she wanted, had her own friends, her own life. And so did he. It happened a lot to cops and their wives. Sooner or later, the job did them in. They were luckier than most. At least they were still married. A lot of their old friends weren't. Like Rick.

Fernanda wandered into the living room like a ghost. She stood and looked at him for a minute, and then sat down.

"Have they called?" Ted shook his head. He would have told her if they had. She knew that, but had to ask. It was all she could think of now and had all day.

"It's too soon. They want to give you time to think about it and panic." The negotiator had told her that too. He was upstairs, waiting in Ashley's room, with a special phone plugged into their main line.

"What are they doing in the kitchen?" she asked with no real interest. She never wanted to see the room again, and knew she'd never forget what she'd seen there. Ted knew it too. He was relieved to know she was selling the house. After this, they needed to get out.

"Cleaning it up." She could hear a machine pulling out the granite. It sounded like they were knocking the building down, and she wished they would. "The buyers may want to put in a kitchen," he said, trying to distract her, and she smiled in spite of herself.

"They put him in a bag," she said, staring at Ted. The scene kept running through her mind over and over, even more than the one in the kitchen, which had been unforgettable too. "With tape over his mouth."

"I know. He'll be okay," Ted said again, praying it was true. "We should hear from them in a couple of days. They may let you talk to him when they call." The negotiator had already told her to ask for that when they did, to prove that he was alive. There was no point paying ransom for a dead kid. Ted did not say that to her. He just sat there, looking at her, as she stared at him. She felt dead inside. And looked it outwardly. Her face was somewhere between gray and green, and she looked sick. Several neighbors had asked what had happened earlier. And someone said they'd heard her scream. But when the police canvased the neighborhood, no one had seen anything. The police had given out no details.

"Those poor men's families. This must be so awful for them. They must hate me." She looked at Ted searchingly, feeling guilty. They had been there to protect her and her kids. Indirectly, it felt like her fault, as much as the kidnappers'.

"This is what we do. Things happen. We take the risk. Most of the time, things turn out okay. And when they don't, we all know that's what we signed on for, and so do our families."

"How do they live with it?"

"They just do. A lot of marriages don't survive." She nodded. Hers hadn't either, in a way. Allan had chosen to bail out rather than face his responsibilities, and left her with a mess, rather than trying to clean it up himself. Instead, he had left her to do it. That had been occurring to her more and more recently. It had occurred to Ted too. And now she had to face this. He felt sorry for her. All he could do to help her was do everything he could to get back her son. And he intended to. The captain had agreed to let him stay at the house for the duration. It was going to start getting dicey once they called.

"What am I going to do when they ask me for money?" She'd been thinking about it all day. She had none to give them, and wondered if Jack could drum some up. It was going to take a miracle, she knew, depending on how much they wanted. Probably a lot.

"With any luck at all, we'll be able to trace the call, and move in on them pretty quick." If they were lucky. If. Ted knew they had to find them fast, and free the boy.

"What if we can't trace their call?" she said almost in a whisper.

"We will." He sounded sure, to reassure her. But he knew it wasn't going to be as easy as he wanted to make it sound. They just had to wait and see what happened when they got the call. The negotiators were standing by.

She hadn't combed her hair all day, but looked pretty anyway. She always did to him.

"If I get you something to eat, will you try to eat it? You're going to need to keep your strength up, for when they call." But he knew it was too soon. She was still in shock from everything that she'd seen and survived that day. She just shook her head.

"I'm not hungry." She knew she couldn't eat. All she could think of was Sam. Where was he? What had they done to him? Was he hurt? Dead? Terrified? A thousand terrors were racing through her head.

Half an hour later, Ted brought her a cup of tea, and she sipped it, sitting on the floor in the living room, hugging her knees. He knew she wouldn't sleep either. It was going to be an interminable wait for her. For all of them. But hardest for her. And she hadn't told the other kids. The police had agreed that she should wait until she heard something. There was no point panicking them, and it would. The local police at both locations had been notified, and they were on standby for both Ashley and Will. But now that they had Sam, Ted felt the other two were safe, and his superiors agreed. They weren't going to try to grab the other two. They had all they needed now with Sam.

She lay on the rug in the living room, and didn't say anything. Ted sat near her, writing reports, and glancing at her occasionally. He went to check on his men, and after a while, she fell asleep. She was lying there asleep on the floor when he got back. He left her there. She needed the sleep. He thought of carrying her to her room, but he didn't want to disturb her. He lay down on the couch himself sometime around midnight, and dozed for a few hours. It was still dark when he woke up and heard her crying, lying on the floor, too grief-stricken to move. He didn't say a word to her, he just sat down on the floor next to her and held her, and she lay in his arms and cried for hours. The sun was coming up when she finally stopped, thanked him, and walked upstairs to her room. They had cleaned the blood off the hall carpet. Ted didn't see her

again until almost noon. They had still heard
nothing from the kidnappers. And Fernanda
looked worse by the hour.

Jack Waterman called her that afternoon, the
day after the kidnapping. The phone rang, and
everyone jumped. They had already told her
that she had to answer the phone herself, so
the kidnappers didn't get scared off by the
cops, although they would suspect they were
there, since there had been cops in the house
when they came for Sam. She answered and
nearly burst into tears when it was Jack. She
had been praying it would be them.

"How's your flu?" he asked, sounding casual
and relaxed.

"Not so good."

"You sound awful. I'm sorry to hear it.
How's Sam?" She hesitated for an endless moment, and in spite of her best efforts not to,
burst into tears. "Fernanda? Are you all right?
What happened?" She didn't even know what
to say. She just went on crying, while he got
increasingly distraught. "Can I come over?"
he asked her, and she shook her head, and then
finally agreed. In the end, she'd need his help
anyway. All hell was going to break loose once
they asked her for money.

He was at her door ten minutes later, and he
was stunned when he walked into the room.

Half a dozen visibly armed plainclothesmen and FBI agents were walking around the house. One of the two negotiators had come downstairs for a change of scene. Ted was talking to a small group in the kitchen, which looked surprisingly clean. And Fernanda stood in the midst of it, looking grim. She burst into tears again when she saw Jack. She didn't know what to say, as Ted led the rest of the cops and agents into the kitchen and closed the door.

"What's going on here?" Jack asked, looking horrified. It was obvious that something terrible had happened. It took her another five minutes to get the words out, as they sat next to each other on the couch.

"They kidnapped Sam."

"Who kidnapped Sam?"

"We don't know." She told him the whole agonizing story from start to finish, including Sam's removal in the canvas bag, and the murder of the four policemen in her kitchen.

"Oh my God. Why didn't you call me? Why didn't you tell me the other day?" He realized now that it had been happening then, when she canceled their date in Napa. He had honestly believed they had the flu. What they had was infinitely worse. He could hardly believe the story she told him, it was too terrifying for words.

"What am I going to do when they ask for ransom? I have nothing to give them to get Sam back with." He knew it better than anyone. It was a tough question. "The police and FBI think that the kidnappers believe I still have all of Allan's money. That's what they think anyway."

"I don't know," Jack said, feeling helpless. "Hopefully, they'll catch them, before you have to come up with the money." It was going to be impossible to find cash for her in large amounts, or even small ones. "Do the police have any leads as to where they are?" For the moment, there were none.

Jack sat with her for two hours, with an arm around her, and he made her promise to call him at any hour, if she heard anything or wanted company. And he made a bleak suggestion before he left. He told her that she should probably sign over a power of attorney to him, so he could make decisions, and move funds for her, if there were any, in case something happened to her. What he said was as depressing as having watched the police cut her children's hair, for a DNA match in case they were found dead. Essentially, Jack was saying the same thing. He told her he would send the papers over for her to sign the next day. And a few minutes later, he left.

She wandered into the kitchen, and saw the men drinking coffee. She had sworn she would never go into the room again, but she just had. It was almost unrecognizable. All the granite had been removed, and they'd had to replace the kitchen table, and had with a plain functional one, the four men's blood had soaked into the wood of the one she had. She didn't even recognize the chairs. The place looked like a bomb had hit it, but at least there was no evidence of the horror she had seen there the day before.

As she walked into the room, the four men guarding her stood up. Ted was leaning against the wall and talking to them, and he smiled at Fernanda as she walked in. She smiled in response, remembering the comfort he had offered the night before. Even in the midst of the agony she was living through, there was something peaceful and reassuring about him.

One of the men handed her a cup of coffee, and offered her a box of doughnuts, and she took one and ate half of it, before she threw it away. It was the first thing she had eaten in two days. She was living on coffee and tea, and on the edge of her nerves. They all knew there was no news. No one asked. They made small talk in the kitchen, and after a while, she went upstairs and lay on her bed. She saw the negotiator walk past her open door to Ashley's room. She never took her clothes off any-more, except to shower. It was like living in an armed encampment, and everywhere around her were men with guns. She was used to it by now. She didn't care about the guns. Only her son. He was all she cared about, all she lived for, all she wanted, all she knew. She lay on her bed, awake all night, from the sugar and the coffee, waiting for news of Sam. And all she could do was pray that he was alive.

Chapter 16

When Fernanda woke up the next morning, the sun was just coming up over the city in a golden haze. She didn't realize it until she went downstairs and saw the paper one of the men had left on the table, it was the Fourth of July. It wasn't a Sunday, but all she knew as she sat and looked at the sunrise was that she wanted to go to church, and knew she couldn't. She couldn't leave the house in case they called. She said something to Ted about it, as they sat in the kitchen a little while later, and he thought about it for a minute and asked her if she'd like to see a priest. It even sounded strange to her. She liked taking the children to church on Sundays, but they had objected to going since Allan died. And she had been so disheartened that she hadn't gone much lately herself. But she knew she wanted to see a priest now. She wanted someone to talk to and to pray with her, and she felt as though she'd forgotten how.

"Is that weird?" she asked Ted, looking embarrassed, and he shook his head. He hadn't left her in days. He just stayed at the house with her. He had brought clothes with him. She knew some of the men were hot bunking in Will's bedroom. They took turns sleeping one at a time, while the others kept watch over the house, the phones, and her. As many as four or five men used the bed in shifts in any twenty-four-hour period.

"Nothing's weird if it gets you through this. Do you want me to see if I can get someone to come out, or is there someone you want me to call?"

"It doesn't matter," she said, looking shy. It was strange, but after the past few days together, she felt as though they were friends. She could say anything to him. In a situation like this one, there was no pride, no shame, no artifice, there was only honesty and pain.

"I'll make a few calls" was all he said. Two hours later, there was a young man at the door. He seemed to know Ted, and walked in quietly. They spoke for a few minutes, and then he followed Ted upstairs. She was lying on her bed and he knocked on the open door.

She sat up and stared at Ted, wondering who the other man was. He was wearing sandals, a sweatshirt, and jeans. She had been lying there, willing the kidnappers to call, when he walked in.

"Hi," Ted said, standing in her doorway, feeling awkward, as she lay on her bed. "This is a friend of mine, his name is Dick Wallis, he's a priest." She got off her bed then and stood up, walked over to them, and thanked him for coming. He looked more like a football player than a priest. He looked young, somewhere in his mid-thirties, but as she spoke to him, she saw that his eyes were kind. And as she invited him into her bedroom, Ted went quietly back downstairs.

Fernanda led the young priest to a small sitting room off her bedroom and invited him to sit down. She wasn't sure what to say to him, and asked him if he knew what happened. He said he did. He told her then that he had played pro football for two years after college, and then decided to become a priest. He told Fernanda as she listened raptly to him that he was now thirty-nine, and had been in the priesthood for fifteen years. He said that he had met Ted years before when he was briefly a police chaplain, and one of Ted's close friends got killed. It had put a lot of things in

question for him about the meaning of life,
and how senseless it all was.

"We all ask ourselves those things at times.
You must be asking yourself those same questions right now. Do you believe in God?" he
asked her then, and took her by surprise.

"I think so. I always have." And then she
looked at him strangely. "In the last few
months, I haven't been so sure. My husband
died six months ago. I think he committed
suicide."

"He must have been very frightened to do
something like that." It was an interesting
thought, and she nodded. She had never
thought of it that way. But Allan was afraid.
And had opted out.

"I think he was. I'm frightened now," she
said honestly, and then started to cry. "I'm so
afraid they'll kill my son." She couldn't stop
crying now.

"Do you think you can trust God?" he asked
her gently, and she looked at him for a long
time.

"I'm not sure. How could He let this happen, and let my husband die? What if my son
is killed?" she said as she choked on a sob.

"Maybe you can try to trust Him, and trust
these people here to help you and bring him
back. Wherever your son is right now, he's in

God's hands. God knows where he is, Fernanda. That's all you need to know. All you can do. Leave him in God's hands." And then he said something so strange to her that she had no idea what to say in response. "We're all given terrible trials sometimes, things that we think will break our spirit and kill us, and they make us stronger in the end. They seem like the cruelest blows, but in a funny way they're like compliments from God. I know that must sound crazy to you, but that's what they are. If He didn't love you and believe in you, He wouldn't give you challenges like this. They're opportunities for grace. You'll be stronger from this. I know it. This is God's way of telling you that he loves you and believes in you. It's a compliment from Him to you. Does that make any sense?"

She looked at the young priest with a wistful smile and shook her head. "No." She didn't want it to make sense. "I don't want compliments like this. Or my husband's death. I needed him. I still do."

"We never want challenges like this, Fernanda. No one does. Look at Christ on the cross. Think of the challenge that must have been for him. The agony of betrayal by people he had trusted, and death. And afterward came the resurrection. He proved that no challenge, no matter how great, could end His love for us. In fact, He loves us more. And He loves you too." They sat quietly for a long moment then, and in spite of what seemed to her like the insanity of what he was saying about the kidnapping being a compliment from God, she felt better, and she wasn't even sure why. Somehow the young priest's presence had calmed her. He got up after a while, and she thanked him. He gently touched her head before he left, and said a blessing over her, which comforted her somehow. "I'm going to pray for you and Sam. I'd like to meet him one day." Father Wallis smiled at her.

"I hope you will." He nodded, and left her then. He didn't look anything like a priest, and yet in a strange way she liked what he had said. She sat alone in her room for a long time after that, and then went downstairs to find Ted. He was in the living room, on his cell phone, and he ended the call when she walked into the room. He'd been talking to Rick, just to pass the time. There was no news.

"How was it?"

"I'm not sure. He was either terrific, or nuts. I'm not sure which," she said, and smiled.

"Probably both. But he helped me a lot when a friend of mine died, and I just couldn't make sense of it. The guy had six kids, and his wife was pregnant with another one. He was killed by a homeless man who stabbed him for no reason, and just left him there to die. No act of bravery, no hero's death. Just a lunatic and a knife. The homeless guy was nuts. They had let him out of the state mental hospital the day before. It just didn't make sense. It never does." The killing of the four men in her kitchen and the kidnapping of her son didn't make sense either. Some things just didn't.

"He said this is a compliment from God," she shared with Ted.

"I'm not sure I agree with him. That does sound nuts. Maybe I should have called someone else." Ted looked sheepish.

"No. I liked him. I'd like to see him again. Maybe after this is over. I don't know. I think he helped."

"That's how I always felt about him. He's a very holy person. He never seems to waver from what he believes. I wish I could say as much for myself," Ted said quietly, and she smiled. She looked more peaceful. It had done her good talking to the priest, however odd his words.

"I haven't been to church since Allan died. Maybe I was mad at God."

"You have a right to be," Ted said.

"Maybe I don't. He said this is an opportunity for grace."

"I guess all hard things are. I just wish we got fewer opportunities for grace," Ted said honestly. He had had his share too, though none as bad as this.

"Yes," she said softly. "So do I."

They walked to the kitchen then to find the others. The men were playing cards at the kitchen table, and a box of sandwiches had just arrived. Without thinking, she picked one up and ate it, and then drank two glasses of milk. She didn't say a word to Ted while she did. All she could think of was what Father Wallis had said about this being a compliment from God. Somehow it sounded weird, but right, even to her. And for the first time since they'd taken him, she had the overwhelming sense that Sam was still alive.

Peter Morgan got to Lake Tahoe in the Honda only two hours after Carl and his crew arrived with Sam. When he got there, Sam was still in the canvas bag.

"That's not very smart," Peter told Malcolm Stark, who had put the bag in a back bedroom, and dumped it on the bed. "The kid's got tape over his mouth, I assume. What if he can't breathe?" Stark looked blank, and Peter was glad he'd come. Addison was right. They couldn't be trusted with the boy. Peter knew they were monsters. But only monsters would do the job.

Carl had questioned him about why he'd come to Tahoe, and Peter said that after the killing of the cops, their boss wanted him to come up.

"Was he pissed?" Carl looked concerned.

Peter hesitated before he answered. "Surprised. Killing the cops complicates things. They're going to be looking for us a lot harder than if it was just the kid." Carl agreed. It had been rotten luck.

"I don't know how you missed the cops," he said to Peter, still looking annoyed.

"Neither do I." Peter kept wondering if something Addison had said in his FBI interrogation had tipped them off. Nothing else could have. He had been impeccably careful in watching Fernanda. And up until then, Waters, Stark, and Free had made no mistakes that he knew of. Once they ran into the police in Fernanda's kitchen, they had had no choice but to kill them. Even Peter agreed. But it was still shit luck. For all of them. "How's the kid?" he asked again, not wanting to seem too con-

cerned. But Stark still hadn't gone to the back
room to get him out.

"I guess someone should check," Carl said
vaguely. Jim Free was bringing the food into
the kitchen, and they were all hungry. It had
been a long day, and a long drive.

"I'll do it," Peter volunteered casually, sauntered into the back room, and untied the knot
in the rope tying the bag. He opened it gin-
gerly, terrified that Sam had suffocated, and
two big brown eyes met his. Peter put a finger
to his lips. He wasn't sure whose side he was
on anymore, the boy's mother, or theirs. Or
maybe just the boy's. He pulled away most of
the bag, and gently peeled the duct tape off his
mouth, but left his hands and feet tied. "Are
you okay?" he whispered, and Sam nodded.
His face was dirty and he looked scared. But at
least he was alive.

"Who are you?" Sam whispered.

"It doesn't matter," Peter whispered back.

"Are you a cop?" Peter shook his head.
"Oh." Sam said no more, he just watched, and
a few minutes later, Peter left the room and
walked into the kitchen where the others
were eating, and someone had put a pot of
pork and beans on the stove. There was
chili too.

"We'd better feed the kid," Peter said to

Waters, and he nodded. They hadn't thought of that either. Nor even water. They had just forgotten. They had bigger things on their minds than food for Sam.

"For chrissake," Malcolm Stark complained, as Jim Free laughed, "we're not running a daycare center here. Leave him in the bag."

"If you kill him, they won't pay us," Peter pointed out practically, and Carl Waters laughed.

"He's got a point. His mother is probably going to want to talk to him when we call. Hell, we can afford to feed him once in a while, he's getting us a hundred million bucks. Give him lunch." He looked at Peter when he said it, and assigned him to the job. Peter shrugged, put a slice of ham between two pieces of bread and walked it into the back room, and once there, sat down on the bed next to Sam, and held it to his mouth. But Sam shook his head.

"Come on, Sam, you've got to eat," Peter said matter-of-factly, almost as though he knew him. After watching him for over a month, he felt as though he did. Peter spoke to him as gently as he would have to his own children, trying to get them to do something.

"How do you know my name?" Sam looked

puzzled. Peter had heard his mother say it a hundred times by then.

Peter couldn't help wondering how she was doing, and how badly shaken up she was. Having watched how close she was to her children, he knew what it must be doing to her. But the boy was in remarkably good shape, particularly after the trauma he'd been through, and a four-hour ride tied up in a canvas bag. The kid had guts, and Peter admired him for it. He offered him the sandwich again, and this time Sam took a bite. In the end, he ate half of it, and when Peter looked back at him from the doorway, Sam said, "Thanks." Something else occurred to Peter then, and he turned back to ask him if he had to go to the bathroom, and Sam looked awkward for a minute, and Peter guessed correctly what had happened. He had wet himself long since. Who wouldn't. He got him out of the bag then completely. Sam didn't know where he was, and he was afraid of the men who had kidnapped him, including Peter. He took him to the bathroom, and waited while he went, and carried him back again and left him on the bed. He couldn't do more for him. But he covered him with a blanket before he left, and Sam watched him leave.

Peter came back before he went to bed that
night, and took him to the bathroom again.
He woke him to do it, so he wouldn't have
another accident. And gave him a glass of
milk and a cookie. Sam devoured both, and
thanked him again. And when Sam saw him
appear the next morning, he smiled.

"What's your name?" Sam asked cautiously.

Peter hesitated before telling him, and then
decided he had nothing to lose. The child had
seen him anyway. "Peter." Sam nodded. And
Peter came back a while later with breakfast.
He brought him a fried egg and bacon. He
rapidly became the official baby-sitter. The
others were happy not to do it. They wanted
their money, not baby-sitting for a six-year-
old kid. And in an odd way, Peter felt as
though he was doing it for Fernanda, and
knew he was.

He sat with the boy for a while that afternoon, and came back again that night. Peter
sat on the bed next to him, and stroked his
hair.

"Are you going to kill me?" Sam asked in a
small voice. He looked frightened and sad, but
Peter had never seen him cry. He knew how
terrifying this must be for him, but he was
remarkably brave, and had been since it
happened.

"No, I'm not. We're going to send you home to your mom in a few days." Sam didn't look as though he believed him, but Peter looked as though he meant it. Sam wasn't so sure about the others. He could hear them in the other room, but they had never come in to see him. They were more than happy to let Peter do it. He told them he was protecting their investment, which they thought was funny.

"Are they going to call and ask my mom for money?" Sam asked softly, and Peter nodded. He liked the boy better than he did the others. By a long shot. They were a nasty lot. They'd been talking about the cops they'd killed and how good it felt to do it. Listening to them made Peter feel sick. It was a lot more pleasant talking to Sam.

"Eventually," Peter said in answer to his question about their asking Fernanda for money. Peter didn't say when they would, and wasn't sure himself. In a couple of days, he thought, which was the plan.

"She doesn't have any," Sam said quietly, watching Peter, as though trying to figure him out, which he was. He almost liked him, but not quite. He was one of the kidnappers after all. But he'd been nice to him at least.

"Any what?" Peter asked, looking distracted.

He was thinking of other things, like their escape. Their plans were set, but he was nervous about it anyway. The other three were heading to Mexico, and from there to South America with false passports. Peter was going to New York, to try to see his daughters. And then he was going to head for Brazil. He had some friends there from his days of dealing drugs.

"My mom doesn't have any money," Sam said softly, as though it was a secret he was supposed to keep, but was sharing with Peter.

"Sure she does." Peter smiled.

"No, she doesn't. That's why my dad killed himself. He lost it all." Peter sat on the bed and stared at him for a long moment, wondering if he knew what he was talking about. He had that painful honesty and sincerity of kids.

"I thought your dad died in an accident, he fell off a boat."

"He left my mom a letter. She told my dad's lawyer he killed himself."

"How do you know?"

Sam looked embarrassed for a minute, and then confessed, "I was listening outside her door."

"Did she talk to him about the money?" Peter looked worried.

"A lot of times. They talk about it almost every day. She said it's all gone. They have a lot of 'bets' or something. That's what she always says, there's nothing left but 'bets.'" Peter understood better than he did. She was obviously talking about debts, not bets. "She's going to sell the house. She hasn't told us yet." Peter nodded, and then looked at him sternly.

"I don't want you to say this to anyone else. Do you promise?" Sam nodded, looking very somber.

"They'll kill me if she doesn't pay them, won't they?" Sam said with sad eyes. But Peter shook his head.

"I won't let them do that," he whispered. "I promise," he said, and then left the room to go back to the others.

"Christ, you spend a lot of time with that kid," Stark complained, and Waters looked at Stark with disgust.

"Just be glad it's not you. I wouldn't want to do it either."

"I like kids," Jim Free volunteered. "I ate one once." He laughed uproariously at that. He'd been drinking beer all night. He'd never been convicted of hurting a child, and Peter assumed it was bullshit, but he didn't like it anyway. He didn't like anything about them.

Peter didn't say anything to Waters till the next morning, and then he looked at him with concern, as though he'd been worrying about something.

"What if she doesn't pay up?" Peter asked him directly.

"She will. She wants her kid back. She'll pay whatever we ask." They had actually been talking the night before about asking for more, and taking a bigger cut.

"And if she doesn't?"

"What do you think?" Carl said coldly. "If she doesn't, he's no use to us. We get rid of him, and get the fuck out." It was what both he and Sam had feared.

But Sam's confession the night before about his mother's finances put a new spin on things for Peter. It had never occurred to him that she was broke. Although he had raised the question once or twice, Peter had never seriously believed that she was. Now he felt differently about it. Something about the way Sam had repeated what he'd overheard told Peter that it was true. It also explained why she never went anywhere, or did anything, and there was no help in the house. He had expected her to lead a far grander life. He thought she just stayed home because she loved her kids, but maybe there was more to it than that. And he had the feeling that the conversations Sam had heard between his mother and her lawyer were all too real. Still, having "no money" was relative to different people. She might still have some left, but not as much as they had once had. The suicide note was interesting though. If that were true, there might really be nothing left of Allan Barnes's fortune. Peter was profoundly worried, thought about it all day, and what it might mean to him, and the others. And worse yet, Sam.

They sat around for two more days, and then finally decided to call her. All four of them agreed that it was time. They used Peter's untraceable cell phone, and he dialed her number. She answered on the first ring herself, and her voice sounded hoarse. It cracked as soon as she heard who it was. Peter spoke quietly, silently aching for her, and identified himself by saying he had news of her son. The negotiator was listening on the phone, and they were already frantically working on tracing the call.

"I have a friend who'd like to speak to you," Peter said, and walked into the back room while Fernanda held her breath, and gesticulated wildly to Ted. He already knew. The negotiator was listening on the line with her, and they were recording the call.

"Hi, Mommy," Sam said as tears filled her eyes and she held her breath.

"Are you okay?" She could hardly talk, she was shaking so hard.

"Yeah. I'm fine." Before he could say more, Peter took the phone away as Waters watched. Peter was afraid that, to reassure her, Sam would say he had been nice to him, and he didn't want the others to hear it. Peter took the phone back, and spoke clearly to her. He sounded well spoken and cool, which surprised her. From what she'd seen in her house four days before, she expected them to be goons. And this one obviously wasn't. He sounded educated, and polite, and oddly gentle in his tone.

"Your son's bus ticket home will cost you exactly a hundred million dollars," Peter said without batting an eye, as the others listened to him and nodded their approval. They liked his style. He sounded businesslike, polite, and cool. "Start counting your pennies. We'll be calling you shortly to tell you how we want it handled," he said, and cut the line before she could answer. He turned to the others, and they sent up a cheer. "How long do we give her?" Peter asked. He and Addison had talked about a week or two at the most, to complete the transaction. At the time, they had agreed that longer than that was unnecessary, but after what Sam had said, he wasn't sure that time was the issue or would make a difference. If she didn't have it, there was nowhere she could dig up that kind of money. Even if Barnes had a few lingering investments. Maybe she could cough up a million or two, if that. But from what Sam was saying about her debts, and his father's suicide, Peter even wondered if she had that. And even a couple of million divided five ways was pointless.

The other three got drunk that night, and he sat talking to Sam again for a long time. He was a sweet boy, and he was sad after talking to his mother.

And at her end, Fernanda was sitting in the living room in shock, looking at Ted.

"What am I going to do?" She was in the depths of despair. She had never dreamed they'd ask for that kind of money. A hundred million was insane. And they obviously were.

"We'll find him," Ted said quietly. It was the only choice they had now. But they hadn't been able to get a trace on the line. He cut it off too fast anyway, although with the device they had, they could have, if he'd been calling from a traceable line. But he was using a cell phone that couldn't be traced. It was one of the few that couldn't. They obviously knew what they were doing. At least she had talked to Sam.

She called Jack Waterman while Ted was talking to the captain. She told him what the ransom was, and he sat in stunned silence at his end. He could have helped her come up with half a million dollars, until she sold the house, but beyond that, she had almost nothing in the bank. She had about fifty thousand currently in her account. Their only hope was finding the boy before the kidnappers killed him. Jack prayed they would. She told him the police and FBI were doing everything they could, but the kidnappers had gone underground. All four of the men they knew about had vanished. And the regular network of reliable informants knew nothing.

Two days later, Will called home, and he knew the minute he heard her voice that something had happened. She denied it. But he knew her better. Finally she broke down and cried, and told him that Sam had been kidnapped, and he begged her to let him come home from camp.

"You don't need to do that. The police are doing everything they can, Will. You're better off in camp." She thought it would be too depressing and upsetting for him at home.

"Mom," he said, sobbing into the phone, "I want to be with you." She called Jack and asked him to go up and get him, and the following afternoon, Will walked into the house, and burst into tears as he threw himself into her arms. They stood holding each other for a long time, and spent hours that night talking in the kitchen. Jack had hung around for a while, and finally left, not wanting to intrude. He chatted with Ted and the other men for a few minutes, and they told him there was nothing new. Investigators were combing the state, but so far, no one had reported seeing anything suspicious, the police were looking for the men in the mug shots, but no one had seen them, and there had been no sign of Sam, or anything he owned or had been wearing. The boy had disappeared without a trace and so had they. They could have been anywhere by then, over a state line somewhere, even in Mexico. Ted knew that they could stay underground for a long time, too long for Sam.

Will slept in his own room that night, and the men slept in Ashley's. They could have slept in Sam's, but it seemed sacrilegious to them somehow. At four in the morning, Fernanda still couldn't sleep, and went downstairs to see if Ted was awake. He was lying on the couch, with his eyes open, thinking. The rest of the men were in the kitchen, talking, with their guns in evidence, as they always were. It was like some strange kind of emergency room, or intensive care unit, where people stayed awake all night, wearing guns and waiting to minister to her. There was no longer any clear definition to day or night. It was all the same. There were always people on cell phones, and wide awake.

She sat down in a chair next to Ted, and looked at him with a despairing glance. She was beginning to lose hope. She didn't have the money, and the police hadn't found her son. They didn't even have a single lead as to where they were hiding. And all of the police and FBI were adamant that they couldn't go public. They said it would just confuse things and make it worse. And if they infuriated the kidnappers, it was almost certain they would kill Sam. No one was willing to take the risk. And neither was she.

Ted had gone home for a few hours that night, and had dinner with Shirley. They had talked about the case, and she said she felt sorry for Fernanda. She could see that Ted did too. She had asked him if he thought they'd find the boy in time, and he said he honestly didn't know.

"When do you think we'll hear from them again?" Fernanda asked him once he was back at her house. The living room was dark, and the only light in the room was from the hall.

"They'll call soon to tell you how they want you to deliver the money," he reassured her, but she couldn't see what difference that would make. They had agreed that she was going to try to stall them. But sooner or later they would realize that she wasn't going to pay. Ted knew he had to find Sam before then. He had called Father Wallis that afternoon himself. There was nothing for them to do but pray. What they needed desperately was a break. Both the SFPD and the FBI were pumping their informants, but no one had heard a word about the kidnappers or Sam.

As it turned out, the kidnappers called her again the next morning. They let her speak to Sam again, and he sounded nervous. Carl Waters was standing over him as Peter put the phone to his ear, and Fernanda could barely hear more than his voice saying "Hi, Mom," before they took the phone away again. The voice on the phone told her that if she wanted a conversation with her son, she was going to have to pay the ransom. They gave her five days to come up with it, and told her they'd give her delivery instructions the next time they called, and hung up again. Listening to them this time, she was frantic. There was no way to pay. And once again, the call they had made could not be traced. All the police knew was that none of them had reported to their parole agents that week, which was old news. They knew who had done it. What they didn't know was where they had· gone, and what they had done with Sam. And all the while, Phillip Addison had the perfect alibi, and was sitting in the South of France. The FBI had checked his phone records out of the hotel. He had made no long-distance phone calls to cell phones in the States, and they kept no records of incoming calls. And from the time the FBI began monitoring his calls, several hours after the kidnap, there hadn't been a single call from the kidnappers. They'd had their instructions, and were handling it on their own. Peter was doing all he could to protect Sam. Carl and the others were getting ever more anxious for the money. Ted and Rick and the networks, agencies, and informants they were using were coming up with nothing. And Fernanda felt as though she were going insane.

Chapter 17

The last call from the kidnappers came to tell Fernanda she had two days left to deliver the money. And this time they sounded impatient. They didn't let her talk to Sam, and at her end, everyone knew time was running out. Or maybe already had. It was time to make a move, but there was none to make. With no leads whatsoever as to their whereabouts, there was nothing the police could do. They were working every source they had to beat the clock, but without a lead, a tip, a trace, or a sighting they were getting nowhere.

Peter explained the delivery instructions to Fernanda when they gave her the two-day ultimatum. She was to wire the entire hundred million into the account of a Bahamian corporation, rather than the one they'd originally planned to use in the Cayman Islands. The

Bahamian bank had already been instructed to
deposit it through a series of dummy corporations, and from there ultimately Peter's and
Phillip's shares were to be wired to Geneva.
The other three shares were being wired to
Costa Rica. And once Waters, Stark, and Free
reached Colombia or Brazil, they could have
it transferred there.

Fernanda knew none of the complicated
details. All she knew was the name of the
Bahamian bank where she was supposed to
wire a hundred million dollars within two
days, and she had nothing to send. She was
counting on the police and FBI to find Sam
before they reached the deadline, and she was
ever more panicked that they wouldn't find
him in time. Hope was dwindling by the hour.

"It's going to take me longer than that to access the money," Fernanda said to Peter during
the call, trying not to let panic creep into her
voice, but it was there anyway. She was fighting for Sam's life. And despite all their efforts
and impressive technology and manpower,
thus far neither the FBI nor the police had
helped. Or at least they had gotten no results.

"Time is running out," Peter said firmly.
"My associates aren't willing to wait," he said,
trying to convey his own desperation. She had
to do something. Every day, Waters and the

others were talking about killing Sam. It mattered nothing to them. In fact, if they didn't get their money, they thought it a suitable revenge. The boy meant less to them than a bottle of tequila or a pair of shoes.

They didn't even care that Sam had seen them and could identify them. The unholy threesome were planning to disappear into the wilds of South America forever. They had illegal passports waiting for them just north of the Mexican border. All they had to do was get there, pick them up, disappear, and live like kings for the rest of their days. But she had to pay the ransom first. And hour by hour, day by day, Peter came to understand that Sam had told the truth. She had nothing to wire into the Bahamian account. Peter had no idea what she was going to do. Nor did Fernanda. He would have liked to ask her, but he could only assume someone was telling her what to do.

Jack had already told her that the biggest loan he could get for her, against the house, was an additional mortgage for seven hundred thousand dollars, which she couldn't support the payments on anyway. And not knowing the circumstances, or even if they had, the bank told her they couldn't approve it or give her the money for thirty days. Waters and his friends wanted it in two.

She had nothing to work with, nor did Ted, Rick, and an army of FBI agents, who swore they were leaving no stone unturned, but to Fernanda, they seemed no closer to finding Sam than on the day he was taken. And Peter felt that too.

"She's playing games," Waters said in a fury after the call ended. And at her end, Fernanda was in tears.

"A hundred million dollars isn't easy to come up with," Peter said, feeling agonized for her. He could only imagine the degree of pressure this was putting on her. "Her husband's estate is in probate, she has to come up with death taxes on his estate, and his executors may not be able to release it to her as fast as we want."

Peter was trying to buy her time, but he was afraid to tell them he now firmly believed she didn't have it, for fear they would fly into a rage and kill Sam on the spot. For Peter, it was a fine line to walk. And for Fernanda too.

"We're not waiting," Waters said darkly. "If she doesn't wire it in two days, the kid is dead, and we're out of here. We can't sit here forever, waiting for the cops to show up." He was in a black mood after the call, said she was dicking them around, and he had a temper tantrum when he discovered they were out of both tequila and beer, and he said he was sick of their food, and the others agreed.

In San Francisco, Fernanda had been sitting in her room all day, every day, crying, terrified that they were going to kill Sam, or already had. And Will was moving around the house like a ghost. He hung out with the men in the kitchen, but wherever you went, and whoever you talked to, the tension was intolerable. And whenever Ashley called, Fernanda kept up the charade that everything was fine. She still didn't know that Sam was gone, and Fernanda didn't want her to. It would just have made things worse to have her hysterical too.

"They're going to kill me, aren't they?" Sam said to Peter with sad eyes, after they had called his mother. He had heard the men talking, and they were angry it was taking so long.

"I promised you I wouldn't let that happen," Peter whispered when he stopped in the back room to check on him after the call to Fernanda. But even Sam knew it was a promise he couldn't keep. And if he did, they'd kill Peter too.

When Peter walked back into the living room, they were all particularly unhappy about the lack of beer, as well as the delay in her coming up with the ransom. Finally, Peter offered to go into town for them and buy some. He had the kind of looks that never drew attention. He was just a nice guy visiting the lake on a vacation, probably with his kids. They nominated him to make a beer run, and told him to bring back some tequila and Chinese food too. They were sick of their own cooking, and so was he.

Peter drove into town and past it on the fateful beer run. He drove through three more towns, thinking about what he was going to do. There was no question. Sam was right. They were running out of time. And from all he knew now, the ransom was a lost cause. The only decision left was whether to let them kill Sam or not. And just as he had risked his life in this to save his own children, he knew now what he had to do for Sam.

He pulled over in the van, near a campsite, and picked up his cell phone. The one thing he knew was that he wasn't going back to Pelican Bay again. There was a momentary temptation to just keep driving, but if he did, when he didn't go back, they would kill Sam for sure.

He dialed the number and waited, and as she always did, Fernanda picked it up on the first ring. His voice was polite, and he told her Sam was fine, and then he asked to speak to one of the policemen with her. She hesitated for a moment, looked at Ted, and said there were no policemen with her.

"It's all right," Peter said, sounding tired. It was over for him and he knew it, and he no longer cared. The only thing that mattered to him now was Sam. He realized as he spoke to her that he was doing it for her. "I assume there's someone on the line," he said calmly. "Mrs. Barnes, let me speak to one of the men." She looked at Ted with anguished eyes and handed him the phone. She had no idea what this meant.

"This is Detective Lee," Ted said tersely.

"You have less than forty-eight hours to get him out of there. There are four men, including me," Peter said, offering them not only information but his alliance. He knew he had to. For his own sake, as much as hers and Sam's. It was all he could do for them.

"Morgan, is that you?" It was the only one it could be. Ted knew he was talking to him. Peter didn't confirm or deny it. He had more important things to do. He gave Ted the address of the house in Tahoe, and described the layout of the house to him.

"Right now, they're keeping the boy in the back room. I'll do what I can to help you, but they may kill me too."

Ted asked him a question then, and desperately wanted an answer. The call was being recorded, like the others, asking for the ransom. "Is Phillip Addison behind this?"

Peter hesitated and then answered, "Yes, he is." It was all over for him then. He knew that wherever he went, Addison would find him and kill him. But Waters and the others would probably do it for him long before that.

"I won't forget this," Ted said, and meant it, as Fernanda watched, not daring to take her eyes off him. She knew something was happening, and she wasn't sure yet what it was, if it was bad or good.

"That's not why I'm doing this," Peter said sadly. "I'm doing it for Sam . . . and for her . . . tell her I'm sorry." And with that, he hung up, tossed the cell phone onto the seat beside him, and took off for the store, where he bought enough beer and tequila to keep them drunk forever. And when he walked into the house, he was carrying four bags of Chinese food, and he was smiling. He had a sudden feeling of freedom. And for once in his life, he had done the right thing.

"What the fuck took you so long?" Stark asked him, but he mellowed as soon as he saw the food and beer, and three bottles of good tequila.

"They took a goddamn hour to give me the

food," Peter complained, and then went to check on Sam. He was asleep in his room. Peter stood staring at him for a long moment, and then turned and walked out of the room. He had no idea when they'd come. He just hoped it would be soon.

Chapter 18

"What happened?" Fernanda asked Ted, looking panicked, as soon as Peter Morgan ended the call.

Ted looked at her and nearly cried. "They're in Tahoe. Morgan told us where they are." It was the break they needed. The only hope they had.

"Oh my God," she whispered. "Why did he do that?"

"He said he was doing it for Sam and for you. He said to tell you he was sorry." She nodded, wondering what had made him change his mind. But whatever it was, she was grateful he had. He had saved her son's life. Or tried to at least.

Everything moved into high gear then. Ted made what seemed like a thousand calls. He called the captain, Rick Holmquist, and the

heads of three SWAT teams. He called the police chief and sheriff in Tahoe, and told them
not to move in. They agreed to defer to both
the FBI and an SFPD SWAT team. Everything had to be executed with the precision of
open heart surgery, and Ted told her they
would be ready to move to Tahoe by the following afternoon. She thanked him and went
to tell Will, who burst into tears.

Ted was back on the phone with a dozen
people the next morning when she got up,
and Will had just finished his breakfast by the
time Ted was ready to leave. Ted told her
there were twenty-five men already on their
way to Tahoe. The FBI was sending an eight-
man commando team, eight more for the
command post, and there were another eight
on the SWAT team, in addition to Rick and
himself. And there would be another twenty
or so local law enforcement officers joining
the task force once they got there. Rick was
taking his best men from the city, marksmen,
sharpshooters, and sending a plane with two
pilots. Ted had chosen their best SWAT team,
and he was sending the hostage negotiator
with them. He was still planning to leave four
men with her and Will.

"Take me with you," she said to him, looking desperate. "I want to be there too." He

hesitated, not sure it was the right thing to do. A lot could happen, and a lot could go wrong with that many men involved. It was going to be a delicate business getting the boy out of the house, even with Morgan's help. Sam could even be killed by the police when they broke in on the others. The likelihood of not being able to get Sam out alive under these circumstances was great. And if the worst happened, he didn't want the boy's mother there. "Please," she said with tears rolling down her cheeks. And even though he knew better, Ted was unable to resist.

She didn't tell Will where she was going. She ran upstairs and got a pair of hiking boots and a sweater, and she told Will she was going out with Ted. She didn't say where. She told him to stay inside with the men. Before he could object, she had run out the front door, and a moment later, she sped away with Ted. He had called Rick Holmquist, and he was driving up himself with four additional special agents and the commando team. There were going to be enough men in Tahoe to start their own police force. The captain had told Ted to keep him informed, and Ted had said he would.

Fernanda was silent as they rolled across the Bay Bridge. They had driven another half-hour before Ted finally spoke to her. He still had qualms about having let her come along, but it was too late to change his mind. And as they drove north, she started to relax and so did he. They talked about some of the things Father Wallis had said. She was trying to do what he had suggested, and to believe that Sam was in God's hands. Ted told her that what had turned it around for them was Morgan's call.

"Why do you suppose he did that?" Fernanda asked, looking puzzled. The fact that he had said he was doing it for her made no sense to her, or Ted.

"People do funny things sometimes," Ted said quietly. "When you least expect them to." He had seen it before. "Maybe he doesn't care about the money after all. If they catch on, they'll kill him for sure." And if they didn't, they were going to have to put him in the witness relocation and protection program when he got out. If they sent him to prison, he was as good as dead. But he might be anyway if the others caught on.

"You haven't been home all week," Fernanda commented as they drove past Sacramento.

Ted looked at her and smiled. "You sound like my wife."

"This must be hard on her," Fernanda said sympathetically, and he didn't comment for a long time. "I'm sorry, I didn't mean to pry. I was just thinking, it must be hard on a marriage."

He nodded. "It is. Or it was a long time ago. We're used to it now. We've been married since we were kids. I've known Shirley since we were fourteen."

"That's a long time," Fernanda said with a smile. "I was twenty-two when I married Allan. We were married for seventeen years."

He nodded. Talking about their lives and respective spouses helped to pass the time. They almost felt like old friends now as they drove along. They had spent a lot of time together, in tough circumstances, in the past week. It had been incredibly hard on her.

"It must have been rough on you when . . . when your husband died," Ted said sympathetically.

"It was. It's been hard on the kids, especially Will. I think he feels his father let us down." It was going to be yet another blow when she sold the house.

"Boys that age need a man around." As Ted said it, he was thinking of his own. He hadn't been around a lot either when his sons were Will's age. It was one of his biggest regrets about his life. "I was never home when my kids were young. It's the price you pay for this kind of work. One of them."

"They had their mom," she said gently, trying to make him feel better about it, but she could see it weighed on him.

"That's not enough," he said sternly, and then looked apologetically at her. "I'm sorry, I didn't mean that the way it sounds."

"Yes, you did. Maybe you're right. I'm doing the best I can, but most of the time I feel like it's not enough. Allan didn't give me much choice in the matter. He made his mind up on his own."

It was easy talking to her. Easier than he wanted it to be, as they sped north toward her younger son. "Shirley and I almost split up when the kids were small. We talked about it for a while, and decided it was a bad idea." He found it strangely easy to confide in her.

"It probably was. It's nice that you stayed together." She admired him for it, and his wife.

"Maybe so. We're good friends."

"I hope so after twenty-eight years." He had told her that several days before. He was forty-seven years old, and had been married to his wife since he was nineteen. Fernanda was impressed by that. It seemed like a long time to her, and a powerful bond.

And then he volunteered something she hadn't expected to hear from him. "We out-grew each other a long time ago. I didn't really see it till a few years ago. I just woke up one day, and realized that whatever it used to be was over. I guess what we have instead is all right. We're friends."

"Is that enough?" she asked him with a strange expression. These were like deathbed confidences, she just hoped that the deathbed wouldn't be her son's. She couldn't bear think-ing of it, where they were going, or why. It was easier talking about him than talking about Sam at this point.

"Sometimes," he said honestly, thinking about Shirley again, and what they did and didn't share, and never had. "Sometimes it's nice coming home to a friend. Sometimes it's not enough. We don't talk much anymore. She has her own life. So do I."

"Then why do you stay together, Ted?" Rick Holmquist had been asking him the same thing for years.

"Lazy, tired, lonely. Too scared to move on. Too old."

"That you're not. What about loyal? And decent? And maybe more in love with her than you think. You don't give yourself much credit for why you stayed. Or why she wants you to. She probably loves you more than you think too," Fernanda said generously.

"I don't think so," he said, shaking his head, as he thought about what she'd said.

"I think we've stayed because everyone expected us to. Her parents, mine. Our kids. I'm not even sure our kids would care anymore. They're all grown up and gone. In a funny way, she's like my family now. I feel like I'm living with my sister sometimes. It's comfortable, I guess." Fernanda nodded. It didn't sound so bad to her. She couldn't even imagine going out and finding someone else now. After seventeen years, she was so used to Allan, she couldn't imagine sleeping with another man. Although she knew that one day she might. But no time soon. "What about you? What are you going to do now?" The conversation was on dangerous ground, but she knew it wouldn't go anywhere it shouldn't. He wasn't that kind of man. In all the days he had been in her house, he had been nothing but respectful and kind.

"I don't know. I feel like I'm going to be married to Allan forever, whether he's here or not."

"Last time I looked," Ted said gently, "it was 'not.' "

"Yeah, I know. That's what my daughter

says. She reminds me regularly that I should be going out. It's the last thing on my mind. I've been too busy, worrying about paying Allan's debts. That's going to take a long time. Unless I get a terrific price for the house. Our lawyer is going to declare bankruptcy to clean up his business debts. When I first realized what he'd done, I nearly died."

"It's a shame he couldn't have hung on to some of it," Ted said, and she nodded, but she seemed remarkably philosophical about it.

"I was never really comfortable with the money he made." She smiled at what she said then. "It sounds crazy, but I always thought it was too much. It didn't seem right." And then she shrugged. "It was fun for a while." She told him about the two Impressionist paintings she had bought, and he was suitably impressed.

"It must be amazing to own something like that."

"It was. For a couple of years. They were bought by a museum in Belgium. Maybe I'll visit them one day." She didn't seem unhappy to have given them up, which seemed noble of her, to him. All she seemed to care about with real passion were her kids. More than anything, he was impressed by what a good mother she was. And she had probably been a good wife to Allan too, more than he deserved, as far as Ted was concerned. But he didn't say that to her. He didn't think it was appropriate for him to do so.

They rode in silence again for a while, and when they passed Ikeda's restaurant and grocery store, he asked her if she wanted to stop and get something to eat, but she said she didn't. She'd hardly eaten all week.

"Where are you going to move when you sell the house?" He wondered if, after something like this, she would leave town. He wouldn't have blamed her if she did.

"Maybe Marin. I'm not going far. The kids won't want to leave their friends." He felt foolish, but hearing her say it, he was relieved.

"I'm glad," he said, glancing at her, and she seemed surprised.

"You'll have to come and have dinner with me and the kids sometime." She was grateful to him for all he'd done. But as far as he was concerned, he hadn't done it yet. And he knew that if things went badly in Tahoe, and Sam was killed, more than likely she'd never want to see him again. He would be part of the memory of a nightmarish time. And perhaps already was. But he knew that if he never saw her again, he'd be sad. He liked talking to her, and the gentle, easy way she handled things, the kindness she showed his men. Even in the midst of the kidnapping, she'd been thoughtful and considerate to all of them. Whatever money her husband had made had never gone to her head, even if it had to his. And Ted had the distinct feeling she was anxious to leave their house. It was time.

They passed Auburn a little while later, and for the rest of the ride, she didn't say much to him. All she could think of was Sam.

"It's going to be all right," he said softly as they drove over the Donner Pass, and she turned to him looking worried.

"How can you be sure?" The truth was, he couldn't, and they both knew it.

"I can't. But I'm going to do my damnedest to see to it," he promised her. But she knew that anyway. He had been committed to protecting them since it all began.

At the house in Tahoe, the men were getting restless. They had been arguing with each other all day. Stark wanted to call Fernanda back that afternoon and threaten her. Waters said they should wait till that night. And Peter cautiously suggested that they give her one last day to get the money together, and call tomorrow. Jim Free didn't seem to care, all he wanted to do was get his money and get the hell out. It was a hot day, and they all drank a lot of beer, except Peter, who was trying to keep a clear head, and slipped away regularly to check on Sam.

Peter had no way of checking without the others knowing, but he was wondering when Ted's men were going to make their move. He knew that when it happened it would be fast and furious, and all he could do was his best to save Sam.

The others were all drunk by late that afternoon. Even Waters. And by six o'clock they were all asleep in the living room. Peter sat watching them, and then went to the back of the house to Sam's room. He said nothing to the boy, lay on the bed next to him, and fell asleep with his arms around him, dreaming of his daughters.

Chapter 19

When Ted and Fernanda got to Tahoe, the local police had taken over a small motel for the entire task force. It was run-down and ramshackle, and had been empty for the most part, even during the summer season. The few guests staying there had been content to leave with a small stipend paid to get them out. And two of the cops were bringing food in from a nearby fast-food place by the vanload. Everything was set up. The FBI had sent eight commandos trained in hostage release and kidnappings, and a SWAT team that had come up from the city was similarly trained. The local cops were swarming, but had not yet been advised of exactly what was happening. There were more than fifty men waiting when Ted got out of the car and looked around. They were going to have to handpick who went in and how they did it. A local captain was handling equipment, road blocks, and local officers. And Rick was in charge of the entire operation, and had set up shop in a room next to the motel office, which he had left for the local captain. There was an entire fleet of communication trucks, and Ted saw Rick come out of one of them, as Fernanda followed him from the car. The organized chaos around them was both terrifying and reassuring at the same time.

"How's it going?" Ted asked Rick, and both men looked tired. Ted hadn't had more than two hours' sleep consecutively in days, and Rick had been up since the night before. Sam was becoming a sacred cause to those who knew about him, which was a comfort to his mother. And Ted had asked one of the officers to set up a room for her.

"We're almost there," Rick said, glancing at her, and she nodded with a tired smile. She looked like she was holding up, but barely. This was beyond stressful for her, although talking to Ted about other things on the drive up had helped for a brief time.

Ted went to get her settled. There were a psychologist from the SWAT team and a female officer waiting in the room for her. And when he had left her with them, Ted came back to Rick in the room he was using as the command post. They had a mountain of sandwiches and boxed salads on a table along the wall, and a diagram of the house and a map of the area taped to the wall above it. The food provided was unusually wholesome, as neither the FBI commandos nor the SWAT team ate fatty foods, sugar, or caffeine, as it slowed them down after the initial high, and they were meticulous about what they ate. The local police captain was sitting in with them, and the head of the SWAT team had just walked out of the room to see his men. It looked like the invasion of Normandy to Ted as he grabbed a sandwich and sat down in a chair, while Rick stood next to him. It looked like they were planning a war. It was a major rescue mission, and the combined brain and manpower was impressive. The house they were setting their sights on was less than two miles down the road. They were putting out nothing over the radios, in case the kidnappers had any kind of monitoring devices, and so the press wouldn't pick it up and blow it for them. They were taking every precaution they could to keep the operation sterile, but in spite of that, Rick looked worried as he glanced at the diagram with Ted. They had gone to the local surveyor's office to get the map of the house, and had blown it up to an enormous size.

"Your informant says the kid is at the back of the house," Rick said, pointing to a room at the back, not far from the property line. "We can get him out, but there's a cliff right behind them, it's straight up from there. I can get four guys down the rock face, but I can't get them back up fast enough, and if they've got the kid with them, they'll be too exposed." He pointed to the front of the house then. "And we've got a driveway the length of a football field on the way out. I can't get in with a chopper or they'll hear us. And if we blow up the house, we're liable to kill the boy."

The head of the SWAT team and the FBI commandos had been conferring for the past two hours, and they hadn't solved the problem yet. But Ted knew they would. They had no way of contacting Peter Morgan to set up a plan with him. They were going to have to make all their decisions on their own, for better or worse. Ted was relieved that Fernanda wasn't in the room with them to listen to the dangers they were outlining. It would have driven her over the edge. They were brainstorming out loud, and so far everything they'd come up with had a high likelihood of killing the boy.

Ted wasn't convinced that wouldn't have happened anyway. With no ransom forthcoming, it was almost certain that they were planning to kill Sam. Even with the ransom successfully delivered, there had been that risk. Sam was old enough to identify them, which made it risky to let him go, even if they got their money. Addison had been aware of that as well, which was why he had sent Peter to Tahoe to keep an eye on the others. In the end, it would have been easier for them to kill him than to return him alive. And with no ransom paid, they had every reason to kill him and dispose of him when they left. Rick and the others in the room with him were verbalizing their many fears. And after another hour of doing so, Rick turned to Ted.

"You realize what the chances are of our getting him out of there alive, don't you? Slim to none. With the emphasis on none." He was being honest with his friend. There was a high probability that Sam was going to die, if he wasn't already dead.

"Then get more guys up here," Ted said tersely, looking angrily at Rick. They hadn't come this far in order to lose the kid. Although they all knew they could. But Ted was on a mission to save him, as was Rick and everyone in the room, and outside. Sam was their mission.

"We have a small army here," Rick bellowed at him. "For chrissake, did you look at how many are outside? We don't need more guys, we need a fucking miracle," Rick said between clenched teeth. Sometimes when they got angry at each other, they did their best work.

"Then get one, make it happen. Get smarter guys in here. You can't just throw up your hands and let them kill this kid," Ted said, looking anguished.

"Does that look like what's happening to you, you asshole?" Rick shouted at him, and there were so many other people talking in the room, you couldn't even hear him yell, or Ted yell back. They were going at it like two angry army sergeants, when the head of the SWAT team came up with another plan, but they all agreed it wouldn't work. It would leave the rescuers vulnerable to open fire from the house. Peter had picked the perfect place. It was damn near impossible to get the boy out of the house and off the property, and one thing Rick already knew, and Ted was coming to understand, a lot of men were liable to die that night, rescuing one boy. But that was what they had to do. The others knew it too.

"I can't just walk my guys into a slaughter," the head of the SWAT team said unhappily to Ted. "We've got to give them a halfway decent chance to get the kid, and get out again."

"I know," Ted said, looking miserable. It wasn't going well, and he was glad Fernanda wasn't in the room to hear it. At nine o'clock that night, he and Rick walked outside. They still didn't have a plan that worked, and he was beginning to fear they never would, or not in time. They had all agreed hours earlier they had to get Sam out by dawn. Once the kidnappers were awake on the following morning, the risk would be too great, and from everything they knew, they didn't have another day. They were planning to call Fernanda sometime the next day for the final word. This was it. Dawn was in nine hours, and time was running out. "Shit, I hate this," Ted said, looking at Rick, as he leaned against a tree. No one had come up with anything that worked. They were sending the plane up for reconnaissance in another hour, using infrared and heat-seeking devices, neither of which would work inside the house. One of the communications trucks was devoted entirely to them.

"I hate this too," Rick said quietly. They were both running out of fire and steam. It was going to be a long night.

"What the hell am I going to tell her?" Ted said, looking agonized. "That the best SWAT team we've got, and yours, can't save her kid?" He couldn't even imagine telling her the boy was dead. And he might already be. Things were not looking good, to say the least.

"You're falling in love with her, aren't you?" Rick said out of the blue, and Ted stared up at him as though he were insane. It wasn't the kind of thing men said to each other, but once in a while they did. And Rick just had.

"Are you nuts? I'm a cop, for chrissake. She's a victim, so is her son." He looked outraged at the thought, and angry at Rick again for suggesting it. But his friend wasn't fooled, even if Ted was fooling himself, which Rick was sure he was.

"She's also a woman, and you're a man. She's beautiful and vulnerable. You've been staying at her house for a week. You didn't have to do that, and you did. You're also a guy who hasn't slept with his wife for about five years, if my memory is correct on that, since the last time we talked about it. You're human, for God's sake. Just don't let it interfere with your job. A lot of guys are putting their lives on the line

here. Don't send a lot of guys in to get slaugh-
tered, if we can't get them or the kid out
again." Ted hung his head, and looked up at
Rick again a minute later. There were tears in
his eyes and he hadn't admitted or denied what
Rick had said about Fernanda. He wasn't sure
himself if he was right. But it had occurred to
him that night. He was as worried about her
as he was about her son.

"There has to be a way to get him out alive"
was all Ted said.

"Some of that's going to depend on the kid,
and the guy you've got inside. We can't control it all." Not to mention luck, and fate, and
the other kidnappers, and the skill of the men
who went in. There were so many unpre-
dictable elements, none of which could be
controlled. Sometimes you had everything
running against you and you came up lucky.
Other times, everything was lined up perfectly, and it all went wrong. It was the luck of
the draw.

"What about her?" Rick asked quietly again.
"How does she feel?" Rick meant about Ted,
not her son. It was a shorthand they both understand, born of many years together.

"I don't know." Ted looked miserable. "I'm
a married man."

"You and Shirley should have gotten divorced years ago," Rick said honestly. "You both deserve better than you've got."

"She's my best friend."

"You're not in love with her. I'm not sure you ever were. You grew up together, you were like brother and sister when I met you. It was like one of those arranged marriages they used to do a hundred years ago. Everyone expected you to get married, and it worked for them. So you did." Ted knew he wasn't wrong. Shirley's father had been his father's boss for most of his adult life, and they were so proud of him when he got engaged to her. He'd never gone out with other girls. Never thought of it. Until way too late. And then, out of sheer decency, he'd been faithful to her, and still was, which was rare for a cop. Their stressful lives and crazy schedules, rarely seeing their wives and families, or being on the same time clock with them, got them into a lot of trouble, and nearly had Ted a couple of times. Rick had always admired him for his iron will, iron pants he used to call it, when they worked together. He couldn't say as much for himself. But his own divorce had been a relief in the end. And now he had found a woman he really loved. He wanted the same for Ted. And if Fernanda was who he wanted, or was falling in love with, it was fine by him. He just hoped they didn't lose her kid. For her sake, as well as Ted's. It would be a tragedy she would never get over, nor forget, nor would he. And more than likely Ted would blame himself, if the mission wasn't a success. But Rick's commitment to get the kid out, and Ted's, had nothing to do with love. It was their job. The rest was gravy.

"She comes from a different world," Ted said, looking worried, not even sure yet himself what he felt for her, but afraid there was something to what Rick was saying, enough to think about. And he had more than once, although he had said nothing of it to her. "She's led a different life. Her husband made half a billion dollars, for chrissake. He was a smart guy," Ted said humbly, looking at his friend in the dark outside the motel. The others milling around were out of earshot.

"You're a smart guy too. And how smart was he? He lost it as fast as he made it, and killed himself, leaving his wife dead broke with three kids." There was truth in that. Ted had a lot more money in the bank than she did at the moment. His future was secure, and so were his kids. He had worked hard for that for nearly thirty years.

"She went to Stanford. I went to high school. I'm a cop."

"You're a good guy. She should be so lucky." They both knew Ted was a rarity in today's world. He was a good and decent man. Rick knew, and often admitted out of love for his old partner, that Ted was a better man than he. Ted never saw it that way, and had always defended Rick to the death. And sometimes had to. Rick had pissed a lot of people off before he left the department. That was just the way he was, and he had done it at the FBI too. He had a big mouth, and never hesitated to say what he thought. He was doing it now too, whether or not Ted wanted to hear it. Rick thought he should. Even if it upset him or made him angry. "I want you to be lucky too," Rick said kindly. "You deserve it." He didn't want to see his friend die a lonely man one day. And they both knew that's where he was headed, and had been for years.

"I can't just walk out on Shirley," Ted said unhappily. He felt guilty already, but also incredibly attracted to Fernanda.

"Don't go there yet. See what happens after this mess is over. One day Shirley may walk out on you. She's smarter than you are. And if she meets the right guy one day, I've always thought she'd be the first one out the door. I'm surprised she hasn't done it." Ted nodded, he had thought of that too. In some ways, she was less attached to the idea of their marriage than he was. She was just lazy, and she said it herself, although she loved him too. But she had said several times recently that she wouldn't have minded living alone, might have preferred it, and felt as though she did anyway, as little as they saw each other. And he felt that way too. It was a lonely life with her. They no longer liked any of the same things or people. The only thing that had held them together for twenty-eight years was their kids. And they were gone, and had been for several years. "You don't need to figure it out tonight. Have you said anything to Fernanda?" Rick was curious about it, and had been since they met her. There was an easy intimacy between her and Ted that had an innocence to it, and assumed a bond neither knew they had. It was a kind of natural closeness that had hit Rick right away. She seemed like the perfect woman for him, to Rick as well as Ted. Ted had felt it, but had never said anything about it to her. He wouldn't have dared, or even wanted to, in the circumstances in which they'd met. And he had no idea if she felt anything for him, except for the job he was doing for her, in trying to protect her and her kids. And with Sam having gotten kidnapped anyway, it was certainly no victory for him, in his eyes at least.

"I haven't said anything," Ted confirmed. "This is hardly the time." They both agreed on that. And he didn't even know if he'd have the guts to when it was over. Somehow, it didn't seem right to him. It was taking unfair advantage of her.

"I think she likes you," Rick suggested, and Ted grinned. They sounded like two kids in high school, or younger. Two boys shooting marbles on the playground at recess, talking about a girl in sixth grade. But it was a relief talking about Ted's feelings for Fernanda, instead of Sam's life-and-death situation for a few minutes. Rick and Ted needed the relief.

"I like her too," Ted said softly, thinking of the way she looked when they talked for hours in the dark, or she fell asleep on the floor next to him, waiting for news of Sam. His heart had melted then.

"Then go for it," Rick whispered. "Life is short." They both knew that, had had ample proof of it over the years, and would again.

"That's for sure," Ted said with a sigh, and moved away from the tree he'd been leaning on while they talked. It had been an interesting conversation, but they had more important things to do. It had been a good break for both of them. Ted particularly. He liked hearing what Rick thought, about all of it. He had unlimited respect for him.

Rick followed him back inside, thinking about what Ted had admitted to him, and as soon as they walked in the door of the command post, they both got swept up in the discussions and arguments again. It was midnight finally when they all agreed on a plan. It wasn't foolproof by any means, but it was the best they could do. The head of the SWAT team said they would start moving toward the house just before dawn, and he suggested to everyone that they try to get some sleep in the meantime. Ted left the office at one o'clock and headed toward Fernanda's room, to see how she was doing.

She was alone in the room when he walked past. The door was closed, but he could see through the window that the lights were on, and she was lying on the bed, her eyes were open, and she was staring into space. And he waved at her. She got up instantly, and opened the door to him, afraid the kidnappers might have called. Her phone lines were being forwarded to a communications truck outside.

"What's happening?" she asked anxiously, and he was quick to reassure her. The hours

since they'd gotten there had seemed interminable to her, and to all of them. The teams
were itching to get going, and tackle what
they had come here to do. Many of them were
wandering around outside in body armor, and
assault suits, and camouflage.

"We're moving soon."

"When?" Her eyes searched his.

"Right before dawn."

"Have you heard anything from the house?"
she asked anxiously. There were still policemen
there with Will, manning her phones, but Ted
knew that as recently as an hour before, no further calls had come in from Peter, nor his colleagues. Ted was sure there was no way he
could call them. He had done all he could do.
And if they managed to save Sam at all, it
would be in great part thanks to him. Without
his lead, the boy would be dead for sure. Now
it was up to them to take the ball he'd handed
them and run like hell. And they would. Soon.

"He hasn't called again," Ted answered her,
and she nodded. News of Sam at this point was
too much to hope for. "Everything is quiet."
They had a PG&E truck stationed near the
driveway to the house, with communications
and surveillance equipment in it, and there had
been no movement there either. In fact, one of
their commandos sitting on top of a hill with

infrared telescopic binoculars said that the house had been dark for hours. Ted hoped they'd all still be sleeping when they got there. The element of surprise was essential, even if it meant no help from Peter. That would have been too much to ask for. "Are you all right?" Ted asked her quietly, trying not to think of his conversation with Rick earlier that night. He didn't want to say or do anything foolish, now that he had admitted it to him, which made his feelings for Fernanda seem that much more real. She nodded, and seemed to hesitate as he watched her.

"I want this to be over," she said, looking frightened, "but I'm afraid for it to be." Right now they could still assume that Sam was alive, or at least they hoped so. Earlier that night, she had put in a call to Father Wallis, and found quiet comfort in his reassurance.

"It'll be over soon," Ted promised her, but he didn't want to assure her that everything would be fine. They were empty words at this point, and she knew it. For better or worse, they would be moving soon.

"Are you going with them?" Her eyes searched his, and he nodded.

"Only as far as the base of the driveway." The rest was up to the SWAT team and FBI commandos. One of the prep teams had already set up a nest for them in the bushes. It was shrouded in foliage, but at least they'd be near when the shit hit the fan, and it would for sure.

"Can I come with you?" He shook his head firmly, although her eyes pleaded with him. There was no way he could allow her to. It was far too dangerous, he couldn't let her do it. If things went wrong, she could get caught in crossfire, or hit with rifle or machine-gun fire if the kidnappers tried to escape, and hit the nest with a blaze of fire on their way out. It was impossible to predict. "Why don't you try to get some sleep?" he suggested, although he suspected it would be futile for her.

"Will you tell me when you leave?" She wanted to know what was happening and when, which was understandable. It was her son they were risking their lives for. And she wanted to be psychically linked to him when they went, willing him to live. Ted nodded, and promised to advise her when the teams moved out, and then she looked panicked. She had come to rely on him. He was her guide through the unfamiliar jungles of fear. "Where will you be till then?"

He pointed. "My room is two doors down." He was sharing it with three other men from the city. And Rick was right next door.

Fernanda looked at Ted strangely for a minute, as though she wanted him to step into her room. And they just stood there for a long moment, looking at each other, as Ted felt as though he could read her mind. "Do you want me to come in for a few minutes?" She nodded. There was nothing surreptitious or clandestine about it. The curtains were wide open, the lights were on, and anyone could see into the room.

Ted followed Fernanda into the room, and sat down in the only chair in the room, while Fernanda sat on the bed and looked nervously at him. It was going to be a long night for both of them, and there was no way that she was going to sleep. Her child's life was on the line, and if the worst happened, she wanted to at least spend the night thinking of him. She couldn't even imagine what she was going to tell the other children, if something happened. Ashley didn't even know that Sam had been kidnapped. And after losing their father six months before, she couldn't begin to imagine the blow it would be to them if Sam was killed. She had talked to Will a few hours before. He was trying to be strong, but by the end of the conversation, they were both in tears. In spite of all that, Ted thought she was holding up remarkably. He didn't think he could have kept himself together as staunchly as she had, if it had been one of his kids.

"I don't suppose there's any chance you'll get some sleep?" Ted smiled at her. He was every bit as exhausted as she was, but it was different for him. It was his job.

"I don't think so," she said honestly. It was only a matter of hours now before the SWAT team and FBI commandos began their raid on the house. "I wish we'd heard from them again."

"So do I." Ted was being equally honest with her. "But maybe it's a good sign that we didn't. I think they were probably planning to call you tomorrow and see if you had the funds for them." A hundred million dollars. It still seemed incredible to him. Even more so that a few years before, her husband could have paid it with ease. It seemed miraculous now that something like this had never happened to him. And in that case, Ted was fairly sure that Fernanda would have been the victim, and not the kids. "Did you eat anything?" There had been cartons of sandwiches circulating for hours, stacks of pizzas, and enough doughnuts to kill all of them. Coffee had been the mainstay that evening for everyone but the SWAT teams, and gallons of Coca-Cola. They all needed the caffeine as they formulated their plans. And now probably most of them were finding it impossible to sleep. Everyone was living on adrenaline. Fernanda was just functioning on anxiety and terror, as she sat wideeyed on the bed looking at him, wondering if life would ever be normal again.

"Do you mind sitting here with me?" she asked sadly, looking like a kid herself. In a few weeks it was going to be her birthday, and she just hoped Sam would be alive to celebrate it with her.

"No, I like it." He smiled at her. "You're good company."

"Not lately," she said, sighing deeply, without even being aware of it. "I feel like I haven't been good company in years. Months anyway." It had been so long since she'd had an adult conversation, or a quiet evening out to dinner with her husband, laughing and talking about ordinary things. Ted was the closest she'd come to that in a long time. And there was nothing normal about these days either. She seemed to be constantly engulfed by trauma and tragedy. First Allan, and everything he had left in his wake. And now Sam.

"You've been through some tough stuff this year," Ted said with admiration. "I think I'd be on a respirator by now in your shoes." Even if things turned out all right with Sam, and he hoped they would, Ted knew she still had a lot of big changes ahead. And after everything Rick had said earlier that night, Ted was wondering if he did too. What Rick had said about Ted's marriage to Shirley hadn't fallen on deaf ears. Particularly that she might leave him one day. Although he never would have, the thought had occurred to Ted too. She was a lot less bound by tradition than he was, and especially in recent years, danced to her own tune.

"Sometimes I think my life will never be normal again." But then again, when had it been? Allan's rocketlike rise to financial stardom hadn't been normal either. The past several years had been insane for all of them. And now this. "I was going to start looking for a house in Marin this summer." But now, if Sam were gone, God forbid, she didn't know what she'd do. Maybe move somewhere else, to escape the memories.

"That's going to be a big change for you and the kids," he said about their moving to a smaller house. "How do you think they'll feel about it?"

"Scared. Angry. Unhappy. Excited. All the things most kids feel when they move. It'll be weird for all of us. But maybe it'll be good." As long as she still had three children, and not two. It was all she could think of now. And eventually they fell into an easy silence. He tiptoed out of the room around three o'clock when she had finally drifted off to sleep. He managed to get a couple of hours of sleep himself after that, lying on the floor of his room. There were two other men on the room's two beds, and he didn't care where he slept by then. He could have slept standing up, Rick always said about him. And once in a while he damn near did.

The head of the SWAT team came to wake him at five o'clock in the morning. He woke with a start and was instantly alert. The other two men were up and halfway out the door, as Ted got to his feet. He washed his face and brushed his teeth, and quickly ran his hands through his hair, as the SWAT team captain asked him if he wanted to ride with them, and Ted said he'd follow them so he didn't get in their way.

Ted passed Fernanda's room on the way out, and saw that she had woken up and was wandering around the room. She came to the door the moment she saw him and stood looking at him. Her eyes were begging him to take her along, and he squeezed her shoulder gently with one hand as their eyes met and held. He knew almost everything she was feeling, or thought he did, and wanted to reassure her. But there were no promises he could make. They were going to do their best for her and Sam. He hated to leave her, but knew he had to. It would be light soon.

"Good luck." She couldn't tear her eyes off his, and she was desperate to go with him. She wanted to be as close as she could be to Sam.

"It'll be okay, Fernanda. I'll radio you the minute we've got him."

She couldn't even speak, as she nodded, and watched him disappear into a car and drive away down the road toward her son.

And at that exact moment, three of his commandos were lowering themselves slowly down the rock face behind the house, on ropes, dressed all in black like cat burglars, with their faces blacked out, and their weapons strapped to them.

Ted stopped the car a quarter of a mile before the driveway, and concealed it in a cluster of trees. He walked silently in the darkness past the scouts in the bushes to the nest the SWAT team had cleared for them. Ted glanced at the men all around him carrying Heckler & Koch MP5s. They were 223mm fully automatic machine guns, used by both the SWAT team and the FBI commandos. There were five other men in the nest with him, as he put on a bulletproof vest, and put on a set of headphones so he could listen to the communications truck, and as he listened to them talking and looked into the darkness, there was a sudden stirring behind him and one of the scouts slipped into the nest, wearing body armor and camouflage. He turned to see if it was one of his men or one of Rick's agents, and he noticed that it was a woman. He didn't recognize her at first, and then realized who it was. It was Fernanda wearing the gear of one of the scouts. She had actually gotten herself there and had conned someone into believing she was a member of the local police, and they had handed her the gear. She'd put it on at lightning speed. She was right there with him, where she shouldn't be, in danger, in the front lines, or way too close to them. He was about to give her hell and send her back. But it was too late, the operation was under way, and he knew how badly she wanted to be there when they got Sam out, if they did. He gave her a fierce look of disapproval, shook his head, and then relented without a word, unable to blame her. He held her hand tightly in his own, as she crouched down beside him, and they silently waited for his men to bring Sam home to his mom.

Chapter 20

Peter lay sleeping next to Sam until five o'clock that morning, and then as though some deep primal instinct told him to wake up, he opened his eyes and slowly stirred. Sam was still asleep beside him, with his head on Peter's shoulder. And the same inexplicable intuition told him to untie Sam's hands and feet. They kept him that way all the time so he couldn't escape. Sam had gotten used to it and come to accept it in the last week. He had learned that he could trust Peter more than the others. And as Peter untied the knots, Sam rolled over and whispered one word, "Mom."

Peter smiled at him, and got up, and stood looking out the window. It was still dark outside, but the sky was more charcoal now than inky. And he knew that soon the sun would be coming up over the hill. Another day. Endless

hours of waiting. He knew that they were going to call Fernanda, and kill the boy if she
didn't have the money for them. They still
thought she was holding out on them and
playing games. Killing the boy meant nothing
to them. And by the same token, if they had
any idea what he'd done, nor would killing
him. He no longer cared. He had traded his
life for Sam's. If he was able to escape with
him, it would be a mercy, but he didn't expect
that to happen. Trying to flee with the boy
might slow them down and put Sam at greater
risk.

He was still standing at the window, when
he heard a sound that sounded like the first
stirring of a bird, and then a single pebble flew
toward him and landed with a soft thud in the
dirt. He looked up and almost beyond his vi-
sion, he saw a stirring, and as he looked again,
three dark forms were sliding down the rocks
above them on black ropes. There was nothing to signal their arrival, and yet he knew
they were there and felt his heart pound. He
opened the window soundlessly and squinted
into darkness, watching them lower themselves down until they disappeared. He put a
hand over Sam's mouth so he didn't cry out,
and gently moved him, until the child's eyes

opened and Peter saw that he was awake. As soon as Sam looked at him, he put a finger to his lips. He pointed to the window as Sam watched him. He didn't know what was happening, but he knew that whatever it was, Peter was going to help him. He lay totally still on the bed, and realized that Peter had untied him, and he could move his hands and feet freely for the first time in days. Neither of them moved, and then Peter went back to the window. He saw nothing at first, and then he saw them, crouching in the darkness, ten feet behind the house. A single black-gloved hand beckoned, and he turned back and scooped Sam off the bed into his arms. He was afraid to open the window any wider than he had, and squeezed him through it. It was a short drop, and he knew the boy's arms and legs would be stiff. He was still holding him when he looked at him for the last time. Their eyes met and held for an endless moment, and it was the single greatest act of love Peter had ever committed as he dropped him, and then pointed, as Sam crawled like a baby into the bushes on all fours. He vanished from Peter's sight then, and then a black hand went up and beckoned him again. He stood staring at it, and heard a sound in the house behind him. He shook his head, closed the window, and lay back down on the bed. He didn't want to do anything to risk Sam.

As Sam crawled across the dirt and into the bushes, he had no idea where he was going. He just went in the direction that Peter had pointed, and as two hands reached out and grabbed him, he was pulled into the brush with such speed and force, it took his breath away. He looked up at his new captors, and whispered to the man who held him with blackened face and black nylon skullcap, "Are you bad guys or good guys?" The man who was holding him tightly to his chest nearly cried, he was so relieved to see him. It had gone like clockwork so far, but they still had a long way to go.

"Good guys," he whispered back. Sam nodded and wondered where his mom was, as the men around him signaled to each other, and flattened Sam down on the ground. He got a faceful of dirt, as long pink and yellow fingers began to streak across the sky. The sun hadn't come up yet, but the men knew it wouldn't be long.

They had already ruled out the possibility of pulling Sam back up the rock face on ropes, it would leave him too exposed to gunfire if his absence were discovered. He was a risk to all his captors now, save Peter, as he was old enough to identify them and tell the police what he heard and saw.

The SWAT team's only hope was getting him out down the driveway, but that left them all exposed as well. They were going to have to make their way out through the thick brush alongside it, and some of it was so dense that there was no way for them to pass. One of them had Sam firmly in his grasp, in powerful arms as they crouched, then ran, then shimmied their way along on their bellies on the ground. And all the while, they said nothing to each other or to Sam. They moved in a precise dance, and made their way as fast as they could, as the sun peeked over the hill, and began to crawl into the sky.

The sound Peter had heard was one of the men going to the bathroom. He heard the toilet flush, and then a swear word as whoever it was stubbed his toe on his way back to bed. And a few minutes later, he heard one of the others. Peter lay very still on the empty bed, and then decided to get up himself. He didn't want one of them coming into the room and discovering that Sam was gone.

He walked on bare feet into the living room, looked out the window cautiously, saw nothing, and sat down.

"You're up early," a voice said behind him. Peter gave a start and turned. It was Carlton Waters. He looked bleary-eyed after their excesses of the night before. "How's the kid?"

"He's fine," Peter said without much apparent interest. He had seen enough of these men to last a lifetime. Waters was bare chested, wearing only the jeans he had slept in, as he opened the refrigerator, foraging for something to eat, and emerged again with a beer.

"I'm going to call his mother when the others get up," Waters said, as he sat down on the couch across from Peter. "She'd better have the money ready for us, or we're done," he said matter-of-factly. "I'm not going to sit here forever, like a sitting duck, waiting for the fucking cops to show up. She'd better get that into her head, if she's jerking us around."

"Maybe she doesn't have it," Peter said, and shrugged. "If not, we've wasted a lot of time." Peter knew the score but Waters didn't.

"Your guy wouldn't be going to all this trouble if she didn't," Waters said, and then got up to look out the window. The sky was pink and gold by then, and there was a clear view of the first turn in the driveway, and as he looked at it, he stiffened, and ran out on the porch. He had seen something move and disappear.

"Fuck!" he said, running back in for his shotgun, and shouted for the others.

"What's wrong?" Peter asked, getting up out of his chair and looking concerned.

"I'm not sure." The other two had emerged sleepily by then, and each of them grabbed one of the machine guns as Peter's heart sank. There was no way to warn the men who were making their way down the driveway on their bellies with Sam. They hadn't gone far enough yet, Peter knew, to be safe.

Waters signaled to Stark and Free to get outside, and then like ghosts they saw them. Peter could see past Waters and the others to a man in black crouching and running, and he had something in his arms. The something he was carrying was Sam. Without warning, Waters fired at them, as Stark let off a machine-gun round.

Fernanda and Ted heard the sounds where they were sitting. They had no radio contact with the commandos. Fernanda squeezed her eyes shut and grabbed Ted's hand. There was no way for them to know what had happened, all they could do was wait. They had lookouts watching for them, but they had seen nothing yet. But from the rattle of the machine gun, he knew they were on their way with Sam. He didn't know if Peter would be with them. It would be riskier for the boy if he was.

"Oh God . . . oh God . . ." Fernanda whispered as they heard the guns go off again, "please . . . God . . ." Ted couldn't look at her. All he could do was stare into the dawning light, and hold her hand tightly in his own.

Rick Holmquist had taken a step out of the nest and was standing, as Ted turned to him. "Any sign of them yet?" Rick shook his head and the guns went off again. They both knew there were a dozen more commandos lining the driveway, in addition to the three who had gone in from the top. And beyond them were an army of men waiting to go in once Sam was out.

The gunfire stopped then and they heard nothing. Waters had turned to Peter and looked at him. "Where's the kid?" Something had aroused his suspicions, and Peter had no idea what it was.

"In the back room. Tied up."

"Is he?" Peter nodded. "Then why the fuck do I think I just saw a guy running across the driveway with him . . . tell me that . . . will you . . ." He slammed Peter backward against the wall of the house, with his shotgun just under Peter's neck, choking him, and both Stark and Free stared. Waters turned to Jim

Free then and told him to go in the back room and check, and he came back running seconds later.

"He's gone!" Stark looked panicked.

"I knew it . . . you sonofabitch . . ." Waters looked Peter dead in the eye as he slowly strangled him, and Malcolm Stark pointed the machine gun at him. "You called them, didn't you . . . you fucking pussy . . . what happened? Did you get scared? Felt sorry for the kid? You'd better start feeling sorry for me. You fucked us out of fifteen million dollars and yourself out of ten." Waters was blind with rage and fear. He knew that whatever happened, he wasn't going back to prison. They were going to have to kill him first.

"If she had the money, she'd have come up with it by now. Maybe Addison was wrong," Peter said hoarsely. It was the first time the others had heard his name.

"What the fuck do you know?" Waters turned back to look down the driveway as far as he could, and took a few steps away from the house as Stark ran after him, but there was nothing to see. The men who had Sam with them were halfway down by then. Rick had just caught a glimpse of them running, and he turned to signal Ted. And then at almost the same moment he saw Carlton Waters and

Malcolm Stark appear, and they started shooting at his men. Sam flew out of one man's
arms, and was grabbed by another. They
passed him along like a baton in a relay race, as
Stark and Waters just went on shooting at
whatever they could see.

Fernanda's eyes were open by then, and she
and Ted were staring down the driveway. She
looked just in time to see one of Rick's FBI
men take careful aim at Waters and bring him
down like a felled tree. He lay facedown on
the ground as Stark ran back to the house with
bullets flying all around him. Peter and Jim
Free had gone back into the house, and Stark
was screaming when he ran in.

"They got Carl!" he shouted, and then
turned on Peter, still holding the machine
gun. "You bastard, you killed him!" Stark said
as he fired a round at Peter. Peter had time to
look at him for only a fraction of an instant before the bullets sawed his body in half, and he
fell at Jim Free's feet.

"What are we going to do?" Jim Free asked
Stark.

"Get the fuck out of here, if we can." They
already knew the brush was too thick on either
side, and there was rock face behind them.
They had no equipment to climb it, and the
only way out was through the front and down

the driveway, which was littered with bodies now, not only Carl's but the men that he and Stark had shot, before they got him. There were three bodies lying on the ground between the front of the house and the road, and Sam saw them as the man carrying him ran. He was like a running back heading for the end zone. He just ran harder and suddenly he was within two feet of Ted and Fernanda. They could see Sam now, as the sun streaked across the road. She was sobbing as she watched him, and then suddenly Sam was in her arms and everyone was crying. His eyes were wide and he looked shell-shocked and filthy dirty, but he was screaming for his mom, and she couldn't make a sound.

"Mommy! . . . Mommy! . . . Mommy!!" She was crying so hard, she couldn't say anything to him, she just clutched him to her, as they both fell to the ground, and she lay there, holding her baby, loving him, as she had every second he was gone. They lay there together on the ground for a long time, and then Ted gently picked them both up, and signaled to some of the men behind them to take them away. He and Rick had been watching them, with tears running down their cheeks, as were the other officers. A paramedic came to help them then. He carried Sam to a waiting ambulance, with Fernanda running along beside him and holding Sam's hand. They were taking him to a local hospital to check him out.

"Who've we got left in there?" Ted asked Rick, wiping the tears from his face with the back of his hand.

"Three guys, I guess. Waters is down. That leaves Morgan and two others. I don't suppose Morgan is still alive by now . . . that leaves two . . ." Inevitably they would have killed him, when they discovered Sam was gone, and particularly after Waters's death. They had seen Stark run back in, but they also knew that there was nowhere for them to go. They had orders to shoot to kill all of them save Morgan, if he was still alive.

The marksmen and sharpshooters came in then, and a man from the SWAT team with a bullhorn. He told them to come out with their hands up, that they were coming in. There was no response, and no one walked down the driveway and into the clearing. And within two minutes, forty men headed up, with tear gas bombs, high-powered rifles, machine guns, and flash bangs, which when thrown, blinded you with light, disoriented you with an explosion and a burst of pellets that flew everywhere and stung like bee stings. The sound of the ammunition being emptied into the house was deafening, as Fernanda drove away in the ambulance with Sam. She saw Ted standing with Rick in the road as they left, wearing a bulletproof vest and talking to someone on the radio. He didn't see her go.

Fernanda heard from one of the FBI men at the motel that the siege at the house had lasted less than half an hour. Stark came out first, choking on tear gas, with bullets in one arm and one leg, and Jim Free came out right behind him. One of the agents told her later he'd been shaking from head to foot, squealing like a little pig. They were taken into custody on the spot, and would be sent back to prison for parole violations, pending trial. They would be tried for Sam's kidnap sometime within the next year, as well as the murder of two police officers and the FBI agent they'd brought down during the siege, and four more men when they'd kidnapped Sam from his house.

They found Peter Morgan's body when they went in. Rick and Ted watched them remove it. They saw the room Sam had been held captive in, and the window Peter had shoved him through for the escape. Everything they needed was there. The van, the guns, the ammunition. The house had been rented in Peter's name. And Ted knew all three convicts by name. The death of Carlton Waters was no loss to anyone. He had been on the street for just over two months. As had Peter. Two wasted lives, almost since the beginning, and ever since then.

Ted and Rick had lost three good men that day, as had the SWAT team, and along with the four they'd killed in San Francisco when they took Sam. Free and Stark would never see the light of day again, for kidnapping Sam, Ted hoped they would be put to death. It was all over for them. The trial was only going to be a formality, if there even was one. If they pled guilty, it would be simpler for everyone, although Ted knew they weren't likely to do that. They would drag it out as long as they could, and file endless appeals, just to live one more day in prison, for whatever that was worth to them.

Rick and Ted stayed on the crime scene until early that afternoon. Ambulances had come and gone, the dead commandos and agent were removed, photographs were taken, the injured seen to, it looked like a war zone. Frightened neighbors who'd been awakened by machine-gun fire at dawn clogged the road, straining to see what had happened, and asking for explanations. The police tried to reassure everyone, and attempted to keep traffic moving. Ted looked exhausted when he got back to the motel, and went to see Sam in Fernanda's room. They had just gotten back from the hospital, and remarkably, he was fine. There were still a lot of questions they wanted to ask him, but Ted wanted to see what kind of shape he was in first. He was lying in his mother's arms and clinging to her when Ted saw him. He was smiling up at her, had a humongous hamburger on a plate next to him, and was watching TV. And literally every cop and agent in the place had come in to see him and talk to him, or just ruffle his hair and leave again. They had laid their lives on the line for him, and lost friends to him. He was worth it. Men had died for him that day. But if they hadn't, Sam would have died instead. And the man who had made the difference ultimately, and helped save him, was dead too.

Fernanda couldn't take her hands off him, and she beamed at Ted as he walked in. He was filthy and tired, and had beard stubble all over his cheeks and chin. Rick had assured him he looked like a bum, when he left him to get something to eat. He said he had to make some calls to Europe.

"So, young man"—Ted grinned at him, as his eyes brushed Fernanda's—"it's good to see you again. I'd say you've been a real hero.

You're a mighty fine deputy." He didn't want
to question him just yet. He wanted to give
the kid a little time and room to breathe, but
there was a lot they wanted to ask him. He
was going to be seeing a lot of the police. "I
know your mom is very happy to see you."
And then as his voice went gruff again, he said
softly, "Me too." Like almost everyone else
who had been working night and day to find
him, he had cried often that day. And Sam
rolled over and smiled up at him, but he didn't
move an inch away from his mother.

"He said he was sorry," Sam said as his eyes
grew serious, and Ted nodded. He knew he
meant Peter Morgan. "I know. He said that to
me too."

"How did you find me?" Sam looked up at
Ted with interest, as Ted lowered himself into
a chair next to him, and ran a gentle hand over
his head. He had never been as relieved to see
anyone, except his own son once when he had
gotten lost and they had thought he drowned
in a lake. Fortunately, he hadn't.

"He called us."

"He was nice to me. The others were scary."

"I'll bet they were. They're very scary people. They're never going to come out of prison
again, Sam." He didn't tell him that they might
even get the death penalty for committing kid-

nap. Ted thought that was more information than he needed. "One of them was killed by the police, Carlton Waters." Sam nodded, and glanced at his mother.

"I never thought I'd see you again," he said softly.

"I thought I would," she said bravely, although there were times when she didn't. They had called Will when they got to the motel, and he had sobbed when he talked to Sam, and when his mother told him. And she had called Father Wallis. Ashley didn't even know Sam had been kidnapped. She was only a few miles away, and Fernanda was going to leave her with her friends for a few days till things calmed down. She had never even known Sam was gone. Fernanda had decided not to upset her, until after it was over. She was going to tell her what happened when she got home. It had been better this way. And she couldn't help thinking about what Father Wallis had said when he met her, that Sam's kidnapping had been a compliment from God. She didn't want any more like this one. He had reminded her of it when she spoke to him that morning.

"What do you say I take you home in a little while?" Ted looked at them both, and Sam nodded. Ted wondered if Sam would be afraid of the house he had been kidnapped in. But he also knew they wouldn't be there for much longer.

"They wanted a lot of money, huh, Mom?" Sam asked, looking up at her, and she nodded. "I told him we didn't have any. I said Daddy lost it. But he didn't tell the others. Or maybe he did, and they didn't believe him." It was a succinct summary of the situation.

"How do you know that?" Fernanda frowned at him. He knew more than she had suspected. "About the money, I mean." Sam looked faintly embarrassed and grinned up at her sheepishly.

"I heard you talking on the phone," he confessed, and she looked at Ted with a rueful smile.

"When I was a little girl, my father used to say that little pitchers have big ears."

"What does that mean?" Sam looked confused as Ted laughed at the old saying. He knew it too.

"It means you shouldn't be eavesdropping on your mother," she scolded, but without fervor. She didn't care what he did now. He had carte blanche for a hell of a long time. She was just glad to have him home.

Ted asked him a few questions after that, and Rick came in a short while later with some of his own. None of Sam's answers surprised them. They had pieced it together surprisingly accurately on their own.

All of the police had vacated the motel by six o'clock, as Fernanda and Sam got in Ted's car. Rick caught a ride with some of his agents, and he winked at Ted as he left, as Ted swung playfully at him in answer.

"Don't give me that," he said under his breath to Rick. And Rick smiled at him. He was glad it had all turned out right. It could easily have been worse. You never knew till it was over. They had lost brave people that day, who had given their lives for Sam.

"It's tough work, but someone has to do it," Rick teased him in a whisper, referring to Fernanda. She was truly a nice woman, and he liked her. But Ted had no intention of doing something foolish. Now that the heat of the moment was over, he was still loyal to Shirley. And Fernanda had her own life and problems to deal with.

It was an easy, uneventful drive home. The paramedics and the doctors at the hospital had found Sam to be in surprisingly good shape, considering the ordeal he'd been through. He'd lost some weight, and he was starving all the way home. Ted stopped at Ikeda and got him a cheeseburger, french fries, a milkshake, and four boxes of cookies. And by the time they pulled up in front of her house, Sam was sound asleep. Fernanda was sitting in the front seat with Ted, and she was almost too tired to get out.

"Don't wake him. I'll carry him in," Ted said easily, as he turned off the ignition. It was a very different trip than the ride up had been, which had been fraught with tension and fears that they might lose him. The past weeks had been filled with terror.

"What do I say to thank you?" Fernanda said, looking at him. They had become friends in the past weeks, and she would never forget it.

"You don't have to. This is what they pay me to do," he said, looking at her, but they both knew it had been more than that. Much more than that. He had lived every moment of the nightmare with her, and would have sacrificed his life for Sam at any moment. It was who he was, and had been all his life. Fernanda leaned toward him then, and kissed his cheek. The moment hung in midair between them. "I'm going to need to spend some time with him, to ask him some questions for the investigation. I'll call you before I come over." He knew Rick would want to question him too. Fernanda nodded.

"Come anytime you want," she said softly, and with that he got out of the car, opened the back door, scooped the sleeping child up in his arms, and she followed him to the front door. It was opened by two policemen with guns in shoulder holsters, and Will was standing just behind them, and looked suddenly panicked.

"Oh my God, is he hurt?" His eyes darted from Ted to his mother. "You didn't tell me."

"It's okay, sweetheart." She put her arms around him gently. He was still a child too, even at sixteen. "He's sleeping." They both cried as they held each other then. It was going to be a long time before they stopped worrying. Disaster had become a way of life all too quickly. Nothing had been normal for so long that they had forgotten what it felt like.

Ted carried Sam up to his room, and laid him gently on the bed, as Fernanda took off his sneakers. He made a gentle snuffling sound, and turned over on his side, without waking, as Ted and Fernanda stood looking down at him. He was a lovely sight, in his bed at home, with his head on the pillow.

"I'll call you in the morning," Ted said to her downstairs, as he stood in the doorway. The two policemen had just left, after Fernanda thanked them.

"We're not going anywhere," she promised

him. She wasn't even sure she felt safe leaving the house yet. It was going to be very odd being on their own again, wondering if there were people out there somewhere, plotting against them. Hopefully, nothing like it would ever happen again. She had called Jack Waterman from Tahoe too. And they both agreed, some public announcement had to be made about the disappearance of Allan's fortune. Otherwise, she and the children would remain targets forever. She had learned that lesson.

"Get some rest," Ted admonished her, and she nodded. It was silly of her, she knew, but she hated to see him go. She had gotten used to talking to him late at night, knowing she would find him there at any hour, and sleeping on the floor next to him, when she could sleep nowhere else. She always felt safe near him. She realized that now. "I'll call you," he promised again, as she closed the door, wondering how she would ever thank him.

The house seemed empty when she walked upstairs. There were no sounds, no men, no guns, no cell phones ringing in every corner of the house, no negotiator listening on her lines. Thank God. Will was waiting for her in her room, and he looked as though he had grown up overnight.

"You okay, Mom?"

"Yeah," she said cautiously. "I am." She felt as though she had been dropped off a building, and was feeling her soul for bruises. There were many, but they would all heal now. Sam was back. "How about you?"

"I don't know. It was scary. It's hard not to think about it now." She nodded at him. He was right. They would all think about it, and remember it, for a long, long time.

As Fernanda got into the shower, and Will went to bed, Ted drove home to his house in the Sunset. There was no one home when he got in. There never was anymore. Shirley was never home. She was either at work, or out with her friends, most of whom he didn't know. There was a deafening silence in the house, and for the first time in a long time, he felt agonizingly lonely. He missed seeing Ashley and Will, Fernanda coming to talk to him, the familiar ease of being surrounded by his men, on a stakeout. It had reminded him of his youth in the department. But he didn't just miss the men, he missed Fernanda.

He sat down on a chair and stared into space, thinking about calling her. He wanted to. He had heard everything Rick had said. But that was Rick, and this was him. And he just couldn't do it.

Chapter 21

Ted talked to Rick the next day, and asked him what he had done about Addison. The state was going to bring charges against him too, and serve him with a warrant for conspiracy to commit kidnap, as soon as he got back to the city. Ted assumed he would. The judge had assured Rick, over his federal charges, that Phillip Addison was not a flight risk. And Ted hoped he was right.

"He's winging his way home as we speak," Rick told Ted over the phone, grinning.

"That was quick. I thought he was supposed to be gone all month."

"He was. I called Interpol yesterday, and the FBI office in Paris. They sent his surveillance guys in to pick him up. We booked him on conspiracy to commit kidnap. And one of my favorite informants called me today. Ap-

parently, our little friend is scientifically ori-
ented, so to speak, and he's been running a
hefty business in crystal meth for quite a while.
We're going to have fun with this one, Ted."

"He must have had a shit fit when they
showed up." Ted laughed at the thought of it,
although there was nothing laughable about
what he'd done. But he was so pretentious
about being "social," from all Ted had heard,
that it served him right to be cut down to size.

"His wife damn near had a heart attack apparently. She slapped him and the agent."

"That must have been fun." Ted smiled. He
was still tired.

"I doubt it."

"You were right about the car bombing too,
by the way. Jim Free told us Waters did it.
They weren't in on it, but he admitted it to
them in Tahoe one night when he got drunk.
I thought you'd like to know."

"At least the captain will know I'm not
nuts."

Ted told him then that they had recovered
most of the money Addison had paid Stark,
Free, and Waters in advance, in suitcases in
lockers in the Modesto bus station. It was going to be damning evidence against him. Free
had told them where it was.

And then Rick changed the subject radically,

as he often did, and got right to the point. "So did you say anything to her when you dropped her off?" They both knew he meant Fernanda.

"About what?" Ted played dumb.

"Don't give me that, you moron. You know what I mean."

Ted sighed. "No, I didn't. I thought about calling her last night, but there's no point, Rick. I can't do that to Shirley."

"She would. And you're doing it to yourself. And to Fernanda. She needs you, Ted."

"Maybe I need her too. But I already have one."

"The one you've got is a lemon," he said bluntly, which wasn't fair either, and Ted knew it. Shirley was a good woman, she was just the wrong one for him, and had been for years. She knew it too. She was just as disappointed in Ted. "I hope you get smart one of these days, before it's too late," Rick said with fervor. "Which reminds me, there's something I want to talk to you about. Let's have dinner next week."

"What about?" Ted was intrigued, and wondered if it was about his upcoming marriage, not that he was any authority on the subject. On the contrary. But they were best friends, and always would be.

"Believe it or not, I want your advice."

"Happy to give it. When are you going out to see Sam, by the way?"

"I'll let you do it first. You know him better. I don't want to scare him, and you may get everything I need."

"I'll let you know."

They agreed to talk again in a few days. And the following day, Ted went to visit Sam. Fernanda was there with Jack Waterman. They looked like they'd been talking business, and Jack left shortly after Ted arrived. He spent all of his time with Sam. Fernanda looked distracted and busy, and Ted couldn't help wondering if something was up with her and Jack. It seemed reasonable to him, and would have been the right fit. He could tell Jack thought so too.

The following day there was a grim article in the newspapers about the financially disastrous end of Allan Barnes's career. The only thing they left out was Allan's presumed suicide. But Ted had the feeling, reading it, that Fernanda had had a hand in it. And he wondered if that was what she had been doing with Jack, and why she looked somewhat upset. He didn't blame her, but it was better to get the word out. So far they had managed to keep everything about the kidnap out of the press. Ted assumed that it would come out eventually, during the trial. But no date had been set, and wouldn't be for a while. Both Stark and Free were already back in prison, after their parole was revoked when they were apprehended.

Sam was remarkably cooperative with Ted. It was amazing what he remembered, in spite of the traumatic circumstances, and what he had observed. He was going to make an excellent witness, despite his age.

After that, things moved quickly for Fernanda and her children. She turned forty shortly after, and the kids took her to International House of Pancakes on her birthday. It wasn't the birthday she would have anticipated a year before, but it was all she wanted this year. To be with her children. Shortly after that, she told them they had to sell the house. Ashley and Will were shocked, and Sam wasn't. He already knew, as he had confessed to her, from eavesdropping on her conversations. Their life had a transitional quality to it, once she made the announcement to them. Ash said it was humiliating for her now at school, once everyone knew her father had lost all his money, and there were girls who no longer wanted to be friends with her, which Will said was disgusting. He was a senior that year. And none of them had shared that they had been targets of a kidnapping attempt that summer. The story was so horrifying that it didn't qualify for school assignments that covered "What I Did on My Summer Vacation." They only talked about it among themselves. The police had warned them to keep quiet to avoid "copycats" and the press. And one of the potential buyers who visited the house gasped when she saw the kitchen.

"My Lord, why didn't you ever finish it? A house like this ought to have a fabulous kitchen!" She looked down her nose at the realtor and Fernanda, and Fernanda had an overwhelming desire to slap her, but didn't.

"It used to," she said simply. "We had an accident here last summer."

"What kind of accident?" the woman asked nervously, and for a moment, Fernanda was tempted to tell her that two FBI agents and two San Francisco policemen were gunned down in her kitchen. But she resisted the urge and said nothing.

"Nothing serious. But I decided to take out the granite." Because it was bloodstained beyond repair, she thought to herself in silence.

The kidnapping still had a quality of unreality to it, for all of them. Sam told his best friend in school, and the boy didn't believe him. The teacher gave him a serious lecture about lying after that, and inventing things, and Sam came home crying.

"She didn't believe me!" he complained to his mother. Who would? She didn't believe it herself sometimes. It was so horrifying she still couldn't absorb it, and when she thought about it, it still frightened her so much, and made her so anxious, that she had to force herself to think about something else.

She had taken the children to a psychiatrist who specialized in trauma after it happened, and the woman was impressed with how well they'd come through it, although now and then, Sam still had nightmares, as did his mother.

Ted continued to visit Sam well into September, to gather evidence and testimony, and by October he had finished. He didn't call them after that, and Fernanda thought of him often, and meant to call him. She was showing the house, trying to find a smaller one, and looking for a job. She was nearly out of money, and trying not to panic. But late at night, she often did, and Will saw it. He offered to get a job after school, to try and help her. She was worrying about college for him. Fortunately, he had good grades and qualified for the University of California system, although she knew she'd still have to scare up

enough to pay for the dorm. It was hard to believe sometimes that Allan had had hundreds
of millions of dollars, although not for very
long. She had never been as broke as she was
at that moment. And it scared her.

Jack took her to lunch one day, and tried to
talk to her about it. He said he hadn't wanted
to approach her too soon, or offend her right
after Allan died, and then there was the kidnapping, and all of them had been so upset,
understandably. But he said he had been
thinking about it for months, and had made a
decision. He paused, as though expecting a
drumroll, and Fernanda never saw it coming.

"What kind of decision?" she said blindly.

"I think we ought to get married." She
stared at him across the lunch table, and for a
minute she thought he was kidding, but saw
he wasn't.

"You just decided that? Without asking me,
or talking to me about it? What about what I
think?"

"Fernanda, you're broke. You can't keep
your kids in private schools. Will is going to
college in the fall. And you have no marketable job skills," he said matter-of-factly.

"Are you offering to hire me, or marry
me?" she asked, suddenly angry. He wanted to
dispose of her life, without having con-

sulted her. And most important, he had never mentioned love. What he said sounded like a job offer, not a proposal of marriage, which offended Fernanda. There was something very condescending about the way he'd asked.

"Don't be ridiculous. Marry you, of course. And besides, the children know me," Jack said irritably. It all made perfect sense to him and love was not important. He liked her. To him, that seemed enough.

"Yes"—she decided that his bluntness deserved her own—"but I don't love you." In truth, his offer didn't flatter her, it hurt her feelings. She felt like a car he was buying, not like a woman he loved.

"We could learn to love each other," he said stubbornly. She had always liked him, and she knew he was responsible and reliable, and a good person, but there was no magic between them. She knew that if she ever married again, she wanted magic, or at least love.

"I think it would be a sensible move for both of us. I've been widowed for a number of years, and Allan left you in a hell of a mess. Fernanda, I want to take care of you, and your children." For a moment, he almost touched her heart, but not enough.

She sighed deeply as she looked at him, and he waited for the answer. He saw no reason to

give her time to think about it. He had made
a good offer, and he expected her to accept it,
like a job, or a house.

"I'm sorry, Jack," she said as gently as she
could. "I can't do it." She was beginning to
understand why he had never remarried. If he
made proposals like that, or saw marriage that
pragmatically, he was better off with a dog.

"Why not?" He looked confused.

"I may be crazy, but if I ever get married
again, I want to fall in love."

"You're not a child anymore, and you have
responsibilities to think of." He was asking her
to sell herself into slavery, so she could send
Will to Harvard. She would rather have sent
him to City College. She wasn't willing to sell
her soul to a man she didn't love, even for her
kids. "I think you should reconsider."

"I think you're wonderful, and I don't deserve you," she said, standing up, as she realized that years of friendship and his handling
their affairs had just been flushed down the
toilet.

"That may be true," he said, yanking on the
chain as hard as he could, as she heard a flush-
ing sound in her head. "But I still want to
marry you."

"I don't," she said, looking at him. She had
never realized it before, but he was more in-

sensitive and domineering than she'd realized over the years, and cared far more about what he felt than what she did, which was probably why he wasn't married. Having made his decision, he thought she should do as she was told, which was not how she wanted to spend the rest of her life. Doing as she was told by a man she didn't love. The way he had proposed seemed more of an insult than a compliment, and showed a lack of respect. "And by the way," she said, looking over her shoulder at him, as she dropped her napkin on the chair, "you're fired, Jack." And with that, she turned around and walked out.

Chapter 22

The house sold in December, finally. Just before Christmas, of course. So they had one more Christmas in the living room, with their tree beneath the magical Viennese chandelier. It seemed fitting somehow, and was the end of a tough year for all of them. And she still didn't have a job, but she was looking. She was trying to get a job as a secretary that would be part time enough to let her leave to pick Ashley and Sam up at school. As long as they were still at home, she wanted to be there for them too. Although she knew other mothers managed with sitters and day care and latchkey kids, if she could help it, she didn't want to. She still wanted to be with her kids, as much as she could.

She had a lot of decisions to make once the house sold. A couple bought it who were moving out from New York, and the realtor explained surreptitiously that he had made an enormous fortune. Fernanda nodded, and said that was nice. For as long as it lasted, she thought to herself. In the last year, she had had constant lessons about what was important. After Sam's kidnapping, she no longer had any question. Her kids mattered. The rest didn't. And money, to whatever degree, was unimportant to her, except to feed her children.

She had been planning to strip the house, and sell whatever she could at auction. But as it turned out, the buyers loved everything she had and paid a huge premium for it, over and above the price of the house. The wife thought she had terrific taste. So it worked out well for all involved.

She and the children moved out in January. Ashley cried. Sam looked sad. And as always these days, Will was an enormous help to his mother. He carried boxes, loaded things, and he was with her the day she found the new house. She actually had enough left over to buy something small, and put a hefty mortgage on it, after the sale of the house. The house she found in Marin was exactly what she wanted. It was in Sausalito, high up on a hill, with a view of sailboats, the bay, Angel Island, and Belvedere. It was peaceful and cozy and unpretentious and pretty. And the children loved it when they saw it. She decided to put Ashley and Sam in public school in Marin, and Will was going to commute for the remaining months of school until he graduated. Two weeks after they moved into the house, she found a job, as curator of a gallery five minutes from her house. They had no problem with her leaving at three every day. The salary was small, but at least the money was consistent. And by then she had a new lawyer, a woman. Jack was still deeply offended by her refusing his proposal. And sometimes, when she thought of it, she thought it was both sad and funny. He had seemed so incredibly pompous when he asked her. She had never seen that side of him before.

What didn't seem funny to her, and never would, was the memory of the kidnapping the previous summer. She still had nightmares about it. It seemed surreal to her, and it was one of the many things she didn't mind about leaving their old house. She could never sleep in it again without an overwhelming feeling of panic that something terrible was about to happen. She slept better in Sausalito. And she hadn't heard from Ted since the previous September. It had been four months. He called her finally in March. The trial of Malcolm Stark and Jim Free had been set for April. It had already been postponed twice, and Ted said it wouldn't be again.

"We're going to need Sam to testify," he said awkwardly after asking her how she had been. He had thought of her often, but never called, in spite of Rick Holmquist urging him to do so.

"I worry about it being traumatic for him," Ted said quietly.

"So do I," Fernanda agreed. It was strange thinking of him now. He had been woven into that hideous experience, almost a part of it, yet not. Her feeling that way was what he had been afraid of, and part of why he had never called. He was sure he would remind them all of the kidnapping. Rick Holmquist told him he was nuts. "He'll get through it," she said, talking about Sam again.

"How is he?"

"Terrific. It's like it never happened. He's going to a new school, and so is Ash. I think that was good for them. Kind of a fresh start."

"I see you have a new address."

"I love my new house," she confessed with a grin, which he could hear in her voice. "I'm working in a gallery five minutes from home. You should come and see us sometime."

"I will," he promised, but she didn't hear from him again until three days before the trial. He called to tell her where to bring him, and when she told Sam, he cried.

"I don't want to do it. I don't want to see them again." Neither did she. But it had been worse for him. She called the trauma therapist, and she and Sam went in. They talked about his being unable to testify, or it being unwise for him. But in the end, he said he would, and the therapist thought it might give him closure. Fernanda was far more afraid it would give him nightmares. He already had closure. Two of the men were dead, including the one who had helped him escape. And two were in prison. It was enough closure for her, and she thought for Sam too. But she showed up at the Hall of Justice with Sam on the appointed day, with a feeling of trepidation. Sam had had a stomachache after breakfast that day, and so did she.

Ted was waiting for her outside the building. He looked just the same as the last time she'd seen him. Calm, and nicely dressed, well groomed, intelligent, and concerned about how Sam was feeling.

"How's it going, Deputy?" He smiled down at Sam, who was visibly unhappy.

"I feel like throwing up."

"That's not so good. Let's talk about it for a minute. How come?"

"I'm scared they'll hurt me," he said bluntly. It made sense. They had before.

"I'm not going to let that happen." He unbuttoned his jacket, flashed it open for a second, and Sam saw his gun. "There's that, and besides they'll be in court in leg irons and shackles. They're all tied up."

"They tied me up too," Sam said miserably, and started to cry. At least he was talking about it. But Fernanda felt sick and looked at Ted, and he looked as unhappy as she did, and then he had an idea. He told them to go across the street for something to drink, and he'd be back as soon as he could.

It took him twenty minutes. He had met with the judge, the public defender, and the prosecutor, and all had agreed. Sam and his mother were going to be interrogated in the judge's chambers, with the jury present, but not the defendants. He never had to see either of the two men again. He could identify them from pictures. Ted had insisted that it was too traumatic for the boy to testify in the courtroom and see his kidnappers again. And when he told Sam, he beamed, and Fernanda heaved a sigh of relief.

"I think you're really going to like the judge. She's a woman, and she's really nice," he said to Sam. The judge looked grandmotherly and warm when Sam walked in, and during a brief recess she offered him milk and cookies and showed him pictures of her grandkids. Her heart went out to him and his mother for all they'd been through.

His questioning by the prosecution took all morning, and when they were finished, Ted took them out to lunch. The defense was going to question Sam in the afternoon, and reserved the right to bring him back at any time. So far, he had handled it very well. Ted wasn't surprised.

They went to a small Italian restaurant some distance from the Hall of Justice. They didn't have time to go too far, but Ted could tell they both needed to get away, and Sam and his mother were quiet over their pasta. It had been a difficult morning, which brought back a lot of painful memories for Sam, and Fernanda worried about the impact on him. But he seemed to be all right, just quiet.

"I'm sorry you both have to go through this," Ted said as he paid the check. She offered to pay half, and he smiled and declined. She had worn a red dress, and high-heeled shoes. And he saw that she was wearing makeup. He wondered if she was dating Jack. But he didn't want to ask. Maybe it was someone else. He could see that she was in much better shape emotionally than she had been in the previous June and July. The move and the new job had done her good. He was contemplating some changes himself. He told them he was leaving the department after thirty years.

"Wow, why?" She was stunned. He was a cop through and through, and she knew he loved his job.

"My old partner Rick Holmquist wants to start a private security business. Personal investigation, celebrity protection, it's a little fancy for me, but he runs a tight shop. So do I. And he's right. After thirty years, maybe it's time for a change." She knew too that after thirty years, he could leave with a pension that would still give him full pay. It was a good deal. And Holmquist's idea sounded like a money-maker, even to her.

The defense counsel tried to make mincemeat of Sam's testimony that afternoon, but couldn't. Sam was unflappable, unshakable, and his memory appeared to be infallible. He stuck by the same story again and again. And identified both defendants from the photographs the prosecution had shown him.

Fernanda couldn't identify the men who'd taken her son, while wearing ski masks, but her testimony about the actual kidnapping was deeply moving and her description of the four men murdered in her kitchen was horrifying. At the end of the day, the judge thanked them and sent them home.

"You were a star!" Ted said, beaming at Sam, as they left the Hall of Justice together. "How's your stomach?"

"Good," Sam said, looking pleased. Even the judge had told him he had done a good job. He had just turned seven, and Ted told him it would have been just as hard even for an adult to testify.

"Let's go for ice cream," Ted suggested. He followed Sam and Fernanda in his car, and proposed Ghirardelli Square for their outing, which was fun for Sam. And even for her. There was a festive feeling to it, as Sam ordered a hot fudge sundae, and Ted got root beer floats for both of the adults.

"I feel like a kid at a birthday party," Fernanda giggled.

She was enormously relieved that Sam's part in the trial was over. Ted said that it was more than unlikely they'd want him back to testify again. Everything he had said had been brutally damning for the defense. There was no question in Ted's mind that the two men were going to be convicted, and he felt certain that however grandmotherly the judge looked, she was going to give them the death penalty at the sentencing. It was a sobering thought. Ted had told her that Phillip Addison was being tried separately in a federal court, for conspiracy to commit kidnap, and all his federal charges, including tax evasion, money laundering, and drug smuggling. He would be going away for a long time, and it was unlikely that Sam would have to testify again in his case. He was going to suggest to Rick that they use the transcript of Sam's testimony from the state's case, in order to spare the boy further grief. He wasn't sure that was possible, but he was going to do everything he could to get Sam off the hook on that one. And although Rick was leaving the FBI, Ted knew he would put the Addison case in the right hands, and would be testifying himself. Rick wanted Addison put away for good, or if possible put to death. It had been a serious matter, and as Ted did, he wanted to see justice served. Fernanda was relieved. It was good to have the whole ugly business behind them. With the trial no longer hanging over them, the nightmare was finally over.

The last of it happened at the sentencing a

month later. It was almost exactly a year to the day since it all began, and Ted rang her doorbell over the car bombing up the street. Ted called her the same day she saw the article about the sentencing in the paper. Malcolm Stark and James Free had been given the death sentence as punishment for their crimes. She had no idea when they would be executed, or even if, given what they might do with appeals, but there was every reason to think they would be. Phillip Addison hadn't even gone to trial yet, but he was in custody, and his lawyers were doing all they could to stall his trial. But sooner or later, Fernanda knew, he would be convicted too. And in the case of the other two, justice had been served. And most important of all, Sam was fine.

"Did you see the sentencing results in the papers?" Ted asked when he called her. He sounded as though he was in a good mood, and he said he was busy. He had left the department, in a flurry of retirement parties for him, the week before.

"Yes, I did," Fernanda confirmed. "I've never believed in the death penalty." It had always seemed wrong to her, and she was sufficiently religious to believe that no one had the right to take someone else's life. But nine men had been killed, and a child had been kidnapped. And since it involved her son, for the first time in her life, she thought it was right. "But I do this time," she admitted to Ted. "It's different, I guess, if it happens to you." But she also knew that if they had killed her son, even putting the defendants to death wouldn't have brought him back or made it up to her for her loss. She and Sam had just been very, very lucky. And Ted knew that too. It could have been otherwise, and he was grateful it wasn't.

And then she thought of something they'd been talking about for a long time. "When are you coming to dinner?" She owed him so much for all his kindness to them, and dinner was the least she could do. She had missed seeing him in recent months, although it was a sign that all was well in both their lives. She hoped never to need his services again, nor anyone like him, but after all she'd been through with him, she considered him a friend.

"Actually, that's why I called you. I was going to ask if I could drop by. I have a present for Sam."

"He'll be happy to see you." She smiled and looked at her watch, she had to get to work. "How about tomorrow?"

"I'd love it." He smiled, as he jotted down her new address again. "What time?"

"How about seven?"

He agreed, hung up, and sat in his new office, looking out the window and thinking for a long time. It was hard to believe it had all happened a year ago. He had thought of it again when he saw Judge McIntyre's obituary recently. He was lucky too that the car bombing hadn't killed him a year before that. He had died of natural causes.

"What are you daydreaming about? Don't you have work to do?" Rick barked at him as he stopped in the doorway of Ted's office. Their new business was already up and running, and they were doing well. There was a sizable market for their services, and Ted had told his last police partner, Jeff Stone, the week before, that he had never had so much fun, far more than he'd expected. And he loved working with Rick again. The security business they were just starting up had been a great idea.

"Don't give me any crap about daydreaming, Special Agent. You took a three-hour lunch yesterday. I'm going to start docking your pay if you do it again." Rick guffawed. He'd been out with Peg. They were getting married in a few weeks. Everything was coming up roses for them. And Ted was going to be best man. "And don't think you're taking a paid vacation while you're on your honeymoon. We run a serious business here. If you want to get married and go running off to Italy, do it on your own time."

Rick wandered into his office with a grin, and sat down. He hadn't been this happy in years. He'd been sick and tired of his work with the FBI, he much preferred running their own business. "So what's on your mind?" Rick looked at him. He could see there was something eating at Ted.

"I'm having dinner with the Barneses to-morrow night. In Sausalito. They moved."

"That's nice. Am I allowed to ask rude questions, like what your intentions are, Detective Lee?" Rick's eyes were more serious than his words. He knew what Ted's feelings were, or he thought he did. What he didn't know was what he intended to do about them, if anything. But neither did Ted.

"I just wanted to see the kids."

"That's too bad." Rick looked disappointed. He was so happy with Peg, he wanted everyone else to be happy too. "Sounds like a waste of a good woman to me."

"Yes, she is," Ted agreed. But there were a lot of issues he couldn't make his peace with, and probably never would. "I think she's probably seeing someone. She looked great at the trial."

"Maybe she was looking great for you," Rick suggested, and Ted laughed.

"That's a dumb idea."

"So are you. You drive me nuts sometimes. In fact, most of the time." Rick stood up and strolled out of Ted's office again. He knew his old friend was too stubborn to convince.

Both men were busy for the rest of the afternoon. And Ted worked late that night, as he always did.

He was out of the office for most of the following day, and Rick only caught a glimpse of him the next evening when he was about to leave for Sausalito, straight from the office, with a small gift-wrapped package in one hand.

"What's that?" Rick inquired.

"None of your business," Ted said cheerfully.

"That's nice." Rick grinned at him, as Ted walked right past him on his way out. "Good luck!" Rick called after him, as Ted just laughed, and the door closed behind him. Rick stood looking at it for a long moment, after Ted was gone, hoping that things went well for him that night. It was time something good happened to him too. It was long overdue.

Chapter 23

Fernanda was in the kitchen with an apron on when the doorbell rang, and she asked Ashley to get it. She had grown about three inches in the past year, and Ted looked startled when he saw her. At thirteen, she suddenly looked not like a child, but like a woman. She was wearing a short denim skirt, a pair of her mother's sandals, and a T-shirt, and she was a very pretty girl, and looked nearly like Fernanda's twin. They had the same features, same smile, same dimensions, although she was taller than her mother now, and same long, straight blond hair.

"How've you been, Ashley?" Ted asked easily as he walked in. He had always liked Fernanda's children. They were polite, well behaved, warm, friendly, bright, and funny. And you could see easily how much love and time she had put into them.

As he walked in, Fernanda stuck her head out of the kitchen, and offered him a glass of wine, which he declined. He didn't drink much, even when he was off duty, which he was all the time now. And as Fernanda disappeared into the kitchen again, Will strolled in, and was obviously happy to see Ted as they shook hands. He was beaming, and they sat and chatted about Ted's new business for a few minutes, until Sam bounded into the room. He had the personality to go with his bright red hair, and he smiled from ear to ear when he saw Ted.

"Mom said you have a present for me, what did you bring me?" He chortled, as his mother arrived from the kitchen and scolded him.

"Sam, that's rude!"

"You said he did . . ." he argued with her.

"I know. But what if he changed his mind, or forgot it? You'd make him feel bad."

"Oh." Sam looked mollified by the correction, just as Ted handed him the package he had brought from work. It was small and square and looked mysterious to Sam, as he took it from him with an impish grin. "Can I open it now?"

"Yes, you can." He felt badly not to have brought something for the others, but this was something he had been saving for Sam since the trial. It meant a lot to him, and he hoped it would to Sam too.

When Sam opened the box, there was a small leather pouch inside. It was the original one Ted had had for thirty years. And as Sam opened the pouch, he looked at it and then stared at Ted. It was the star he had carried for thirty years, with his number on it. It had a lot of meaning for him, and Fernanda looked nearly as stunned as her son.

"Is that your real one?" Sam looked at it and then him with awe. He could see that it was. It was well worn, and Ted had shined it for him. It lay gleaming in the boy's hands.

"Yes, it is. Now that I retired, I don't need it anymore. But it's very special to me. I want you to keep it. You're not a deputy anymore, Sam. You're a full detective now. That's a big promotion after just one year." It had been exactly a year since Ted had "deputized" him after the car bombing when they first met.

"Can I put it on?"

"Sure." Ted pinned it on for him, and Sam went to look at himself in the mirror, as Fernanda glanced at Ted with grateful eyes.

"That was an incredibly nice thing to do," she said softly.

"He earned it. The hard way." And they all knew how, as Fernanda nodded, and Ted watched him prancing around the room wearing it on his chest.

"I'm a detective!" he was shouting. And then he looked at Ted with an earnest question. "Can I arrest people?"

"I'd be a little careful who you arrest," Ted warned him with a grin. "I wouldn't arrest any real big guys who might get mad at you." Ted suspected correctly that Fernanda was going to put it away for him, with other important things, like his father's watch and cufflinks. But he knew Sam would want to take it out from time to time to see it. Any boy would.

"I'm going to arrest all my friends," Sam said proudly. "Can I take it to school for show and tell, Mom?" He was so excited, he could hardly stand it, and Ted looked genuinely pleased. It had been the right thing to do.

"I'll bring it to school for you," his mother suggested, "and I'll take it home after show and tell. You don't want it to get lost or hurt at school. That's a very, very special gift."

"I know," Sam said, looking awestruck again.

A few minutes later, they all sat down to dinner. She had made a roast beef, Yorkshire pudding, mashed potatoes, vegetables, and chocolate cake and ice cream for dessert. The kids were impressed by the trouble she'd gone to, and so was Ted. It was a terrific meal. They were still sitting at the table, talking afterward, when the kids got up and went to their rooms. They still had a few weeks of school before summer vacation, and Will said finals were next week, and he had studying to do. Sam took his new star to his room, just so he could look at it. And Ashley scampered off to call her friends.

"That was some dinner, I haven't had a meal like that in ages. Thank you," he said, feeling as though he could hardly move. Most nights now, he worked late, went to the gym, and came home close to midnight. He rarely even stopped for dinner. He went to a diner sometimes in the daytime. "I haven't had a home-cooked meal in years." Shirley had always hated to cook, and preferred getting take-out from her parents' restaurant. She never even liked to cook for the kids, and liked taking them out too.

"Doesn't your wife cook for you?" Fernanda looked surprised, and then suddenly, for no particular reason, noticed the absence of his wedding ring. The year before, during Sam's kidnapping, it had been there. And now it wasn't.

"Not anymore," he said simply, and then decided he ought to explain. "We split up right after Christmas. I guess it was a long time coming, and we should have done it years ago. But it was hard anyway." It had been five months, and he hadn't gone out with another woman yet. In some ways, he still felt married to her.

"Did something specific happen?" Fernanda looked sorry for him, and sympathetic. She knew how loyal he was to his wife, and how much he valued the marriage, even though he had admitted that things weren't perfect between them, and he had said they were very different people.

"Yes and no. The week before Christmas she told me she was going to Europe with a bunch of her girlfriends over the holidays until after New Year. She couldn't see why I was upset about it. She thought I was standing in the way of her having fun, and I thought she should be home with me and the boys. She said she's been doing that for nearly thirty years, and now it's her turn. I guess she has a point. She works hard, she'd saved the money. Apparently, she had a great time. I'm happy for her. But it pointed out to me that we don't have much anymore. We didn't for a long time, but I thought we should stay married anyway. I didn't think it was right for us to get divorced when the kids were small. Anyway, I thought about it while she was gone, and I asked her how she felt about it when she came back. She said she's wanted out for a long time, but was afraid to tell me. She didn't want to hurt my feelings, which is kind of a lousy reason to stay married.

"She met someone else about three weeks after we split up. I gave her the house, and I got an apartment downtown near the office. It takes some getting used to, but it's okay. Now I wish I'd done it sooner. I'm a little old to be out there dating again." He had just turned forty-eight. Fernanda was turning forty-one that summer, and she felt the same way. "What about you, are you going out with your lawyer?" He had been sure that he had that in mind the year before, and was just biding his time while Fernanda adjusted to her widowhood, and then the kidnapping came along. Ted wasn't far wrong.

"Jack?" She laughed in answer, and shook her head. "What made you think that?" He was very astute. But then again, studying people was his job.

"I thought he had a thing for you." Ted shrugged, thinking maybe he had made a mistake in his assessment, given the way she reacted.

"He did. He thought I should marry him for the children's sake, so he could help me pay the bills. He said he had made a 'decision' about it, and it was the right thing for me to do, for my kids. The only problem was he forgot to consult me about the decision. And I didn't agree with him."

"Why not?" Ted was surprised. Jack was smart, successful, and good-looking. Ted thought he was perfect for her. Apparently, she didn't agree.

"I don't love him." She said it as though that explained it all, as she smiled at him. "I fired him as my lawyer too."

"Poor guy." Ted couldn't help laughing at the picture she painted, getting turned down on his proposal and fired all in the same day. "That's too bad. He seemed like a nice guy."

"Then you marry him. I don't want to. I'd rather be alone with my kids." And indeed she was. Ted had that impression now, just looking at her. And he wasn't quite sure what to say next. "Are you divorced, by the way? Or just separated?" Not that it mattered. She was just curious how serious he was about leaving Shirley. It seemed hard to believe that he was out of his marriage, and it was for him too.

"The divorce will be final in six weeks," he said, and sounded sad about it. It was sad after twenty-nine years. He was getting used to it, but it had been a huge change for him. "Maybe we could go to a movie sometime," he said cautiously. She smiled, and it seemed a funny way to start, after they had spent days on end together, and nights on the floor, and he had been there, holding her hand when the SWAT team brought Sam back to her.

"I'd like that. We've missed seeing you," she said honestly. She was sorry that he had never called.

"I was afraid I'd be a bad memory for all of you, after everything that happened."

She shook her head then. "You're not a bad memory, Ted. You were the only good part of it. That and getting Sam back." And then she smiled at him again, touched by his thoughtfulness. He had always been so kind to her kids, and to her. "Sam loves his star."

"I'm glad. I was going to give it to one of my sons, and then I decided Sam should have it. He earned it."

She nodded. "Yes, he did." And as she said it, she thought back to the year before, everything they had said to each other, the things that had gone unspoken but she knew had been felt by both of them. There had been a connection between them, and the only thing that had stopped it from going further was his loyalty to his failing marriage, and she had respected him for it. And now they seemed to be starting from the beginning. He looked at her, and suddenly they both forgot the last year. It seemed to melt away from them, and without saying a word, he leaned toward her where they sat at the dining table and kissed her.

"I missed you so much," he whispered, and she nodded, and smiled at him.

"Me too. I was so sad you didn't call. I thought you forgot us." They were whispering to each other, so no one would hear. The house was small, and the kids were very close.

"I didn't think I should . . . that was dumb of me," he said, and kissed her again. He couldn't get enough of her now, and wished he hadn't waited so long. He had spent months not calling her, thinking he wasn't good enough, or rich enough for her. He realized now that he should have known better. She was more than that. She was real. And he had known ever since the kidnapping that he loved her. And she loved him. This was the magic she had been telling Jack about, that he had never understood. It was the right kind of compliment from God, not like the other one . . . the easy kind that soothed all the old wounds of loss, and terror, and tragedy. This was the happiness they had both dreamed of, and hadn't had in a long time.

They sat kissing at the dining table, and then he helped her clear the table, followed her into the kitchen, and kissed her again. He was standing with his arms around her, when they both jumped about a foot, as Sam leaped into the room and shouted at them.

"You're under arrest!" he said convincingly, pointing an imaginary gun at them.

"For what?" Ted turned with a grin. Sam had nearly given him a heart attack, and Fernanda was giggling like a kid, looking embarrassed.

"For kissing my mom!" Sam pronounced with an enormous grin and put the "gun" down, as Ted smiled at him.

"Is there a law against that?" Ted asked, as he pulled Sam toward them, and hugged him, including him in the circle with them.

"No, you can have her," Sam said matter-of-factly, wriggling free of their embrace, which he found embarrassing. "I think she likes you. She said she missed you. I did too," he said, and disappeared to announce to his sister that he'd seen Ted kissing Mom.

"It's official then." Ted put an arm around her and looked pleased. "He said I can have you. Do I take you with me now, or pick you up later?"

"You could stick around," she said cautiously. He liked that idea too.

"You may get tired of me." Shirley had, and it had taken the edge off his confidence a bit. It was so hurtful to have someone you cared about no longer love you. But Fernanda was a totally different woman, and Rick was right, he and Fernanda were much better suited to each other than he'd ever been with Shirley.

"I'm not going to get tired of you," she said quietly. She had never felt as comfortable with anyone as she had with him during those weeks, despite the traumatic circumstances. It was an extraordinary way to get to know someone. They just had to wait for their time to come, and it had.

He was standing in the hallway, saying good night to her, and promising to call her the next day. Things were different now. He had a normal life finally. If he wanted to, he could leave his office and go home at night, if he had reason to. No more crazy hours or swing shifts. He was just about to kiss her good night, when Ashley sauntered by, and gave them a

knowing look. But she didn't seem to disap-
prove. She seemed entirely relaxed about seeing them with their arms around each other,
and Ted was pleased. This was the woman he
had been waiting for, the family he had been
missing since his kids grew up, the boy he had
saved and come to love, the woman he
needed. And he was the magic she had
dreamed of, and thought she wouldn't find
again.

He kissed her one last time, and hurried
down the stairs to his car with a last wave to
her. She was still standing in the doorway
smiling when he drove away.

He was halfway across the bridge, grinning
to himself, when his cell phone rang. He
hoped it was Fernanda, but it was Rick.

"So? What happened? I can't stand the sus-
pense."

"It's none of your business," Ted said, still
grinning. He felt like a kid, especially talking
to Rick. With her, he felt like a man again.

"Yes, it is," Rick insisted. "I want you to be
happy."

"I am."

"For real?" Rick sounded stunned.

"Yeah. For real. You were right. About
everything."

"Holy shit! Well, I'll be damned. Good for

you, my friend. It's about goddamn time," Rick said, sounding relieved, and happy for him.

"Yes," Ted said simply, "it is." And with that, he disconnected his cell phone, and smiled the rest of the way across the bridge.